Only Wrong Once

Jenifer Ruff

Copyright

Only Wrong Once is a work of fiction. Any references to historical events, real people, or real places are used fictitiously. Other names, places, and events are the products of my imagination. I attempted to be realistic, but I also exercised my creativity.

Epigraph

"And let's remember that those charged with protecting us from attack have to be right 100 percent of the time. To inflict devastation on a massive scale, the terrorists only have to succeed once. And we know that they are trying every day."

—National Security Adviser Condoleezza Rice - Statement to the 9/11 Commission, April 8th, 2004.

Chapter One

Aleppo, Syria
Present Day – September 19ᵗʰ

The dead lay unattended amidst bombed-out buildings on streets coated with ash and blood. Beside a pile of rubble, Yesenia spotted a body wearing a blue and white hijab, one leg bent at an impossible angle. Her neighbor, before their homes burned, had the same hijab. Yesenia squeezed her eyes shut and clutched her mother's hand. Normally, she was much too old for hand-holding, but anyone could become lost in the shoving crowd and nothing was normal anymore. As far as Yesenia could see, thousands of other Shiite Muslims from her village were packed together, waiting evacuation. Refugees. That's what they were called now. Buses would soon arrive to carry them to safer territories. They huddled under blankets, clinging to valuables. Yesenia pressed her shivering body against her mother's leg for warmth. Eyes lifted to the sky, her mother prayed to leave the war-torn city alive, before the next explosion. She'd been praying almost every hour for months. So far, it hadn't done any good.

Cheers erupted when the buses, dozens of them, finally arrived. An elbow hit Yesenia hard, sending a sudden pain across her cheek, as someone edged in front of her mother. Yesenia was just as desperate to reach the door of the bus, climb the steps, and end up somewhere safe. Anywhere else but here. But so many people were waiting. Yesenia didn't think the buses could possibly hold enough seats for all of them.

The escalating rumble of trucks filled the air, louder than the mob swarming forward to load the buses. In the distance, a rising cloud of dust indicated a convoy approaching. Yesenia held her breath, waiting to see the colors. Green for good, gray or black for bad. They were all evil, as far as she was concerned. They had destroyed her city and her life one nightmarish day after another until both became completely unrecognizable. Her mother pulled her toward the bus, even though there wasn't room to move forward. Her scarf caught on something and yanked away from her neck, but she snatched it back in time. The engines grew louder, joined by angry shouts. A quick glimpse on her tiptoes revealed the front of a truck.

Gray.

Her heart sank.

"Hurry, Yesenia," said her mother. "Don't let go of me." Together, they pressed into the mass of unwashed, pungent smelling bodies and tattered, flowing garments moving toward the buses.

The men from the trucks, ISIS or government? She did not know or care. They fired their rifles into the night sky, scattering the refugees. Looking like crazed demons, they jumped from the truck beds with flaming torches and ran along the line of buses, flinging streams of gasoline, and setting them on fire. Refugees rushed off the buses, pushing and shoving, shrieking and screaming, some on fire. Desperate souls searched for space to roll on the ground and extinguish their flaming clothes. Able to escape the fiery inferno, Yesenia's mother pulled her daughter backward causing Yesenia's ankle to twist and give out. Yesenia dropped her bag and saw it disappear under a stampede of boots. She wanted to scream too, but she

2

could only open her mouth and stare wide-eyed as the flames leapt from the bus windows, consuming their only life-line.

The men from the trucks kept guard, their hardened expressions glowing in the blazing light, their guns and rifles ready, watching the buses reduce to burned-out metal shells.

Yesenia's mother rocked in place on her heels, sobbing.

Yesenia wanted to run, but they had nowhere to go, and at least with the fire they were finally warm. Next to her, a frail, old man, eyes cloudy with cataracts, wailed up at the sky. "Does anyone in the world care if we all perish?"

Yesenia released her mother's hand and whispered through clenched teeth. "No one cares. No one is paying attention to Aleppo." That was one thing she knew for sure.

But she was wrong. Someone *was* paying attention.

Just outside Aleppo, in a hidden compound, one particularly dangerous and powerful man, Muhammad Al-Bahil, had taken note of the city's tragic situation. Aleppo had become the perfect location for his sinister experiment.

Miles away from the war-zones, in a secluded area, a mysterious containment pen was hastily being erected per Al-Bahil's orders. Tall steel posts established the perimeter. Thirty of the healthiest and strongest male villagers from Aleppo had been carefully selected to work on the structure, rumored to be a new refugee camp.

"You'll be paid if you do what you're told," said Kareem, the young man who had chosen them. He tended to speak while looking down or away, then walk off, clearly reluctant to spend any more time with the villagers than required.

"Kareem isn't from Aleppo," said one of the laborers, his eyebrows almost blending with the dirt coating his face. "But with that accent, I don't know where he comes from."

"American?" said a large man with a chemical burn across one side of his face

"Doubtful. He seems nervous, don't you think?"

"He sounds like he's had a fancy education somewhere. And he's not half as strong as the weakest of us," said a man wearing an orange sweatshirt stained with dirt, sweat, and blood. "Did anyone find out what we're building? Is it a camp? Who is it for?"

The man with the chemical burn shrugged. "And who is paying us, the Syrian government?" He grabbed a bottled water from the cases Kareem had provided, staring at it appreciatively before gulping it down.

Later that day, Kareem addressed some of their questions, barely, without meeting anyone's eyes. "I don't know any more than you do. But we should all be grateful for the work when there is none other to be found. Doesn't matter what it is or who is paying us. At least we will have money."

The man in the orange sweatshirt removed a handkerchief and wiped the sweat from his brow. Heads bobbed up and down in silence. A round of gunfire echoed in the distance.

On the fourth day of construction, a pen encircled three acres of camp. The structure was a random conglomeration of heavy mesh wire and steel girts, but it was tall and impenetrable. More trucks arrived carrying hundreds of crates. As instructed, the workers carried them inside the pen and opened them, finding food, water, tents, blankets, and cots. Rumors spread quickly when the laborers told other villagers about the recently arrived supplies. Everyone who couldn't get out of the city wanted to be safe and fed inside the giant walled space.

By late afternoon on the fourth day, Kareem called the laborers together.

"I hope they still need us," said one, standing at attention near the front of the group.

His friend kicked dirt around with his boot and fidgeted with his hands. "Yeah. Me too."

"Your next jobs are to screen potential entrants, select those for admission, and guard the entrance gate," said Kareem, his eyes focused on a spot above the workers. "Only a hundred people will be allowed inside the camp. They must all be healthy, single, and young. Provided you complete the next tasks successfully, all of you who have built this structure will be guaranteed admittance." He looked down and covered his mouth with his hand. "Um, excuse me." He rushed away from the group, stifling a choking sound.

The word spread quickly. Yesenia and her mother lined up outside the one gate, the only entrance and exit. Around them, refugees paced, wrung their hands, and cursed as more were sent away than allowed inside. The newly appointed guards asked them questions.

"Do you have any other family members in the city?"

"Do you have any health issues?"

"Are you over forty years of age?"

"Would anything prevent you from doing physical labor for extended periods?"

The only acceptable answer for all the questions was— no. Most were turned away.

In less than an hour, the quota of one hundred was met. The gate closed.

"There's room for more of us!" shouted a villager.

"In the name of Allah, please let us in," pleaded another.

5

The guards told the remaining refugees, the *unchosen*, to leave while there was still a bit of daylight left. Yesenia, her mother, and hundreds of other villagers were forced to clear the area and trek back to the city against the bitter wind. Yesenia's mother left in tears. Yesenia struggled to put one foot in front of the other and keep going.

Kareem sent the guards back inside and spoke to them one last time.

"You won't have weapons, but you must maintain order inside the camp, no matter what happens. I'll be back in a week to check in. All of you will be rewarded."

Meal packets were handed out and quickly devoured.

Kareem glanced over his shoulder as he walked to a corner of the camp. One young man followed him. Behind a tall stack of crates, Kareem paced back and forth, kneading his hands and sweating, waiting for the other man to join him.

"It's time," Kareem said, when the man stood next to him. Kareem peered out from between the crates one more time, then put on surgical gloves and a mask he'd carried in his bag. He removed a padded box from his coat pocket, opened it, and picked up the syringe nestled inside. "Are you ready, Aamaq?"

Aamaq nodded, his chin quivering. He took off his coat and pushed his sleeve up over his shoulder. "I'll document everything. For as long as I'm able."

"Good. You've been an excellent assistant." Kareem spoke without making eye contact. "Remember, it's going to be fast. Very fast. When they begin to get sick, start handing out the medicine, let them have as much as they want. The pills are placebos, but they have a powerful opioid. They'll help with the pain."

A bead of sweat glistened on Aamaq's lip. He swept a hand over his forehead. "I expect to be dead by the time you return. This is my last chance to say that I trust my family will be provided for."

Kareem put his hand on Aamaq's shoulder and leaned in, although his eyes remained on the syringe. "Of course. Your mother and father will be taken care of for as long as they live. They'll learn of your sacrifice at the right time. You won't be forgotten. You'll be martyred and live in paradise for eternity." With trembling hands, he injected the contents of the syringe into Aamaq's arm. They prayed together briefly before parting.

Kareem exited the camp alone and closed the massive gate behind him. Under the cover of darkness, he peeled off his surgical gloves and dropped them to the ground with his mask and the empty syringe. He had no worries about anyone finding them or caring enough to track him down. Not in Aleppo. He secured the gate with four heavy padlocks and deposited the keys inside his coat pocket. He paused for a moment, staring at the enclosed pen, gulping down breaths, his knees weak.

Nearby, across a charred field, a black Mercedes waited under a copse of trees. The driver spotted Kareem, stepped out of the car, and opened the backdoor for him. Kareem sat down inside. A violent shiver rocked his body. "They're locked in," he said, his American accent still strong from living in the States for over half of his twenty-seven years.

Al-Bahil, the large man beside him in the backseat, nodded. "We've built a giant cage for human lab rats where no one will miss them." His satisfied smile failed to reach his piercing eyes but deepened the scar that ran from his temple to the edge of his thick black mustache.

Kareem bowed his head and twisted his hands together.

Al-Bahil put his hand on Kareem's shoulder, causing Kareem's every muscle to tense. "You scientists are always perfectionists. But now, we rely on Allah. We wait to see how many die and how long it takes."

7

"They were all going to die here anyway, right?" Kareem's voice shook.

Al-Bahil laughed. "If your virus does its job, we'll be ready. Have you identified more jihadists with American passports?"

"I'm working on it." The sick feeling in his stomach grew stronger. His vision turned yellow, then gray. He leaned his head against the window and took deep breaths.

"Work harder, Kareem. You have a critical deadline to meet. My brother's death must be avenged."

Chapter Two

Los Angeles

September 20th

Holly smoothed her dress into place and picked up her spiked heels from the polished concrete floor of her office. She inspected the luxurious couch for any telltale stains and said, "Please hurry up. People are going to be arriving any minute."

Christian stood from the sofa and finished re-buttoning his shirt. "Come here. Just for a second."

Holly didn't move.

Unfazed by her refusal, he walked toward her. With only inches separating them, he ran his fingers through her lush red hair. His deep kiss took her breath away and caused a stir between her legs. "You're so beautiful," he whispered.

"Not now." Holly wet her lips and pulled away. "I have to get ready."

Behind her office door, a gorgeous designer dress hung, waiting to cling to her body in all the right places. The caterers were already buzzing around outside her office, busy setting up tables in the gallery. Fortunately for Holly, they had an established routine and hadn't needed to bother her. She had to admit, the last thirty minutes had been delicious. She turned and began walking to the door, a slight smile crossing her lips.

"C'mere, you," said Christian.

"Can't. I have to get cleaned up. My hair is a mess. Play time is over. I'm expecting a big crowd soon."

"I know, you told me. They're coming to admire the latest creations of Mira Renault. Some young artist you're currently promoting."

Raising one brow, Holly spun back around to face Christian.

"Don't look so shocked. You think I don't listen?" He laughed. "So, you're going to come out and see me in a few days, right? I'm going to make dinner for you."

"I told you I'll visit." She scooped her black panties off the floor and frowned. She'd almost left them behind.

"But you didn't say when."

She slipped the panties back on. "Just as soon as I run out of the excellent product you're selling." Holly gave Christian her most seductive look. She didn't like to make promises, but she didn't want to upset him either. He had something she needed beyond his sexual talents—an unlimited supply of prescription pain pills. Pills she happened to need. Pills she didn't want to be without. Not quite yet.

"I don't want you taking more than one of the oxy a day. And I don't know if I can wait that long."

"Listen, Christian, if you come out here, promise you won't show up unannounced."

Christian nodded.

She opened the back door. "Come on."

Christian stood up and put his hand on her shoulder. He kissed her again until she backed away, holding the door ajar as if waiting for a dog to go out and do its business. After he left, she entered her office bathroom. She set out make-up and brushed her hair, pausing to admire her reflection. She planned to make a grand entrance once the gallery filled with her chic crowd of friends and potential buyers. She tapped a thin line of coke onto a small jade slab. Just one. She picked up her ivory straw and inhaled.

Ready for business.

Quinn spotted his wife in the middle of her gallery and made his way across the room. "You look beautiful, Holly." He placed his hand on her elbow and leaned forward for a quick kiss, but only caught the side of her mouth.

"Thank you." Holly glanced at the digital clock above the door. "Nice of you to stop by," she said, her sarcasm poorly masked. She wanted Quinn at her show, but only if he wanted to be there. She hated feeling like she'd forced him.

"Simpson," she said to the man next to her, "have you met my husband?" She tilted her head down and lifted her eyes.

"Quinn Traynor." Quinn extended his hand.

"Simpson is my father's newest film director at Amore," said Holly. "He directed two successful mainstream films before he switched over. The allure of bigger money won out over critic's accolades, didn't it, Simpson?"

Simpson smiled. "True. Are you in the industry, Quinn?" Simpson's gaze traveled over Quinn's lean, well-muscled physique, evident even under his sports coat. His eyes lingered on Quinn's face and square jaw.

Holly laughed. "Oh, Simpson. You're way off. My husband may look the part, but he's never been involved in the porn industry. He works for the FBI. He's an expert on counterterrorism. He keeps us safe." Holly loved announcing what Quinn did for a living. Along with his handsome looks and his "protector" image, it was one of the things she found most attractive about him. She had a "thing" for secret service men ever since she snuck away and watched one of her father's movies, "The President's Naughty Daughter," at the impressionable age of eleven. Her father was out with his latest twenty-something girlfriend, and the nanny sound asleep. She locked the door, and seated herself inches away from the television, keeping the volume so low she could barely hear the sound. She didn't know what she expected to see, but it sure wasn't *that*. At first, she was shocked and horrified at the president's daughter, whose naughtiness wasn't like anything she could have anticipated. And she was fascinated by the dreamy secret service agent assigned to protect the floozy. The images cemented themselves in her brain. Over the years, she had revisited them more times than she could ever count.

When Holly met Quinn for the first time, he wore a dark suit and aviator sunglasses. Holly imagined he had just stepped away from the president's side. She didn't waste a minute. She walked right over to Quinn, batting her eyelashes, working her hips, and making sure he noticed her spectacular body.

"May I ask what do you do for a living?" she said.

Quinn narrowed his eyes but smiled. "I have a government security job."

Good enough, so long as he looked and dressed like he did.

Now, years later, Simpson was asking the same type of questions. "Counterterrorism?"

"Yes. Intelligence and Analysis," said Quinn.

"Tell me about it, Quinn. It sounds fascinating."

"Like any job, sometimes it is, but most of the time it isn't."

"He can't tell us anything. Believe me, I'd love for him to entertain us with a few stories. But he can't," said Holly.

Holly accepted a champagne flute from an attractive woman carrying a tray. "Thank you, sweetie." She winked. "Simpson, you follow me. I have a piece you might like." Over her shoulder she added, "Quinn, go ahead and introduce yourself around."

She guided Simpson to one of the priciest paintings, a giant canvas with bold red and black strokes titled *Power Surge*. "This one reminds me of you. It's so powerful." She leaned in close, pressing her breast against his arm while he stared at the painting. "I have to move along and be social now. You admire the painting and think about what I said." She gently squeezed his upper arm before sauntering away.

Holly surveyed the gallery, temporarily bestowing her gaze on various guests, deciding who to visit next, until she spotted someone she didn't expect to see. Her smile disappeared. Christian stood just inside the front entrance wearing a black Armani sports coat over a grey shirt. He fit in well with the crowd, but she didn't want him around. He wasn't in the market for a painting, but more importantly, she didn't want her lover mingling with her husband. And where was Quinn now? What would he do if he knew? How could he ferret out terrorists if he couldn't detect an affair being conducted under his nose? Maybe, if he spent a little more time at home and less at work, there wouldn't be the need for any affairs.

She followed Christian's fixed gaze to a corner of the gallery where one man stood alone. Of course, it had to be Quinn. Her heartbeat quickened. Was Christian about to cause a scene? Would tonight's gallery show be memorable for reasons beyond the art? She imagined the two men fighting over her. The thought of a rivalry over the honor of her affection made her blood rush.

Across the room, Quinn removed his phone from his coat pocket. He glanced at the screen and raised it to his ear, lowering his chin toward his chest. Holly knew what would follow.

In record time, Quinn began the usual routine. The one leading to his polite escape; the one that made her blood boil. He found Mira Renault, the artist on display, and congratulated her, briefly holding her hand in his own. Next, he located Holly and quickly moved to her side.

I'm sorry, Holly," he said, his voice low. "I'm going to have to leave. Something came up."

"Of course it did." Holly wrapped her finger around a small section of hair and began to twirl it, a habit whenever she was irritated.

Out of the corner of her eyes, she spotted Christian walking toward them.

"I'll see you at home tonight." Quinn's statement almost sounded like a question.

"Fine." Holly's body tensed. Christian moved steadily closer, only a few feet away now, his eyes locked on Quinn.

Quinn turned, focused on the exit. He walked briskly past Christian, brushing his shoulder, without giving him so much as a sideways glance.

Holly forced a breath through her mouth and sighed, not with relief, but disappointment. *He's always ready to save everyone and everything. Except for our marriage.*

Chapter Three

Los Angeles

September 20th

The distinctive white shell of the Hollywood Bowl rose in the distance against the Hollywood Hills. Hundreds of people mingled across the grounds waiting for the beginning of the evening's main event, part three of a classical concert series. Groups of friends, families with picnic dinners, and couples holding hands talked and relaxed in the cool September air.

Looking straight ahead, Quinn walked up to a white van with the AT&T name and logo parked near an entrance. He slid the door partly open and stepped inside. The interior of the surveillance vehicle barely provided enough height for his six-foot two-inch frame. Cameras and camera monitors covered a large part of one side wall. "Hey, I'm here."

Agent Rashid Usman, who could read, write, and speak five Arabic languages, sat slouched in front of a wall of monitors. Light from an overhead video feed gleamed off his bald spot. He used two fingers to adjust his glasses. "You didn't have to leave your wife's gallery event. I only called to say we're moving forward with Redman. We've got this."

"I know. I wanted to come."

15

Rashid grinned and shrugged. "Okay, you're the boss." He focused on one monitor with a zoomed-in view. In the center of the screen, a man stood alone inside the crowded entrance. His name was Dylan Redman. He was average height with a mess of dark hair, piercing brown eyes, and olive skin.

Quinn shifted his gaze from Redman to another monitor. A man and woman around Quinn's age, mid-thirties, sat on a blanket. The woman sipped from a glass of red wine and smiled at her companion. The man's hand rested on her knee.

"People rarely realize when they're being watched," said Quinn.

Ten yards from Redman, a body-builder sold concert programs from behind a metal cart. His biceps strained against the fabric of his tight T-shirt. "Program?" he yelled, shading his eyes from the setting sun. He waved a handful of programs to attract attention and shook his head when no one expressed interest. Three teenagers passed within a few feet of his cart, laughing, smiling, and ignoring him. The body-builder scowled. "Get your programs here!"

"Humph. Very convincing." Quinn broke into a smile. "So, what have I missed?"

"Nothing yet. Redman's been standing there for twenty-seven minutes. He reminds me of a street performer who can't remember his act."

"Or one with a serious case of stage fright, more likely."

Rashid's lips parted unconsciously and his eyes zoomed in on an attractive woman jogging across his monitor. She wore tiny earbuds. Long, straight blonde hair swung from side to side in a ponytail. Her black stretch pants and running top revealed an exceptionally toned body. "Three times she's run down that walkway past Redman, and he hasn't noticed once."

Quinn's eyes also followed the jogger onto the next monitor. She passed a handsome man in his early twenties on his cell phone. He wore an expensive dark suit and Italian loafers. His free hand made jerking, animated gestures through the air. Like everyone else wandering through the plaza or headed into the concert, he looked too self-absorbed to pay attention to what was happening around him. "I see everyone is in place."

"Yep. And no one here has noticed anything odd about Redman. Blows my mind. It's seventy degrees and he's wearing a big ugly coat. Makes him look like he marched out of a psych ward."

"He's not different enough to warrant attention. He's only different enough to ignore."

Rashid laughed. "Even if I didn't do this for a living, I think I'd notice there's something up with this guy. Wouldn't you? There are enough shows about terrorism for people to recognize the classic signs by now. The thousand-yard stare, sweating, and especially that coat."

"People are here to enjoy themselves. They can't do that if they're worrying about terrorists."

"A little awareness wouldn't hurt once in a while."

A breeze lifted Redman's dark hair away from his forehead, revealing a wide-eyed, pained expression. Drops of sweat formed trails down the sides of his face. He gazed at the highway overpass in the distance. His fingers twitched against his side.

Rashid suddenly sat up and leaned forward. "I can't see him. Lost visual. Maybe a bus just arrived. There are too many people."

Quinn watched without blinking. *This was supposed to be easy.*

The crowd thinned and Redman appeared again on the monitor in exactly the same position as before. Quinn took a deep breath. "You think he's having second thoughts?"

"No. Impossible. He was as ready as I've ever seen and very impatient. He thinks I'm an ISIS cell leader. If we didn't set this up for tonight, he would have done something else soon. He told me he made a new contact, a guy in Syria whose group has a fool-proof project."

"He used the word *project*? Really? Like it's some sort of school assignment?"

"Yes, that's what he called it—a project."

"Do you know who it is? The contact?" Quinn said.

A young family walked at a leisurely pace toward Redman and would pass him in a few seconds. Two children wearing matching outfits, one on either side of their father, had to lift their arms almost overhead to hold on to his hands. The mother pushed a baby carriage. Redman glanced in their direction. Rashid watched the scene intently as he answered Quinn. "I don't know who the contact is yet. Redman said the guy used to live in America. Hold on…he's doing it!"

Redman's hand moved away from his side, parting his coat. He squeezed his eyes shut and pressed the button.

An alarm sounded inside the surveillance van. A computerized voice indicated the "bomb" had been activated. At the same time, Rashid turned on his headset. "Done. Get the bastard!"

Redman opened his eyes and his mouth fell open in shock. The muscular man selling programs, Ken, wrapped his hand around Redman's arm and held it in a grip like a vise. Rick, the handsome young man from the bench held the other arm, trapping him. The blonde jogger, Stephanie, prevented him from moving forward. She quickly pulled Redman's coat closed to cover the explosive device. Their movements were quick and natural, like three people had simultaneously recognized an old friend and rushed over to catch up with him.

An elderly man and woman, clutching their tickets, gawked at the foursome. Stephanie offered a friendly wave. The woman's face slowly relaxed and the man waved back.

"What happened?" Redman said, as the agents led him to the surveillance truck.

Stephanie's pleasant smile remained, but her voice, barely above a whisper, indicated her disgust. "You have the right to remain silent...."

When Stephanie finished reading his rights, Rick burst out with, "You've spent the last three weeks sharing your big plans with an agent from the FBI's Counterterrorism Unit. The bomb we gave you is authentic looking, but harmless, if you haven't figured that out yet. Everything was recorded. You'll be locked up for a long, long time. Not exactly the paradise you imagined, is it? Or are you relieved you didn't blow yourself to bits?"

Ken rolled his eyes. A vein in his temple flickered.

"We don't usually share all that info," Stephanie whispered, shooting Rick a warning look.

"Oh, sorry." Rick was almost breathless with excitement.

Redman's head dropped. He trudged along in silence between the agents toward the surveillance truck. Inside the vehicle, all pretenses were dropped. Stephanie removed Redman's coat and fake bomb while the other agents held him. He was handcuffed, patted down in search of other weapons, and pushed inside a small temporary holding cell. Ken clanked the steel door shut and locked it, glaring at Redman.

"If he took much longer I could have gotten my full cardio work-out in." Stephanie opened a bottled water, took a long swig, and turned to Rick. "You did okay. For a new guy. Very convincing as a yuppie banker in your fancy suit."

"Thanks. I think it's a Saint Laurent. Went smoothly, didn't it?"

19

"Try not to be so excited next time. We don't owe him any explanations," said Ken.

Rick's face was still flushed. "Yeah. Okay. Got it. What an adrenaline rush! Now what?"

Rashid lowered his voice so Redman couldn't hear. "We'll take him in for interrogation. See if we can find out who his new contact is."

Redman lifted his head and looked around the truck. His gaze settled on the gas masks hanging from the wall in one corner. The corners of his mouth turned up slightly. His eyes shone with an intense and crazy gleam. "This was nothing. Nothing compared to what's coming."

"You're right that you accomplished nothing. We could see that," Rick said. "Still puts your ass in jail for a long time."

"For Christ's sake, stop talking to him." Ken narrowed his eyes.

Redman pressed his chest against the steel cage. "I should be thanking you. All of you. Now I'll be here to see America brought to justice. Because it's going to happen. Soon. America will suffer like never before."

Stephanie pulled a cord above the cage. A black shade descended over its front, effectively silencing Redman.

Chapter Four

Syria
September 21st

Kareem had been summoned by Muhammad Al-Bahil. He was used to it by now, still, he hated having to rush out of the lab. He'd learned that working slowly and patiently produced better results, but today he had no choice. When Al-Bahil said come—you did. When he said jump—you did. Over the past year, the instructions he'd given Kareem involved actions far worse than *come* and *jump*. And so far, Kareem had done everything Al-Bahil told him to do. He had seen what happened to those who didn't. Blinded, mutilated, or executed, depending on how they had displeased him. Al-Bahil made sure everyone in the compound witnessed the consequences of disloyalty.

It was hard to believe only a year had passed since the day Al-Bahil walked into Kareem's busy Damascus University lab with two formidable men dressed in black moving like shadows behind him.

"Which one of you is Kareem Sarif?" Al-Bahil focused on one of the lab assistants. The young graduate student didn't hesitate before pointing out Kareem, probably anxious for Al-Bahil to move on to someone else's space.

"Kareem, I want to talk to you." Al-Bahil's stare sent a shiver down Kareem's spine like the temperature had just dropped ten degrees.

Kareem stepped away from his research, glancing over his shoulder at the vials left out on the counter, and sat down with Al-Bahil in a private room. He wiped his suddenly sweaty palms on the sides of his lab coat and tried to block out the bodyguards and their penetrating stares. He had no idea who Al-Bahil was, yet he understood he was a powerful man with a commanding presence. Back then, Kareem's life revolved around scientific exploration. He had largely managed to ignore the hostilities building around the Middle East. He only wanted to be left to his virology research, his passion.

"Tell me about your virology skills," said Al-Bahil.

Kareem crossed his fingers under the table when he answered, hoping his work was about to be recognized and esteemed on a global level. His hopes wavered when Al-Bahil's questions focused more on what he could do, than what he had already accomplished. Was he being interviewed for a specific job? Perhaps Al-Bahil was a billionaire with a child or spouse in desperate need of a cure for a currently incurable disease. Explanations flew through his mind, propelled by his ego. But he'd never come close to guessing the real reason and he hadn't asked. Anyone in Al-Bahil's presence instinctively understood he was not to be questioned.

"Allah had a plan for you before you were even born. An important plan. One that will have a positive impact on the world," Al-Bahil said after the interview, if that's what it could be called.

With a persistent knot in his stomach, yet feeling like he could now conquer the world, Kareem was hired at a ridiculous salary, five times what the University was paying him, for a "top-secret" job. Men arrived to pack up his personal belongings and move him from his university apartment into a new rent-free apartment in Al-Bahil's modern compound outside the city of

Aleppo. Just before he left the University, Kareem had his first huge clue that he might be in over his head, although in hindsight there had been many others along the way.

"Bring samples of Ebola, Marburg, Lassa, and Machupo with you," Al-Bahil said, as if it was no big deal to *borrow* highly contagious viral samples from the University's maximum containment lab.

"Um, excuse me?" Kareem hoped he'd misunderstood.

"You'll need samples of those viruses to continue your work." The way Al-Bahil's eyes bore into Kareem's soul made it clear he wasn't used to telling someone to do something more than once. "You can get them, can't you?"

Kareem only nodded, reasoning that he had been trusted with those viruses at the University of Damascus, he would now trust himself with them elsewhere so his important research could continue. He believed what he needed to believe because it felt too late to turn back.

A private lab with innovative equipment, everything he required, was waiting for him at Al-Bahil's private compound. A bioreactor, high-performance liquid chromatography, a PCR thermocycler, and a qualified lab assistant—Aamaq. A continuous loop of ISIS propaganda, much of it well-made and inspiring, he had to admit, although he did his best to ignore it, played out in video and intercom feeds throughout the day. Only after Kareem was comfortable in his lab, and feeling a bit like he'd won the lottery, like he was indeed special and chosen, did he learn why Al-Bahil had spent months searching for a scientist with Kareem's background and capabilities. Kareem's American passport and flawless English were simply huge bonuses.

Al-Bahil's plan, further weaponize an already lethal virus to facilitate its spread, was not a beneficial use of Kareem's skillset. But, Kareem reasoned, *having* a weapon and *using* it were two different things. Possessing a weapon and being properly afraid to use it was the whole point of nuclear bombs.

Kareem had learned that somewhere. The weapon's very existence could deter violence. Kareem had come up with many other similar arguments to have with himself while moving forward with Al-Bahil's "project".

Al-Bahil put Kareem in charge of every step of the project. He gave him all the support he needed, and everything he requested as soon as he asked. That alone was empowering. In his new lab, Kareem worked hard, focusing on scientific goals, not the man or the objectives driving the work. But the minute he injected Aamaq with the virus in Aleppo, he catapulted the hypothetical secret project into the real world. One step closer to no turning back. Instead of feeling powerful, Kareem felt like a small rat caught in a trap.

Al-Bahil continued to emphasize that everything Kareem was doing was predestined. Allah had chosen Kareem and provided him with the skills necessary to wage a holy war. Kareem had no choice but to believe. How else could he wake up each morning, get dressed, and go into the lab to continue the work? How else could he have directly infected Aamaq and sentenced the strongest Aleppo villagers to death?

And now, he had to get to moving if he was to meet Al-Bahil in time. Alone inside his state-of-the-art laboratory, fully covered in his PPE, personal protective gear, he stood in front of the monkey cages. The monkeys were more agitated than usual, a result of their physical discomfort. They shook the bars of their cages and paced. One large male hissed and snarled at Kareem. Most of their food lay untouched inside the cages. The female with the blue band lay curled in a fetal position in the corner of her cage. Her fever was advanced. A thin trail of blood emerged from her nose. She had been infected the same day as Aamaq. The powerful virus replicated faster than Kareem originally predicted.

"You don't know it, girl, but you just might be part of something amazing. Genius level amazing. Let's see if this makes a difference for you." He gripped her limp arm in his glove and injected a syringe of cloudy colorless liquid. The monkey didn't try to pull away, not like she had when Kareem first infected her.

The other monkeys watched his every move. They weren't as sick as the blue-banded one. They would be soon. They had already learned Kareem wasn't their friend. Aamaq had always fed them. Kareem only prodded them with needles and made them sick.

Kareem backed away from the cages. The monkeys watched him go, releasing their tight grips on the metal bars and slumping to the bottom of the cages. He transcribed some notes into his data recorder and left the room to begin the decontamination process. He was about to head out and meet Al-Bahil, when he heard a voice calling from outside the locked door. An old man's desperate face pressed against the window, peering inside, scanning the room. He leaned back from the window to knock a second time. The worried face belonged to Aamaq's father. Kareem closed his eyes, summoning the strength he needed to lie again. Head down, he walked to the lab door and opened it.

"Aamaq hasn't been home all week. Are you sure you don't know where he went?" Aamaq's father clasped and unclasped his fingers.

Kareem shook his head. "I'm sorry. He hasn't shown up here for work either. I promise I'll call you if he does."

"Something happened to him." Aamaq's father pulled at strands of hair from his beard.

"I'm sorry. I'll pray for him."

The father's eyes darted around the lab, as if he might find his son hiding under one of the long tables.

"He's not here," Kareem said, his voice gentle.

Aamaq's father left, muttering or praying to himself, Kareem wasn't sure which. He finished his work, turned off the lights, and left the building, locking the outer door behind him.

The subject Al-Bahil called him to discuss—recruiting—weighed heavily on Kareem's mind. He'd told Kareem to find recruits willing to join the jihad. Recruits with American passports. Kareem wasn't a salesperson. He could teach microbiology principles with his eyes closed, but he had no experience convincing people to fight a holy war. Especially when he was weakly clinging to his own conviction like holding on to a thread in a strong gust of wind. He'd already found three Americans willing to give up their lives and travel to Syria, which surprised him. But they hardly needed convincing of anything; they were already on board. Kareem was simply their connection. Based on his limited communications with them, one, an airport employee, seemed to have an IQ far below average. Another was a quiet professional, an engineer, and Kareem had no idea where or how the man developed his convictions. The third, Dylan Redman, the most motivated, troubled, and possibly insane, had mysteriously stopped all communications.

Kareem knew Al-Bahil was going to ask for a status update. He would be disappointed with Kareem's report. He would insist Kareem find more people.

There *was* one person Kareem knew in America who could help him. Someone who might, someday, welcome the mission, if he could only be convinced of its merit. The man was Kareem's own cousin, Amin. He lived in Charlotte, North Carolina.

But how could Kareem convince him when he wasn't himself convinced?

Chapter Five

Charlotte, North Carolina

September 21st

After a long but typical day at Continental Bank, Amin Sarif held his kitchen cabinet door open and stared at the nearly empty shelves. A can of sardines he couldn't remember buying, a can of soup a year past its expiration date, stale crackers—he should throw them out once and for all—along with packets of sugar and ketchup. He opened his freezer again to make sure he had run out of frozen pizzas. Empty. It was too late to be eating dinner anyway. He could skip it. He hadn't intentionally fasted since he was in high school. Why not give it the old college try? But the growling inside his stomach got the best of him. He could try fasting another day. He was undeniably hungry. He would go to the grocery store and stock up, fill an entire cart.

He removed his white dress shirt and striped tie and changed into a short-sleeved polo. He grabbed an umbrella, but didn't open it. His car wasn't far from his apartment. Head down, he ran through the rain toward his Chrysler 200, opened the door, and slid inside. Drops of water fell from his short dark hair. He lifted the edge of his shirt to wipe his glasses dry before turning his key in the ignition. The car turned over, but didn't start. He tried again. Same result. The lights were on, the windshield wipers were going, but the engine wasn't running. Amin groaned, dropped his head against the steering wheel, and shut his eyes. He knew nothing about fixing cars. He listened to the rain pattering his roof. When he opened his eyes, he noticed a glowing red light near the gas gauge. The needle pointed to E. Impossible. He had filled the tank yesterday on his way home from the bank. There had to be something wrong with the gauge. But his car wouldn't start, and an empty tank provided a good explanation. He turned on his phone's flashlight, climbed out of the car, and bent down to look underneath for a leak, a drip, or a puddle of gas. Nothing under the car looked or smelled like gasoline.

He stood up and saw the circular gas door sticking straight out, open. The gas cap dangled from its cord.

He screwed the cap back into place and assembled the evidence in his mind. Had every drop been siphoned? How? Some special vacuum for stealing other people's gas? Was that a thing you could buy on Amazon? Was the theft random, or did someone have a problem with him? Not him *personally*, but his nationality. These days, he was never sure what others thought he represented. He was a long way from being a devout Muslim. He hardly ever went to mosque, hadn't since he started college, unless he was visiting with family. Anyone who thought they knew what Amin stood for was most likely wrong, since he hardly knew himself.

His stomach rumbled. There was no one he felt comfortable asking for a ride to the gas station. No one he knew well enough to trouble. He opened his umbrella and walked the four blocks to the nearest convenience store telling himself it wasn't his fault. He was a nice guy. People liked him. But he was shy. And he spent too much time working and not enough time doing anything else.

Inside the Mini Mart, Amin selected a plastic container with a sandwich. Stocking up on groceries would have to wait until his car was running again. He looked around for gasoline containers and didn't see any.

"That all?" a woman not much older than himself asked in a flat voice from behind the register. She looked at Amin and yawned before turning toward the door to watch another customer enter. Women generally treated him that way, even though he was always neat, clean, close-shaven, and well-dressed. The woman who worked at the men's grooming salon said he was a good-looking guy. So how come it seemed like he wore an invisibility cloak when women were around?

"I couldn't find the gasoline containers. Do you know where they are?"

"The red plastic ones?"

"Yes."

"We're out."

"Then this is all, thank you."

He tried not to notice the magazines stacked behind the counter. Bold women stared down at him from glossy covers. *They* certainly looked interested—half-naked and practically begging him to come closer. He should be disgusted, that's how he had been raised, but he honestly didn't care, aside from being curious.

Amin walked back to his apartment with a tightening in his throat, glancing over his shoulder when the light of the streetlamps failed to reach him, half-expecting whoever stole his gas to pop out of the darkness and assault him. Had he ever felt this lonely before? Maybe his first two days at the University of Michigan, when his insides cramped from the pain of missing home. When he had to sit alone in a corner of the library in case he accidentally allowed a tear to fall. But he recognized homesickness then. His anguish was temporary. Normal, even. He'd waited for it to pass, and it did. What he now felt was different. Instead of dissipating, it had accumulated at a slow and steady pace. At twenty-seven-years old he shouldn't feel so empty. This was his life. He wanted to change it. But how?

He returned with his dinner at the same time his neighbor, Julia, unlocked the door to her apartment. Julia was around his same age. She had light brown hair and light freckled skin which suggested she was at least part Irish. She wore a low-cut blouse to accentuate her bosom and she wasn't alone. The hand on her elbow belonged to a tall, gangly man with long sideburns.

"Hey, Amin." She always had a big smile and it made Amin uncomfortable for reasons he didn't understand.

"Hey," her male companion echoed, grinning. Amin had seen him around the last few weeks, Julia's latest boyfriend. Amin had heard amorous sounds traveling through his thin bedroom walls on more than one occasion. He had to blast his music and wrap a pillow around his head. The sounds involved her current companion and at least two others over the past few years—a stocky red head and an intellectual-looking man from Jamaica. Julia didn't seem to prefer a type.

"Hello," Amin answered, leaning away from Julia and her friend. He unlocked his door and entered his quiet apartment, unsettled by the melancholy feelings Julia had aroused.

His apartment gave off the faint, indescribable odor of absence, as if no one really lived inside. He sat down at his kitchen table, shoulders slumped forward, and turned on his personal computer. By the time his old Dell booted up, all that remained of his sandwich were unwanted onions, pushed to one corner of the container. His work laptop was newer and faster, but he didn't use it because he wanted to check for new emails from his cousin in Syria. Continental Bank monitored employee internet activity and some of his cousin's messages were, well, ...*questionable.*

Amin and his cousin were close when they both lived in America, until Kareem's family moved back to Syria before the start of high school. Kareem went to college in Damascus, majoring in bio-chemistry before completing a Ph.D. in microbiology. He was now an accomplished research scientist working to find a cure for some of the most dangerous viruses on the planet. He'd already been recognized in a magazine called *Virology Today*, although no one except other virologists and Kareem's family would ever see the article. Being a finance guy himself, Amin understood little about what Kareem did from day to day in his lab.

Amin welcomed the opportunity to become close friends with his cousin again. Family was forever. Their conversations became more frequent, though some of Kareem's comments alarmed him. Maybe they were supposed to be sarcastic, but they might be construed as extreme. A brief glance at their last string of instant messages reaffirmed Amin's worries.

Kareem: *I'm concerned for you. How can you find spiritual purity surrounded by lust and greed in America? I think you should come here.*

Amin: *It's not so bad. We shower every day. That helps with the purifying. Ha-ha.*

Kareem: *Americans waste water like they waste everything else. It's disgusting. I know what's on your television. I remember.*

Amin: *Then I guess you don't want to know what the bachelorette supposedly did in the fantasy suite this season. Ha-ha.*

Kareem: *I don't know what you're talking about.*

Amin: *It was a joke. Never mind. I'll get you the complete season box set for your birthday. Maybe it's a little sexualized and materialistic here, but it's not the "Great Satan" like you wrote in a previous message. And I'm so busy with work, it keeps me out of trouble.*

Kareem: *Our main focus should be fulfilling Allah's prophecy.*

Amin: *Unfortunately, I also have to listen to my boss, if I want to stay employed.*

Kareem: *Forget your boss. Your future depends on living according to Allah's word. It's hard for you to see clearly* *because corruption is too prevalent there. You have to move past your fears, get out of your box. Be brave. Live the life you're supposed to live.*

Amin: *What fears? What box?*

Kareem: *I'll pray for you. I have to go now.*

Amin: *Back to the lab?*

Kareem: *I'm in the lab now. Working miracles here. But this is something new. Recruiting. It's only temporary.*

Amin: *Like for a pharmaceutical company?*

Kareem: *Check out the link I sent you. Must go. Later.*

Those messages were a few days old. After reading them for the second time, Amin made an important decision, one that made him feel brave. He would speak with his aunt and uncle, Kareem's parents and tell them his concerns. He planned to share some of Kareem's recent opinions about America being an "evil cesspool". As far-fetched as it sounded, he worried his cousin might become one of those radicals who despised Western civilization and joined a militant group. How would his aunt and uncle respond when he told them? They might be shocked, or worse—offended. Or did they have some of the same concerns? He wasn't sure, but a pressing sense of duty compelled him to speak with them and find out. Sooner rather than later.

He found his most recent email from Kareem and opened the link inside—he had nothing else to do; the Bachelorette was being recorded. The link opened a website, in English, called *Muslims Unite*. He explored tentatively, as if the site was booby-trapped and one wrong click would sink his operating system. He searched for information to help him understand Kareem. If he gained a better understanding, he could voice his concerns to his aunt and uncle. Listen and learn. Help Kareem. That's what he was thinking when something did capture his attention—a man interpreting the Quran.

The Quran has the solutions to everyone's problems, regardless of their complexity or when they occurred. Its message comes straight from Allah.

The words reminded him of the Iman he grew up with at mosque. Most of the services went right over his head, but some memorable snippets offering wisdom and guidance managed to sink in, only to be forgotten in recent years. He might need wisdom and guidance now more than ever. He listened and a sense of hope grew inside him—until Julia's moans traveled through his living room wall, surrounding him, as if they were coming from his own bedroom, growing louder and more urgent. He reached for his iPad and earbuds and had just cranked up the volume when Kareem contacted him via Skype. Amin pulled out his ear buds and pushed a button, allowing music to blast through his kitchen before accepting Kareem's call.

"I can barely hear you," Kareem said. "Why is your music so loud?"

Amin considered turning off his music and letting Kareem hear evidence of his amorous neighbor's sexual activity. Was it possible Kareem would be more intrigued than incensed? Would they have a good laugh like they would have when they were younger? He didn't want to find out. Amin hardly needed to provide Kareem with more evidence of America's immoralities. Kareem already had his share of ammunition.

"I'm unwinding," said Amin in explanation.

"Oh. Hey, it would be great if you came to visit me. I have a lot I want to talk about with you. We could work together on this project I'm involved with."

Chapter Six

Los Angeles
September 21st

The Los Angeles Counterterrorism team sat at technology-covered desks in a windowless open area, called the War Room, focused on their computer monitors. Except Rick. He stood behind Rashid, asking questions, most likely. His body swayed from side to side and he fiddled with a pen against his thigh. The kid, Quinn couldn't help thinking of Rick that way, was good-natured and brought a new sense of eagerness into the department, but he needed to tone everything down. Although he had some valuable work experience, internships acquired through powerful connections, he was the youngest member of the team. Only twenty-four.

Ken stood up, stretched, and walked over to Quinn. "He's not up to the job," Ken said quietly, tilting his head toward Rick.

Quinn made eye contact with Ken and held it. His voice was barely above a whisper. "Rick isn't going anywhere. So, all of us will have to help him wise up before he messes up. Clear?"

Ken nodded, his lips pressed tight together. His biceps tensed and quivered.

Quinn cleared his throat and spoke to his team. "I just got out of that National Security Council meeting. What's going on here?"

Stephanie answered first. "An escalation of attacks on Christian churches across Egypt. Bombs planted under pews. Islamic State immediately claimed responsibility online through the Amaq News Agency. It's already in the news."

"Also, Al-Shabab—"

Rick interrupted Stephanie with, "That's Somalia's Islamic extremist rebels, right?"

"Yes," said Stephanie. "They immediately claimed responsibility for the car bomb targeting Somalia's new military chief. He survived, but thirteen others died. Death toll still growing."

Quinn nodded, his face solemn. Ideally, he only wanted to hear about planned attacks before they happened, when they could still be stopped. "Do we have anything to follow up on from Redman? Anything more about his contact?"

Rashid turned in his chair. "He's been under interrogation since last night. Just comfort denial, non-stop noise, no water boarding. He's a real messed up piece of work, but not really a hardcore terrorist. There have been plenty of tears, and plenty of regret."

"Regret at being caught?"

"That too, but he's consistently alluded to a planned attack on mass transit. Three major cities. He didn't know which. And something else, he didn't know the details, only that it was a top-secret project targeting American citizens. He regrets not waiting to be a part of either of those plots."

"Hmm," Quinn said. "I thought his comments in the van might have been idle threats. A prisoner's only means of intimidating his captors. And the contact?"

"First name is Kareem. He used to live in America. He's somewhere in the Middle East now. Redman believes Kareem is powerful, with the means to do something huge. Much bigger than strapping on explosives."

Ken chuckled. "If he was powerful, why would he be chatting with Redman?"

"Right," said Rashid. "But Redman believes otherwise."

"Did you find interactions with Kareem on his computer or phone?" said Quinn.

Rashid shook his head. "Redman was following dozens of Twitter, Facebook and Instagram sites for jihadists, but we found no personal correspondence with Kareem, or anyone else with a specific plan. Besides his interaction with me."

"So how were they communicating?"

"I don't know yet. I found one unusual thing. Frequent visits to a website, the Yoga Institute of Paris. The first visit was two days before his arrest."

"Yoga in Paris?"

"Yes. He's never been to Paris. Maybe he does yoga, tons of people do. But, I haven't found proof of it yet."

"Sounds like you've got something to follow up on." Quinn rubbed his chin. "I'll be out of the office tomorrow and Friday, for the training I promised to do. Let me know if you find anything new."

"Maybe I'm just being paranoid, but it seems every time you go somewhere, something big happens," Rashid said.

"Hopefully, not this time."

After Quinn left the War Room, Rick turned to his team members. "So, what was Redman's deal?" he asked them.

"He's been in lots of trouble," Rashid said. "Claims it wasn't his fault. Right now, he's blaming everything on prejudice against Muslims, although he was hardly a devout Muslim of any sort. He recently got himself hooked on ISIS propaganda over the internet and discovered a new purpose."

"Does it ever bother you that we're often, you know, targeting Muslims?" Rick leaned back in his chair toward Rashid. "If you don't mind me asking."

"Well, you're assuming I'm Muslim because I'm Arab."

"Oh, sorry, man."

Rashid laughed. "It's okay. I am Muslim, but not devout. And we hardly target *all* Muslims, just the ones who hang out in IS chatrooms."

"Oh. Listen, I hope that wasn't offensive to ask about," Rick said.

"It wasn't."

"In the spirit of getting to know all of you," Rick continued, "Stephanie, I hear you're quite the tennis player."

Stephanie grinned. "Number one singles at Cornell."

"Wow. You remind me of Sharapova. You know, with the long blonde ponytail. I heard you spent two years in Afghanistan, posing as a tennis instructor?"

"Checking up on Stephanie?" Rashid asked. There was an odd tone to his voice, meant to be joking and barely missing his mark.

Ken crossed his arms. "How do *you* know that? You shouldn't have access to that info."

Rick shrugged apologetically. "I just wanted to know who I was working with."

"It's okay. The rest of the team knows." Stephanie smiled. "I lived on a private compound. I had one student. Son of an Al-Qaeda leader. My mission was to earn the boy's trust during our daily lessons and obtain information on his father's whereabouts."

"Nice," said Rick. "A little glamorous spy action and you get to play tennis."

"Does it sound glamorous? Because it wasn't. No one was happier than me when he was found and I was out of there. And my tennis game got worse. No competition."

"If you're still looking for competition, I played on my high school team. I know it's not college, but we were decent."

"I might consider taking you up on your offer." Stephanie tilted her head to the side.

"Sounds like fun," Rashid said, but his voice didn't sound like he thought so.

"What led you to an FBI career?" Rick asked, still facing Stephanie.

"My older brother was killed in the Twin Towers. He was a stockbroker."

"Jeez. I'm sorry. I knew about the tennis, but not—"

Stephanie shrugged. "Changed my life. No question. I was in college. Switched my major from pre-vet to computer science so I could stop terrorists, exactly what we're doing. And yes, sometimes my job feels personal. I think that's a good thing."

Rick nodded.

"And you?" said Ken. His stare reminded Rick of the red-tailed hawk in his parents' neighborhood, when it was about to swoop down on its prey. "Why are you here?"

They knew who he was, or more specifically, who his father was—Senator John Webster. The presidential nominee's pick for vice-president in the last election. A polished and powerful statesman. Public opinion was split almost evenly between loving and hating him.

"I wanted to work for the FBI in Counterterrorism," said Rick. "The Los Angeles field office was an easy first-choice decision." He grinned. "My father convinced me to go for Intelligence and Analysis, said it would be exciting but relatively safe."

"True," said Rashid. "The opportunity to apprehend Redman was an unusual one."

"So, the position pretty much landed in your lap?" Ken sneered.

"Look, Ken, I can't erase my father's influence, but I'm more than capable of doing this job and doing it well."

"We'll see about that." Ken folded his muscular arms across his chest.

"What's your problem with me?" Rick stood with his hands on his hips.

"What's my problem? Do you even have to ask? My problem is that the FBI isn't a place for people who aren't up to the job."

Rick held Ken's gaze for as long as he dared. Now that Ken's opinion was out in the open, Rick didn't have to wonder if he was being paranoid anymore. He'd have to work harder until he proved himself, and then keep working just as hard. He couldn't wait until his unit had their next big case.

Chapter Seven

Los Angeles
September 22nd

Holly stepped from her bedroom into the art-lined hallway and coughed. A few feet away from the front door, Quinn turned and set down his suitcase. "You're up. Good morning."

"Where are you going?" she asked, pushing a section of glossy hair away from her sleep-laden eyes.

"I'm on my way to Georgia to give a lecture at FLETC."

A sigh of exasperation escaped her collagen-plumped lips. "I don't know what that stands for."

"It's the DHS Federal Law Enforcement Training Center." He glanced at his watch. "I still have some time. I can sit back down and have coffee with you before I go."

Holly spun around and walked in the opposite direction, already twirling her hair around her finger. Her lack of a negative response translated into a yes, so Quinn followed. In the kitchen, he pulled a bar stool away from the counter and sat. Holly busied herself with the espresso machine.

"I'm sorry I left your gallery party early."

"It's fine," Holly said, still facing away from him. Quinn knew that "fine" had multiple meanings.

The machine hissed and frothed. Holly dropped her head forward and rolled it slowly from side to side. One hand kneaded the muscles in her neck. When she finished, she straightened her decorative canisters, the ones she'd had handmade for the kitchen counter. Her hands moved gently around them, aligning each to perfection. As far as Quinn knew, they contained Holly's herbal teas and detoxifying vitamins—things that didn't concern him.

"We don't need three of these bottles on the counter. I mean, jeez, you have enough anti-bacterial products for an army." She grabbed two bottles and tossed them under the sink. "So why do they need you there anyway? In Alabama?" she asked, still facing away.

"Georgia. I'm teaching part of a training course for emergency responders, like firefighters, police, paramedics. I'll talk about the precautions they need to take with chemical and biological threats. I agreed to do this a year ago. Things kept coming up and I kept cancelling. This is the first time it's worked out where I can go down to help."

"You kept cancelling? Really? What a surprise." Holly finally turned around. She frowned, shot her index finger up to her face and pressed against one nostril, preventing a drop of blood from escaping her nose. "The air is dry in the house. When will you be back?"

"Tomorrow night." He shared this information with her previously—where he was going, why he was going, and when he would return—at least he thought he had. But he kept calm, as if disclosing the information for the first time. He glanced at the open seat next to him but Holly remained standing. She picked up the morning paper and gave it her full attention. Quinn thought hard about what to say next. He wanted to tell Holly about the drops in the bathroom cabinet to soothe her bloodshot eyes, but the comment and its implications might make her angry

41

and starting an argument was the last thing he wanted to do. He wanted to connect in any small way that might lead to things feeling okay between them. Ask about her plans for the day? Tell her he wasn't looking forward to the flight to Georgia? She'd been so irritable lately. It might be best to say nothing. He stood and moved closer. Standing behind her, he wrapped his arm gently around her waist and leaned forward, silently inhaling the scent of her face cream and the minty toothpaste she'd used. Holly's shoulders stiffened as his chest gently met her back. He swallowed his dismay and held his ground, his body barely touching hers, reading *The Los Angeles Times* over her shoulder.

"Humpf," Holly said, as she read the front-page headline.

A smug TV celebrity, notorious for bad decisions, stared at him from the front page. One day out of a much-publicized rehab stint and she had driven her convertible onto the strand in Manhattan Beach. No one was hurt, but the scene—her confused stumble from the car and subsequent retching in the sand—had been recorded on every bystander's cell phone. Front-page worthy news? Shouldn't be. Quinn imagined what the dominant headline might have been if Rashid hadn't spent weeks diligently analyzing the results of scanning software to find Dylan Redman, if he hadn't built a relationship with him and stepped in to provide fake explosives. Redman could have attained real explosives from another source. Pictures of military personnel carrying body bags from the Hollywood Bowl amidst family members wailing on their knees might have replaced the drunk celebrity's mug shot.

Quinn's team had done their jobs well, protecting the public from the plotting, hating, and killing. A screw-up would be public knowledge in a heartbeat, but his teams' successes stayed hidden, as intended, without public celebration. As much as Quinn wanted to highlight the arrest, let the public know his team was doing their job, he didn't want communications from Redman's new contact to cease. Not until they identified him. Unfortunately, there were plenty of other Dylan Redmans out there.

42

When Quinn arrived at the FLETC training center and stood at the front of the auditorium, he saw a sea of faces in every shade of skin color staring back at him from the rows of seats. He recognized the attentive look of an ex-military man with cropped hair, and the eagerness of a young trainee who sat on the edge of his seat, staring up at Quinn as if an attack was imminent and he might be placed in charge. Quinn smiled and nodded to acknowledge them.

Exactly on time, Quinn said, "Welcome, everyone, and thank you for being here, not that you had a choice." He smiled. "I'm Quinn Traynor, Assistant Special Agent in Charge of the Los Angeles Counterterrorism Unit. I oversee the FBI's Los Angeles office and the Joint Terrorism Task Force. We work closely with DHS."

A few heads nodded.

"I'm going to talk about biological terrorism. This training is designed to help you protect the public and yourself, in the event of a biological attack, should you be called on as a first responder." He paused. "Tell me, what comes to your mind when I say bioterror?"

A middle-aged man wearing a polo shirt and khakis near the front raised his hand. Quinn pointed to him.

"Billion-dollar bio-weapons facilities in North Korea and North China with the capabilities for controlled deployment."

"Excellent. That's what I expected to hear and it certainly fits the definition. But biological weapons also include any natural organism that can cause disease, incapacitation, or death. Viruses. Bacteria. Herbs. Fungi. All can become tools of terror."

He clicked on his laptop to start the presentation the FLETC had created for the training.

"The use of biological agents for warfare dates back thousands of years. A few examples—in 300 BC, the Romans killed their enemies and destroyed their morale by contaminating their water supply with dead animals. In the early 1300s, the Mongols catapulted plague-infected corpses over the walls into what is now Crimea. They forced their enemies to flee the city, possibly starting the epidemic plague that killed 25 million in Europe. Russian troops did the same against the Swedes in the 1700s when they flung corpses over the city walls of Reval. That's the last known incident of using plague-infected corpses."

Quinn suddenly stopped speaking. His words echoed in his head. The last known incident of using plague-infected corpses. *Not exactly.* He looked up and over the audience, unblinking, as if he'd forgotten how to read the notes on his laptop.

"Is he okay?" whispered someone in one of the center seats.

A slight shake of his head, and Quinn returned to the present. He looked down at his laptop as if seeing if for the first time. "Sorry, I was saying, um, yes… in the 20th century, bio-warfare became more sophisticated. In several countries, weaponized bio-agents were produced and stockpiled in huge facilities. Botulinum. Aflatoxin. Anthrax." He looked away from the notes and focused on faces in the front row. "If you're old enough, you'll remember September 2001. Members of Congress and the media received letters tainted with anthrax spores. Twenty-two people became sick and five died."

Quinn scanned the audience. A young woman to his left was writing furiously across a notebook like a college student, even though there wouldn't be a test. Next to her, the head of a large man slumped forward. Quinn couldn't see his face and thought his eyes might have been closed. Was he bored already? Did he think terror attacks could only happen to other people in other countries? Quinn wanted to smack the back of the guy's head, but instead, he continued. "A single gram of odorless, colorless toxin, impossible to detect, can kill ten million people. It only takes a few particles to start an epidemic. Terrorists can disperse them using almost any mechanism, a plane flying over a crowded venue, a ventilation system, vectors, such as mosquitoes or rodents, the food or water supply, and, last, but not least, a carrier on a suicide mission."

"Category A agents pose the biggest threats. These are anthrax, botulism, plague, smallpox, tularemia, and viruses that cause hemorrhagic fevers, such as Ebola, Marburg, Lassa, and Machupo. All of them are naturally-occurring, except for smallpox, which has been eradicated. None are indigenous to the United States. They're the most dangerous because they're easily transmitted and have high mortality rates. Genetic manipulation can make them even more aggressive."

Quinn continued, explaining in detail the first response protocols for a biological attack. When finished, he asked, "Does anyone have questions?"

A young man with a shaved head raised his hand. Quinn pointed to him.

"Is the point of a biological attack to kill as many people as possible?"

"Good question. The main goal is to create fear. The direct casualties associated with the outbreak would be minor compared to the financial and economic damage. The ensuing fear-induced panic could cripple a country. Imagine the scenario of a contagious epidemic. Most people would be too afraid to go to work, so our basic infrastructure would be paralyzed. Public order collapses. Basic services fail. The result—complete chaos— is what radical terrorists are aiming for."

Heads nodded.

"Other questions?" Quinn asked.

A young woman raised her hand. Her porcelain skin and wavy red hair reminded Quinn of Holly. "I'm sorry if this is a

45

stupid question, but, if we're talking about terrorist groups, like ISIS, for example, why do they hate us?"

"Another good question. If we're talking about Islamic terrorists, there are a few reasons. Radicals believe the Quran commands them to punish or eliminate all infidels—non-believers. Citizens of the United States, Europe, and Israel are their main targets. They also want to punish western civilization because western military forces are preventing them from taking over other countries and building an all-powerful, radical Islamic State without borders. Their greatest accomplishment would be an attack on western civilization so destabilizing that it would create a spiraling power vacuum in the Middle East. We'd have to direct our money, our law enforcement, and our intelligence inward. We'd have to pull our troops back home. Militant groups could exploit our absence, overthrow our proxy governments, and confiscate money from oil resources, growing even more powerful. If the United States pulled its military presence and money out of the Middle East, ISIS, for example, could take over the entire area."

"What do they hope to gain, like, personally?" a woman a few rows back called out.

"Extremists believe they're doing the will of Allah and if they do their part they will be rewarded with a lifetime in paradise. Recruits are conditioned and brainwashed to believe this. Unfortunately, ISIS is extremely successful in this regard. They're a powerful recruiting machine. They spend millions on propaganda, very effective propaganda, and it's all over the internet."

He looked around the auditorium to see if any other hands were raised and saw none. He put both hands on the podium and leaned forward. "Here's something I'm sure you've heard before, but it's important. To successfully protect our nation, we must be right one hundred percent of the time. No mistakes. To be successful as a terrorist—you only have to get lucky once." He paused. "All of us must work together to keep the country safe. That's it. Thank you."

Several people stood up immediately to leave. Others clapped politely. Quinn felt a quick surge of resentment. They weren't worried about the highly-motivated terrorists who wanted nothing more than their annihilation. They were probably just grateful he finished speaking so they could hurry over to the lunch buffet. Frowning, he shut down his computer and slipped it into his bag.

"Hey, Quinn."

Quinn raised his eyes to see a DHS agent he had worked with in the past. "Hey. How's it going?"

"Good, man. I heard you were here and wanted to say, hi. I just stepped in at the end of your presentation. You had some good questions."

"It's good when people ask questions at the end, means at least a few are still awake."

The DHS agent laughed. "In your answers there, you didn't mention the millions of jihadists with raging appetites for mass murder. Those who find fulfillment through executions and view the murder of infidels as holy and beautiful." He snorted. "That's what I wish they all knew."

"I do too. Sometimes. But that evil and the depth of that hatred surpasses what the average American is prepared to believe."

"True. And changing the jihadist's motivation isn't going to happen in this lifetime."

"Nope. Our best strategy is prevention and defense."

The man nodded. "Because it's getting crazier out there."

This time it was Quinn's turn to agree.

"Are you going to get lunch?" said the DHS agent.

"Oh, uh, no. I need to check in with my office."

"See you around then."

"I'll be back tomorrow morning."

The next morning, after a long run on unfamiliar streets, Quinn taught a training session on chemical weapons and left the auditorium with the last of the trainees. Stepping into the hallway, he spotted a woman ahead of him with smooth brown hair wearing a white lab coat. A surge in his heartbeat propelled him forward. He wove through the crowd, hurrying to catch up with her before she disappeared.

"Madeline," he called.

She didn't turn around. Only a few yards away, and she glanced to her right. Quinn saw her profile, a roman nose and full cheeks. He stopped and someone bumped into him from behind. "Oh, sorry," said Quinn. His shoulders slumped forward with a heavy sigh. It wasn't her. He was angry with himself for his surge of anticipation. He didn't like what that said about him. He was supposed to fly home in the morning, but he decided on the spot to skip the evening's events and get an earlier flight home.

His phone buzzed with an incoming message from Rashid.

Redman died.

What? How the hell did that happen? He stepped into an empty classroom, closed the door and called Rashid. "How did Redman die?" he said when Rashid answered.

"Don't know yet. He met with a public attorney this morning, returned to his cell in the Federal Detention Center. I had him taken to an interrogation room. I walked in and he started seizing. I called for help. Medics were there in minutes, but failed to resuscitate him. He died right in front of me. If he had some sort of medical condition, he didn't mention it when he was processed."

"Damn," Quinn said. "We'll have to wait for an autopsy."

"There was nothing I could do."

"I'm sure there wasn't."

"Civil rights groups are going to protest, even though they didn't give a damn about him two days ago, when he tried to take out everyone at the Hollywood Bowl. I mean, did you see him press the button right when a young family with three little kids walked by?"

"I know."

"And, unfortunately, we still don't know how he was communicating with his contact, Kareem. I'm sorry. I know it could turn into a big headache for us."

"We'll figure it out." Redman wasn't a high-profile terrorist with irreplaceable inside intelligence, but he was evil. The image of him detonating his bomb as the young family passed had been seared into Quinn's memory.

"Okay," said Rashid. "Are you going to the boondoggle thing tonight? Some sort of celebration, forget what they call it. Everyone who has ever done the training says it's worth the trip."

"Yeah, I've heard. But I'm skipping it, if I can get an earlier flight. I'm going to go home and spend some time with my wife."

"Oh. Good. Safe trip and all that."

Quinn boarded an afternoon flight and landed at LAX before nineteen hundred hours. Driving down Pacific Coast Highway, the ocean breeze welcomed him home and the setting sun illuminated the horizon with an array of purple and pink tones. He pictured Holly greeting him with her beautiful smile and a deep kiss inside the front hallway—happy to see him arrive home earlier than usual. He imagined the scent of her perfume, still intoxicating after so many years. When he reached the driveway, he braced himself for reality, expecting irritation in some form regardless of the time he had arrived. Lately, Holly always found something to set her off.

The first time he met Holly, she exuded beauty and confidence and seemed to fear nothing. Her carefree attitude was a welcome distraction from his career. All those things still held true, so what had changed?

He unlocked his front door. The house was dark, quiet, and empty. He exhaled through his mouth, long and slow. Built-up tension dissolved across his forehead and shoulders at the thought of unwinding in front of the television. He locked his weapons in the bedroom safe and changed into shorts and a West Point T-shirt. He microwaved three frozen dinners and ate them standing in front of the window, mesmerized by the ocean waves crashing onto the shore in the distance. When the plastic trays were empty, he grabbed a jar of peanut butter and a spoon, turned on the television, and sorted through a stack of mail while the Clippers played the Warriors in the background.

A crack of thunder surprised him. He crossed the house and opened the back door to witness a sudden downpour accompanied by a quick drop in temperature. After a few minutes of watching the rain, he grabbed a water bottle and walked out to the garage to bench, curl, and squat. An hour later, his shirt was stained with sweat and Holly still wasn't home. He tried to reach her on her cell. When his call went directly to her voicemail, he left a message, took a shower, and went to bed. He stayed awake for a while worrying about his wife, but eventually the effects of a long day made him succumb to sleep.

Chapter Eight

Los Angeles
September 23rd

Digging her toes into the sand, Reese tipped her face up toward the moon, stuck out her chest, and flung her arms back. "Oh, my God! Seriously. I love this stuff!" She had been grinning like the Cheshire Cat since she'd swallowed the pills Holly gave her. Minutes later, she'd been hit with the overwhelming urge to go for a walk on the beach.

With a deep laugh, Holly dropped her high heels onto the beach and sashayed over to put her arm around her best friend. "Look at you! Someone is feeling good tonight."

"I am. And it's not just the drugs. I *love* my new job. I mean, did you see my boss's house?" She turned to face the beach-front house they had left moments ago. Four stories of giant windows stared back at them. "And he's insanely hot."

"So is his wife," Holly said.

"She's a little on the plump side, a size six, at least. But don't worry. Yes, I would screw him in a heartbeat, but I am *not* going to do anything to mess up this opportunity."

"Good. I hope you can remember that."

Reese laughed. "Thanks so much for coming out with me to his party, sweetie."

"Are you kidding me? You're my best friend. Plus, I wanted to see his house. So many blank walls in need of art. I made some recommendations. I hope I'll be hearing from him."

"I can always try to remind him." Reese spread her arms wide and spun around in a circle until she stopped, facing the ocean. "Like I said, it's not only the drugs, but seriously, you've got to get me more of them. Where did you get them?"

Holly smiled knowingly. "A new friend."

"Your new friend needs to patent them quick. Everyone will want to feel like this all the time."

"He doesn't make them. He's a distributor. I should send some to my father for his studio. They'll help his actresses loosen up more than whatever it is they're using now, don't you think?"

"Absolutely. So, is there any particular reason you called your supplier a new friend, as opposed to a new dealer?"

Holly laughed. "Yes." A grin spread across her face. "I slept with him. A few times. His name is Christian."

Reese grinned. "Really?"

A crack of thunder startled the women. They froze, staring at each other with wide eyes and open mouths. A large raindrop splatted on top of Holly's head. Another hit Reese's nose. They broke into hysterical laughter.

"It's about to pour. Come on!" Reese grabbed Holly's hand.

"Wait!" Holly looked around for her shoes before scooping them out of the sand. She quickly pulled her tight skirt up around her waist so she could move more easily.

"I hope none of my new colleagues see you in your underwear," Reese said, breathy from running.

"I look amazing in my panties!" Large raindrops suddenly pelted them from every direction. "Oh no! Oh shit!" yelled Holly.

They hurried back the way they had come, giggling and shrieking like children, aside from the profanities, as their hair and clothes quickly became drenched. The rain fell harder and faster. They sprinted across the wet sand toward the beach-front mansion.

"Go to your car. It's closer!" Reese yelled.

Still laughing, Holly ran with her head down. "I'm so frickin' cold. How did it get cold so fast?"

"I don't know. It never rains here. What the hell?"

Holly saw her red Mercedes convertible and yelled, "Shit!" The top was down. The car sat open and exposed like a giant water barrel.

"Oh, my God!" Reese shrieked through her laughter. "Quick. Get it up! Get it up!" She opened the passenger door and sat down. Rain continued to douse her.

Holly's keys slipped from her hand. She dropped to her knees and searched the ground. Her wet hair hung heavy, plastered across her eyes. One side of her skirt had slid back down, partially covering pink panties. "I can't find the keys. Help! Shit! Fuck! Damn it! Where did they go?"

Reese laughed hysterically. "Stop! Cut it out! I'm going to pee my pants."

"We're so wet, no one will notice. Wait! Don't. Not in my car." She fumbled around on the ground. "Ah-ha. I've got them!" Holly stood up, tossed her shoes into the back seat, and fired up the car.

"Get the top up!" shouted Reese. She reached across the driver's seat, pressing against Holly's firm breasts for the button to operate the top. In an instant, a compartment opened in the back of the car and the top smoothly and silently unfolded into place.

Holly leaned forward, one arm across her abdomen, catching her breath from running but mostly from laughing so hard. Steam filled the car, making it impossible to see in or out of the windows.

"You look like hell," Reese said. "There's mascara running down your cheeks."

Holly wiped drops of rain from under her eyes. "You're not exactly runway-ready yourself."

"We're not going back in there like this. Let's go home. Okay?"

Holly nodded. "I should go anyway. I think Quinn is supposed to be home tonight."

"Supposed to, huh?" Reese scrunched up her face. "I wouldn't hold my breath if I were you."

Holly maneuvered her sports car out of the circular driveway and onto Pacific Coast Highway. Rain fell hard and steady. She leaned forward, using her hand to rub condensation off the windshield. The Mercedes meandered across the center line and back into the right lane.

Holly's phone rang, a few lyrics from Beyoncé. She rummaged through her purse with one hand to find it and glanced at the screen long enough to see it was Quinn calling. The car crossed the center line again.

"Watch out!" Reese screamed and grabbed Holly's arm.

Holly looked up, straight into the headlights of an oncoming car. She yanked the steering wheel to the right. Her phone sailed into the door. The muscles in her arms and neck automatically grew rigid, bracing for impact. The other car swerved sharply to get out of her way, avoiding a head-on collision. They heard the crunch of metal bending and the screech of it tearing away as the back ends of the cars collided and one ricocheted off the other. Holly slammed on the brakes. Her gaze flew to her review mirror in time to see the other car spin around, veer off the side of the road, and disappear over the dark embankment.

The Mercedes came to a stop in the break-down lane. They were alone on the road.

"Oh. My. God," Holly's entire body trembled. An intense and horrifying alertness followed. She could feel her heart pounding in her temples.

"What are you doing? You can't stop here!" Reese said.

"That car just flew off the side of the road. We have to see if they're okay." Holly's voice rose with her panic.

"Wait. How much did you drink?"

"I don't know. Not much. A few mixed drinks? I'm not drunk. It was an accident."

"You had at least three drinks. And pills. You were looking at your phone. We'll both be blamed for this. They'll make us use a breathalyzer and take a urine test. You'll have a mug shot. My boss will find out about it. I don't want to lose my job."

Holly stared blankly ahead at the road. The windshield wipers slashed back and forth in silence. She tried to figure out what to do, but it was impossible with her heart beating madly in her chest like she'd snorted way too many lines. She reached for the door latch. "We have to check and see if someone needs help."

"No. We don't." Reese wrapped her fingers tightly around Holly's wrist. "It was just a fender bender. We have to drive away, before we're both arrested and taken to jail."

Cars whizzed past on both sides of the road, none of them aware of what had just occurred. An image of Quinn flashed into Holly's maze of frantic thoughts. How would he feel about bailing her out of a jail cell tonight? He always did the right thing. He was all about saving people. He would have jumped from his car and ran across the street the minute it happened.

"I'm sure they're calling for help on their phone right now, if they need it. Please, just drive away. I don't want you to catch the blame for this. It wasn't really your fault. It was raining and no one could see well, but that's not how it will play out in a court room."

Holly swallowed the lump in her throat and shifted the car into drive, but kept her foot on the brake.

Reese looked out the back window. "The police might be here any minute. Let's go. Drive." She released her grip on Holly's wrist like it was a done deal.

Holly pressed her foot on the gas pedal and drove, feeling suddenly sober and anxious. They remained silent until they were a few miles away from Reese's apartment.

"It stopped raining," Reese said, as if they could have a normal conversation.

"Did that *really* just happen?"

"Just forget about it."

"My car is damaged."

"We'll look when we get inside my garage."

Holly drove into the underground garage for Reese's building. She parked in a lit corner and turned off the car. "I'm afraid to look."

Reese got out and walked around the back to the driver's side. "Oh, shit."

"What? Is it bad?"

Reese exhaled loudly, puffing out her cheeks. "It's obvious you've been in a wreck. But it can be fixed."

"What does it look like?"

"The back thingy is sort of torn off and hanging down."

"What back thingy?"

"I don't know what it's called. Come look at it. It's not that bad. I shouldn't have made a big deal about it."

Holly remained in the driver's seat. "I can't take the car home. Quinn is going to see it and ask what happened and…"

"And what? Figure out you hit someone and turn you in?"

"I don't want him to know about any of this." Holly covered her face with her palms and shook her head.

Reese stood with her hands on her hips and waited. "You've had this car almost two years. Isn't the lease up soon anyway?"

Holly looked up. Her eyes were dry. "It's only been a year. And it can't be turned in like this. In case something *did* happen and the police are looking for it."

"They're not."

"You don't know that. I'll leave the car here and talk to my father tomorrow. He'll know somewhere I can take it where they won't ask questions."

"I don't know if it's such a good idea to leave it here. It's not private. Your garage is private."

"Reese! You're the one who insisted we leave the scene. And you're trying to convince me nothing happened, like I've got nothing to worry about."

"Okay. Calm down. Don't say *the scene* as if it was a major accident. For all you know the only damage is to your car. Everything is going to be fine. I have a car cover I can put on it. No one is even going to know it's here."

"Okay. Go get it," Holly said. "I'll feel better once it's covered."

Holly waited in the driver seat. She debated calling Quinn, but didn't. Reese returned ten minutes later carrying a blue car cover stuffed into a giant trash bag. She had changed out of her wet clothes into a pink hoodie and black leggings, and pulled her hair back. "Got it."

Holly stepped out to assess the damage. A massive dent marred the back side and part of the rear spoiler sagged toward the ground.

"See? It's not so bad. Totally fixable. And I don't see any missing parts. So, that's good." Reese put her arms around Holly and hugged her. "Do you want to stay here tonight?"

"No, I better get home. I'll take an Uber."

Reese clasped Holly's shoulders. "Take a deep breath."

Holly inhaled slow and deep, but looked away.

"Look at me." Reese waited until Holly turned. "Accidents happen. It's not a big deal."

Holly wrapped her arms around her chest and hugged herself tightly. Accidents happened all the time. But leaving the scene of an accident? Not so much.

Chapter Nine

Los Angeles
September 24th

Quinn woke to the creak of the front door, followed by thumping noises and the soft squelching sound of the refrigerator opening and closing. A glance at the watch he never removed told him it was zero two hundred hours. Light flooded the bedroom. He squinted, his eyes adjusting to the glare and Holly's figure inside the doorway. Her hair was wet and curling. Smudges of black mascara sunk into tiny creases below her eyes. And she'd been drinking. He could always tell. The only good side was that when Holly was intoxicated, she wanted sex, which wasn't the worst thing he could think of. It might help them reconnect. It would certainly be a good start.

"Hey." He sat up in the bed.

"When did you get home?" Holly said. She removed her necklace with a sharp tug and tossed it toward the Art Deco dresser, where it hit the edge and slid to the floor. She wrapped her arms around her shoulders, shivered, and leaned against the wall.

"Around nineteen…I mean, around seven. Where have you been?"

"With Reese. Her new boss had a party. She wanted me to come."

"I didn't hear the garage door open or close."

"I didn't drive. I had a drink at Reese's apartment so I left my car there and took an Uber."

"You could have called me. I could have picked you up."

"Oh, too late."

"Looks like you got caught in the rain. That was something, wasn't it? The storm?"

"Yes. I need to take a shower." She pulled off her soaked blouse and let it fall to the carpet, revealing her eighteenth birthday gift—perfectly shaped breasts, still as good as new. She stumbled stepping out of her skirt but steadied herself against the bathroom door frame. Quinn heard the door click shut behind her. He was surprised she hadn't shed her clothes and joined him in bed like she usually did after a few drinks. He got out of bed and picked up her necklace, along with her wet blouse, panties, and bra. He dropped the clothes in the hamper, turned the light off again, and returned to bed. He intended to wait up, but it seemed like the shower ran forever. He fell back asleep before she tiptoed across the floor and quietly slid onto the opposite side of their king-sized mattress.

Quinn watched Holly snoring, a short, soft whistling sound, against her pillow. Sleeping more than a few hours challenged him. His mind was constantly on overdrive. He worried about what could go wrong if his team didn't do everything right. Nightmares often plunged his subconscious into worst case scenarios. Someone from the watch list being more of a threat than realized or someone flying under the radar slipping into a crowded mall with a semi-automatic or a suicide vest, renting a helicopter and spraying a chemical weapon over the Dodgers Stadium, touring the water treatment plants and poisoning the water supply. His imagination had no limits while he slept.

Holly's tangled hair fanned out above her head in every direction like a peaceful Medusa. He gently moved a section covering her forehead. She stirred and opened her eyes. Just as quickly, she closed them. He placed his hand on her backside and moved closer, his thighs against hers. He trailed his fingers slowly along her hip and stroked her inner thigh. His breath quickened. Suddenly, she turned over and scooted away, toward the edge of the bed.

He lay next to her for a few more minutes, aching inside. The emotional distance between them seemed even greater when they were only inches apart. With a lump in his throat, he got out of bed and went for a long run in the crisp morning air.

Later, he was changing a kitchen light bulb when Holly appeared. She wore a short ivory-colored robe he had never seen before that showed off her long legs. Her arms were wrapped tightly across her chest. Despite sleeping late, she looked like she had been awake for most of the night. She glanced around the kitchen. "Did you get the newspaper?"

"Yeah, but I guess I left it by the front door. You know, I don't have anything planned for the day. I'm wide-open for whatever you want to do."

"Oh. Sorry. I have plans. Meeting Dad for something." Holly uncrossed her arms and walked off to retrieve the paper.

"I'll go with you," Quinn called after her.

Holly was back and spreading the paper out on the kitchen counter. "What did you say?"

"I'll go with you to see your father. What is it about?"

She looked startled for just a second. "Thanks, but it's not a good idea. Coming with me, I mean, because, um, I have a spa appointment after." Her eyes moved to the left when she told him her plans for the day, a sign she wasn't being truthful. "I'm also checking out a new gallery with Reese." She looked down to scan the newspaper pages.

Quinn frowned slightly at the mention of Reese's name. "Do you want to meet for dinner? Rick was talking about a new place in Malibu. He's the young new guy."

"The senator's son?"

"Yes. I can't remember the name of the restaurant now, but I'll get it."

"I'll let you know as soon as I'm free. Okay?"

"Sure."

"I have to get ready." She walked away but turned around after a few steps. "Quinn?"

"Yeah?"

"I would like to spend the whole day with you, but I already made these plans. I'm sorry."

"Oh. It's okay. I should have asked you sooner."

Holly had been unusually nice. None of her comments were facetious. He watched her walk away. There was less of a side to side sway in her hips, like her whole attitude had been taken down a notch. Something was going on. Holly was hiding something.

Quinn rubbed his chin. He wasn't a quitter. Besides that, he was Catholic. Or at least he had grown up Catholic. When he was young, he'd spent countless hours over the holidays listening to his grandfather grumble about the divorce rate in the context of the world going to hell in a handbasket. Quinn wasn't going to give up on this marriage, but he wasn't sure what he needed to do. There was so much distance between them that needed to be closed. Talking about the more dangerous aspects of his job had always made Holly excited, like lead-him-to-the-bedroom excited, which made them feel closer. Yet, he couldn't share anything that wasn't about to be public knowledge. Unless…he suddenly had an idea for later.

"Quinn, I'm home," Holly called, walking in from the garage. Her usual confidence had returned, along with the sway in her hips.

"Great. I'm starving. We have a reservation."

"I have to change my clothes. Give me fifteen minutes."

"Sure." Quinn opened the garage door. "Wow. What's this?" A Porsche Cayenne filled Holly's side of the garage, next to Quinn's Ford F-150.

"It's temporary. My father needed a red Mercedes for a shoot. I'll get it back in a few days. You can drive us in this one. It's fun. I'm going to shower. Be right out."

Quinn entered the bedroom and saw Holly's clothes on the floor outside the closed master bathroom door. He was bending down to pick them up when he heard her voice. She said, "He's going to have it fixed." There was a long pause, followed by, "He didn't ask. I didn't see anything about it anywhere, did you?" Another pause. "You were right, Reese, everything is going to be fine."

Holly came out a few minutes later and met him in the kitchen.

There were three knocks at the front door.

Holly spun around, her eyes wide and the color draining from her face. "Someone is here."

Quinn looked at her strangely.

"Who do you think it is?" Holly gripped the side of the counter.

"No idea." Quinn headed toward the door and opened it to find out. "It's a package from UPS."

"Oh." Holly's shoulders relaxed and she exhaled as if she'd been holding her breath.

"Is everything okay?"

She picked up her purse and smiled. "Of course, let's go."

That night, after a romantic dinner at the restaurant Rick recommended, Holly removed the four decorative pillows from her side of the bed, folded down the duvet, and slid under the cool sheets.

Quinn placed his hand on the curve of her hip. "We had a big day this week, my team did. I'm proud of them."

"What happened?" Holly asked, her ear against the soft pillowcase, facing away from her husband.

"So, you know how Rashid analyzes the results of our scanning software? It searches for key phrases in different languages. He looks for anything that sends up a red flag warranting further investigation. Well, yesterday, he intercepted some troubling conversations. Men with assault rifles planning to make a statement at Universal Studios. The assault teams weren't available, so we had to go." Quinn averted his eyes, struggling to look serious, "We showed up at their apartment with a SWAT team."

"Who knows this?" she said. "Is it public knowledge?"

"No. No one knows. It's top secret. You can't tell anyone. Okay?"

Holly nodded and her lips appeared to relax into a conspiratorial smile.

"It was tense. Really tense. We surrounded their apartment and tried to burst in and catch them off guard, but they were prepared. At one point, I didn't know if we would all make it." In the past, Quinn had explained the primary responsibilities of his job, gathering and monitoring intelligence, but she didn't question the plausibility of his story.

With her eyes glued to Quinn's, Holly's fingers found his arm. She gently stroked the surface of his skin with her nails, satisfying an itch Quinn didn't know he had. He kept the Hollywood-style details flowing as best he could until his story reached its heroic conclusion. The good, brave guys won and the bad guys were captured. By then, Holly had already removed his shirt. Her hair cascaded around her face as she sat on her knees and leaned over him to trail kisses from his neck down his torso.

"Holly?

"Hmm?"

"Don't share what I told you with anyone. I could lose my job. Promise?"

"I won't," she murmured, without looking at Quinn. She sat up, pulled her shirt over her head—revealing those perfect breasts—tossed it on the floor and returned to being a loving wife.

Quinn stretched his quads and hamstrings on the beach in preparation for a long morning run. Facing away from the ocean, he could see the top of the house he and Holly had purchased four years ago, thanks to her father and the incredibly lucrative porn industry. The white stucco siding and blue tiled roof rose high into the air, competing with the surrounding homes for the ocean view. He was used to the incredible house and location by now, but from time to time, it still caused him embarrassment. No government employees he knew owned anything so expensive. He looked away when his phone beeped. He was not expecting the text he received from one of Holly's friends.

Holly told me about the terrorists you stopped. We were going to take the kids to Disney on Saturday. Is it safe now?

A few minutes later, a second text arrived, from Reese. **My new office is close to where you arrested the men with the assault rifles. Have all the terrorists been captured? I feel like I should tell my boss, just in case.**

Quinn pounded through the sand. He'd thought fabricating a story was a good idea, knowing how the dangerous aspects of his job used to be a huge turn on for Holly. He'd made a mistake.

It took two miles to decide how to respond without embarrassing Holly or himself. He had no choice but to call both women before they spread his fake story to all their friends. He leaned into a lifeguard stand while he made the first of the two calls. "Hey, sorry to give you a scare," he said when Reese answered, "but there's nothing to worry about. Everything Holly told you is from an episode of SWAT Team. She was joking. Trying to see who watched the show."

"Oh!" she exclaimed. "I think I saw that one. I thought it sounded familiar. Well, she had me fooled. Although, I don't know that it's funny at all, Quinn."

"Sorry. If you don't see it on the news first, you're not going to hear it from me. You know that."

"If you told me what you know I'd be running out to stockpile food, right? Ha-Ha."

Quinn laughed politely. What Reese didn't know allowed her to function normally—to agonize over choosing the perfect outfit for an event, to stress about the last five pounds of weight she wanted to lose, or the late payment on her credit card. He would allow her that ignorant bliss, to some extent. "It's important to keep a one-month supply of water and non-perishable food on hand. One gallon of water per day, per person. It never hurts to be prepared."

"I've seen the water gallons and all the jars of peanut butter at your house. It looks like you have a few months' worth.

66

Holly doesn't even like peanut butter, it's almost all fat, did you know that?"

"I've got a year's worth of supplies. Peanut butter has an incredible shelf-life."

After making the second call, his heartbeat had returned to normal and his adrenaline rush had disappeared. The ocean breeze stirred up goosebumps on his sweaty skin. He dropped to the sand for fifty pushups before continuing his run. Images of another woman, the one he thought he saw in Georgia, entered his mind. He blocked them out by running faster. He was wrong about what Holly needed. She didn't want to connect, she only wanted to hear his stories so she could entertain her friends. And after insisting she keep his information secret, she had apparently insisted the same thing to everyone she told. He tightened his jaw and began to sprint, his muscles burning, his lungs taking steady gulps of breath, desperate for more oxygen.

Chapter Ten

Kareem – Syria
September 24th

Forty miles away from Aleppo, in an underground bunker beneath the most extravagant building in his residential compound, Al-Bahil sat on a throne-like chair behind an ornate desk, smoking a cigar. His open-necked shirt revealed a mass of black hair. Bowls of nuts and a tin of cookies had been set out before him.

"Kareem, my genius scientist. Come in."

To enter the room, Kareem had to walk between Al-Bahil's two bodyguards. Dressed in black, as always, with their military-style automatic rifles, one reached his arm forward, causing Kareem to quickly step back.

"Chill," said the guard. He stared at Kareem before extending his arm again, handing half a Twix bar to the other bodyguard. Then they both laughed as if Kareem was an insignificant fool.

Kareem felt his face grow warm with anger as he continued into Al-Bahil's office.

A phone lit up on top of the desk. Al-Bahil picked it up. "What is it?"

Kareem listened to Al-Bahil breathing loudly into his phone. He struggled with where to aim his gaze and settled on his hands.

Al-Bahil smiled. "Really? Praise Allah." There was a long pause. "Send the details. Great news." Another pause. "Peace be upon him." He put his phone down and slapped his desk. "That was great news. Usama Onamar has died. Do you know who he is, Kareem?"

Kareem's mind raced through possibilities. "No," he said softly.

"He was a wealthy oil baron. He willed an enormous sum to our organization. Millions."

"Great news," Kareem forced a smile.

Al-Bahil laughed deeply. "Maybe I should finally buy a new car. The Mercedes has seen better days, hasn't it?"

Kareem offered a half-smile, unsure of the right response.

"Do you know why I haven't bought a new one, Kareem?"

"No. I don't know. Because the one you have still works?"

He laughed again. "Funny, but no. And it's not that we couldn't afford one. We can afford a thousand Mercedes. Ten thousand of them, maybe more, I don't know what they cost. I set up that fancy lab for you here, didn't I? But it isn't wise to order luxury vehicles with bullet-proof windows and impenetrable siding. Someone may want to know where those vehicles are going, and who they're for. And we don't want that, do we?"

"No, we don't," said Kareem. Al-Bahil was preoccupied with his own safety and wouldn't do anything to jeopardize it.

That's why he'd built a compound in the middle of nowhere. It was also the explanation for why the school had such a large presence in the center of the compound, even though there were hardly any children there. Schools implied youthful innocence, lives to be spared at all costs. Western militaries would never drop a bomb in the vicinity of a school building.

"So, Kareem, you've just returned from Aleppo, from your *other* lab." He slapped his desk and laughed. "Was your experiment a success?"

Kareem nodded. "There was no one left alive."

"How long did it take?"

"Less than a week before symptoms developed. Three days for some. Once symptoms appeared, death was almost immediate, within a day or two."

"How is that possible?"

If Kareem had been asked the same question back at the University of Damascus, he would have smiled and said with confidence, "Because I'm amazing." Instead he said, "I used RNA from the strongest strains of virus."

"Hmmm." Al-Bahil pressed his meaty lips together.

"Aamaq captured some good data before he died."

"Humpf. Not sure why you need it. Now, what is the status on recruitment?"

"Well, I have three Americans. They don't know what they'll be doing yet, but they know they'll be returning to the States to help your... I mean, to help the cause. They'll do it."

"Only three?"

"They're from opposite coasts, two from California and one from Massachusetts. I'm working on more." He hadn't heard from Redman in days, the man might have had a change of heart, but claiming to have three recruits sounded much better than only two.

"Three isn't enough. Why haven't you found more? You still sound like an American." He said this as if it disgusted him. "Use your connections."

"I will. I'm working on it."

"They'll go through our program first and watch our new recruiting movie. Have you seen it yet?"

"No, not yet."

"You need to watch it then. Today. It's amazing. It could be an Oscar winner. You know. Like the Titanic."

Kareem nodded. "A blockbuster."

"I want to meet them and speak to them personally before they return to America. Make sure that happens." He picked up a handful of nuts and put them in his mouth.

Kareem nodded. "Okay."

"Will you be ready for November sixth?"

Kareem wanted a few more weeks. He had one more piece of the project to complete. Something critical wasn't finished. Something he didn't want Al-Bahil to know about. A scientific breakthrough. But he couldn't ask and risk being discovered.

Al-Bahil leaned forward. "I won't let my brother's death go unmarked. If you claim that after infecting only Aamaq, all of the men from the Aleppo experiment died, the virus is effective enough. You'll be ready." He peered at Kareem, challenging him, and Kareem felt his breath catch in his chest.

"Our plan will succeed. And we may never need another. The United States will be decimated." Kareem swallowed hard and did his best not to look away.

"That's what I needed to hear from you. Sometimes I doubt your allegiance."

Kareem bowed his head.

71

"Am I wrong to doubt your allegiance?"

Kareem felt his gut clench. He was trapped. He couldn't tell Al-Bahil he was wrong, but he couldn't let his allegiance be doubted. He shook his head and hoped a humble gesture would suffice.

"You can go now."

Kareem turned to leave. The burden of responsibility pressed strongly against him. Or maybe it was moral ambiguity crushing his chest like a massive pile of stones. If he was going to mentally survive, he needed to focus only on the job ahead and push the emotions aside.

From behind him Al-Bahil spoke again. "Watch the movie. And don't forget, if you're falling short with recruitment, there *is* one more person you know who has an American passport. You know him well. He should be easy to inspire."

Kareem wished he had never spoken of his cousin. He gritted his teeth, suppressing the urge to shout, *Find your own fucking recruits, you fat asshole.*

Allah would not be pleased with him.

Chapter Eleven

Charlotte

September 24ᵗʰ

Amin's cubicle on the 34ᵗʰ floor of the Continental Bank Building reminded him of a child's living room fort, the ones with blankets stretched across the back edge of chairs. Temporary. Insignificant. A box. Perhaps it was *the box* Kareem was talking about when he said, "give up your fears, get out of your box." Which was a rather perfect description because Amin felt most comfortable *thinking inside his box,* working with numbers and spreadsheets.

He was concentrating on his monitor and a forecast spreadsheet when Doug, his third boss in as many years, plodded over, his breath wheezy, and leaned heavily against one of Amin's gray fabric cube walls. Amin turned to face Doug, wondering if the wall could support all his weight. Inside his dress shirt, Doug's gut hung over the edge of his suit pants. "I need to talk to you about these numbers. Stop by my office when you have a chance." He finished with a grunt.

"I'll be there in a few minutes." Amin immediately clicked and saved his spreadsheets. In the adjacent cube, which shared a wall with his own, he heard Melissa, his colleague, tapping out an irritating rhythm with her pen. Melissa brought in home-baked goodies to share at least once a week. Today she'd brought "rich" caramel brownies and coconut chocolate-chip cookies. She wasn't helping Doug any with his weight. She had an MBA from a prestigious business school. She wasn't married, didn't have children, but she was a "big sister" for two elementary-aged girls who, she explained, needed a good role model. Pictures of a smiling, light-complexioned Melissa with two different dark-complexioned little girls were pinned to her cube walls. The pictures captured their trips to Panthers games, Hornets games, the Nutcracker ballet, and the Discovery Place museum. Amin respected Melissa for her kindness and her intelligence. During their weekly finance review team meetings, when Melissa diplomatically pointed out where Doug had made mistakes, Amin sometimes forgot she was a woman. He suspected she was a lesbian. His religion expected him to be concerned for her, but he didn't care. He had developed a complete apathy toward her potential lesbianism, or anyone else's for that matter. Her sexuality was her business. Live and let live. One more reason he was a poor excuse for a devout Muslim. His college friends might say, "good for you, you've become more open-minded", but his parents would say he was now immune to morally conflicting situations. Who was right? Did it matter?

Amin walked through the center of the building and its maze of cubes to the outer corridor. He passed several offices, the ones with the floor to ceiling window views, all with closed doors, until he reached Doug's corner space.

"Shut the door." Doug didn't look up when Amin entered. "How are things?"

"Fine," Amin answered, uncertain which "things" they were talking about.

"Good. Unfortunately, the bottom line isn't so great around here," said Doug. "There are hundreds of layoffs in the pipeline, all coming from the internal support departments—HR, IT, Operations, and Finance. It's fallout from the recent acquisition of Future's Bank. We all need to prove our worth these next few weeks. Particularly with the upcoming forecast. We can't afford any mistakes."

"I understand," Amin glanced at an empty plate covered in brownie crumbs on Doug's desk.

"Just wanted to let everyone know. That's all. You can go." Doug rolled his big leather chair away from his desk as if he was about to stand up, although he remained seated.

"Thank you." Amin returned to his cube, his spreadsheets, and his numbers. He had barely started when Melissa entered his space.

"Knock, knock," she said.

Amin rotated his chair. "Yes?"

"There's a flu shot clinic in the lobby for employees. We should go. We're supposed to have a bad flu season this year."

"Hmm." Amin cupped his chin. "I've never had a flu shot before. I never get sick."

"Never? Are you sure?"

"I can't remember a single time. I have an amazing immune system. I have never seen a doctor aside from annual check-ups. Remember when everyone in the department had a bad cold, and I didn't catch it?"

"Actually, I do remember. I was jealous." Melissa smiled.

Amin shrugged. "I've got some sort of super immunity. Seriously."

"Well, it's up to you." Melissa turned and walked away.

Although he truly believed he didn't need one, saying so suddenly seemed arrogant. Wouldn't it be his rotten luck to get sick this year, for the first time ever, because he was so certain it wasn't possible? The shot would cost him nothing aside from a few minutes of his time. And it couldn't hurt. "Okay. Why not?"

he said to himself, clicking and saving again before hurrying to the elevator banks. "Melissa, wait up. I'm coming with you."

Amin stood in a line with Melissa and other Continental employees in the lobby. He let his eyes trace the etchings on the marble floor. When his turn arrived, he removed his suit jacket, sat in one of the upholstered chairs, unbuttoned his shirt cuff, and bunched his sleeve up over his elbow.

The health care provider, an attractive woman with very dark skin, opened a sealed packet and removed a syringe. She smiled at him and made eye contact. "This won't hurt. Just a quick sting. Are you ready?"

"Yes." He found himself suddenly nervous and offering unnecessary information as he watched the needle head toward his arm. "It's my first flu shot. First one ever. I can't quite remember what it's going to be like. The shot, I mean, what it's going to feel like to get a shot." He tensed all his muscles. The tip of the silver needle was on his arm and then it quickly disappeared into his skin. Before he registered the sting, the woman was finished, pressing a piece of folded gauze against the prick mark.

"All done," she said, cheerfully, glancing over her shoulder at the line of people waiting.

"That was quick and easy," Amin said.

"Of course it was."

At home, while eating his take-out dinner—empty shelves again—Amin thought about revisiting the Muslims Unite chat room. Inspirational guidance backed by ayahs from the Quran might lift his spirits. He scrolled through the site, absentmindedly kneading his shoulder, a little sore from the vaccination. He paused to check out a post analyzing the lyrics to an offensive rap song—heroin, ho's, robbing a pimp, and gunning down the "po-po". Amin shook his head. The author of the post acted as if Americans had collectively chosen the song to represent the morals of the country. Amin was tempted to write, "Get over it. I've never heard this song before. It may have a small following, but it is not a mainstream song," but he moved on instead. Continental Bank was the main topic of a thread titled *Greed and Capitalism*. The CEO had recently been granted a twenty-five percent salary increase and would gross twenty-seven million. Amin quickly calculated the CEO's annual salary to be seven hundred seventy times his own. He let out a low whistle with his breath. Did that make him seven hundred seventy times less valuable than the guy in charge? He frowned. It didn't help that the bank had announced a recent salary freeze for employees at Amin's level.

The words "What is your purpose?" caught his attention. The "Learn More" button led to a video, in English, about following Allah's call. Images of young Muslim men surrounded by friends and pretty wives temporarily transported Amin to a world with possibilities for self-fulfillment. The soundtrack struck a hopeful chord, like watching a movie where the underdog team wins the game, the bad guys get what they deserve, and the audience cries happy tears. When the video ended, a live-chat session box popped up. A real person on the other end of the connection had typed, *Hi. What do you do for a living?* Easy to answer—finance. Amin leaned back in his chair and drummed his fingers against the counter, wondering where the conversation might lead. He took a chance and responded, which led to—*What do you do for fun?* Not so easy. *Where do you see yourself in a year?* In my cube – although I hope not. Half an hour later, after pondering some soul-searching questions, he finally shut his computer down.

Chapter Twelve

Charlotte

September 25th

On Saturday, for the first time in a very long while, Amin attended the Charlotte Islamic Center's afternoon service. He had a few reasons for going. One was to be a good son. Muslims believed that raising a virtuous child benefited them after death and he didn't want to deprive his parents in their afterlife. During the service, his mind wandered. *Should I have used a higher interest rate for the margin model? Did Doug ever answer my questions about the forecast assumptions? Can I eat pizza again tonight or should I try and find something with a vegetable? Are all my suits at the dry cleaners?* When the service ended, he felt more of a misfit, more aware of a gaping disconnect, than when he arrived. The time he spent inside the mosque seemed inconsequential in relation to the rest of his life. He was thinking about going into the office to knock out some work, when a heavily accented stranger spoke to him.

"Hello. Have I seen you before at daily prayers?" the older man asked. He wore a prayer cap, a sign of traditional respect.

"I come whenever I can," Amin said, stretching the truth. "I'm Amin Sarif." He extended his hand.

The man shook his hand. "I'm Maran. Sarif, you say? Where are you from originally?"

"I was born here, but my parents are from Iraq."

"Where in Iraq?"

"Mosul." Amin cast his eyes downward to acknowledge the current turmoil in his ancestral city.

"I'm from Mosul! And my wife as well. Thank Allah we don't live there now. The Islamic State is holding on to its self-proclaimed caliphate. It's a tragedy, a constant battle between the Iraqi army, police, and the militants." Maran shook his head and closed his eyes briefly. "Millions of civilians are trapped. The U.S. is providing support in the form of airstrikes, but those do the most damage to the city. They're perceived as the real enemy."

Amin nodded. He had little to contribute to the conversation unless he offered some of Kareem's opinions, but he wasn't going to go there.

"Where are your parents now?" Maran asked, as they walked out of the mosque together.

"My parents live in Michigan. My father is an engineer at Chrysler."

"And what brought you to Charlotte?"

"A job. I work at Continental Bank, in finance."

"And what else do you do here in Charlotte?"

Amin thought, *I should have waited to find a job in Michigan where I had friends and family.* "I'm afraid not a lot, I spend most of my time at work. I'm trying to change that."

"Oh. Ah, here comes my family." Maran's eyes beamed. "I'll introduce you. This is my wife, Nina, my teenage son, Rehan, and my lovely daughter, Isa."

Amin's mouth went dry, his palms grew sweaty. Isa exuded warmth and beauty. Her large brown eyes were so luminous a Disney princess could have been modeled after her. Dark slacks and a flowered blouse looked lovely on her petite figure. Unlike her mother, her head was uncovered and her long hair hung loose. Maran continued to talk about Mosul and possible family connections, but Amin was only tuned in to Isa.

Throughout the following days, Isa's image occupied Amin's thoughts. Over the past few years, when he did pray, which wasn't very often, he had consistently asked for a pretty and kind Muslim woman who could understand his sense of cultural misplacement. Ideally, one who had already figured out how to handle the dichotomy between America's "anything goes" culture and her family's religious loyalties and expectations. He believed his prayers had been answered. He planned to go to the mosque the next week, same day, same time, hoping to see Maran and Isa again.

He had just finished his cheesesteak sandwich in the food court. As he passed the small convenience store, he remembered running out of toilet paper at his apartment. If he bought one of the single rolls they sold inside, he would be set for a few days. He went into the store to make the purchase.

"We're out of bags," said the cashier. "Can you handle it?"

Amin laughed. "Yes, no problem." He only had the one roll of toilet paper.

He was leaving the store when he heard his name.

"Amin!"

It was Isa, and she sounded excited. Amin's face lit up. She remembered his name! Her lovely dark skin and raven hair stood out amongst the dozens of uptown workers threading their way around her. She wore a fitted navy pants suit and white blouse. His heart beat faster.

"I'm Isa. Remember we met outside the mosque?"

Amin nodded. He remembered all right. He hadn't stopped thinking about her since. Mesmerized by her beauty, his eyes followed the graceful gestures of her hands when she spoke. He couldn't believe she had spotted *him* in the lunch hour crowd.

"My father introduced us. He introduces himself to everyone." She laughed. "It's nice to see you again. Do you work around here?"

"Yes, I work in the Continental Bank building. How about you?"

"I work in the Hearst Tower." She turned and pointed in the building's direction before laughing again, a melodic sound reminding Amin of someone who was simply happy to be alive.

They spoke for a few minutes, long enough for Amin to learn Isa worked as an IT programmer at another big Charlotte bank. Giddy anticipation accompanied his every word and gesture. Their conversation ended when Isa said she was going to be late for a meeting. They had to say goodbye. Walking back to his office, Amin considered everything he had learned about Isa. Beautiful. Nice. A college graduate. An IT specialist. Middle Eastern descent but raised in America. He imagined her trapped between two worlds, like him, wanting to fit in somewhere and unsure of which way to lean. Might they create their own middle-ground world together? He was all the way back to his cube when he realized he'd been holding the roll of toilet paper the whole time. He felt his face grow hot. Oh well.

After seeing her uptown, Amin made a point of buying his lunch from the same place at the same time. He was rewarded the following week when he saw her again. He spotted her first, because he was desperately looking. Black pants, red heels, red blouse, her gorgeous hair grazing her shoulders. She was speaking to another woman as they carried take-out containers toward a trash can. Amin tossed his drink into a nearby receptacle, pressed his shoulders down and back, and hustled to catch up with her.

"Hello, Isa. What a nice surprise seeing you here again." He tried to temper his excitement, but it wasn't easy. How many times had he thought about seeing her, looking into her beautiful eyes, and having her smile back at him?

"You too, Amin." Her smile was genuine. Her friend also smiled at him. Isa said, "This is Joyce. We work together. Joyce, this is my friend, Amin."

"Hi, nice to meet you." Amin dipped his chin.

"And I'm late for a meeting. Again." Isa laughed, a sound he had replayed in his daydreams. "Sorry I have to go. I'll see you soon, I hope?"

"Yes." Amin nodded. Her silky pants swished between her legs as she walked away with her friend. To whomever might be listening, he said a silent prayer of gratitude. He believed he and Isa had a connection. Next time he saw her, he would ask her to dinner. He would say, "Isa, are you busy this weekend?" Or maybe, "Would you like to catch dinner with me on Saturday night?" He would practice a few lines in his head so when the time came he wouldn't be flustered. He wasn't going to let his shyness get the best of him. His thoughts were interrupted when he noticed she had turned around and was walking back in his direction. His heart beat faster.

"There's a social at the mosque on Friday night. My father would be overjoyed if my brother and I went with him. I was thinking of finding an excuse, but, any chance you'll be there?"

"Yeah. Sure. I can be. Sounds like the sort of thing my father would want me to do if he were here," Amin said with a conspiratorial grin that quickly disappeared. "I mean if he were here in Charlotte. He's alive."

Isa laughed. "Good. Wonderful. Here's my email." She handed him her business card. "Okay. I'll plan to meet you there. See you later."

Over the next few days, he planned his outfit—charcoal grey pants, the black cashmere sweater his mother bought for his birthday, and polished black leather shoes. He planned some small talk to avoid awkward moments with nothing to say. Although he couldn't imagine that happening, not with Isa, he didn't want to take a risk. He practiced saying *Have you been to Ilios Noche or Carpe Diem*—restaurants from a list of supposedly good ones he'd read about in the Charlotte Observer but never visited. *What sort of IT work do you do exactly? Where did you grow up, Isa? What sorts of things do you do for fun?* All good questions. He allowed himself to imagine beyond the mosque social, beyond their first date. He daydreamed about attending a concert at the National White Water Center and visiting the Mint Museum, two things he'd seen others do on the Channel 14 news.

At work on Friday afternoon, Amin was anxious with excitement.

"You're in a good mood," Melissa said. "What's going on?"

"Maybe I am," he answered, raising his eyebrows mysteriously in a manner that was out of character and caused Melissa to smile.

On his way home to change, with only an hour remaining before the event, he felt like a nervous teenager. Something good was about to happen, something for which he had been waiting a long time.

A message from Kareem appeared on his phone. **I need you to come visit me.**

He smiled at the request, and responded without much thought. **Can't. I have a lot going on. You should come here.** He wanted to share his excitement about Isa with someone. But he would wait until he had something more than simple anticipation to share. He also needed to call Kareem's parents to discuss his concerns about Kareem's extreme views. Soon. He was in too good a mood to ruin it right now with a somber discussion.

He had to remind himself to breathe as he walked up the steps to the mosque and down into its basement. He wiped his hands against his pants and scanned faces looking for Isa's family. He intended to tell Isa's father he was going to ask her out to dinner. Maran would appreciate his respect. He spotted Maran and his wife and walked over to say hello. Maran put his hand on Amin's shoulder as if he were already family. "Amin. Hello. Great to see you again."

Amin's eyes opened wide when Isa rounded the corner, until he saw she wasn't alone. A tall man wearing a suit walked at her side and was speaking to her. They stopped in front of Amin and Isa's parents.

Isa's father spoke to the man by Isa's side. "This is Amin. His family is from my home city." He turned back to Amin, bursting with enthusiasm, "This is Isa's fiancé. I thought you might have a few things in common and would make good friends."

An angry voice in Amin's mind yelled *What the Fuck!* The rest of his body responded in a way that left him queasy and empty inside. His forced smile threatened to crack and reveal his despair. He shook the man's hand and congratulated the couple, avoiding Isa's face completely. He quickly made up an excuse and hurried to the bathroom. He thought he heard Isa calling his name as he fled, but he didn't turn around and he didn't slow down.

Why had she led him on if she was seeing someone else? Engaged! After a minute in the bathroom, he exited the mosque without saying goodbye to anyone, hurrying to disappear before anyone witnessed his pain. The future happiness he had built in his mind would never exist. His ability to assess a woman's feelings—complete garbage. He was grateful, at least, that he hadn't shared his feelings or his grand plans with anyone else.

He remembered Kareem's text – *Come visit me.* For the first time, he actually thought about visiting his cousin, just to escape his embarrassment.

Over the next few weeks, he avoided the food court all together and ordered his sandwiches from the Pita Pit in the opposite direction. He didn't return to the mosque.

Chapter Thirteen

Los Angeles
September 27th

Quinn heard keys turning the lock at twenty-three-hundred hours. He swung his feet off the leather ottoman and muted the television before the front door swooshed open. He heard Holly's purse drop to the floor followed by the tap, tap of high heels moving across the hardwood floors, the clunk, clunk of them being tossed to the ground. He moved toward the edge of his seat and set his Dos Equis bottle down.

"What happened to my pumpkins?" Holly's irritated voice traveled down the hallway and into the family room.

"What's wrong with the pumpkins?" Quinn asked, although he had a pretty good idea.

"I definitely did not arrange them like they are now."

"Sorry. I accidentally walked into them when I was leaving for work. I was looking at my phone. I thought I put them back how you had them."

"Not even close. But, forget it. It's not a big deal. I'll take care of it,"

"Holly," he called, before she could pass the family room. "We need to talk."

Sighing, Holly walked toward him on the plush family room carpet, flicking the light switch on her way. "What do we have to talk about?"

"Please sit down." He patted the space next to him on the couch. His phone beeped and he glanced at it. Couldn't help himself. The text came from a friend in the FBI's legal department.

Sorry to bother you so late. Call me tomorrow. Need to talk about Redman. Cynthia Fryberg, civil rights attorney and publicity whore, is breathing down my neck. I have some questions for you.

Holly watched Quinn with crossed arms from a few feet away until he looked up.

"I want to talk about us. I don't want our marriage to be like this." He pressed his palms against his jeans.

"Like what, exactly?"

"You seem unhappy and I feel like I'm walking on eggshells every time I talk to you."

"Really? Because you could have fooled me that you give a damn."

"Please sit down."

Holly rolled her eyes and sat down, angling her back against the arm of the couch so a full cushion separated them. She ran her fingers through her hair and sighed. "There's only one problem with our marriage. You're never around. Ever."

Quinn wanted to point out that he was home tonight, he had been home all last weekend, and she was the one who had been out, but he held his tongue. He turned off the television so he wouldn't be distracted. "Things come up at work and I can't leave until they're resolved. You know that. You knew what it would be like when you married me."

"It's harder than I thought it would be." Holly bit her lower lip and lowered her forehead, resting it against her closed fist.

"What can I do to make things better?"

"Be around more. All I want is for you to be around."

"I'm not going to quit my job. I don't think you really want me to, do you?"

She looked up. "I don't know. I'm just tired of being alone all the time."

"We've got the best security system money can buy, short of having armed guards at the door. You must feel safe."

"I never said I didn't feel safe. I feel plenty safe. I'm lonely!"

How could she be lonely? Quinn wondered. She always seemed to be out with friends doing social things, but arguing with her wasn't going to help. "You changed your mind about children, and I've respected your choice, even though…" Quinn swallowed the taste of bitterness rising in his throat. "Look, we could get a dog."

"I don't want a dog or I would have a dog!" Holly looked up and met his eyes with a defiant stare that ended with a vigorous head shake. "Don't you get it? I want you home more. And I want to be able to plan things with you and then actually do them. When is the last time we took a vacation?"

"Umm. We went to Tahoe."

"That was so long ago, I can't even remember when that was."

"You're right. Maybe it's been too long."

Holly's glared without blinking, as if challenging him to admit that their uncomfortable situation was all his fault.

"Why don't you plan a vacation?" He tried to push away the discomfort his suggestion generated. "We can go anywhere."

"I know we *can* go anywhere, because I'm the one who has the money to pay for it. That's not the issue. The real issue is, can you make yourself available? Remember the last time we tried to go away? You cancelled at the last minute."

Quinn felt the quick pain of her verbal blow, but resisted the urge to fight back. He made a good living, but he didn't have a go-anywhere-buy-anything type of salary. *She's lashing out because she's not happy, and she's not happy because of me.* He swallowed hard and reached his arm forward, placing his hand gently on her arm. A peace offering. Holly looked down at his hand. Something in her eyes changed.

"I know," he said. "And I'm sorry. It won't happen this time. I promise."

"I'm sorry I told our friends the story you said not to tell."

"And I'm sorry I had to make something up. I wish I could tell you everything." He looked down. "No. That's not true. I don't want my work on your mind or in your life in any way, because it's disturbing. I want you to be happy."

"I just wish your everyday work wasn't so totally separate from our life." Holly sighed.

He cupped her chin with his hand and looked deep into her eyes. "The whole point of my job is to keep the people and things I deal with away from you, to prevent them from interfering with your world. When you bring home a new painting, it improves our surroundings. Sharing my job would not improve anything. Every day, I'm thinking about keeping you safe. So, how about the vacation?"

Her shoulders relaxed. "Okay. Where should we go?"

Quinn felt the tension dissipate. "Wherever you want. Skiing?"

"No, I'm thinking Caribbean."

"That sounds great t—"

"Or France," Holly said, interrupting. "'I haven't been to France since I was thirteen." Her eyes glistened with excitement.

"France isn't safe right now."

"Really? Why? What do you know?"

Quinn only shook his head.

"How about Italy?" Holly asked.

He shook his head again.

"Italy isn't safe either?"

"We could go to Spain."

Holly rubbed her hands together. "Okay. Spain, it is. Can we go soon? I have a show scheduled for next week, but I can have someone else cover it."

"How about at the beginning of November?"

"That long from now?"

"It will give both of us time to plan and really enjoy the trip, not be rushed." Quinn reached for his phone so he could check his calendar. "How about leaving on Saturday, November 5th?"

"Okay. I'll find a resort, or a chateau." Holly's voice rose with excitement. "Maybe we can ski too." She folded her legs to the side and scooted closer to Quinn, weaving her arm through his and nestling her neck against his chest. He wrapped his arm around her shoulder and gently pulled her against him. Together they sat, staring at the black television screen. Holly sighed again, but snuggled against his shoulder,

"Here's something I can tell you about my job. I think Rashid has a thing for Stephanie."

"Doesn't surprise me. She's beautiful. And if he works as much as you, he probably doesn't have a chance to meet anyone else."

"They can't date if they're working together."

Holly laughed. "I don't think you have to worry about that."

"How come?"

"Umm…let's see. He's short."

"He's not tall, but he's not short."

"He has a bald spot. He wears glasses."

"You make him sound like George Costanza."

Holly tipped her head back and laughed, but Quinn didn't.

"He's brilliant. He has too many IT degrees for me to remember all of them. Fluent in five Arabic languages. He almost beat me when we ran a 5k together. Under twenty-one minutes. He's a great guy."

Holly shrugged.

"Besides, you know, there's a significant discrepancy between your father's appearance and that of his girlfriends."

"Well, they're not after my father because of his looks, Quinn. They're after my inheritance. Take away his money, and my father's companions would look very different. If Stephanie is as smart as you say, she'll wait for someone who is brilliant *and* handsome, or brilliant *and* rich. But, like I said, she'll end up alone if she works the hours you do." Holly lifted her head away from his shoulder. "How old is she anyway? Thirty-something?"

"Thirty-five. Your age."

"Too old to have children now."

"No, she's not. And neither are you."

"This again? I don't want children, Quinn. I only want you." Holly frowned and scooted a few inches away.

Two steps forward, one step back.

Chapter Fourteen

Los Angeles
September 28th

In the center of the FBI building, Quinn dropped his cell phone in a box outside the secure conference room where all intelligence briefings took place. The windowless room-inside-a-room had one secure phone and no Wi-Fi. Nothing the team shared in the room would be discussed outside until it became public knowledge.

He entered the meeting in time to see Stephanie leaning toward Rashid. His face sort of lit up when she spoke to him. She laughed and turned to her right, presumably to share the same anecdote with Rick. Rashid's smile slowly deflated like a leaky balloon.

Quinn nodded to Jayla, his assistant. Jayla had smooth dark skin and long, thin microbraids. Seated next to Ken and his bulging muscles, she looked even more slender than she was. She started the PowerPoint presentation using the only computer permitted inside the room, an encrypted laptop connected with its own unique and permanently secured cable.

"Since this is your first intelligence meeting, let me give you a summary of what we do," Quinn said to Rick. "Jayla shares updates, current intelligence on terrorist activities, from all the federal agencies. We speak up if we have anything to add, or to share what we've done to mitigate or monitor each situation. She'll capture all of our information."

Jayla tossed a section of braids over her shoulder and smiled at Rick.

"Let's get started," said Quinn.

The slides projected on to the white wall at one end of the room. Jayla read the information aloud.

TOPSECRET//NOFORN//FVEY

SEPTEMBER 2017 INA SPECIAL FORCES' ASSETS HAVE SECURED INTEL DURING A ROUTINE RAID IN FALLUJAH INDICATING ABU BAKR AL-BAGHDADI IS IN CONTACT WITH KNOWN USPER KABIR ASSAD AND MAY BE IN THE PLANNING STAGES OF FACILITATING TRAVEL TO MEXICO FOR THE PURPOSE OF ILLEGALLY ENTERING THE US HOMELAND THROUGH THE MEXICO/US BORDER AREA. //DOD

USPER KABIR ASSAD IS KNOWN TO FBI AND IS CONFIRMED TO HAVE BEEN RADICALIZED BY ANJEM CHOUDARY IN THE UNITED STATES AND TRAVELED TO TURKEY WITH THE INTENTION OF CROSSING INTO SYRIA AND JOINING IS //FBI

USPER KABIR ASSAD NO LONGER HOLDS A VALID US PASSPORT AND HAS BEEN PLACED ON THE NO FLY LIST PER DHS BUT MAY BE SEEKING ALTERNATE MEANS TO ENTER A COUNTRY WITH WEAKER TRAVEL RESTRICTIONS AND TRAVEL TO MEXICO/US BORDER //DHS

SEPTEMBER 2017 LOCAL FBI UNDERCOVER AGENT INTERCEPTED COURIER MESSAGE TO ABU BAGDADDI INDICATING KABIR ASSAD HAS ACQUIRED VISA WITH THE INTENT TO HEAD TO MEXICO AND CROSS SOUTHERN BORDER AND START A CELL.

SECRET//NOFORN//FVEY

SEPTEMBER 2017. A LOCAL ALLY IN SUDAN TURNED OVER A COPY OF OIL BARON/ISIS WARLORD USAMA ONAMAR'S HANDWRITTEN WILL. THE SIGNATURE HAS BEEN VERIFIED. ONAMAR INDICATED THIRTY MILLION DOLLARS BE RELEASED

TO FIGHT JIHAD AGAINST THE WEST. THE MONEY IS EXPECTED TO BE FUNNELED TO MUHAMMAD AL-BAHIL IN SYRIA.

FIVE MEMBERS OF MUHAMMAD AL-BAHIL'S EXTENDED FAMILY FROM THE WATCH LIST HAVE LEFT THE SAN DIEGO AREA FOR IRAN.

SECRET//NOFORN//FVEY

SEPTEMBER 2017 DHS AGENT PICKED UP KURDISH CONVERSATION IN ISIS CHAT ROOM. RADICALS READYING AN ATTACK ON THREE U.S. PUBLIC TRANSPORTATION LOCATIONS USING PEROXIDE-BASED EXPLOSIVES. THE TARGET CITIES ARE CHICAGO, PHILADELPHIA, AND BOSTON. TARGET DATE REPORTED TO BE NOVEMBER 6TH. HASAAN FAYAD IS THE SUSPECTED RINGLEADER. HE SPENT TIME IN A TRAINING CAMP IN NINAWA CITY.

Rashid and Quinn made eye contact before Jayla reached the end of the last sentence. Rashid moved his body toward the back of his chair and straightened his shoulders. "That's what Redman mentioned. So, he may have had some real intelligence after all."

"One of our own undercover agents in a New York City mosque received the same intel," said Ken. "The people talking about it weren't involved. They'd just picked up on some chatter."

"Any info picked up in there makes me skeptical." Stephanie placed both hands on the table. "The radicals in the New York mosques have known for years that they've been infiltrated with undercover agents. They're careful. It could be counter intelligence."

"Maybe they don't know about the undercover agents because they're amateurs," Ken said. "They're planning to use peroxide based bombs? I mean, come on. Anyone can make those. It doesn't get more amateur than that. According to my source, they couldn't decide if they wanted to strike in New York on the subways and trains, or if that was cliché and they should attack somewhere in the Midwest where we least expect it. My source also reported the same target date. November 6th."

"That's the anniversary for the death of Anwar Al-Bahil. The U.S. took him out with a drone strike last year." Quinn's stomach turned when he remembered the other reason the November 6th date had stuck out in his mind—his vacation with Holly. They had booked a red-eye, departing the evening of November 5th. They would arrive in Spain on November 6th.

"Anwar Al-Bahil was a former ISIS cell leader, correct?" said Rick.

Quinn nodded.

"So, you think the attack is retaliation for his death?" Rick leaned forward.

"Normally I would," said Quinn. "But a retaliation attack would likely be spearheaded by his brother, Muhammad Al-Bahil, who essentially replaced Anwar."

"The same guy who just received an influx of thirty million from the oil baron, right?" said Rick.

"Yes. Muhammad Al-Bahil controls a relatively small ISIS cell, but a huge amount of money. And now he has a new influx of cash to plot with. But if this subway attack was *his* plan, it wouldn't be so sloppy. No one would label his plans as amateur. If he wanted to avenge his brother, he'd employ something more sophisticated and new. Or something so simple that we might not suspect it. He likes to think of himself as revolutionary and techno-savvy. Bombing in the subways? Doesn't sound like him."

"Do we know where Muhammad Al-Bahil is?" Rick asked.

"Somewhere in Syria," Ken said. "He's well-hidden and well-protected. He's a behind the scenes guy. You won't find him outside rallying the troops like his brother did. He has a son with special needs. The son is in his twenties and Al-Bahil seems to have a soft spot for him. The only times he's been seen in public, he's been with that son."

"Apparently, fathers act against rational judgement for the sake of their sons." Ken remained facing straight ahead, but as he spoke, his eyes darted to Rick. His comment went unacknowledged.

"Maybe Redman's contact, Kareem, *is* linked up with Muhammad Al-Bahil. If so, Redman was correct in saying this Kareem guy is capable of something huge and terrible," said Rick.

"More likely, Redman and his supposed contact, Kareem, both picked up chatter on the internet," Ken said.

"Well, one of the updates claimed part of Muhammad Al-Bahil's extended family recently moved out of the United States, which would indicate they're anticipating trouble of some sort," Rick said.

"True, but I've been following them myself. None of them even live in those targeted cities," Stephanie said. "So, the subway attacks don't explain why they would be leaving the country. Something else is going on."

The agents were quiet until Stephanie spoke again. "What do we know about Hasaan Fayad, the alleged leader of the November 6th plan?" She turned to Quinn, who turned to Rashid.

"Until now, Fayad has been a follower known to associate with ISIS cell leaders, but not a leader," said Rashid. "He's lived in Chechnya and the Sudan. Online comments show his pledge of support for the Islamic state. He was detained for questioning in London a few years ago, and MI6 recovered a memory card with photographs of the Sears Tower."

"Do we know where he is now?" Stephanie asked.

"I'd start looking in Chicago," said Rashid. "It's one of the target cities and he's familiar with the area."

"Like I said, I don't think this plot is sophisticated enough for Al-Bahil." Quinn rested his index finger against his cheek. "But regardless, we need to find Hasaan Fayad and whoever else is planning to carry out these subway attacks."

"Agents in NY are working on it," Ken said. "I'll touch base with them right after this."

"I want us to work on it with them. Make this our number one priority until we've put an end to the threat. I'll notify officials in those three cities and get them prepared," Quinn said. He turned to Jayla. "Keep it classified as top secret, but either DHS or us will need to pass it on to local law enforcement eventually, so they can set up counter measures." He paused and looked around. "If this plan is real, let's destroy it." Heads nodded around the table. Rick grinned.

"Anything else for today?" asked Quinn.

No one responded. Ken and Stephanie stood up.

"Quinn, you received two calls from our legal department today," said Jayla. "Don't forget. They need to talk to you about Redman's death."

"Got it," said Quinn. "One more thing, everyone, before you go. This isn't classified, but, um, I'm going to be taking a vacation at the beginning of November." He intentionally didn't mention the exact date.

Stephanie let her mouth fall open and stared at him with her remarkable blue eyes, feigning shock. "Am I hearing things?" She turned to Rick. "Quinn never ever takes vacation."

"Good for you." Jayla smiled.

"Where are you going?" Rashid asked.

"Spain, with Holly."

"Wonderful," said Stephanie. "Don't think we can't handle things while you're gone, you know."

"I know," Quinn said.

"Everything is going to be fine," Ken said. "You're going to love Spain."

"Not so fast," Rashid said. "I hate to break it to you, but the last time Quinn left for a few days is when Redman died, remember?"

"Think positive," Quinn said with a laugh. "Nothing bad is going to happen except me getting killed by my wife if I *don't* go on this trip."

Chapter Fifteen

Charlotte
September 28th

"Hell week has begun," said Melissa, when Amin arrived at his cubicle in the morning.

"Yep, except technically, it's a week and a half," said Amin.

Melissa moaned.

Once a quarter Amin, Melissa, and their colleagues lived, slept, and breathed quarter-end reporting and financial forecast updates. They input thousands of data points and assumptions into one massive model. Fitness routines were put on hold. Diets suffered. Back problems flared. Family events went unattended. Days passed without reading or listening to the news, turning on the television, or checking personal emails. Aside from a few hours of nightly sleep, hell week rudely took over, pushing everything else aside.

Amin spent hours on the phone with his business partners, Continental Bank "speak" for hundreds of other cube-dwellers like himself. He asked their opinions on the reasonableness of his assumptions, new initiatives that might impact the forecast, and the direction of interest rates. He built spreadsheet models with Melissa and downloaded the recent actuals from the general ledger. They analyzed historical trends and met or spoke with all their business partners again to garner agreement with their projections. Amin and Melissa checked and rechecked, uploaded and downloaded, scrutinizing their work for a single mistake hiding amongst the thousands of calculations. The possibility of an error lurked around every formula and assumption; even one could wreck the department's credibility and cause huge personal embarrassment. Finally, they created the PowerPoint deck for Doug to present to the higher-ups and prepped him to explain their work.

With Amin's job fully consuming every waking minute, he had less time to dwell on everything his life lacked, less time to take action and make some changes, less time to think about Isa and what might have been. And not enough time to call his aunt and uncle about Kareem's escalating anti-western views.

At seven pm on Friday, five days into hell week, he glanced at his cell phone and saw three missed calls from his father. He was about to check for voicemail when his phone lit up. His father calling again. He clicked the icon to save his spreadsheet and picked up the phone.

"Dad?"

"Amin, I'm sorry. I have some terrible news."

Instantly alarmed by the tone of his father's voice, Amin took a deep breath, bracing himself for what was to come. He assumed the worst—something had happened to his mother.

"What is it?"

"Your aunt and uncle were killed in Mosul."

Amin's stomach dropped. His face felt tingly. "What? How?"

"They were having lunch at an outdoor café. Celebrating their thirtieth wedding anniversary. They were caught in crossfire."

Amin's uncle, a professor, wore a perpetually thoughtful expression. As far as Amin knew, he was calm and composed in all matters. His aunt, a dark beauty, had always been exceptionally kind and gentle toward him and Kareem. Both were suddenly dead? It just couldn't be. It just couldn't. He struggled to process the surreal news.

"Your mother and I are traveling to Mosul tomorrow. We'll wash the bodies. Have you heard from Kareem?"

"I don't know. I…" Amin lost his train of thought picturing an image of his aunt and uncle lying in the ground shrouded in white fabric, the reminder everyone is equal in the eyes of Allah. "He doesn't have my work number, and I've been really busy this week." He cringed and heard his stupid, selfish-sounding words echoing in his mind.

"We're leaving tomorrow. We'll call when we get there. We won't stay long."

"Should I go with you? Meet you there?" Amin asked.

"Can you?"

He stared up at the ceiling. "I don't know. Not until the end of the week. It's my quarterly—." He stopped mid-sentence. "What kind of attack? Who killed them?"

"We're not sure."

Amin heard a tapping noise and turned to find Melissa standing next to his cubicle. "Doug is waiting for us. Are you ready?"

He held up one finger. Had she heard his end of the conversation? He wished he had an office with some privacy.

"All right, I'll wait," Melissa said.

"Hold on, Dad, please." Amin turned his face to the side and passed Melissa. He hurried to the hallway bathroom and entered a stall with his cell phone. "What kind of attack was it?" he asked again, from the sanctuary of the empty men's room.

"We don't know who was involved. It doesn't matter. They were in the wrong place at the wrong time. That's all."

Amin was silent until he remembered his concerns regarding his cousin. "If their deaths involved a military strike from the U.S., or any Western country, Kareem is going to go berserk. He's becoming an extremist. I wanted to tell you. I was planning on talking to his parents..." A low moan escaped his mouth. He gulped. He kicked the side of the marble stall. "This is terrible," he said when he could speak again.

"I know. It's a terrible thing, but indeed we belong to God, and indeed to Him we will return," his father said, quoting the Quran. "Call Kareem as soon as you can. He needs us now."

"I will. I'm sorry, Dad. I'm really sorry. I'll call you later tonight, okay?"

Amin walked back to his desk leaning forward, clutching his shoulder with his hand. He could clearly visualize his uncle and aunt seated at a café with smiling faces. That picture gave way to images of chaos and a bloody massacre. He didn't know what triggered the brutal scene in his mind, but he wanted to erase it. He shuddered and began to rub his arms up and down.

Melissa popped her head out of her cube. "Ready?"

Amin nodded and followed her into Doug's office. The shock of his uncle and aunt's violent deaths clouded his mind. It was too much to handle. He discovered Doug looking at him expectantly.

"Not in the mood to discuss interest rates, Amin?" Doug snorted.

"I'm sorry. What was that?"

Melissa repeated Doug's question. Doug rolled his eyes. Amin willed his brain to focus.

That night, when he finally returned to his apartment, he searched the internet looking for a recent attack in Mosul. Using different sources, a few sentences here and there, he pieced the tragic incident together. A contract security firm, ex-military Americans guarding an oil company executive, had been traveling their daily route from office to residential compound. Their intimidating procession of vehicles, Amin pictured bullet-proof Escalades with blacked-out windows just like in the movies, passed through a crowded area of the city where traffic was lucky to inch forward. A rocket-propelled grenade launched from a roof and penetrated deep inside the engine compartment of the second vehicle. The explosion flipped the vehicle over. The Americans fired their M4s in a semi-circle around them, unsure of who or how many were attacking. The streets were crowded with donkeys, carts, and people. Everyone scrambling for cover looked like a suspect. Kareem's parents died instantly, caught in the gunfire, attempting to run away.

Fox News briefly mentioned the massacre under the headline, "Violence Erupts in Mosul Marketplace." Happening so far from home, in an area where violence wasn't uncommon, the story held little interest for most Americans. *The world is so big, we can't pay attention to all of it unless it affects us personally,* thought Amin.

When it was late enough in Charlotte to be morning in Syria, Amin tried to Skype with Kareem. His cousin didn't respond, but Amin discovered he'd recently sent an email. It contained a single sentence. **If Americans had stayed in their own country and minded their own business, my parents would be alive right now.**

Amin's weekend dragged by, each minute marked by the audible click of the wall clock's hands, inside the tallest building in Charlotte. Stiff dark hairs poked out around his unshaven face. He ate leftover stale bagels and donuts from the break room, cheese crackers and trail mix packages from the vending machines. He wasn't hungry anyway. An uncomfortable nausea took residence inside him. He attributed it to too much caffeine. He turned a container of ibuprofen upside down and shook. Nothing came out. "No way," he said out loud. Somehow, he had used up a half-full bottle of pills during the week.

On the other side of his cube wall, Melissa sighed and said, "Yessss?" in a weary, exasperated tone when Doug plodded over for one of his random progress checks. She cursed when he left. "Sorry, if you heard that. My TMJ is back and my jaw just popped out. And Doug just asked for another rework of my model."

"No need to apologize to me." Hearing her exhaustion helped Amin manage his own frustration.

They experienced a brief respite on Monday afternoon when Doug presented their initial report. Amin sent another note to Kareem, expressing sympathy and concern. He said a quick, silent prayer. *Please grant Kareem strength, peace, and understanding.* Reluctantly, he redirected his attention to the accumulation of emails he had received throughout the week. He scrolled through the pages, the words "action required" and "urgent" flickering by. After less than a minute, he closed his eyes and dropped his head in his hands. He heard silence in the adjacent cube, as if Melissa was too tired to tap her pen. He said another silent prayer. *No mistakes and no changes. Please just let us be done with this.*

He held his breath when he heard Doug's heavy footsteps, but he walked to his office without stopping. Seconds later, he heard the ping of an instant message saying, "Come to my office."

Amin heard Melissa's chair squeak when they pushed away from their desks at the same time. They walked to Doug's office in single file and stood across from his desk, waiting. Amin took a deep breath. His gaze traveled to the Krispy Kreme donut box peeking out of Doug's trash can.

"We're good to go." Doug made a face and shifted his weight in his chair before loudly breaking wind. All of them successfully pretended it hadn't happened, but Amin's exhaustion made it more difficult than it would otherwise had been. He bit down on his lip to keep a straight face while Doug continued speaking. "The presentation went well. Just minor changes. You two should be out of here before dinner tonight. Send it to me when you're finished and I'll check it. I have to be somewhere so, see you tomorrow." He handed Melissa a ream of papers and left.

"These don't look like minor changes," Melissa grumbled.

Amin scanned the list of Doug's requested changes and shook his head in agreement.

"Done by dinner? Maybe he eats dinner at midnight, but I don't," Melissa added, massaging her lower back with one hand.

"I don't think Doug ever stops eating dinner, so dinner time could be *any* time for him," Amin said with a slight grin.

Melissa's jaw dropped. She stared at Amin, wide-eyed. "What did you just say?"

Amin's face froze.

"You tried to make a joke. Well, I'll be! We are so completely over-worked and sleep deprived that you actually made a joke." Melissa held his gaze for one more second before she doubled over and burst out laughing. Amin's stiff and aching body suddenly relaxed, and he laughed too. He laughed in a way he hadn't for weeks or months, maybe even years, propelled into hysterics by Melissa's uncontrollable snorts. He laughed the way people do when nothing is funny, but circumstances have traveled beyond ridiculous. His abdominal muscles cramped from the effort and he wiped tears from under his eyes. Next to him, Melissa tried to catch her breath. For a minute, he was transported back to grade school and a memory he shared with Kareem. One of Kareem's many science experiments, a handmade volcano, had exploded gallons of purple foam onto their heads, the kitchen, the curtains, and the ceiling. It was hilarious, and they laughed through the entire clean up that followed. Thoughts of his recently deceased aunt and uncle led him to pull himself together, but a smile remained on his face.

"We needed that," Melissa said. "Let's go to a conference room and sort this out. I'll order some dinner to be delivered, and this time we're expensing it. I'm not eating plastic wrapped food from the vending machine again."

Amin followed Melissa, feeling a bit lighter than before.

Hours past a reasonable dinner time, Amin arrived back at his apartment. He hung up his sports coat and tie and saw that he needed to take his dirty shirts to the cleaners right away or start recycling them. Before he went to bed he spoke to Kareem via Skype. It was the first time they had spoken since the death of Kareem's parents.

"How are you doing?" Amin asked.

"I'm doing exactly what I need to. I wasn't always sure about it, but now I am. Damn! It feels good."

Amin expected subdued sadness or depression. Kareem's conviction surprised him. His tone had an angry edge. But everyone grieved differently. "What are you talking about?" asked Amin.

"I'm moving forward with something important. Something I was holding back on, but not anymore. Everything happens for a reason, and I'm right where I need to be. How about you?"

Kareem's energy rivaled Amin's exhaustion. "I finished a big project at work. Forecast reports."

"Don't take offense, but does any of that matter? Does anyone care what you do at Continental Bank?"

"Huh?" said Amin, although he knew what Kareem meant. No one cared about or appreciated his work. Certainly not his boss. Aside from those few silly moments with Melissa, his work might be slowly and gradually sucking the life out of him. But it was all he had. Besides his family.

"If you died next week, how would you feel about wasting your life helping the richest people in the richest country become richer? Do you think that's what Allah put you on this earth to do?"

"I don't know." Amin sighed, lacking the stamina for his defense. Kareem was right. Amin's efforts did nothing to make the world a better place, he was only helping to ratchet the CEOs multi-million-dollar salary to a new level of obscenity. At this rate, he would grow old feeling alone and unfulfilled in his cube. But he wasn't about to admit it or complain about it. Not yet. He massaged his temples to soothe his returning headache.

"Come visit me," Kareem said.

Amin almost laughed out loud. Taking a vacation right now was absurd. Even if he wanted to, he couldn't. "I can't. But maybe someday."

"I hope it's soon. I can give you a purpose that matters. I have to go now. I have a meeting."

"What type of meeting?"

"Something I'll share with you when you visit me. Take care of yourself. You look like crap. You're not on the right path brother, but I can help."

Kareem signed off and the screen went blank.

"I'm sorry about your parents," Amin said, although no one was listening.

Chapter Sixteen

Charlotte
October 1st[th]

With hell week behind them until next quarter, Amin logged in to his computer and began scrolling through unread emails. He had no meetings scheduled and planned to be caught up by the end of the day. That's when he noticed something new had just been added to his calendar. A 1:00 PM meeting with Shelly Venne in Human Resources which included a message to bring his laptop. An ominous chill swept through his body. The request was out of the ordinary. Out of the ordinary rarely meant anything good. Amin had done nothing wrong. He thought of the emails from Kareem, but all correspondence with his cousin had been on his personal computer. In the last eight days, he had worked one hundred hours, if not more. The forecast reports were mistake free. And surely, if he was going to be in trouble, it would have come from Doug first, not from someone in human resources whom he had never met. He walked to Doug's office to ask if he knew anything about the meeting request from HR. Doug's door was closed. Amin's knock went unanswered. He returned to his cube.

Amin busied himself with account reconciliations and did his best to push his worries aside and concentrate on his work. At

109

noon, he decided to grab some lunch and return in time for the mysterious meeting.

Melissa heard his chair hit the edge of his desk when he slid it back in place. Still seated, she scooted her chair away from her cube and asked, "Are you going to get something to eat?"

"Yes, would you like me to pick something up for you?"

"No. But thanks. I brought something from home. Can we meet when you get back? To go over these new general ledger numbers?"

"Maybe around one thirty."

"Long lunch?"

"I have an appointment with HR at one o'clock."

"What for?"

"I don't know. It popped up on my calendar today. It didn't say. Only that I needed to bring my laptop."

Melissa's expression changed immediately to one of concern. "Amin, that's not good."

"Do you think I'm being laid off?"

"I don't know. You don't deserve it. You've done great work. Both of us have. It's just, well, what else could it be?"

Amin looked down at his cube and chewed on his inner cheek.

"I don't want you to freak out. Maybe it's nothing important, but you don't want to walk in there and be blindsided."

"Thanks, Melissa. I appreciate your concern. I'll let you know what happens."

Amin walked to the deli, letting his shoulders and face relax, resigning himself to the fact that he was going to be fired. He had never been fired from anything before. He wasn't sure if he felt embarrassed or angry. There wasn't a whole lot of feeling happening inside. He was mostly concerned because losing his job would mean losing his identity. Who would he be without his work? What would he say when people asked him questions about what he did and who he was?

"Amin!"

Isa, one arm waving above her head, tried to break through a tight double row of people waiting in line at Starbucks. Isa, who had a fiancé. Amin quickly looked away. Knowing he was about to be fired, seeing Isa was more than he could handle today. He picked up his pace, walking in the opposite direction, blending into the noontime lunch crowd. Isa called his name twice more before he could no longer hear her.

Doug sat waiting, along with Shelly, the HR representative, when Amin arrived for the one o'clock appointment.

"Thank you for coming, Amin," Shelly said as if it had been his choice. "I'll get right to the point of our meeting. The bank needs to downsize and we're cutting back on our non-revenue producing roles. Unfortunately, your job has been eliminated, effective immediately."

"I see." Amin ran his hand over his head. A lightheaded sensation came and went.

"It's not a reflection on you or your work."

"Not at all," said Doug. "It's just one of those unfortunate things."

"You'll receive a severance commensurate with your years of service here. Two weeks of pay for every year you've been with the bank." Shelly handed Amin a piece of paper with the figures. He read it carefully, surprised by his own lack of indignation.

"I'll need to take your laptop. You can put it right there, please." She pointed to the desk before him. "I can't allow you to open it again, so please put it right there."

"What if I had something personal I needed to download?"

"That would be unfortunate. I'm only following policies." Shelly's mouth formed a tight smile. Amin placed his laptop on the desk along with the charging cord and the mouse. He sat back down and crossed his arms over his chest.

"Sorry, Amin. Best of luck," Doug said.

"Thank you," Amin said, as if they had done him a favor. He reached out to shake Doug's hand while wondering if Doug would grow fatter and eventually have a heart attack at work. "So, that's it?"

"That's it." Shelley placed her hands on the table.

"I need to get my things from my office, I guess."

Shelly bent over to retrieve the empty box she had waiting. She handed the box to Amin as she stood up and opened her office door. "You can put your personal belongings in here. Security will escort you to your desk."

Amin cocked his head. "Another part of the bank's firing policy process?"

"Yes." Shelly glanced to her desk as if she had already mentally moved on to her next appointment. Doug remained seated.

A big tall guy from security stood waiting outside the door. The man looked past him and said, "Ready?"

Amin and the security guard walked silently to the elevator. Amin wrapped his arms around the box, feeling conspicuous. He couldn't think of anything he would miss if he left everything behind, but it seemed like a good idea to check and make sure. The elevator stopped twice on the way up. Each person who stepped inside noticed his box and avoided eye contact. Amin's face grew hot. When they reached the thirty-fourth floor, he walked to his cube for the last time, the security guard a few paces behind. At least he wouldn't miss his office area much. He wondered if an unescorted ex-employee had ever run around like crazy after being fired. He pictured someone vandalizing the cubes, lifting them up and tossing them over, probably not possible, and throwing around pens, paper clips, and staplers. The thought made him smile. The guard stood nearby, stone-faced.

"I'm so sorry," Melissa said, immediately at his cube. "You don't deserve this." She shook her head, the creases in her forehead pronounced. "The bank is downsizing in all the departments, you can't take this personally. I'm sure they'll be calling you back soon for another position."

Amin nodded. "I'm okay. Sorry I won't be helping you with the general ledger numbers." He offered a half smile. He opened and closed his cube drawers one at a time and removed his few possessions: a mug, a fork, a neatly folded paper bag, and a Panther player bobble-head from the finance department holiday gift exchange. He placed them in the box. He added a framed picture of himself laughing with some friends from college. He dropped a half package of crackers in the trash can, took a last look around, and left everything else. Leaving his cube without his laptop felt strange, like he had left a limb behind.

Melissa put her hand on his arm. A tear hung in the corner of her eye. "I'm not okay with this."

A spark of gratitude welled up inside him. Melissa seemed to genuinely care about his job loss. More than he did, perhaps. Unfortunately, her concern couldn't change his situation. "Good bye, Melissa. It's been a pleasure to work with you."

Melissa surprised him with a big hug before he left. "You take care. We'll keep in touch," she said.

"Damn," he said inside the parking garage when he realized that just yesterday he had paid the parking fee for the next three months. He drove back to his apartment, went straight to bed, and slept for four hours.

He knew something was different when he woke up, but for a few groggy seconds, he didn't remember why he was home in bed at a time when he was always in the office. He now had nothing to do. Nothing at all. He thought about calling his parents, but didn't want to burden them with his terrible news. He wished he'd done a better job of keeping in touch with friends from high school and college. He wished he hadn't spent so many hours in his cube. And if those were his biggest regrets, maybe losing his job was a good thing after all. Maybe now he could have a life. A girlfriend. A family. A purpose. He wondered where to start.

With an emptiness in his soul, he cooked and ate his last frozen pizza and opened his personal computer. He spent two hours in the Muslims Unite chat room searching for soul-lifting guidance. When it was late enough to call Kareem, he dialed. His cousin answered right away.

"I had one hell of a shitty day, Kareem."

"What happened?"

"You're probably going to love it." Amin laughed and proceeded to tell his cousin about losing his job and being escorted to his desk when he had nothing worth taking home and could have spared himself the embarrassment. He kept talking, sharing the story of Isa, his dream woman, and finding out about her fiancé.

"Come visit me. Now that you've been canned, this is the time. There will never be a better time. The time is now."

Amin's heartbeat picked up. He acknowledged the instant feelings of excitement and apprehension. "I would like to see you. But no offense, Syria isn't on the list of my top vacation spots. Is it even safe for visitors?" He opened a new page in his browser and typed, *Is it safe to travel to Syria?*

"You know how you hear about a hurricane somewhere? The news makes it seem like the whole entire state is flooded, because the media goes ape-shit over carnage and disasters, when in reality, it's only one or two unfortunate and shitty neighborhoods, and everyone else is going about their business as usual. That's how it is here."

Amin rubbed the back of his neck and thought of Kareem's parents who were simply eating lunch when they were shot and killed. He said, "That's not what it says on the internet. Listen. The U.S. Department of State continues to warn U.S. citizens of increased threats from terrorist groups throughout Syria. U.S. citizens should avoid travel throughout the country. Foreigners may be targets for terrorist attacks, assassination and kidnapping for ransom or political gain."

"I live here and I'm telling you, you'll be fine. If you want, I can take you to look at areas where it looks like an earthquake hit, I'm not saying they aren't here, there are plenty, but I promise you, you will be fine."

"How can you know that?"

"I live hours away from the main city in a compound built exclusively to keep its occupants safe. No one even knows it exists. I'm going to have someone protecting you every step of the way here. Trust me. I'll arrange to have someone drive you from the train station right to my neighborhood."

"Can't you do it? Pick me up?"

"Can't. I'm up against a tight deadline. Shit. I sound like you, don't I?"

"Maybe I shouldn't be traveling until I have a new job lined up. I'll find a new position and ask to start after I get back from visiting you."

"You're always trying to find a reason not to do something, aren't you? Some things never change. You just reminded me of when we were kids and you wouldn't sneak into an R-rated movie with me. You made a big deal of it. I forget the movie. What was it? Now it's bugging me."

"The Virgin Suicides. And I did go with you. And we got caught. Did you forget that part? The security guards asked for our tickets and made us wait in an office. They called *my* parents."

"Oh, yeah. Ha! The scary movie theater security guys! Well, you know what? You survived. Listen. The whole trip here and back can be free if you're willing to help out with a few things. My employer will pay for everything." Kareem's voice rose with contagious excitement.

"Your employer? What do they need help with?" Amin asked.

"Um…finance-related stuff."

"How do you know they'll want me?"

"Believe me. They'll want you. You'll have a free trip and you won't have to do much work. You won't be stuck at a desk all day like you were at the Bank of Satan." Kareem spoke with the utmost conviction and confidence.

Amin thought about what he had going on in Charlotte. The answer—nothing. He wanted to help Kareem. He wanted to help himself. The trip offered an opportunity to escape his boredom, surround himself with devout Muslims, spend time with his cousin, and, somehow, change his attitude about westerners before it was too late. Only one reason existed to say no—the fear of stepping away from his comfort zone. Enough of that. For once, he wasn't going to let fear stop him from doing something new and interesting.

"Okay. I'll come."

"Yes! Way to go, man! As your President would say, it's going to be a really, really, great trip. Believe me. It's going to be the best trip ever. You're not going to believe how very great it will be." Kareem laughed.

Amin couldn't help but smile at his cousin's eagerness.

"I'll get it all set up now, before you can change your mind. All you have to do is pack a suitcase. It will take a few days to get here, but it won't cost you anything. They'll fly you in through Paris or Amsterdam, better rates, you know, and someone will meet you there."

"What? Wait. Paris? How do I go the rest of the way? Won't it take days?"

"Bring a good book. A few good books. You can brush up on the Quran. No one flies into Syria. The instructions might seem a little strange, but you'll have to trust me. Okay?"

"What instructions?"

"Instructions for traveling."

"Oh, uh—"

"Email me a recent headshot. I'll get back to you asap with details. Don't even think about talking yourself out of this. Don't even think about it. Pack your things. You're coming!"

Chapter Seventeen

Charlotte – Amsterdam – Syria

October 5th

Amin locked his apartment door with one hand. The other clasped a small suitcase containing his essentials. He paused to study a meticulously constructed bird's nest of moss, straw, and the blue cellophane of an Oreo wrapper tucked between the wall and the light fixture next to his door. He'd never noticed it before, but it made him feel hopeful. He wasn't sure exactly what lay ahead, but he was ready for an adventure.

He wondered if things would be strange with his cousin when he first arrived in Syria. When they were younger, Amin was quiet, intellectual, and as a rule follower, content to hang back and watch others have fun. None of that had changed. Kareem was always the leader, hell-bent on proving he could do whatever he set his mind to doing. Yet, despite their differences, Amin and his cousin were almost inseparable. On a few occasions, Amin had been grounded for following his cousin's lead against his better judgement. But, for the most part, it had been worth it.

The last time he saw his cousin, he was twenty years old. Kareem and his parents had visited Amin's family in Detroit. The cousins exchanged college experience stories and watched a

118

lot of television. Kareem led a search through the house to find liquor they could "borrow," but there was none to be found. Kareem had always added an element of risk and excitement into Amin's life where none existed. Those same twinges of excitement were back. He felt like a child again, almost giddy. He inhaled the cool air deeply and opened the back door of his Uber ride.

"Airport, right?" the young driver asked with enthusiasm. Acne covered his chin, but it didn't appear to have affected his confidence.

"Yes."

"Where are you flying to?" He smiled into the rearview mirror and shifted his Volkswagen into drive.

"Amsterdam." Two thousand miles separated Amsterdam from his destination in Syria. Days of travel. The equivalent of driving two thirds of the way across America. Yet he hadn't argued with the plan. He was following Kareem's directions, like he always had.

"Oh, cool. Amsterdam is supposed to be a blast. Hey, if you tell me when you're coming back, I can put it in my calendar and pick you up."

"I'm not sure when I'm coming back, but thank you anyway."

"That's cool. How come you don't know when you're coming back?"

"I'm going to do some work overseas. I don't know how long it will take, so the company bought me a ticket with an open-ended return."

"Oh, yeah? What company?"

Amin felt his face grow hot. He didn't know the name of the company. "Umm, it's a recruiting company."

"Oh, cool."

"Yes. I lost my job at a bank, I mean I didn't lose it, I got let go. This new company is paying for my trip."

"You lucked out, man."

The driver chatted all the way to the airport, and Amin surprised himself by holding his own in the conversation, thanks to his upcoming adventure.

"Bye, man. Have a great trip," the driver said once Amin was out of the car with his suitcase.

"Thank you for the ride." Amin patted the top of the car and turned away.

He waited in a long and winding security line. When the TSA agent examined his license, he caught an older woman with fluffed gray hair staring at him. An uncomfortable awareness hit him. She was probably concerned because of his heritage and all the recent talk about banning Muslims from entering the country. As if all Muslims were demented extremists. Dark scruff lined his lower face. He'd missed a few shaves since he lost his job. But still, in his collared shirt, L.L.Bean vest and REI boots, he looked like any young professional. He wanted to yell, "I'm American. Are you?" But he didn't. *Whatever, lady,* he thought to himself. He lowered his gaze toward his shoes. He wished he could let the world know that even though he was Muslim, and just barely, he was still first and foremost a lonely American.

Amin moved slowly through the crowded customs area and stepped outside. He raised an arm to shield his eye from the bright Amsterdam sunshine. A group of young people wearing flannel shirts, backpacks, and sturdy walking shoes rushed past, forcing him to step backward. Small cars wove through the airport lanes with alarming confidence. His eyes roamed his surroundings. Although Kareem told him someone would meet him there, he was surprised when he spotted a printed sign bearing his name. A dark-suited stranger with neatly-trimmed facial hair held the sign across his chest. Kareem said his company had employees all over Europe and this man was one of them. Kareem might be higher up in his company than Amin had imagined. If so, no wonder Kareem wasn't impressed with Amin's banking job.

Amin walked over to the man holding the sign. "Hi. That's me."

"Identification?" the man asked, his voice deeply accented.

"Oh, sure." Feeling more cautious than usual, he slowly took out his passport and handed it to the stranger.

The man studied the first few pages and handed it back with a large envelope.

"What's this?" Amin asked, holding the envelope up between both hands.

"Allah Akbar," the man said in a soft voice before turning and walking away.

Amin looked around to see if anyone had heard and chided himself for his instinctive response. People didn't often say *Allah Akbar* out loud in Charlotte, but so what? The man had given him a blessing. He wished his automatic reaction had been a grateful one. "Thank you," Amin called after him, too late to be heard. "Well, okay, then," he said quietly to himself. Feeling a little absurd, and the least likely person to be part of a mysterious game, he passed several occupied seats before selecting an empty bench. He sat down and looked around again before opening the envelope and sifting through its contents. He found six items inside. A train ticket to Istanbul, instructions to walk the short distance to the train station, a thin stack of local currency, a disposable cell phone, a Turkish passport full of stamps with a name that wasn't his own and a document in Arabic, which, to the best of his understanding, stated the name on the new passport had been hired as a financial analyst by the Syrian embassy.

He stared at the passport, chewing on his cuticles. Had there been a mistake? But no, because his picture stared back at him, just not his name. He didn't know what to make of it. He wanted to call Kareem, but the last time they spoke, Kareem made it clear Amin wasn't to use his old cell phone once he left the States. He had mumbled something about the finance work being secretive. Private is the word he had used, not secretive. At the time, it sounded acceptable. Now, not so much.

Amin turned the new phone over and around in his hands. He pressed the power button and found Kareem's name and number already programmed inside. An attempt to call his cousin and say "What the hell is going on?" was met with unanswered rings. He stuffed the phone and the documents back into the envelope. He wrapped his hand around the back of his neck and tried to massage out the tension. He didn't want to irritate Kareem before he even arrived by messing up the directions he had been given. Although mysterious, they were simple enough to follow. The fake passport was most troubling because it was, of course, illegal, and he had never done anything illegal before. Never. And especially not in a foreign country. He'd seen enough movies to understand that the justice systems in other countries were radically different from in America, and not in a good way.

"Trust me," Kareem had said. Could he trust Kareem? If he couldn't trust him, he had no one.

A young mother holding her child's hand smiled and walked past. Amin made an effort to lift the corners of his mouth in return. He sat in the sunshine gnawing at his lower lip and trying to justify his situation. Maybe Kareem worked for the Syrian government, the Syrian equivalent of the CIA. They must have scientists. That would explain all his secretive work. And if Amin was going to be working for them too, it made sense he would need a cover story. Ten minutes passed before he removed his real passport from his front pocket, stuck it between the pages of a novel, and zipped it inside the inner pouch of his carry-on. Taking hold of his suitcase and clutching the envelope, he stood and headed to the train station. At least he didn't have to board a plane with the fake passport. Perhaps he wouldn't need it at all.

He saw an airport café with a sign for waffles. He was hungry. He removed his wallet and held it in his hand. His instructions had been clear—do not use your own credit cards. He had his own cash, but he would have to exchange it first. He felt uncomfortable spending the money from the envelope, like it would open some sort of Pandora's Box with no return. He exhaled loudly to fortify his decision, and pulled a few of the foreign bills from the envelope.

Carrying a chocolate crepe and a large coffee, he boarded the train. His fare included a private sleeping car. His seat allowed him a prime view of the passing landscape while he ate his breakfast, but the food and coffee didn't sit well in his nervous stomach. After a few miles, he dozed off and slept fitfully between stops, his mind whirling with concerns. His boring cube at the bank didn't seem so awful anymore. His sleeping car was about the same size, but after only a few hours, it made him feel like a caged animal. Why did he ever think he needed an adventure? And what sort of adventure was this? Why hadn't he insisted Kareem provide more detailed information? Why was he following these directions now, with every part of his conscience and common sense protesting? What was wrong with him? What would Isa think of him now? He wondered if he still had anything left to lose.

He slept for most of the two days, walked through the train cars, and used cash from the envelope to buy meals from the dining car. He finished two entire novels, long ones. At stops, he paced around to stretch his legs. Adrenaline surged through his body each time his passport was requested. He handed over the new one with a slightly shaking hand, nd it was always returned without issue.

When he stepped off the train in Istanbul, he immediately spotted a large printed sign bearing a name he recognized—the fake name on his new passport. He looked around before approaching the man waiting for him. The man looked right at him and dipped his head with apparent recognition. Amin nodded back and walked over to show his new passport. Without saying a word, the man, who was about forty years old, tilted his head for Amin to follow. He led him to an older-model, black Mercedes sedan and opened a back door. Amin put his hand on the roof and looked around as if the view might be his last glimpse of freedom. What was the alternative? He'd already come this far. He swallowed the panic threatening to choke him and lowered himself into the back seat. There was no conversation, only silence. He worried the driver could smell his fear.

"For you." The driver gestured to a cooler in the back seat. The cooler held drinks, protein bars, and several containers. The containers held grilled chicken, grilled lamb, and vegetable and bean salads Amin didn't recognize.

"Quite a spread," Amin said.

The driver fiddled with the air conditioning knobs and said something in an apologetic tone. Amin tried to call Kareem again. Again, the phone call went unanswered. He retrieved his own phone and looked at Kareem's contact information to confirm the phone numbers matched, which they did.

He ate, sweated, and worried through two bathroom stops, mostly in silence aside from quick prayer sessions with the driver, until they reached a checkpoint at the Syrian border. The car inched forward in a packed single line of vehicles and stopped when they reached the guard station. A chill gripped Amin's heart and traveled from his neck down to his toes. His skin felt clammy. What had he gotten himself into?

The guards spoke in Arabic. The driver answered them, took out his own passport, and turned to Amin. "Your passport and work papers."

Amin's jaw dropped open. "You speak English?"

The driver smiled and shook his head.

Amin scrambled to open the manila envelope and hand over the new documents.

After a minute of scrutiny, the guards handed everything back, and the driver moved forward.

"Almost there," said the driver. "Eight more hours."

Amin lay his head back, closed his eyes, and moaned. He didn't know why Kareem wanted him to visit so badly, but if Amin had fully understood what the trip involved, hour after hour of silent travel, he would be back in his apartment watching The Bachelorette.

Chapter Eighteen

Syria

October 7th

With few main roads to choose from, the driver took a rural route where they were safe from ground fighting. Amin saw smoke rising into the distant sky, darkening the horizon, but he couldn't tell how far away. The lack of scenery became torturously monotonous from the back seat of the warm car. The terrain was mostly desert, the foliage scarce and far between. An occasional buzzard represented Syria's wildlife. Amin forgot about the danger of air strikes and the ongoing war between President Assad's troops and rebel forces. Each time they approached an area with a more concentrated population, he saw signs of destruction, burned and exploded buildings in the distance, but he saw nothing to indicate they were in present danger, which allowed him to dwell on the endlessness of the drive. Eventually they stopped somewhere in Northern Syria. It was late afternoon, the driver needed a few hours of sleep. Amin got out of the car and stretched. His body felt the same way it did during hell week, tense, cramped, miserable. He was desperate to use his muscles and get his blood flowing. He set off on a brisk walk, pumping his arms.

He explored in concentric circles so he wouldn't get lost. The town was a maze of winding alleyways with tarp-covered windows. Overhead, sheets and tunics billowed from clotheslines strung between the walls. Faded awnings stretched out on rickety poles from buildings that looked more like storage facilities than homes or businesses. There was little to see in the way of vegetation. He pictured the neighborhoods in Charlotte. Nearly every yard was manicured to perfection and seasonal flowers were strategically placed in the medians of city streets. He had never appreciated that landscaping until now.

At one intersection, a group of women wearing blue burkas moved silently across the street like a band of ghosts. A skeletal man hurried through, dragging two goats on leashes behind him and paying no mind to the moving cars. A new model silver Range Rover zipped by, reminding Amin he was still in the 21st century.

When he looked to his left before crossing, he found himself standing a few inches away from a man who looked like he'd just stepped out of a Walking Dead episode. Amin had never seen anything like him before in real life. His forehead and one side of his face were covered with scar tissue and lesions. Part of his jaw, the skin and bone, was missing, his face sunken in as if melted. The man stared into Amin's eyes, searing his burned face into Amin's memory. Amin wondered what could have caused such trauma.

Unsettled by the man's burns, Amin decided he'd had enough exercise. He retraced his steps back to the Mercedes, eager to get back inside. The vehicle, with its crappy air conditioning and now smelling like chicken and pickled vegetables, had become his home away from home, his new safe box from which he took comfort.

"Here," the driver announced, stirring Amin from sleep. He opened his eyes but didn't see anything to indicate the trip was finally over. After driving a few more miles on dirt roads through deserted landscape, the driver again said, "Here. Now."

A huge compound of homes surrounded by a stucco wall appeared as if it had dropped out of nowhere. The compound looked more recently built than anything else Amin had seen in Syria. The driver entered a code and a gate swung open.

A large one-story building sat in the center. The playground equipment on both sides clearly marked it as a school. Goats and chickens wandered around inside the fence.

They drove down a single-lane road to a tall building. "Wait," the driver told Amin.

Was this where Kareem lived and worked? Was his ridiculously long trip finally over? After sitting for so long, he felt a sudden lightness when Kareem appeared and walked toward the car, his smile welcoming under his full beard, wearing baggy pants and a loose tunic.

Amin got out of the car and the cousins awkwardly embraced.

"You made it." Kareem slapped Amin's shoulder.

"Yeah. To say it took longer than I expected would be the biggest understatement ever."

"You got to sleep, right? So, you're not tired?"

"I don't know if I'll ever need to sleep again. Hey, were you always so tall?" Amin laughed.

"It's been a long time since we've seen each other."

"Yes. And all I can think of is getting a shower and changing my clothes."

Kareem laughed. "I forgot how Americans don't like to be uncomfortable."

"I don't like to stink is what it comes down to." Amin waited until the driver handed him his bag and drove away. "I'll tell you what makes me uncomfortable. Carrying a fake passport. What's the deal with that?" he whispered.

"Oh. It's so they don't have to worry about taxes and all that when they pay you. It makes it less complicated."

"That doesn't make sense. Who are *they* and why would it be less complicated to pay someone with a made-up identity?"

"Don't worry, cousin."

"A cab driver asked me what company I was going to work for and I didn't know the name."

"The Yoga Institute of Paris."

"What? Are you joking? You don't work for a technology company?"

"You'll be working for the Yoga Institute of Paris."

Amin cocked his head. "Are you messing with me?"

"That's all you need to know about it for now." Kareem smiled and placed his hand on Amin's shoulder. "But I hope that will change soon."

Before Amin could ask for clarification, a young man rushed toward them. He was lean, with cords of muscle rippling across his arms. He wore a T-shirt under a hoodie, Levi jeans, and Nike sneakers. His hair and beard were neatly trimmed. He was alarmingly handsome, glistening with sweat and dirty as if he'd been working outside, but something about his behavior was a little strange. He projected an eager innocence. His eyes and smile were bursting with excitement. He set his sights on Amin and exclaimed, "Your cousin is here!"

"Yes. Amin, this is Mustafa. He's been excited to meet you so he can practice his English."

"Good to be meeting you, Amin. Welcome. Kareem works many hours in his lab. I can help guide you here. We go to mosque. Together," said Mustafa.

"Hi. Going to mosque more often is something I was hoping to improve on here."

"I repair the mosque every day. Make it better. I will show you." Mustafa's grasp of the English language was far from perfect, but good enough for Amin to understand him.

Kareem moved his cousin forward. "It's almost time for evening prayers. We need to get ready. Amin's had a long trip."

"Good. Good. See you tomorrow. Yes?" Mustafa said.

Amin laughed at the man's enthusiasm. "Sure. Thank you."

Once inside the building, Kareem said, "He's different. You know?" He circled his finger by the side of his head.

"I thought so, but I wasn't sure."

"He's slow, but extremely well-educated. His father tried to stick him in my lab to help there, but he didn't like being inside. He prefers manual labor, and he's some sort of genius at building and repairing things. Whatever you do, treat him well."

"Yeah. Of course. I try to treat everyone well."

"His father is important. Really important. He's my boss. You'll meet him too."

Kareem unlocked the door to his apartment and they stepped inside. "You probably can't tell this is a nice place, because of what you have to compare it to, but it is."

The space was small, but new.

"Not everyone has a microwave and air conditioner." Kareem grinned. "Most people don't."

"I couldn't live without a microwave. This isn't much different than my apartment. Except I don't have those." He lifted his chin toward a wall with a giant banner and a poster. The banner had the word *Allah* written in Arabic. "What does that poster say?"

"What have you done for Islam lately." Kareem opened the door to an extra room with a mattress on the floor. "You can stay in here."

Amin dropped his bag on the ground. "I've got to shower, seriously, and change my clothes."

"Okay, make it fast." Kareem pointed to the one bathroom.

Amin used the gray soap in Kareem's shower to scrub himself more thoroughly than usual. He wanted to put the long trip and the fake passport behind him. He could have stood under the hot water longer, but he got out and quickly dried off with a threadbare faded towel. The small bathroom was filled with steam so he opened the door a crack to air it out. He heard Kareem speaking in a stern voice, "Understand?" Amin's Arabic was extremely limited, but he'd heard and used the phrase "don't understand" and "sorry, I can't understand" enough times to easily recognize that word.

A man who sounded like Mustafa answered Kareem with, "Yes, yes," in an eager voice.

Kareem spoke again, but Amin didn't catch any of the words.

He quickly dressed. When he entered the kitchen, Kareem was alone.

"Can I get a drink of something?"

"Where are my manners? I've got orange nectar or Coca-Cola."

"Water?"

"That too." Kareem poured him a glass of water from a carafe inside the refrigerator. He watched Amin drink it.

"Oh, I brought you a few things." Amin got his bag from the extra room and handed over a bag with the gifts he'd selected. "They're not wrapped or anything."

131

Kareem lifted a silver thermos from the bag. The side said, **Keep Calm and Call a Microbiologist**. Inside the thermos was a key chain with the universal symbol for virus. And lastly, two boxes of Nutter Butters.

"Not sure how well those traveled. You used to scarf them down like there was no tomorrow. Wasn't sure if they had them here or not."

Kareem smiled. "They don't. These are great gifts. Thank you." They looked at each other and the moment became one where they might have hugged had they been more comfortable together.

"We better get going now. The mosque isn't too far, but we don't want to be late."

They went back outside and started walking in the direction of the mosque. "Do you walk everywhere?" said Amin.

"Yeah. Pretty much. My lab is close. The stores are close. We don't always have great internet inside my building. There's a café a few miles away with the best service. If we go into the main part of the city there are some good restaurants."

"That dog looks like he's starving." Amin gestured toward a mangy looking animal whose ribs protruded through filthy hair. The creature began to follow them from a safe distance.

"Probably is." Kareem picked up a rock and threw it in the dog's direction. The rock missed and the dog scrambled away with its tail tucked under. Amin cringed.

"Is it safe, walking around? I mean, do you feel safe here?"

Kareem shrugged. "Inside the compound, you couldn't be safer. Did you see the school? There's no way you can miss it. Even the Americans know not to drop their bombs on those, if they ever found this place, which they won't. And here, on the

132

outside, I know which areas have buried explosives in the streets. I avoid those."

"That's not very reassuring. You're kidding, right?"

"You'll get used to it. There's no crime here. None. The punishment for just about everything is death or amputation. Steal something – lose a hand, blasphemy against Muhammad or the religion – death. You know what happens to homos here? They get pushed off a tall building."

Amin pictured Melissa screaming as she plummeted from the top of the Hearst Tower. His hand flew to his mouth. His stomach lurched.

"Pre-marital sex or adultery – death by stoning."

This time an image of Julia popped into his head, even though she wasn't married and couldn't commit adultery. He shuddered.

"A girl was stoned to death a few years ago for opening a Facebook account. Immorality is not looked upon lightly."

"How can you tolerate it? It's so barbaric."

"Nah. The punishments are intended to purify, so the recipient can meet Allah free of sin. Most of us accept them. Sort of like how Catholics go to confession."

"Except . . ." Amin didn't even bother to point out the difference. His cousin's use of the word "us" disturbed him. He'd finally arrived, the trip had taken forever, and now he already had a powerful urge to leave as fast as he could. Feeling homesick and uneasy, he stepped behind his cousin and followed him closely the rest of the way to the mosque, where men moved inside from all directions wearing pajama-like tunics, but also dark pants or khakis and jackets.

The mosque had seen better days. Parts of the outside structure had crumbled into piles of concrete rubble. Stacked stone and scaffolding suggested it was currently being repaired.

Amin stepped inside and scanned his surroundings. What he saw made his jaw drop. No wonder everyone wanted to come inside. "Wow. I wasn't expecting *this*."

Kareem nodded. "Not too shabby, eh?"

Amin let his eyes feast on the richly colored carpet, intricate archways and alcoves, illuminated walls, ornately carved ceilings, and iridescent paint. All in pristine condition.

They cleansed with the water provided, even though Amin had recently showered, and sat down on the ground in the front. The service began with prayers and a lesson from the Quran. Amin understood almost none of the spoken language, but that didn't lessen the experience. Everyone stood to face Mecca for the salat, led by the Sheikh. Devout intensity surrounded Amin like a charged electric current, encouraging his mind and soul toward a higher level of spirituality. He stole quick glances at the men around him, many had closed their eyes. He was willing to bet none of them were compiling mental to-do lists for afterwards, like he usually did during a service. He followed their lead by closing his eyes and tried to absorb their energy.

Despite traveling for days, Amin left the mosque with an air of readiness, a floating sensation, so mesmerized by the experience that Kareem's disturbing comments were temporarily pushed aside. He looked forward to returning for the next service. A glance at his cousin surprised him. Kareem looked determined, angry even.

"Back to your place?" said Amin.

"Yep. So, this is where I live." Kareem opened his arms, making a half circle. "What do you think? Are you glad you came?"

Now was the time to muster his courage, the sooner the better. "Yeah. And now that I'm here, one of the reasons I came, I want to talk about some concerns I have. Concerns for you."

"Hmmm. I'm listening," Kareem raised his eyebrows. His mischievous grin instantly returned a memory Amin had forgotten until now: Kareem and Amin seated next to each other on Disney's Space Mountain roller coaster. From the first drop, Kareem had screamed as if he was being murdered. Amin spent the whole ride worrying and wishing the ride would end for his cousin's sake. When the cars finally slowed to a stop, Kareem's face bore the same exact grin he had now. He hadn't been one bit afraid, he was screaming like a mad man for the sheer joy of it.

"I'm going to come right out and say it. I'm worried you might be developing some extreme views. You know, like taking too literal an interpretation of the Quran. Becoming someone who believes Allah is calling them to put an end to western civilization."

"And?"

"What do you mean, *and*? I don't want that to happen to you. Obviously. For many reasons."

"I'll keep that in mind." Kareem's grin was gone, replaced by the same angry look he had leaving the mosque.

That hadn't gone well at all. Amin tried again. "Allah calls us to be peaceful, merciful, and forgiving above all. Even when it's difficult."

"And *you* would know what Allah wants?"

Amin placed his hands on his hips, unsure of how offended he should be. "Yes. I may not be the most devout, but . . . I'm trying. And yes, I think I have a good idea about that part."

Kareem appeared to be considering Amin's words. Amin didn't want to push him and put a strain on the visit his first night there. He had been hoping for more of a conversation ending with a mutual understanding. Not...whatever had just transpired. He dropped the subject, for now. The decision was made for him anyway because Mustafa hurried over.

"Hello, hello." Mustafa's smile stretched from ear to ear, showing all his teeth.

"Hello. The mosque is beautiful," said Amin. Speaking to Mustafa came easily. Amin didn't worry he was being judged in any way.

"Yes. Yes. So beautiful. It needs much work. I would like to use your help. A big strong American." Mustafa raised his arms and flexed his biceps.

Amin laughed. Perhaps, by Syrian standards, he was well-fortified by frozen pizzas, but no one would describe his average stature with minimal muscle tone as big or strong. "I'd be happy to help tomorrow if I haven't started working yet." He turned to Kareem. "Any word on that?"

Kareem shrugged his shoulders. "They're not ready for you yet, um, for the financial stuff. I have to work in my lab. So, go ahead."

Mustafa thumped Amin's shoulders. "I'll come tomorrow for you. Eat big foods. Big work."

Chapter Nineteen

Syria
October 20th

Amin woke to the sound of explosions. He jumped out of bed and rushed into the kitchen. Kareem stood next to the counter, a spoon of yogurt between his lips, looking unconcerned.

"What's going on?" Amin said.

"What? That? It's so far away."

"It doesn't sound far away."

"It is. Believe me, that shit is loud. Don't worry about it. I told you we're safe here. Listen, I'm sorry to leave you already, but I have to go to my lab. I'm finishing up something important."

"It's okay. What is it you're working on? In layman's terms, please."

There was a loud pounding on the door before Kareem could answer. "*That* would be Mustafa," Kareem whispered. "His name means the chosen one, but I think he's chosen you as his new friend. I hope you're up for a day of free labor."

"Sure. I'm definitely here to experience something different. No worries."

Most of the other men around the mosque avoided Amin, but Mustafa stuck to his side like a personal escort. Together, they walked around the outside of the building, moving bags of cement and building materials.

"Who is this?" A man asked. He stepped right up to Amin. Faced with his angry eyes, Amin let go of his wheelbarrow handles and took a step back.

"Kareem Sarif's cousin."

"Oh." The man lowered his head and nodded. He left and spoke to a small group of men. Each man looked Amin's way. They were talking about him, loud enough for him to overhear, but he couldn't understand them. He could only tell they were impressed. Apparently, Kareem was well respected there.

"How long have you lived here?" Amin asked, dumping his wheelbarrow of stones on the pile Mustafa started.

"A long time. Maybe. Not long. This mosque is hundreds of years old," said Mustafa.

"Okay." Amin had already grown accustomed to Mustafa's non-sequiturs.

"It was burned inside when my father moved everyone here. We fixed the inside first. America gave millions. Now the outside. Important work. Saving history."

"America paid for the inside of this mosque?" Amin tried to hide his surprise but had to know if he'd heard correctly.

"Yes. You didn't know?"

Amin shook his head. "No. I didn't know. America helps a lot of countries with a lot of things around the world."

"They should have told you."

Amin couldn't help but smile.

"They bomb buildings and then send money to fix them. Better to not bomb first."

Amin nodded.

They worked silently for a bit, aside from grunts of exertion, until Amin started another conversation. "Kareem says you live with your father."

"He's near. He can't come outside. He works really hard. Planning. Like Kareem."

"I know all about that sort of life." Amin thought of his former cube.

"Do you know Jennifer Aniston?"

"Jennifer Aniston?"

"Friends. Know anyone from Friends?"

"The TV show? No." Amin laughed. "That show finished a long time ago. Ten or fifteen years ago."

"Buffy the Vampire Slayer?"

Amin shook his head, grinning. "I don't know any TV or movie stars."

"Poor man." Mustafa adjusted his smile to show a bit of sympathy.

Mustafa wasn't one for intellectual conversation, or political opinions, which was a relief. He was the most pleasant person Amin had ever met, and he took pride in his work. The tasks they completed were physically tiring but simple, and the time passed with Amin's mind in a semi-meditative state. He didn't worry about his forecast models or his dry cleaning. He did occasionally think about Isa, her long gleaming hair, her sweet and confident smile. He couldn't help himself, even though it made him cringe with disappointment.

There were no available seats in the crowded café. Amin leaned against the wall under a fan that wasn't doing much to disperse the smell of body odor. Although the temperature was cool outside, too many bodies crammed into the small space made the interior hot. Under his shirt, beads of sweat rolled down between his shoulder blades. A cold glass of Syrian tea, even more sugary than North Carolina's sweet tea, brought little relief.

Amin had been in Syria for a week without seeing much of his cousin. He worked longer hours in his lab than Amin had at Continental Bank. It surprised him how often his cousin had found the time to reach out to him in the past few months. And strange he had been so insistent about this visit when he hardly had time for visitors. Amin spent most of the day with Mustafa, not Kareem, and in the mosque. In the evenings, he had wandered through most of the shops and restaurants alone.

He returned to Kareem's apartment with take-out for dinner, grilled chicken with rice and chickpeas. He found Kareem hunched over the kitchen table, writing.

"Hey. You're here," said Amin. "Good. I bought food for two."

"Do you still have enough cash?"

"Plenty. What are you working on?" Amin asked. He saw a short line of block letters and numbers, like a code, in the middle of the page.

Kareem leaned forward and put his forearms on the table, essentially blocking Amin's view. "It's for my job."

"Tell me more about what you do."

"I work with viruses in a lab. My lab. But right now, I'm also doing some recruiting work. I told you about it."

Amin slid an envelope out from under Kareem's elbow to read it. The return address was for Paris, but the recipient lived in Chicago. "For the yoga company in Paris? That's random."

140

"It's really—." Kareem looked down at the papers, pausing as if he was going to say something important. He looked up and met Amin's gaze, and Amin could tell his cousin agonized over an explanation that would make sense. Kareem sighed and his words rang with a sense of resignation. "The company is in Paris, but the owners are here. Mustafa's father is the main guy. He needed someone who could translate letters into English. No shortage of opportunities here for people fluent in English."

"What are they recruiting for? Yoga teachers?"

"They hold…spiritual workshops."

"How did you go from working in a lab to doing recruiting for spiritual workshops?"

"When Mustafa's father asks you to do something, it's not a question. He's not the kind of guy anyone says no to."

"Can I help you?" Amin looked down at the letter Kareem was writing.

"No, I've got it. I can wrap it up for now." Kareem quickly folded the letter and slid it under a pile of envelopes, all with the Yoga Institute of Paris in the return address.

"Okay," Amin said under his breath. He massaged his biceps on one arm. "I'm sore. From working on the mosque every day."

Kareem nodded, maintaining eye contact with his cousin. "So, how's it going?"

"Better than expected. It's good for me, the manual labor. There's a first time for everything. And Mustafa is a good man. Imagine what life would be like if everyone was as happy as him all the time."

Kareem nodded.

"So, have you heard anything more about when I start the financial work? I'm not complaining, but it has been a week already."

Kareem picked up the letters and envelopes on the counter. "It turns out they may not need you for the finance work after all. Their needs change. We'll find out soon. But no worries. They'll need you for something else. Definitely."

"Who is this *they* again?"

"Same people who own the yoga company. They're investors. Mustafa's father is one of them."

"Investors in what?"

Kareem stared deep into his cousin's eyes before answering. "In our future."

Waiting inside Al-Bahil's office to discuss the "future" of his project, Kareem rubbed his clammy hands on his pants. The guards were laughing and eating something just outside the door. He flinched at a loud SMACK, and turned to look over his shoulder. One of the guards made eye contact and winked, the other cracked his knuckles. They were trying to mess with him, and it was working. He turned back around and did his best to pretend they weren't there, always watching.

A toilet flushed and not even a second later, Al-Bahil entered the room. No way had there been time for handwashing. In spite of his anxiety, the microbiologist in Kareem cringed with disgust, but it was nothing relative to what he had been summoned to discuss.

"Where were we?" Al-Bahil, scooped up a handful of nuts. "Ah, the recruits. We need more."

Kareem swept the back of his hand across the film of sweat on his forehead. "What about the people designated for the subway attacks? Are any of them American citizens?"

"No."

"They can't leave the country and go back in?"

"No."

Sometimes Al-Bahil acted as if Kareem should be honored he was given a private audience with him, and he should not show disrespect by asking questions. Kareem was not just anybody. He was an accomplished scientist who couldn't be easily replaced. He was necessary.

"You were hardly successful finding recruits. It's good you have that cousin."

Kareem nodded.

"It's time to consider the ultimate sacrifice. Considering your failure, it's required." Al-Bahil stared hard at Kareem.

Kareem paled, choking back his anguish, and nodded again. His body began to tremble. Apparently, he wasn't necessary any longer.

It didn't matter, he told himself. He'd accomplished more than most people do in a lifetime. Even if no one would ever learn of it.

Chapter Twenty

Los Angeles
October 25th

It was another beautiful day on the Southern California coast, until Holly merged onto the 110 Highway and inched along, stuck between two huge trucks. Gone was the breeze she'd enjoyed near the beach. Traffic had just begun moving, from ten miles an hour to forty-five, when her phone rang. She answered without looking to see who it was. She'd been more careful driving since the unfortunate accident with Reese.

"Hi, gorgeous. What are you doing?" said Christian.

"Driving."

"Come out and visit me."

"I can't. I have a previous commitment."

"Where are you going?"

"I'm visiting my ex-stepmother for lunch."

"Your ex-stepmother? Where does she live?"

"In a mental hospital."

"Seriously?"

"Pretty much. That's what the place would have been called a few decades ago. Now it's called a rehab facility. Essentially, it's a long-term spa for older people who can't handle life. She's lucky my father makes enough money to keep her there. Rehab-resorts are *not* the worst places to spend one's time, and this one is more like a country club."

"How long have they been divorced?"

"I don't know. She lived with us when I was in middle school and part of high school. They got divorced after. She hasn't been in rehab all that time though."

"How come you're going to see her? A special occasion?"

"I try to go once a month. She doesn't have anyone else. She's lonely."

"She doesn't have any other children?"

"No. Just me. Her ex-step-daughter."

"That's nice of you, then. No one wants to be alone when they're older. Someone needs to be there for her. My grandmother lived with us for a few years before she died. She had Alzheimer's."

Holly's mood suddenly changed. Christian's story introduced some unpleasant questions. Who would take care of Holly when she was older? What if she got Alzheimer's? Who would visit her in a rehab-resort if she ended up not being able to cope someday? Not Quinn. He'd probably never retire. And his job was dangerous. He could die and leave her even more alone than she already felt. Dying terrified her. Dying alone would be so much worse. She didn't want to die alone from Alzheimer's or any other way.

"I have to go." Holly hung up before Christian could say goodbye.

At the rehab resort Holly noticed several of the "guests," that's what they called the people living there, visiting with younger people who were nicely dressed and mostly attractive. Presumably, their children. Babies grew up to be children, and children, grew up to be adults, hopefully good-looking ones, who might turn out to be enjoyable company someday.

Maybe having a baby wasn't the worst idea after all.

Thoughts of making babies turned to thoughts of romantic dinners and fabulous wine in Barcelona. She couldn't wait to have Quinn all to herself for a whole week. When was the last time they had been together for so long? Their honeymoon. They went to a couples' only resort in the Caribbean. They both ended up with terrible sunburns the first day, and had to be so gentle with each other in bed. Quinn was tender, kissing her everywhere her skin wasn't red, the best places. Pretty soon her body was on fire, and not from the sun burn, but feverish with desire. They couldn't get enough of each other. It had been wonderful. Just remembering gave her a sensual longing for him. They were so happy in those days.

She sent Quinn a text.

It's me. Just wanted to say I love you.

Chapter Twenty-One
Syria
October 25th

Amin woke in the second bedroom with aching muscles, appreciating the correlation between his soreness and his physical efforts. Due to all the manual labor, he'd slept well again.

He found Kareem eating at the kitchen counter again. "Morning. I waited up for you last night? Were you working?"

Kareem nodded, his mouth full.

"I wanted to tell you, I'm planning to go home on Tuesday."

Kareem let his spoon drop to the counter. "Already?"

"I'll have been here for three weeks. And the financial work...I don't know what happened with that, but I need to earn a living. My skills are getting rusty."

"But, you never..." Kareem stopped mid-sentence and shook his head.

Amin waited a few seconds before saying, "What were you going to say? I never what?"

"Nothing." A heavy sigh escaped Kareem's lips as he ran his hand roughly from his cheek to his chin.

"You know, I was thinking, I haven't spoken to a woman or even seen one up close since I arrived. That's weird. I think it's why I can't get Isa out of my mind."

"The girl you told me about? The one who turned out to be engaged?"

"Yeah."

"Forget her. She's not worth the agony," Kareem said in a soft voice. "Sorry, my friend, but I have to go back to the lab."

Amin thought they were on the verge of a heartfelt conversation. But he was wrong.

"It's not usually like this," said Kareem. "I don't usually work this much. There's something important I need to finish as soon as possible. Deadlines. You know how it is." He stood up, put his empty plate and glass in the sink, grabbed a set of keys, and left, leaving Amin wondering what was going on with his cousin.

Why did Kareem look disappointed about him leaving? What did he expect? They were hardly spending any time together anyway. Amin sighed, choosing not to waste any more time trying to figure out Kareem. He ate breakfast alone and headed to the mosque to help Mustafa, who was always thrilled to see him, although, he might have been thrilled to see anyone.

On his way to the mosque, Amin heard shouting from a loudspeaker in the distance. The sounds came from the mosque. A series of energetic proclamations. After each, the men nearby responded with a wholehearted-sounding "Ameen". A different voice would take up the chant in the same stirring tone, and again the men answered together, passion ringing from their voices, "Ameen."

"Hey, Mustafa," Amin said with a smile. Mustafa hadn't seen him coming and looked startled at first.

Mustafa's most noticeable "difference" stemmed from his unwavering pleasant attitude. But not today. He greeted Amin with a look that was half-smile, half-grimacing apology.

"What's wrong?" said Amin.

Mustafa shook his head. His grimace deepened when the voices resumed over the loudspeaker.

"What is being said?" Amin asked.

Mustafa patted him on the shoulder. "No worry."

"Please tell me."

"May Allah make their children orphans and make their wives widows. Send disease and epidemics to destroy them. Drench them in their own blood."

"Holy shit." Amin shook his head. "Who are they talking about?"

"Non-believers. Christians and Jews. Infidels."

Now that he understood the meaning of the announcements booming loudly across the square, the hair on the back of his neck stood up and a shudder rolled over him. Anyone who managed to grab a loudspeaker and broadcast similar pleas across uptown Charlotte would have hell to pay for their hate speech. But Syria was not Charlotte. And all the men he could see were actively responding while continuing their business, as if they heard these chants on a regular basis. Nothing seemed out of the ordinary for them. So why did Mustafa alone look so uncomfortable?

"At least they only want to kill the men. Not the women and children. That's something." Amin lifted an eyebrow to make sure Mustafa recognized his sarcasm. Mustafa still looked pained. Amin guessed why. "Are they talking about Americans too?"

Mustafa nodded. "But not you."

"Why not me? How do you know?"

"Because, you know, you're not a Christian or a Jew, and you're helping."

Amin assumed Mustafa meant helping repair the mosque. He wished he hadn't asked about the chants. Too bad Mustafa hadn't made up a different story. Told him they were singing "Hi-ho, hi-ho, it's off to work we go." Ignorance is bliss.

"The filthy French are worse than Americans," Mustafa added, as if his comment would boost Amin's confidence.

The prayer bells rang and Mustafa's smile returned. "Time to pray."

Each time the men were called to prayer, Amin and Mustafa went inside and cleansed. It became a ritual, a break, a chance to recharge physically and emotionally five times a day. Amin didn't understand the spoken messages ringing through the mosque, and now, he didn't ask, preferring not to know. Instead, he prayed for confidence, goodness, and compassion. He prayed for his family. He prayed for starving dogs and people he saw who looked like they could use prayers. He prayed to counteract the prayers from the loudspeaker. The more he prayed, the more natural the process became and the more fulfillment he received. To be good at anything—piano, soccer, spreadsheets—took practice. Day after day of practice. Perhaps praying was the same. It seemed to be the case. He'd logged in more consecutive practice days than ever before.

A few hours later, when Amin returned from the building site, coated with a layer of sweat and dirt, Kareem greeted him inside the apartment door.

"Welcome back. I have some big news. Guess what I'm going to do?"

"No idea. Tell me."

"I'm going to visit you in North Carolina. I'm going to the States."

"Oh." Amin paused to process the news and conceal his concern. To add to his confusion, Kareem's unsmiling, serious expression was more suited for announcing his own funeral than a trip overseas. "You don't look very excited," said Amin.

"Oh. I am. It's just, I have a lot to do to get ready. You know?"

"Well, it will be great to have company if I have to go back the same way I came. That's for sure."

"I can't go with you. I'm still not finished with something in the lab. I can't leave until I'm done. I won't be far behind." He looked around his apartment as if surveying all his possessions.

"So, you're leaving a few days after me?"

"Yeah."

"Should I just wait, then?"

"No. Just in case something comes up. I don't want to hold you up any longer. Unless something completely unforeseen happens, I'll be there by the sixth of November, you can count on that. Oh, one thing. Before we go back, we both have to get a vaccination."

"Huh?"

"A vaccination. You know, a shot."

"I don't need any vaccinations," Amin said.

"We both have to get this before we can leave."

"Who says? I didn't hear anything about this before."

"The European and Asian countries don't require it. But the U.S. is paranoid about people bringing sicknesses into their country. It's not a big deal, just come with me."

151

"I'm not letting someone stick a needle in me without finding out what it's for."

"It's like a flu vaccine."

"I had one two months ago. I don't need another." Amin was starting to get annoyed. He felt a knot tighten inside his stomach.

"They paid for your trip. Get the shot. Please."

"You just said the U.S. Government required the vaccination. So, who is this *they*? Your employer? The investors? The yoga people? Why do they need me to get a vaccination?"

"Please trust it's the right thing to do and come with me."

Amin narrowed his eyes. "I'm going to google it."

"Good luck getting internet service."

Not for the first time, Amin felt a chill of apprehension in his cousin's presence. "I don't need a vaccination. I'm not getting one."

"All right. Don't get all upset about it." Kareem frowned

"*All right?* So now I don't need one anymore? Just like that? Because now I'm really confused. What the hell is going on?"

"I'll see what I can do to get you out of it, okay?" Kareem said in a quiet voice. "There are other ways…" All at once he looked exhausted and sad.

"What did you say?" Amin stepped closer to hear even though he experienced a strong urge to put distance between them.

"Don't worry."

A shiver ran down Amin's spine. For once, he hadn't gone along blindly with whatever his cousin said. The realization didn't leave him feeling any less unnerved.

Chapter Twenty-Two
Syria
October 29th

Amin sat on the remaining section of a toppled wall outside the mosque opposite graffiti spray-painted on a fence. He'd asked Mustafa what the words meant. The answer— Remaining and Expanding. Amin mistakenly thought the slogan referred to the work at the mosque.

He watched the villagers, intending to leave Syria with a solid understanding of the deeply religious but alarmingly hostile society. At first, he was wary of the men because he didn't understand most of what they said. Now, he was more worried because of what he did understand.

The women wore burkas and scarves, some colorful and printed, some dull and plain. They stepped carefully through the streets carrying baskets, groceries, and children. They didn't have to wear the head to toe ghost wraps he had seen on the way through Syria. But there were no tight yoga pants in the mix. And no power suits. How would Melissa feel about wearing a burka? How would Isa feel?

"I'm finished. Let's go back," Mustafa said, interrupting Amin's thoughts, which was just as well. Almost a month had

153

passed since he learned Isa was engaged and he was still feeling the sting and letting her sneak into his thoughts. He had to move on.

"Kareem is giving me his television. Now I'll have two." Mustafa flashed his grin and his perfectly straightened teeth, not the norm in Syria.

"Why is he giving you his television?"

"He is leaving. Going to America."

"Oh. To visit me. But he's coming back."

"He said he's leaving and I could have it." Mustafa's smile was so genuine, Amin didn't want to set him straight by telling him the television might not be a permanent gift.

In Kareem's apartment, Amin helped disconnect the wires behind the TV. Mustafa wrapped it in a blanket he had brought with him, and carried it away like a cherished child.

Kareem returned shortly after. "Hey. I'm glad you're back. Before I forget, I need your mailing address in Charlotte."

"Why?"

"I need to have something mailed to you."

"Why not give it to me now?"

"Cuz I don't have it yet. It's something good. Consider it a gift for hosting me next week."

Amin raised an eyebrow with concern. "Hey, you know Mustafa took your TV, right? That's okay?"

Kareem's eyes settled on the empty space the television had occupied. "Yes, I told him he could have it. I don't need it. I have no use for a television anymore."

Amin waited for a better explanation, but got none.

"Have a drink with me." Kareem removed a dark unlabeled bottle and two glasses from a cabinet. He poured out generous equal measures of the amber liquid, picked up one glass, and gestured toward the other.

It was the first time that alcohol had been mentioned since they'd been together. "I didn't think you drank," Amin said.

"I don't usually. Tonight is special. And Muslims can drink. Muhammad drank."

"Our parents never drank."

"We're not our parents. It's your last night here. Come on. Punishment is only eighty lashes, but no one is going to know."

Amin couldn't tell if he was joking. Kareem pushed the drink closer and his mischievous grin appeared. The same grin from their youth. The one leading to purple foam exploding from his science experiment volcano and covering the kitchen walls and curtains. The one that made Amin want to punch him at the end of the Space Mountain roller coaster ride.

"No, thanks. I don't want to be hungover."

"Who said anything about getting drunk or having a hangover? Here. Drink this." He lifted the glass and extended his arm so Amin could take it. "Half of it. Don't be rude."

Amin forced a laugh. With his heart beating faster, he turned his back on Kareem and filled a glass of water from the faucet. Facing the wall, he attempted to get a grip on his emotions. Kareem was acting insistent about the drink. *Too* insistent. Amin had a bad feeling there was something besides alcohol inside the bottle. It could be anything, after all, his cousin was a scientist. Or maybe he wanted him drunk. Amin turned around and attempted to keep his voice light. "I'm tired. I think I'm going to turn in early." He left the room. Behind him, he heard a low noise like a growl.

Amin woke abruptly to a sudden and sharp burning sensation in his shoulder. His eyes flew open. "What the—?" His eyes registered nothing in the darkness. His hand pressed instinctively against his shoulder. The pain left as quickly as it arrived. He pushed himself into an upright position. Kareem's figure came into focus, hovering above his mattress.

"Sorry." Kareem's hands were clasped behind his back.

"What the hell happened? It felt like something bit me." Amin spit out the first logical explanation his mind chose.

"Yeah. You got bit. I was going after it. Guess I wasn't fast enough."

"What was it?"

"A spider. A huge one. Be glad you didn't see it."

"Shit." Amin massaged his arm, trying to get a grip on his fear and confusion. It had to be the middle of the night. "Do I need to go to see a doctor?" He knew a spider didn't bite him. A scorpion, maybe, but even that explanation seemed far-fetched. Kareem had wanted him to get a vaccination. It was no coincidence that his "bite" felt identical to the shot he received in the lobby at Continental Bank. He slid back on his bed, away from Kareem, uncomfortable with the way his cousin peered down at him. The strong scent of alcohol wafted off his breath.

"Why are you awake?" said Amin.

"I couldn't sleep. I didn't try hard enough to convince you of anything important. I didn't have time. I thought it would happen on its own. Maybe I suck at this. But I don't suck at science, that's a real promise."

Amin wasn't sure if Kareem laughed. He squinted to get a better view of his cousin's features. He was definitely drunk and it looked like he might be crying. Amin's situation reminded him of a horror film where everyone watching knows what is happening except the victim. The darkness and uncertainty were

156

freaking him out. "What are you talking about, Kareem? Are you okay?"

"Yeah. Just tired." He backed out of the room. "I have to go back to my lab and work on something." A tear dropped from the corner of his eye.

"Now? Isn't it the middle of the night?"

Amin's question was met with silence and now he was certain his cousin had been crying. Weird. He closed his eyes, but his unease prevented him from falling asleep again. He was glad he only had one more night in Syria. He'd had enough of his cousin's strange behavior. Not strange. No. Strange didn't begin to describe it. Creepy was more accurate. Creepy and disturbing. Maybe Kareem needed more time to process his parents' death. Maybe. In any case, it was past time for Amin to go home and find a new job. He shivered under his sheet and blanket, though it wasn't cold, waiting for the sun to rise.

Still awake when morning light filled the sky, he heard boots trudging past outside the apartment. The footsteps stopped. He heard a man speaking in Arabic, and then his cousin's voice, unmistakable because of his U.S. upbringing. Amin struggled to hear the bits of the hushed conversation reaching him from below his open window.

He thought he understood the word *sick*, but his Arabic was weak so he didn't spend much time wondering what Kareem meant in case he had said something entirely different. Taking shallow breaths, he got down on his hands and knees and crawled closer to the window. He pressed his ear against the wall, below the sill where he wouldn't be seen. Using all the concentration he could muster, he strained to hear more. The only other words he understood came from Kareem. "Peace be upon him."

Amin heard his cousin enter the apartment, heard him turning on the kitchen faucet, and clinking a mug down on the counter. He waited, counting down the seconds until enough

157

time had passed before getting up and heading straight into the bathroom. He passed his cousin, who knelt in silence on his prayer mat. It was still early for morning prayers.

Heavy eyes with dark circles reflected at Amin from the bathroom mirror. Not enough sleep and too much worrying. His arm felt sore, the same way it felt after he and Melissa got the flu vaccine. With one hand pressing into each side of the sink, he stared, digging deep inside himself for strength. Something wasn't right, but he didn't want to confront Kareem. A coward, that's what he was. Or maybe he didn't want to know what was going on. What he wanted was *out*. Soon he would be home. Soon. And it couldn't be soon enough.

Chapter Twenty-Three
Syria
October 31st

Amin opened the door to the hallway with caution, unsure of what he would find. Kareem sat at the kitchen table. His mouth a determined straight line.

"Were you in your lab all night?" Amin asked. He dug his hands into his pockets and tried to sound more lighthearted than he felt.

Kareem looked up at him, stifled a yawn and rubbed his eyes. He looked like he hadn't slept much either. "Yeah. Just got back. Oh, you shaved for your trip home."

"Yeah."

"Hey. There's someone I want you to meet today."

"Who?"

"Mustafa's father. Don't look so nervous. I'm sure Mustafa has told him everything he knows about you. Seeing you're his new best friend."

Amin glanced toward the clock. "I have a long trip ahead of me. Do I have time?"

"Bring your suitcase. You'll leave from there." He lifted a box of cereal from the counter. "Breakfast?"

"No. Not hungry this morning."

They left the apartment to find Mustafa, so Amin could say goodbye. After, Kareem led the way through the compound in solemn silence. Amin's shirt grew damp with perspiration. He felt sorry for anyone who might sit next to him on the long trip home.

"We're almost there," Kareem said. "It's the furthest point from the front gate. We call it the palace."

At the back of the compound, a large and almost palatial building loomed. The size was similar to an average, new one-family home in Charlotte, but here, relative to the other structures, it looked significant and obscene. A familiar black Mercedes sat parked near an arched stone entrance with guards positioned on each side.

"See, the driver is already waiting to take you back."

Kareem nodded at the guards and they stepped aside. The cousins entered an ornately decorated foyer. Fancy columns divided the space, but the marble floor was covered with the type of cushioned metal chairs found in a cheap hotel's banquet room. Kareem led the way down a flight of stairs until they were underground and standing in front of another guarded door flanked by Al-Bahil's ever present personal bodyguards. In the hallway sat two young men. Americans. Their clothes and shoes were a give-away. Both had scruff on their faces, not beards. One, a large Caucasian, wore a T-shirt and athletic shorts. The other man, smaller statured, appeared neat and of Middle-Eastern descent. His eyeglass frames were the same as Amin's.

"Kareem, hey," said the larger one. He raised his hand to his forehead in a half salute.

"Hey," Kareem said, looking uncomfortable. He put himself between Amin and the Americans, blocking their views of each other.

Amin scrunched up his face, willing Kareem to either introduce him to the Americans or provide an explanation for why he wasn't.

"He should be available in a minute." Kareem glanced around like he was looking for somewhere else to go.

"Mustafa's father?" asked Amin.

The Caucasian man turned and his eyes lit up when Amin spoke. "You're American! I'm Spitz. From Boston." He looked to Kareem. "Is he...doing the same thing as we are?"

From the way Kareem's expression changed— like he might be in desperate need of a toilet—Amin knew Kareem had heard Spitz's question, but he didn't respond.

"Um, I'm here to meet someone," Amin answered, filling in the awkward silence his cousin had created.

"Me too. I'm waiting to meet Muhammad Al-Bahil. I'm waiting for my turn to serve. Him and me both are." Spitz gestured toward the smaller man and nodded as if he had said something profound. He rubbed his left shoulder with his right hand. "We were supposed to come later, but he wanted to see us now."

Amin waited for further explanation but got none. Spitz's words reminded Amin of bravado masking fear. He was either low on the IQ scale, slightly brainwashed, or both.

"Allah Akbah," Spitz said, bowing his head.

Amin stepped back and nodded politely. He turned to his cousin. "You knew there were two other Americans here?"

Kareem nodded.

"Where have they been?"

161

"Look, we should go," Kareem whispered.

"What are they doing here?" Amin asked again.

"This is taking longer than I expected and you should get going," Kareem grasped Amin's shoulder and turned him around, pushing him back out the door.

"You don't want me to meet Mustafa's father?" Amin said outside once they were alone.

"No, I changed my mind."

"It seemed important to you a few minutes ago? What's going on?"

"Let's go. The driver is waiting."

Amin stopped. "I'm totally confused. What just happened in there? Who were those Americans?"

Kareem narrowed his eyes. "Look, all this time I've been trying to help you change your life so you had a purpose. I mean, seriously what else do you have to live for? Some girl who doesn't even know you exist because she's engaged to someone else?"

Amin kept his chin raised. He was tired of being put down. He found strength knowing he wouldn't have to put up with it much longer. "I did find some purpose here. One that isn't driven by spreadsheets and numbers. I haven't missed any daily prayers. I helped repair a mosque every day with my bare hands. I'm on my way to fulfilling the five pillars of Islam. I was going to ask you to come with me to…." He sighed and lowered his voice, but his anger rang through. "You don't think this has been life changing for me? You don't think I've grown stronger in my faith?"

Kareem squeezed his eyes closed for a second. "You're my family. I was trying to look out for your eternal future, not provide you with a few weeks of entertainment. It takes more than what you've done to secure your place in the kingdom of heaven. Don't you want that? Don't you want to do more?"

"I don't know what you're talking about. You're freaking me out. Do I want to become a jihadist? Is that what you're asking? I mean, seriously, is that what we're really talking about here? Huh? Because the answer is no. I don't want any part of it for me or for you." Amin's voice became a rushed whisper. He glanced around to make sure no one could hear them.

"You would turn your back on Allah and what he asks of us? What kind of Muslim are you? One who says his prayers and helps build buildings, but doesn't take the true risks required?" Kareem face grew red with anger as his voice rose.

"Our religion asks us to be peaceful and to help those in need. That's what it asks of us."

Kareem shook his head and spit onto the ground next to his feet. "No. Allah doesn't expect us to stand by and watch what's happening in the world, just let the West take over and kill people like my parents. America is a massive evil empire. Their power is unlimited and they're trying to crush Islam. *You* aren't really an American. That's not who you are. We need to rise against them, whatever it takes. And you're in a position to help. Allah put you specifically in a position to help."

"I *am* an American. I'm a Muslim and an American, and I'm not helping you rise up against anyone." Amin's heart beat madly against his chest.

Kareem stared his cousin down. "I am going to answer his ultimate call." He pointed a finger at Amin's chest. "And you, you—Amin, are going to help, whether you choose to or not."

"What the hell are you talking about?" Fear gripped Amin's insides along with the urge to wrap his hands around Kareem's neck and squeeze the life out of him, which scared him even more.

Kareem's laughter ceased, the skin between his eyes pinched together. "It's too late. It doesn't matter anymore. You can continue to be ignorant." He moved closer, towering over

Amin, and for a second, Amin thought his cousin might strike him. Instead, Kareem laughed, but there was nothing humorous about the sound. "Some of us are loyal followers. And then there's those of us who are too afraid." He spun around and stomped away without turning back.

"Kareem!" Amin shouted at his cousin's retreating figure. "Fine, be that way. Fuck you!" Amin kicked at the ground with his boot. He lifted his suitcase as if it carried three times its weight. He wanted out of Syria. Kareem was right. He was afraid. And it wasn't Syria, or the threat of an attack making him uneasy and fearful. It was Kareem.

He walked over to the waiting Mercedes and its driver and left without saying goodbye to his cousin. His head swarmed with questions, concerns, and fear. He wished he were back home already.

Chapter Twenty-Four

Syria
November 1st

A drop of sweat slid down Kareem's neck and under his shirt collar. He hadn't bothered with the heavy plastic protective suit he usually wore. He kept the lab temperature set at sixty-two degrees, so his perspiration could only be blamed on an abundance of nervous energy. He had to kill the monkeys today. They appeared to be okay, but he couldn't let them go, in case their symptoms returned. And there would be no one to take care of them anyway. The female with the blue band stared mournfully into his eyes, chirping, reaching her hand through the cage for a cracker. He'd been extra generous with her food because of the scientific breakthrough she represented.

He'd always disliked watching the monkeys suffer, and more so with this current group. They had survived against all odds, the result of his brilliant work. While manipulating the virus, he had purposefully ignored the daily prayer intentions blasting from the mosque loudspeaker— "May Allah make the infidels suffer." He had used the most aggressive viral strains, aiming for swift deaths. One to two days of symptoms, at most. And it had worked. In the end, it wouldn't be monkeys suffering.

The last piece of his project, the only part not commissioned by Muhammad Al-Bahil, was now complete—an antidote, essentially, a cure. It wasn't merely a vaccination, a weak version of the disease that stimulated an immune system to produce disease-specific antibodies. And it wasn't an anti-viral that inhibited the development of the virus, like the drugs used to help with HIV, hepatitis B and C, and influenza. It was better. Kareem had developed a true viricide, a chemical agent designed to destroy its target virus.

He'd worked almost around the clock to finish the cure, but still didn't have time to test it, not properly in the lab. Still, his cure was undeniably ground breaking. In any other context, Kareem would be heralded a scientific genius, possibly even win a Nobel Prize. But no one else knew about it, and Kareem had to make sure no one ever did. Unless? No, he wouldn't even consider not following through. His path was inevitable. He had developed the cure for no other reason than intellectual accomplishment. That's what he'd told himself just about every day for the past few weeks.

When Kareem was a teenager in the States, a bumper sticker on the back of an old Honda caught his attention and its powerful message stuck with him. The sticker said, *if you're living like there's no God, you better be right.* It wasn't about Allah—the car's owner was a Jesus freak, with a fish decal and a WWJD sticker on the opposite side of the bumper—but it could have been. Now, he could twist the bumper sticker's advice around to make sense of everything. He was doing the ultimate to fulfill Allah's plan. Al-Bahil had convinced him of that. If Allah was real, and Kareem didn't follow through with his chosen destiny, he would have an eternity in hell to pay for it. And if Allah wasn't real, none of it mattered. Everyone died eventually. Same as the monkeys. Ashes to ashes. A more profound rendition of the sentiment existed, he'd heard it in mosque or from his parents, but he didn't remember it exactly.

The female with the blue band shook the sides of her cage and held her hand out again. He handed her another cracker and smiled at his own accomplishment. Her recent blood tests had revealed irreparable organ damage, but she was up and about. Alive. If he had more time, he would infect another batch and then give them the antidote the moment they became symptomatic. If only he could. If only Allah didn't have a bigger plan for him. He choked back a wave of self-pity.

"We all make sacrifices," he said to the monkey.

An hour later, he had euthanized the animals and disposed of their carcasses.

He took one last look around the lab—the gleaming stainless-steel counters, his shelves of chemicals, his vials of viruses—his home away from home for the past year. Everything was in place. Nothing had been left behind. Who would use the lab when he was gone? Would it sit empty and unused, all the equipment going to waste, or would Al-Bahil find a new scientist?

Normally, his next step would be to enter the disinfecting stalls and douse himself with a powerful spray for oxidizing and destroying viral proteins. But there was no longer any need to follow safety protocol. Glancing over his shoulder, he entered a small office. From inside a desk drawer, he removed a padded toiletry bag containing two travel-size shampoo bottles. Into them, he poured the cloudy contents of a glass vial he'd stored in the refrigeration unit—his cure. He closed the containers, placed them in the toiletry bag and put the toiletry bag inside his larger one. He took one last look around, a deep breath, and a long slow exhale.

He noticed the time. Now he had to hurry.

Kareem locked the door to his lab, fumbling with the keys on the virus keychain Amin had given him and dropping them in haste. Shutting down the facets of his life took more time than he had left, but it was never okay to be late for a meeting with one of the leaders of the Islamic Holy War. Al-Bahil was expecting a final update.

Kareem rode a bike to the palace, the strap of his bag wrapped around his shoulder and the bag itself tucked tightly under his arms. With the acuity of someone who knew his days were numbered, he noticed every detail along his way.

The guards stopped him in front of the mansion.

"Wear this." One of the guards kept his distance and tossed Kareem a face mask with a heavy plastic shield that would cover his eyes, nose and mouth.

Kareem didn't see the point in explaining that his virus wasn't contagious until symptoms appeared. He put the face shield on and the guards allowed him to pass and walk straight to the underground bunker where Al-Bahil's guards took one look at him and stepped back, keeping their distance.

Al-Bahil's office door was slightly ajar. Kareem overheard him speaking Arabic, not in a commanding voice, but softly, with an occasional laugh. Kareem knew instantly he was addressing his son, Mustafa. Considering the seriousness of the mission, how could the warlord feel lighthearted, even for a moment? It was the opposite for Kareem. Even though their future actions were called for and justified, knowing what was going to happen made it difficult for him to breathe, think, and swallow. Just being in his own skin had become a challenge. His appetite was gone, replaced with a burning sensation like a tiny ball of fire inside his gut. A growing fury fueled his resolve, though he hadn't consciously decided where to aim it.

He sat down on one of the seats where he had last seen the two Americans, *his* recruits. They would be nearing Paris by now. He wondered how they were doing, if they were freaking out or acting stoically brave. He hoped it was the latter, and, at the same time, he hoped he too would be brave in the end. He tried to control his breathing while unconsciously picking at his lips.

The door opened all the way and Mustafa emerged, radiant and smiling like a playboy stepping off the polo fields without a care in the world. Despite Al-Bahil's intense hatred of western civilization, his son's clothes epitomized the western world. Kareem repressed the urge to reach out and slap him, and reminded himself the man was "different". Too kind and pleasant to ever make it as an international terrorist.

"Kareem. Whoa. At first I didn't recognize you with that mask," Mustafa said. "You have different clothes and no beard."

"Well, I want to fit in with the Americans."

"Don't get close to him!" Al-Bahil's voice boomed from inside his office.

"Okay," said Mustafa, looking unconcerned. He pointed to Kareem's sweatshirt. "What is mit?"

"M.I.T. A college in Massachusetts. In the states. I almost went there." *How different things might have been.*

"Oh. Have a good trip. You were a good friend. Send me a picture if you meet Jennifer Aniston."

He almost told Mustafa the Friends episodes he watched were decades old, and Jennifer Aniston was old now too, but he didn't have the energy. Instead he said, "Yeah. Thanks. Enjoy my TV. And keep up the good work on the mosque."

Mustafa smiled, patted Kareem on the shoulder, and left.

"Kareem!" Al-Bahil called, his harsh tone was all business now. Kareem hoped he wasn't still angry about not meeting Amin before he returned to America. He stood up and entered his office. Al-Bahil held up a hand. "Stop right there, don't come any closer."

Kareem stopped in the doorframe.

"Are you ready?" Al-Bahil asked.

Kareem nodded.

"And the others?"

"On their way back to Los Angeles and Boston via Paris. I have confirmation the tickets were delivered to the correct addresses. I sent them. They should have them."

"Should. I hate hearing should! Americans are stupid and lazy, infamous for fucking up. Do you trust them?"

"They don't have to do much to get this right. They'll be symptomatic by November 6th." He said a quick, silent prayer for his statement to prove true. They needed to be sick enough to infect people, but not so sick they couldn't walk around in public. The timing was critical. The monkeys had died more quickly than expected, the ones he hadn't attempted to cure, but they were smaller, and they had a different build-up of immunities.

"All they have to do is leave their damn houses at the right time. Walk around. Breathe on people. Cough. Shake hands."

"Yes. The virus will spread quickly. And it will be happening just hours after the subway system attacks."

"Ah, if they succeed."

"Why wouldn't the subway attacks succeed?"

Al-Bahil's eyes traveled over his desk. "They weren't meant to succeed. I left clues everywhere to confuse them. That's why I told you to share the plan with some of your recruits. I wanted America's defense scrambling all over the country. Busy like bees in every subway system. If they stop us, they'll be busy celebrating, getting drunk, getting fatter, laying with women, thinking they've won and they're so smart. If the attacks do succeed, if they're even more stupid and lazy than I think, they might tighten up their security. The only time they take us seriously is right after we strike. But there's nothing they can do to prevent this virus from destroying them. They can't keep their own citizens from reentering. They have no idea what is coming." Muhammad's eyes sparkled with glee.

170

"Right," said Kareem.

"They're so busy fighting amongst themselves, the Americans. Democrats against the Republicans." Al-Bahil laughed and dropped his head back. "This could be world changing. America's apocalypse. An Islamic State without borders. Let there be no doubt, we will be responsible for the change Allah wants. He is pleased with us. Allah is pleased."

Kareem nodded.

"And you have your ticket?"

"I sent it to my cousin's address. Just in case the United States won't allow me entry."

"They will. You have an American passport. And you look just like one now."

Kareem shrugged. "I haven't been back in ten years."

"Your cousin and those other two Americans, they will be rewarded."

Kareem dropped his gaze. "My cousin doesn't know. He's...not a martyr."

Al-Bahil stared for what seemed to Kareem like minutes. His eyes were small slits, his lips pressed tightly together. Kareem's body tensed.

"That's a shame for him," Al-Bahil finally said.

"Yes, it is. But it had to be that way." Kareem wanted to offer Amin the chance to be brave, the chance to be a hero, along with the benefits of paradise, but somehow, he knew his cousin wouldn't be a willing jihadist by November 6th. Perhaps he had always known. He deeply regretted their last interaction, his outburst of anger, the things he'd said. What a terrible lapse in judgement. He'd been stressed. Who wouldn't be in his situation? But what if Amin talked to someone about his concerns? Although what could he say? No, Amin wouldn't talk.

He didn't have the confidence. That was a good thing for Kareem.

"Do you have other family there? Family you might have warned?" There was no mistaking the threat in his tone.

"No." Kareem looked out the window, steeling his features and doing his best to block out the clear image of his uncle and aunt in Michigan.

"They better not fail." Al-Bahil said again. "*You* better not fail."

"There's no way we can."

Al-Bahil nodded. "I have a going away present for you. She's waiting in your apartment right now. She's beautiful."

"Oh." He looked confused until the meaning registered. "Oh. Umm, thank you."

Al-Bahil dipped his chin before shifting his attention to his computer. Kareem took it as a signal to leave. He stopped moving when Al-Bahil spoke again.

"Hey. About your parents——everyone has a role to play in Allah's plan. Their role was to inspire you. They did that by dying at the hands of infidels. Your conviction is strong now. I can tell. You've changed."

Kareem nodded and set his jaw. Al-Bahil was correct.

"Take that off." Kareem pointed to the girl's hijab.

With trembling hands and an expression like she was walking over shards of glass, the young woman removed her scarf.

Al-Bahil was right. The girl was beautiful. Slender, with raven black hair. She stood in the corner of his almost empty apartment looking down at her feet and shaking so hard her whole body appeared to be vibrating.

"Look at me. I want to see your whole face."

She slowly lifted her chin. Her long brown lashes were wet with tears. It was understood Al-Bahil had presented him with a virgin.

Kareem set his jaw. She wasn't going to make him feel like garbage. He was about to sacrifice his entire life, including all his skills and talents. She could deal with one fuck and then move on with the rest of her life, provided no one had seen her come in or out of his apartment and no one ever found out.

"Take off your clothes and go sit on my bed."

Without saying a word, she did exactly as she was told, her tears falling faster.

"Did you bring a condom?"

She shook her head slightly. Her eyes darted right, left, and then back to her feet.

"You don't even know what it is, do you?"

She shook her head again.

Kareem sighed.

Now this was a dilemma. If she became infected, the virus could wipe out the whole compound before they knew what hit them.

Or was it an opportunity?

Chapter Twenty-Five
Charlotte
November 3rd

Amin strode through the Charlotte airport flexing and contracting his recently developed muscles. He considered joining a gym to maintain his strength. At the same time, his heart remained heavy with thoughts of Kareem. He'd spent countless hours analyzing their last conversation and what his cousin meant about answering Allah's ultimate call. Why did he say Amin was going to help whether he wanted to or not? Almost two days of travel now separated them, but Kareem's ominous words still haunted him, leaving Amin paranoid and profoundly disturbed. He thought the comments must have something to do with Kareem's impending visit, if it was still happening. He hoped not, but would that mean he and Kareem were lost to each other forever? He wasn't sure he wanted to lose his cousin.

The alarm on his phone rang.

"Excuse me? Can you tell me which way is East?" he asked a nearby airport employee.

The uniformed man pointed without hesitation. Amin ducked into the restroom to quickly wash in preparation. Once cleansed, he rolled out his mat in an empty corner of the terminal and faced the blue-grey wall. Quietly he prayed, touching his forehead to the ground. He focused on his intentions, carefully piecing his thoughts together. Prayers of gratefulness for getting the hell out of Syria in one piece, arriving safely back home, and for fully-functioning air-conditioning. Prayers committing his service to Allah. Prayers asking for guidance. And lastly, most fervently, a prayer for his cousin who was far more messed up than he had realized. When he stood up, he discovered people staring at him. A businessman, an entire family, an elderly couple. He smiled at them, attempting to project the peace and confidence he was trying to cultivate in his heart. Peace he might have associated with his trip, had it not been for his cousin.

He walked through two terminals to concourse B, the location of a California Pizza Kitchen. Outside the window, luggage carts zipped around on the tarmac while he savored a pepperoni pizza. Strange, the things he had missed about home. He considered picking off the pepperoni, but pepperoni wasn't really pork. It wasn't real meat, according to Melissa who had, on occasion, advised him regarding his food choices. And besides, he had already decided he needed to be realistic. Not all the devout Muslim rules made sense in today's society. He had to be reasonable if he was going to stick with his faith. His thoughts and intentions mattered most, not his consumption of pepperoni.

A yellow cab drove him from the airport and dropped him off at his apartment. For four years he had rented the space, but he entered as if seeing it for the first time. The inside smelled musty. Each room in the two-bedroom unit seemed excessive and large compared to Kareem's smaller spaces. Oddly, it also made him feel trapped. He dropped his bag on the bed and removed his shoes. He opened the fridge. Moldy cheese, two brown oranges and a half-gallon of sour-smelling curdled milk. Breathing through his mouth and wishing he had thrown them out before he left, he placed them in a bag, walked outside, and tossed the bag in the dumpster. He was headed back to his apartment when Julia's door opened.

"Amin! Where in the world have you been?" Julia smiled like a long-lost friend happy to see him.

Amin experienced a twinge of guilt. The few times he thought of Julia in Syria, he prayed she moved out during his absence so he would no longer be privy to her sexual exploits.

"I was visiting family."

"I was worried about you. I have all your mail. Come in and I'll get it."

Amin hadn't considered what would happen to his mail. He reluctantly followed her, noticing the pumpkin decorations outside her door. His eyes moved cautiously around her apartment, expecting to see something he shouldn't see. What, he wasn't sure, but he couldn't help himself from looking. The color and light surprised him. Comfortable-looking furniture—a white couch, blue chairs, and polka dot pillows—filled her living room. A coffee table held books, a mug, and a vase with fresh flowers. Lamps cast a warm glow over the room and illuminated a large oil painting. The space, smelling like fresh baked bread, didn't look anything like his own, even though the floorplans were identical.

"It smells nice in here," he said.

"Just a candle." Julia reached into a wicker basket and handed him a stack of envelopes and flyers. "Let me know next time you leave town and I'll get this for you *before* it's overflowing."

"Thank you," Amin said. "I guess I have bills to pay."

Julia laughed. "Don't we all, unfortunately. Well, welcome home."

"Thanks." He glanced down at the pile. "Thanks for taking in my mail."

"We both missed Halloween. Some trick or treaters weren't too cool with it. I think I cleaned a dozen eggs off our doors the morning after."

"Oh. Thank you for doing that."

"I almost forgot. You have an envelope from Paris in that pile. I wasn't poking through your mail, I promise, but I happened to see it. My Dad collects stamps. If you wouldn't mind, I'd like to give him those stamps, if you don't need them. He'd appreciate it."

Amin transferred the stack to one hand and sifted through the items with the other until he came across a business sized envelope marked Priority Express. The now familiar Yoga Institute logo was in the left-hand corner. Amin remembered Kareem asking for his address and mentioning a surprise gift. He presumed the gift was in the envelope—a restaurant gift certificate perhaps—but Kareem's name was listed as the intended recipient.

"You can just stick the stamps or the whole envelope in my mailbox when you're done with it, if it's all right with you."

"Sure. It's not addressed to me. It's for my cousin. He's planning on visiting. I think. After he opens it, it's yours. And thanks again." During the short walk back to his apartment, he debated opening the envelope. But it wasn't his to open. And maybe, more than that, he didn't want to know what was inside. After their fight, would Kareem still come?

Chapter Twenty-Six

Los Angeles
November 3rd

Holly admired herself in the mirror, practiced a few poses, and adjusted her new scarf. Perfection. Every piece of hair on her head was cooperating beautifully. Her hip bones were almost visible under her tight skirt. That would change with a pregnancy. But that celebrity—what was her name, oh yeah, Christina O'Hare—just had her third child and snapped back to a size zero within a few weeks. And Christina O'Hare wasn't any younger than Holly. Holly looked and felt even better than usual, and she wanted to be appreciated. Today was the ideal day to tell Quinn she wanted to have a baby. She'd given the matter a lot of thought. He was going to be thrilled. Maybe they would go straight home and start trying right away. Or to a nice hotel, which would be even more exciting. She might be pregnant before they left for Spain. She had a feeling today would be an unforgettable day.

She sent Quinn a text. **Hi, babe. Call me when you have a chance. I miss you.**

Yes, he might wonder who had stolen her phone. They hadn't exactly been sweet to each other lately, but she wanted a fresh start. She waited patiently for his response, four minutes, then five, her enthusiasm receding. "Call Quinn," she told her phone.

"Hello," Quinn said.

"Hi, it's me." She was surprised he answered, but glad.

"What's going on?"

"I have something special to tell you. I want to tell you in person. Spend the day with me, Quinn. We'll go somewhere nice for lunch and go shopping to buy some new things for our trip. And after you hear my news, you just might want to take me home to celebrate."

"I can't, Holly. I can't leave work today."

"Just for lunch then."

"Holly, I can't."

"You always say that. Every time I ask it's the same thing. Surely you can leave for a few hours."

"I'm sorry."

"What the hell is so important that you can't leave for an hour or two to have lunch with me? You get four weeks of vacation every year and you don't take any of it. You're at work almost every weekend."

"I'm taking a week off to go to Spain with you in a few days." Quinn sighed. "What is it you want to tell me?"

"I wanted to tell you somewhere nice, so it would be special."

"I'm sorry. Can't it wait until I get home?"

"Forget it. I don't know why I even asked." She hung up on Quinn and called Reese.

"Hey sweetie. What's going on?" Reese said.

"Quinn just blew me off again."

179

"Is something important happening, like an attack somewhere?"

"No. There's nothing like that. We would have heard something if there was."

"Want me to send him a text? I'll let him know how wrong he is."

Holly laughed. "He is wrong. But no, I can handle it. What are you doing?"

"I was about to go out and grab a bite. Do you want to come?"

"Yes. I would love to. Where should we meet?"

"Hmmm. How about the Improper Penguin?"

"Perfect. I can be there in thirty."

Holly touched up her lip gloss, grabbed her purse, and left the house. She drove down Pacific Coast Highway and met Reese walking in through the front entrance. Perfect timing. They sat at an outside table with a view of the ocean and ordered lemon splash martinis and chilled appetizers. By the time their drinks arrived, Holly's phone had alerted her of three texts.

"Who keeps texting you?" Reese asked, taking a sip of her drink.

"Christian."

"Ooh. He's a doll. A doll with a nice ass."

"He claims his good looks come from the skin product line he sells—Fisque and L'aron. It's just a ruse for his drug business. But he sells his clients at least one expensive beauty product along with every bag of pills, coke, or meth."

"Hmm. You never told me that."

"Good idea, isn't it? He's one of the top sellers for that company because of it. My last purchase came with a small jar of intense firming day crème. I tried it. I have to admit it's good stuff – the pills *and* the lotion."

"He has a lot to offer a woman, doesn't he?"

Holly laughed. "But he's needy. He's always texting me. Asking what I'm doing. Asking me to come over. Asking me questions. Asking me out to dinner and to go to the movies, like he's my boyfriend or something."

Reese raised her eyebrows. "How cute. Sounds like he might have fallen for you. Sweetie, why don't you go meet him after our lunch? Since your husband doesn't have time for you. Consider this your revenge."

Holly's peach colored lips formed a sly smile. "You're right. Maybe I will. I need to stock up on *products* for my trip anyway."

"It's always good to be stocked-up for a rainy day." Reese turned to a passing waiter and gestured to her empty drink. "When you get a chance?"

"Quinn can be a serious bore sometimes. Maybe I'll slip a little something into one of his drinks and see what happens." Holly lifted her chin and smiled.

"That's the spirit, sweetie. Now text Christian back and go visit him after lunch. He'll cheer you right up. And can you pick up a few of those pills for me? You know the ones?"

"Of course."

"Just let me know how much it is."

"Consider it an early Christmas present."

"Ooh, that reminds me. Give me your phone. You must watch this video. It's that couple we met last week at the studio."

"Edward and Matthew?"

"Yes! They do these song parodies. There's a few of them. So hilarious! Believe me when I tell you, you're going to die laughing."

After lunch, Holly called Christian and headed east to visit him in the San Fernando Valley. She had friends in Los Angeles she could ask for prescription pain killers. She didn't *need* to venture outside the city. But today, her trip to the valley was as much about getting revenge on Quinn as it was about the goodies Christian had for her. She smiled, thinking of how glad he'd be to see her. At least someone would be.

The temperature rose with each mile she drove. The mountain ranges and the lack of an ocean breeze worked together to trap a layer of gray smog over the valley. Eventually she pulled over and raised the top of her car to surround herself with air conditioning. She thought, who would want to live out here? Way too hot. But the houses had some space in between them rather than being an arm's width apart like her contemporary home two blocks away from the beach. And the area seemed as quiet as a ghost town, which allowed Christian the discretion his business required.

Holly glanced in her rearview mirror. A black sports car followed her. A young man with sunglasses and a hoodie sat behind the wheel. *What if Quinn sent someone to spy on me? What if he knows what I'm doing?* Her eyes repeatedly darted to the mirror and back. *I'm being paranoid. I don't need to worry. He's too busy chasing down terrorists and analyzing other people's business to pay attention to me. But what if he does know?* A little spark of hope fired up inside her. She eased up on the gas. The sports car drove around her and sped away. He hadn't been following her. The realization brought disappointment instead of relief. She wanted Quinn to care enough about her to send a tail, just in case.

Holly wondered how much farther she had to drive, but after her accident with Reese, she was nervous about glancing at

182

her phone. Over a minute had passed since her phone last provided directions. She took a quick look at the screen. It was black.

"No! No! Damn it." She fumbled around inside the middle compartment, searching unsuccessfully for a car charger and cursing the stupid videos she'd watched at the Improper Penguin. They had drained her phone battery. The Mercedes had its own navigation system, but she didn't have the slightest clue how to turn it on, she had always relied on her phone.

She crept along the suburban neighborhood at ten miles an hour, squinting to read house numbers and regretting her decision to drive to the valley. Finally, she spotted someone she could ask for directions. A man with olive skin stood alone on the sidewalk. He wore an average sort of white-collar work outfit; one Holly thought would only suffice in a boring office where no one cared or knew any better. She stopped her car against the curb and rolled down her window.

"Excuse me," she called, the car idling.

The man turned slowly, as if he was thinking about whether to respond. Holly thought he was a little out of it. Aimless. Slow. She wondered if he was on something. He staggered from the sidewalk to her side of the car. Covering the short distance seemed to take forever.

"Umm, hi. Can you tell me where 7816 Rancho Verde is?" *Rancho dried-out brown is more like it.* "Which direction at least?"

He paused to concentrate. Or maybe he didn't understand. It wasn't a difficult question—either he knew or he didn't. Why was it taking him so long? Holly pressed her lips together and raised her eyebrows, waiting for a response, aware of the cool air from inside her car exiting through the open window. After a long and awkward pause, the man took a few unsteady steps toward her. Smudges covered his eyeglasses. He gripped a business envelope between his fingers and it shook along with his hand. He leaned against the driver side of the car, one arm on the back edge of the window, too close for Holly's comfort. Beads of liquid dotted his brow and lip. Circles of sweat darkened his shirt under his arms and across his chest. He looked sickly and smelled strange. She wished she hadn't stopped to ask him, but by then, there was little else to do except wait for his response. He lowered himself down, moving even further into the open window. Holly shifted away toward the passenger side. His eyes were bloodshot, hardly any white left around his irises. *What the hell is wrong with this guy? He's so gross. I would stop using in a heartbeat if something compromised my looks like that.*

"Rancho Verde is behind you," he mumbled. With no warning, his eyes opened wide with apparent surprise and he coughed, without moving away from Holly's open window. A spray of liquid hit her arm and face. She grimaced and tilted farther toward the interior of her car.

"Thank you." Holly jammed her finger against the button to raise her window. She shifted the car into gear and shook her head. She wanted to erase his face from her mind, but couldn't resist a peek in her rearview mirror for the same reason people paid to see freak shows. The mirror revealed the man crouched on the ground. Maybe he was too messed up to remain on his feet. Holly shuddered, and kept driving. She pulled a Kleenex from her purse and wiped her arm and cheek in disgust.

When she finally located Christian's rental home—an uninspired, small terra-cotta ranch with nonexistent landscaping—all she could think was, *Really? This* was the best he could do? So far from the beach and the cool air to live in a place like this? It was a lot to sacrifice for privacy and discretion. She stood on the uninviting front porch and looked around. Perhaps the drug business wasn't as profitable as she imagined. Then again, nothing was as profitable as the porn industry. Thanks to her father, she'd never had to live in a shack like this, and never would. Yes, she had many reasons for which to thank her father. He took care of the important things in her life.

The front door opened before Holly rang the doorbell, revealing a grinning Christian, sexy in a black T-shirt and jeans. "I've been waiting," he said. His smile revealed his white, almost-perfect teeth.

"I got lost." Her eyes took in the scuffed entryway floors and the pink painted walls. She tried to hide her distaste. The trip already felt like a big mistake.

"Come here," Christian placed his arms around her small waist and pulled her against him, closing the door with his foot. But Holly backed out of his embrace.

"What's wrong?" he asked.

"Do you have an Indian-looking customer who lives a few streets away? Not the Native American kind, but, you know what I mean. A guy?"

"Nope. Doesn't sound like anyone I know." Christian's smile grew wider. "Why do you think he's one of my customers? Did he have beautiful skin?"

"No, he didn't. Definitely not. My phone died and I couldn't find your street. There was no one around except for this guy. I stopped to ask if he knew your address. Oh my God. He was a total wreck, but also nerdy, with those small wire-framed glasses and a plain office type of shirt. I hardly expected someone like him to be an addict."

"Hmmm," Christian said. "People need to know their limits."

"I do," Holly pressed her shoulders back. Suddenly she shivered.

"What's wrong?" Christian reached out to stroke her arm.

"He was just…just awful. That's all. Disturbing and creepy. He coughed on me. Like right in my face. Ugh, I can't stop thinking about him." Holly twisted her diamond ring from side to side between her fingers.

"I'm going to make you forget about him. Come on," Christian said, taking her hand in both of his and leading her toward his bedroom.

"Wait. Maybe you could start me off with something to relax me," she said, offering her most seductive smile.

Christian stroked her hair. "How about waiting until later?"

"Seriously? Are you trying to convince me *not* to use your drugs?"

"No, I just thought it would be…. Never mind. I've got you taken care of, don't you worry. I know what you need."

"I need a pill," said Holly.

Christian nodded and gestured with his arm. "Right this way."

"Okay then, whatever." Holly followed him down the hall and into his bedroom.

An hour later, Holly stretched her arms overhead and laid back against Christian's pillows. "*That* was certainly worth the trip out here. It was exactly what I needed."

Christian smiled. He kissed her shoulder, her neck, and her cheek. "I told you I would take care of you. You'll have to visit more often."

"Hmmm." She suddenly remembered Quinn and felt a wave of sadness dampen her good mood. She sat up and placed her feet on the floor. "I better go."

She dressed and left Christian's house, having received everything she'd come for. The prescription pain pills were stacked neatly inside her Fendi purse beneath a jar of age-defying eye cream and nighttime lip conditioner.

A combination of sex, Oxy, and guilt had erased the awful man with the bloodshot eyes from her mind.

Chapter Twenty-Seven
Los Angeles
November 3rd

For three weeks Quinn's team had worked with other federal agents to dig up intelligence to prevent the mass transit plot. Only three days remained before the subway attacks. They still hadn't located Hasaan Fayad, the alleged leader. They were running out of time.

Ken cracked his knuckles. "Chatter is high across the internet. We've intercepted an abnormal amount of contradictory information. The attacks are on. The attacks are off. They're using peroxide bombs. They're using petrol bombs. They're using TNT. The target cities change. They change again. Fayad is not in charge. Then he is. It's ISIS. Then it's Al-Qaeda. We've been spinning our wheels following up on false leads."

"Consider that we first heard of this plot from Redman, a total outsider. This organization, whoever it is, they're controlling us like puppets. Feeding us dead end cues on purpose," Rashid said. "At this point. I don't know what else to think."

Quinn listened, twisting the remnants of a paper napkin between his hands.

187

"Listen," said Stephanie. "I know we need to catch them *before* they attempt this attack, but let's remember, no one is going to bomb the subways. It may not be ideal, but we can shut the transportation systems down if we must. If it comes to that."

Stephanie touched Quinn's arm. He flinched. "Sorry," she said. "I wanted to get your attention. Come with me to the break room for a minute. It's almost fourteen hundred hours. I have to eat something. You should too." She gestured toward the hallway with a tilt of her head.

"Okay." Quinn got up and followed her out.

Inside the break room, Quinn opened a refrigerator and pushed aside Sprites and root beers. "We need more cans with caffeine."

"There's more in the other fridge," said Stephanie. "Do you have an itinerary for your big trip?" She reached under Quinn's arm to remove a yogurt from the shelf before the door closed.

"Uh..." He paused as if the trip was the farthest thing from his mind. "I think Holly does. She met with a travel agent who planned it out for her."

"So, it's just going to be a surprise for you?"

"You could say that."

"Do you even know where you're going?"

"Spain."

Stephanie laughed. "That's not what I mean. Which cities?"

"Right now, I'm just focused on catching Hasaan Fayad and stopping the bombings."

"There's always going to be something about to happen at work. You need to be able to walk away from it occasionally. Once a year, anyway, at least."

"Yeah? Tell me, Stephanie, when was your last vacation?"

Stephanie leaned against the counter and opened her yogurt. "September. I spent a week with my parents in New Hampshire. I'm always with them on the 9/11 anniversary, if I can help it."

"Oh. That's right."

"Besides, I don't have anyone to go away with, so it's different."

Quinn didn't know what to say. Was he supposed to say he was sorry? There had to be plenty of men who wouldn't mind spending time with Stephanie, assuming she was into men, sometimes it was impossible to know and she'd never spoken of a boyfriend. Anyway, he wasn't in the mood to chat about personal situations.

Quinn's phone lit up. He looked at his screen and sent the call to voicemail.

"No one you want to talk to right now?" Stephanie said.

"It's a woman from the Los Angeles Times. She wants information on Redman. I can't comment. But I do owe our internal legal department a call, though I'm not going to deal with it today. We're running out of time on this one."

"Then we have to pick up the pace."

Quinn smiled. "Yes, we do. Come on, let's get back to work."

Stephanie hurried to finish her last spoonful of yogurt and said, "Nothing like a leisurely lunch."

They tossed their empties into the recycling bin and walked at a brisk pace back to their work area. The rest of the team was still busy chasing down leads. Quinn stopped close to Rashid and said, "How are you holding up?"

Rashid put down his phone and spun around in his chair. "Fine, and—"

Ken interrupted from behind him. "You don't look fine. Your breath is rank."

Rashid grinned. "*Thanks*, Ken, luckily my appearance doesn't affect my work. *I* just located Hasaan Fayad." With exuberance, he thrust his fist toward the ceiling.

"What? Seriously?" A smile spread across Ken's face.

Stephanie rushed across the room and leaned forward to get a look at Rashid's monitor. "How did you do it?"

"Facial recognition software on live videos feeds shared by the Gendarmerie Nationale. Found him walking into a pharmacy. There's a ten second delay. I called American agents in Paris. They're on their way there now."

"So awesome, Rashid," Stephanie said, beaming.

"Thanks. I got lucky."

"Excellent work, Rashid," Quinn said.

"And it happened when we were taking a break." Stephanie nudged Quinn in the shoulder. "Maybe we should take breaks more often."

Rashid pointed to the scene on his monitor. "There they go. Those are our guys heading inside. There's no way they don't catch him."

"Who wants to bet me that Mr. Holy Wars isn't picking up a prescription for a venereal disease?" Ken said.

"I don't care what he's picking up, as long as we get him," Quinn said, his hands curled into fists.

After a flurry of video and phone conferences, Quinn spoke to his team in the briefing room. "Here's the latest. Fayad's interrogation is going well. We'll have some solid intelligence soon. However, if the terrorists learn he's been picked up, they're likely to move their timeline forward—a better-now-than-never philosophy. They could strike immediately. The terror alert in Boston, Philadelphia, and Chicago has been raised to red. They need our expertise on the ground."

"So, we keep the public safe without causing panic—not easy," Stephanie said.

"I know what's coming. I'll arrange for immediate flights, just let me know who is going where," Jayla said, her fingers poised to type.

Quinn lifted his gaze to the ceiling and paused before making eye contact with each of his agents. "Stephanie, head to Philadelphia. Ken, you're going to Chicago. Rick, you'll go with me to Boston. I'll contact the other agencies and direct defense personnel to each mass transit stop. Local law enforcement will be expecting us."

Rashid leaned forward. "I can go to Philly too, or Chicago if you want me there instead."

"Thank you, Rashid, but you'll be our point person here. Once Fayad gives up names, locate them before they can get to the subways."

Rashid sighed quietly and lowered his head.

"No one is better than you at piecing together information from cyberspace," Stephanie said before leaving.

Carrying their laptops and the bags they each kept in the office stocked with necessities and a change of clothes, Quinn and Rick waited to board the red eye bound for Boston. Rick leaned forward in his seat, one hand on his knee, his toes tapping against the floor. "So, I know we're trying to find them before they get to the subways, obviously, but in case that doesn't happen, what's in play to stop them?"

"Every subway entrance is manned with officers checking bags. Same in Chicago and Philly."

"Lots of overtime pay these next few days," Rick said.

"Yes. They've got dogs trained to detect peroxide. Undercover agents and police will patrol for any unusual type of behavior—standing too long, moving against the crowd, wearing bulky clothes, looking uncomfortable, sweating, peroxide burns, lips moving silently, anyone with no body hair. Anyone suspicious will be pulled aside and questioned."

"No body hair? Never heard that," Rick scratched his jaw.

"Certain sects purify themselves before a suicide bombing by removing all their hair."

"Oh."

"And some don't, because they know it might give them away."

They boarded the plane, sat, and opened their laptops. Two hours into their flight, Quinn smiled and shook his head in disbelief. "Fayad has already given up names."

"Names?"

"Names of the terrorists who planned to carry out the bombings."

"That was fast."

Quinn frowned and chewed on his bottom lip. "Yes, it was."

"What sort of techniques did they use?"

"Don't know. Didn't ask. The suspects are spread around the East Coast. I'm sending names and photos to Rashid now."

"Can I help find anyone?" Rick asked.

"No, not yet. Once Rashid tracks these guys, we'll direct teams to their locations. If we land before they're apprehended, we'll head out to the assigned station. Until the last terrorist is accounted for, there's no guarantee the subways are safe."

Rashid suddenly stopped typing and linking data on three different keyboards. He jumped up from his chair and pounded the desk. "We got them! The information was good! We got them!" He turned to share the exciting moment with his colleagues before remembering he and Jayla were the only ones in the work room. He high-fived Jayla, sat back down, and smiled up at the ceiling.

"All of them?" Jayla said.

"In Philly. Two men and two women. Both married couples. They had explosives and a document outlining the plans in each city. Names, locations, everything. Agents are scanning the documents right now. It's only a matter of time before we catch the other suspects."

Jayla's expression reflected her exhaustion from long, stressful hours. She smiled and adjusted the dark-rimmed glasses that had replaced her contacts sometime during the night. "I'll contact Quinn and make sure he knows. Sometimes they don't have the best reception in flight."

"We got them in Boston!" Rashid shouted ten minutes later. He gestured excitedly with his hands and Jayla laughed at his excitement. "Three people. All in one house. Every name on the list. And duffel bags and briefcases with the bombs. They didn't know Fassad or the Philly terrorists had been arrested."

"I guess they didn't have time to warn the other groups before they were cuffed," said Jayla.

Rashid tugged at his ear and narrowed his eyes. "Apparently, they didn't have a contingency plan in place.

Usually, with groups spread out like this, they communicate at arranged times. Failure to check in means something is off."

"Maybe it's a two or three-hour window and none of the ones who were caught missed it yet."

Rashid offered a slight nod. "Yeah, maybe. But, it's strange."

"Arrested in Chicago," he said shortly after. A prickling sensation crossed his scalp. He should have been more elated than when the first and second groups were arrested. But instead, he remained seated, his voice subdued when he said, "I can hardly believe our luck."

Quinn communicated the good news to Rick, Ken and Stephanie. "Local law enforcement will stay in place to check bags and monitor everyone who gets on the subway for the rest of the day. But it's over. Head back. We'll be of more use following up on the incoming intelligence. Much shorter trip than planned, but it's good our efforts weren't required after all." Quinn allowed himself to smile, even though his body was tight and tense with need for sleep. The U.S. had successfully prevented terrorists from striking without a single government agent or civilian getting hurt.

"Now what?" Rick asked.

"Work with the intelligence and information coming out of the interrogations. See which of the terrorists might be willing to work out a deal in exchange for information that could nab us a bigwig."

"Find a hotel?" Rick raised his shoulders.

"Probably not worth the trouble for only a few hours of sleep. We can grab something to eat when we land and then find a conference room. Get some work done until the first flight out."

Quinn ignored his growling stomach. He would be boarding a plane for Spain in the next few days. He'd soon have plenty of opportunities to eat some decent meals and catch up on his sleep. The mass transit attacks, for those who knew about them, would be remembered as a botched plot. The line "No one from those countries has ever attacked us," spoken many times by the public after the President's refugee ban, rang in his head. Thank God, those words were still true. He dropped his head back against the seat and tried to shake the unnerving sense that something was wrong.

Chapter Twenty-Eight

San Fernando Valley
November 4th

Frank Hayes knew a thing or two about sick people. His father died of lung cancer years ago, but he remembered well. At the bitter end, his father's skin turned ashen. His emaciated body grew too weak to stand. It took all his father's energy to sit in his leather recliner hacking up bloodied globs of clotted tissue into a never-ending procession of Kleenex. So, when Frank returned to his modest valley ranch house from walking his dog and spotted his neighbor outside, he knew right away something was wrong. His neighbor leaned heavily against the top of his stair rail, barely able to hold himself upright. From afar, the man reminded him of his ailing father just before his bed-ridden days, bent over, wracked with pain. But his father had been eighty. His neighbor couldn't be older than mid-twenties. Frank watched with suspicion as the man took a few precarious steps toward his house and collapsed, half-in and half-out of the front door. One hand slid down uselessly against the doorframe. Eyeglasses hung from one ear, threatening to fall.

Frank tied his dog's leash to the mailbox. "Stay." He turned and walked slowly toward the house, almost on tiptoe. "Raj?"

Two days ago, Frank couldn't have said for sure that his neighbor's name was Raj. He was quiet for such a young man. The ideal neighbor. They only exchanged waves when Raj, in his Honda and presumably on his way to work, drove past Frank and his schnauzer during their morning walks. Frank knew most of his other neighbors, especially those who walked their dogs every day. He even knew the well-dressed "lady's man" down the road who had men and women going in and out of his rental home all day buying fancy beauty products, lotions and exfoliating creams, someone had told him—of all things. How weird was that? But he didn't know much about Raj. According to another neighbor, Matilde, who seemed to know everything about everyone, Raj was a radiation engineer who worked at the nuclear facility. But come to think of it, Frank had seen more of Raj in the past few days than he had since the guy moved in six years ago. More than once, he happened to spot Raj walking to or from his mailbox. Two days ago, they had a brief conversation. Frank couldn't remember exactly what was said, aside from their names. Something about the weather? Raj seemed reluctant to make eye contact so Frank ended up looking down at the letters in his neighbor's hand. He wasn't being nosy, and he didn't mean to see the words *Paris, France* in large print on the top envelope, but he did. Raj impressed him as a serious man, certainly polite, but a little odd and a little lonely. He hardly seemed like a savvy world traveler. Frank couldn't help but wonder what sort of friend or business dealing Raj had in Paris.

"Raj?"

Frank approached the open front door. Raj didn't respond. He crept forward until he stood a few yards away. Raj lay unmoving in a fetal position on the porch floor. Streaks of dark fluid trickled from his eyes and nose and down his cheeks. Frank inched nearer, close enough to confirm his suspicion. The streaks were blood.

"Oh, no. Oh, God!"

He jerked backward, away from the house, aware of an acrid smell. Down by his foot, a large puddle of bloody vomitus was slowly being absorbed into the earth. Frank's face twisted in horror. Images from a scary movie flashed before his eyes. The characters had died of radiation poisoning, blood streaming from their eyes and noses. Their bodies were toxic to everyone who went near them. Raj looked exactly like those doomed movie characters. Was Raj emanating toxic waves right at that very moment? And was Frank absorbing them?

"Raj! Can you hear me?" Frank yelled. Again, no response.

Frank wasn't going to risk contaminating himself. He returned to the mailbox to untie his dog's leash and ran back to his house to call an ambulance.

"My neighbor is unconscious inside his front door. He may be dead." His breath coming fast, Frank gave the dispatcher the information necessary to reach the correct address.

"I'm sending help," the dispatcher said. "Can you check if he's breathing while you wait for the ambulance, sir?"

"No. I'm calling from my house." Frank stared out the window, his eyes darting to his neighbor's house. "I don't want to get too close to him. He's bleeding from his eyes and nose. He vomited blood. I have good reason to believe he has radiation poisoning. He works at the nuclear power plant. The people you send out need to wear hazmat suits or they could be contaminated. Please. Don't put anyone's life in danger."

"Okay, sir. I'll alert the medical team to the information you've provided. What nuclear power plant does he work at?"

"The nearest one, I guess. San Louis Obispo."

"Thank you. I'll make a note of that."

"Contact them and find out if he was exposed to radiation. They may have a leak."

"I'm sure someone will do that, sir."

Frank hung up and hurried to his sink. He pushed up his sleeves and scrubbed his hands and arms with soap under hot water.

Minutes later, a siren signaled the arrival of a fire truck. His dog barked sharply. Frank rushed back outside to meet the firemen at the curb.

Two men, one bald and one with a full head of light colored hair stepped out of the fire truck wearing protective suits.

"I think he's already dead. I think he has advanced radiation poisoning." Frank clasped his hands and squeezed them tight. "He works at the nuclear facility."

A third man, younger than the others, studied Frank. "Who are you?"

"Frank Hayes. I'm a neighbor. I'm the one who called 911. I told them I'm sure he's been exposed to radiation. They told you that, right?"

"Yes, they told us. Thank you for your concern, sir," the bald fireman said as he put on gloves. "We're a hazardous materials response team. We've already heard from the nuclear facility. They have sensors that alert to radiation leaks, and they insist they don't have one. But we're going to check here anyway. We've got a Geiger counter, it detects radiation."

"I know what it does," said Frank.

"How about you stand over there beside the fire truck until we get back?" said the bald man just before securing his helmet.

"You don't have to tell me twice." Frank walked backwards the short distance he had moved from the firetruck. "Not gonna argue 'bout that. Glad you're here." He paced around for several minutes while the firemen assessed the situation.

"The victim is deceased. Radiation levels are at zero," said one of the firemen. "We need to set up the decon tent and put biohazard tape around the area, but first, call the CDC."

199

Twenty minutes later, a Taurus sedan raced to an abrupt stop in front of Pivani's house. The driver's side door swung open before the motor cut off. A slender and attractive woman in her mid-thirties exited the car. Her smooth brown hair touched her shoulders and her perfect nose was just shy of being sharp. Her eyes were hidden behind sunglasses. She didn't waste a second before addressing the paramedics at the curb. "Hi. I'm Dr. Madeline Hamilton with the CDC."

"You sure got here fast," the youngest paramedic said.

A slight smile crossed her face, friendly and professional. "As fast as I could. I'm with the CDC's Outbreak Response Team and I'm actually out here in LA for a conference. Just good timing. Otherwise there wouldn't be anyone here until tonight."

She tossed her sunglasses onto the seat of her car before walking around to the trunk. She removed a large bag and put it on the sidewalk. Quickly, before the young paramedic even realized what he was seeing, she removed her blouse, revealing her toned and shapely back in a camisole, and climbed into her own plastic protective suit. She bent over to tuck the feet of her suit into plastic boots. Her graceful movements concealed under the spacesuit-like gear, she walked toward the porch, studied her surroundings at every step as she slowly eliminated the distance between herself and the body.

When she reached Pivani, she continued her investigation for a few moments without touching anything. Eventually she lifted Pivani's eyelids, pressed her gloved fingers against his cheeks, turned his hands, and peeled his shirt up to examine his torso. A rash covered most of his chest and abdomen. She used a metal tool from her bag to scrape a drop of blood from his cheek and placed it on the hand-held DxH device.

Carrying the DxH device in front of her, Dr. Hamilton moved away from the house, halfway back toward the fire trucks. She removed her helmet and placed it on the ground. Her forehead shone with sweat and her hair was no longer smooth.

She carefully removed her gloves and tossed them into a bucket of chlorine and bleach the paramedics had set out for her. She scrubbed her hands with sanitizer. She returned to the body and took pictures without touching anything.

"What's that machine?" the bald paramedic asked when she moved away from the body again.

"It's a diagnostic tool developed after the West African Ebola outbreak. It can diagnose any hemorrhagic fever in one minute, once symptoms present," said Dr. Hamilton.

The DxH emitted a faint beep. Behind her face screen, Dr. Hamilton's brow furrowed.

"What did the machine tell you?" the bald paramedic asked, a nervous edge to his voice.

"The results are inconclusive. It's not a known hemorrhagic fever, but it's something similar."

The medics nodded and paced as if they were suddenly full of nervous energy. The youngest reached for the dispatcher radio.

"Wait," Dr. Hamilton held up her hand. "Put that down." She turned her head and looked at each of the paramedics. "Don't say anything about this yet, to anyone. Clear?" Again, she waited until each of them nodded. "Okay, then. I'm just going to call my boss. Toss me my phone, please. It's on the front seat of my car."

When her boss answered the phone in Atlanta, Dr. Hamilton said, "It looks bad. I'm going to need an epidemiological investigative team, body removal, a decon tent, and a quarantine order for the house, no, not just the house, the whole street."

After the call, Madeline stared at the horizon, turning her phone over in her hands. She had one more call to make— possibly more important than the first—although she prayed it would turn out to be unnecessary. Sometimes she just had a feeling about certain situations, and this was one of those times. She took a deep breath to brace herself against her suspicions before calling the FBI to speak with her old friend.

"Quinn Traynor, please." She prayed the call wouldn't go to voicemail.

Chapter Twenty-Nine

Los Angeles
November 4th

The plane from Boston landed at LAX under blue sky and a late-morning sun.

"Can we grab something for lunch?" said Rick. "I'm starving."

"Me too. Let's make it quick."

"Do you have the keys? You drove to the airport, right?" Quinn asked after they had grabbed sandwiches from an airport kiosk.

Rick rubbed his eyes and laughed. "Yes. I've got them." He climbed into the driver's seat and started one of the FBI's cars. "Are you going into the office when we get back?"

"Yes. I need to check out a few things before I leave on vacation."

"The intelligence you're going to look at, is there something specific concerning you, or are you just searching for new leads?"

"Both." Quinn turned to stare out his side window, dozed off for a few minutes, and said little else until they were pulling into the field office lot. He should have felt relief, the weight of apprehension and responsibility lifted from his chest and shoulders, but he didn't. "Something about the whole plot didn't sit right with me from the beginning."

"How so? A full arsenal of bombs was found with the terrorists in each target city. The right guys were caught. I mean, I know I'm new to this department, but, jeez, it was impressive. The coordination across agencies... So, what is it? Do you think there are more of them?"

Quinn shook his head. "Think about this with me. Their plan was vague but hardly a secret—discussed amongst jihadists online and in mosques. Even Redman, knew something about it. Once we located Fayad, he gave up enough intel to find the terrorists in a matter of hours. Terrorist organizations don't plan a revenge attack for years to go down so easily. ISIS leaders are grossly misguided, but their motivation is unparalleled. It's almost as though they wanted the bombers to be captured."

"Hmm. But why?"

Quinn shook his head. "That's what's bothering me. Terrorists aim to kill, but also to destroy morale. To leave everyone, including civilians, but especially our military and defense, afraid and unable to do our jobs."

"We're not afraid."

"No. But what else could prevent us from doing our jobs?"

"Being too tired? Like spread thin, going in all directions chasing false leads."

"Exactly."

Rick parked the car and they walked together toward the front of the building. "You should go home. Get some rest," Quinn said.

"I'll stick around a bit more. In case something exciting happens. I want to see what comes out of the interrogations. I slept a few hours on the plane. Let me know if you need me." They parted in the hallway, Quinn going to his private office and Rick to the field agents' War Room.

Quinn's office had one window with a view of a few bushes, a Palm tree, and the concrete side of the building next door. He pulled the blinds down to block out the light, sat down at his desk, and rubbed his eyes. He downed the remainder of a Coke, crunched the can, and tossed it into the corner trash bin. He'd lost track of how many cans he'd consumed for the caffeine in lieu of sleep. Holly would be angry if she knew. "Cut out the soda," she always said. "It will make you fat, even the diet ones." Even if she was right, now was not the time to give up his preferred source of energy.

Concerned for the rest of his team, he sent a brief message congratulating them for their success. He suggested they go home and sleep, and come in the next day. If they hadn't already crashed, he knew they had to be feeling just like him— on their last chemical-induced fumes of energy. Quinn closed his eyes for a brief second. He planned to read the case files one more time, trying to pinpoint the source of his discomfort before he left for home. He looked forward to changing out of the clothes he'd been wearing for two days and taking a shower. He was scanning the incoming intelligence from the terrorist interrogations when his phone rang. A glance at the caller ID brought an immediate smile. He had half expected—maybe even hoped—to run into her when he was in Georgia doing the training presentation. He remembered his excitement and subsequent disappointment when the woman in the hallway turned out to be someone else. He wondered what had led to this unexpected contact.

He picked up the phone and heard, "Quinn? Thank God. I was afraid the call would go to voicemail."

"Maddie! Hey." An image of the accomplished doctor filled his mind. He and Madeline grew close seven years ago, around the same time he met Holly. He was working a case jointly with the CDC. In addition to being a medical doctor, Madeline also held a Ph.D. in epidemiology. They consulted each other often on the phone, although it had been some time since he'd seen her in person. She was based in Atlanta, at the CDC's main headquarters.

"Still working eighty-hour weeks?" she asked.

He resisted the immediate urge to share how he and his team had just helped prevent terrorist attacks in three cities. "Actually, I'm about to leave for vacation in a few days. What's going on?"

"I'm here in LA."

"You are? So…"

"This isn't a personal call. I was attending a conference and something came up. I'm in the San Fernando Valley. I've got a suspicious dead body. The cause of death is not from any *known* hemorrhagic fever, but something similar. Worse."

"Worse in what way?" *What could be worse?*

"The victim's death appears to have come with little warning. A sudden and violent onset. Nothing I've ever studied in nature has a comparable rate of progression."

"And you're calling me because—?"

"I don't have evidence to back this up yet, just an instinctive reaction. I don't want to say more, but I think you should look into it right away. The deceased man's name is Raj Pivani. You can have anyone from your team call me directly if they need to. I'll be putting an epidemiological case together, no matter what you find."

"Did you say you're still on site now?"

"I am. I've got people coming to remove his body and run tests. I've ordered a quarantine on the premises. I'll make the area available for your team if you can send people out right away. Have them wear full protective gear. Not just masks, but pressurized suits with respirators. Like I said, this is a serious one and I don't know exactly what we're dealing with yet."

Quinn wrote down the name and the address Madeline provided. "Give me thirty minutes to do some research. Can you hold off local law enforcement until then?"

"Yes, absolutely. The containment team is on their way. They'll treat the area as a potential crime scene. But get here as soon as you can, and then call me, I mean, if your research finds anything supporting my suspicion."

"Of course. Thank you, Maddie."

Quinn trusted Madeline's judgement. If she had a gut feeling about an uncommon disease, there was likely something to it. She wouldn't have called if she didn't believe there might be probable cause for bioterrorism. He called Rashid and Stephanie, conferencing them on his phone. "I know I recently told all of you to go home—"

"Yes. You were like go home or else." Stephanie laughed. "But we're still here. Both of us."

"Good. Something new came in. It's urgent. Possible bioterrorism. Here in LA. The victim's name is Raj Pivani. An epidemiologist from the CDC, Dr. Madeline Hamilton, is on the scene in the San Fernando Valley. We have twenty minutes to gather intelligence and determine if our involvement is necessary. If it's not, go home. I mean it this time. And if it is, well...I'm sorry."

"We're on it," Rashid said. He and Stephanie started gathering information on Raj Pivani.

Quinn opened the top drawer of his desk, and removed an electric shaver. He ran it over his face as he looked over the interrogation reports. Something bothered him, but he couldn't put his finger on it. He was missing something, but he didn't know what.

Twenty minutes later, lacking any new revelations, Quinn grabbed another can of Coke and joined Stephanie and Rashid in a conference room. "Okay, tell me what you found on Pivani from the valley." His choice of words sounded odd to his own ears. That's what happened when he skipped a night of sleep, now that he was older. His thoughts weren't as focused. The word *groggy* flashed inside his brain in tall bold letters like it was part of a cartoon reel. The inside of his mouth felt gross. He could use a good gargle with mouthwash.

Stephanie spoke first. "Here's what happened. Frank Hayes, a neighbor who lives across the street from the victim, spotted Pivani just outside his house. Time estimated to be zero nine hundred hours. According to Hayes, Pivani could barely stand. He vomited and collapsed. Hayes called 911, insisting his neighbor had radiation poisoning. All of this is in the police report."

"Okay. Then what?"

"First responders arrived, but before they took a close look at the victim, Dr. Madeline Hamilton from the CDC entered the scene. That's her." Stephanie gestured to the picture she projected onto the wall, Madeline's slender figure obscured by a bulky blue suit. "The local police took this picture an hour ago. Based on the information Hayes provided to the 911 dispatcher, Dr. Hamilton initially thought radiation contamination was a possibility, but the symptoms also sounded like a hemorrhagic fever."

Quinn interrupted. "I know Dr. Hamilton. She spent a year in Sierra Leone working with patients during the Ebola outbreak. She's one of the premier experts on the virus. And she's the person who called me."

Stephanie wrapped her hand around her water bottle. "According to Hamilton's analysis, the victim died of an unknown hemorrhagic fever. Extensive bruising and bleeding from multiple orifices. The viral RNA is being analyzed right now, with top priority rush on the results. There are zero known cases of hemorrhagic fever in the United States. The CDC will have a better idea of what we're dealing with by the end of the day, but they have good reason to be concerned." Stephanie took a sip of water. "I was able to speak with Hayes, the neighbor. He was eager to share everything he knew about Raj, but it's not much. He said Pivani was home all week, which was out of the ordinary. He saw Pivani walking to and from his mailbox every day, presumably waiting for something specific to arrive in the mail. Hayes also said he had a conversation with Pivani two days ago. Pivani didn't appear to be sick in any way, shape, or form. I'm quoting him."

"Okay. Tell me more about Pivani." Quinn directed his attention to Rashid, who had been leaning forward in his chair, listening to Stephanie.

Rashid sat up straighter in his chair and cleared his throat before speaking. "Twenty-eight years old. Born in Berkeley to parents who emigrated from Iraq. No siblings. Educated at Cal Tech. For the past five years, he's worked at the San Louis Obispo nuclear power plant. Last year he was promoted to lead engineer and radiation technical specialist. No close friends or known relationships, per his colleagues and neighbors. They referred to him as nice, quiet, and polite, and, consistently from everyone, as a loner. All of them were of similar opinion. No one claimed to be friendly with him outside the office. A few also used the words disciplined, and normal." Rashid cleared his throat again and continued. "Well, if that was true, he stopped being *normal* four weeks ago. On October 1st, he handed a physician's report to his employer and requested a long term sick leave. His coworkers were surprised. No one had noticed any signs of illness."

"What sickness did he claim to have?" Quinn asked.

"Lupus. The nuclear facility has the report on file in their HR office. But lupus has never been known to leave someone bleeding from every orifice," Rashid said.

"No, it has not," Quinn said, biting his lower lip.

"That's his ID picture from the employee database." Rashid tilted his head toward a picture of Raj projected from his laptop onto the wall. "So—here's where it gets interesting. The day after his sick leave began, Raj boarded a plane for Paris using a ticket he purchased with his credit card in September. He landed at Charles de Gaulle."

"And?" Quinn said.

"*That's* the thing. There is no *and* after he landed. No record of him eating, traveling, or making any purchases until the day of his return four weeks later. Six days ago."

"Could he have been in Paris receiving special medical treatment? Did you check hospitals?" Stephanie asked.

"I checked hospitals and outstanding hospital invoices and found nothing, although it may be too early for them to have put together a bill," said Rashid.

"Damn, you're fast," Stephanie said.

"I still need to look into treatment centers."

"Maybe he was working as a missionary? Or doing something similar where he picked up this new disease?" Quinn suggested.

"I'll need his computer to dig deeper. I also contacted his parents. They believe he was in Europe for an engineering conference. They knew nothing about him having lupus. They sounded convincing," Rashid said.

"Okay. First, that's great work in a short amount of time. One, we have an expected cause of death from an unknown, aggressive hemorrhagic fever, and, two, a red flag timeline—leaving the country with unexplained activity abroad. That's more than enough evidence to arouse suspicion. Let's stay on this until we can either confirm or rule out terrorism," Quinn said.

Stephanie's normally bright eyes were dull and Rashid let his head drop forward as they waited for Quinn to decide on their next move.

"Do you know if Rick and Ken are still here?" Quinn asked.

"Ken probably went straight to the gym," Stephanie said.

"Hold on." Quinn picked up his phone. "I'm calling them."

Rashid and Stephanie discussed their research on Pivani while Quinn made two phone calls. Rick and Jayla appeared in the conference room a minute later, but Ken had gone directly home after his flight from Chicago. With Ken on speaker phone, Quinn brought them up to speed. When he finished explaining the situation, he set his hands on the table before saying, "I know I just briefed you, but," he paused, closing his lips and filling his cheeks with an exhale, "I'm going to call in another unit—"

"No way," Ken said. "I can be wherever you need me to be in just as long as it takes to get there."

"We want this." Stephanie made a fist. "We can always sleep later."

"Okay. Good. Ken, you'll search Pivani's house for anything to either confirm or rule out bioterrorism. You'll need to come back here to get your equipment and...Rick. Rick is going with you. You'll bring Pivani's computer and cell phone back to Rashid."

"Told ya, you'd get the computer." Stephanie jabbed Rashid gently in the arm with her elbow. In response, Rashid managed a slightly awkward smile.

"The CDC is holding the scene for us," said Quinn. "You'll need full PPE. Rick can get it organized while you drive here."

"Okay. I'm leaving now," said Ken.

"Will do." Rick tucked in an errant side of his wrinkled dress shirt. Quinn studied him for an extra second, searching for any sign of reluctance toward working with Ken. Rick blew out a long breath, clasped his hands together and smiled.

"You shouldn't be nervous, but you should be afraid. That fear will keep you safe," Quinn said to Rick. "We don't know what this disease is or how it's spread yet. If you have any questions with the precautions—ask first. Understood?"

"Absolutely." Rick nodded and smiled.

Quinn turned to Stephanie. "Keep digging for info. Contact the physician who wrote the lupus note, if he exists. The note could be forged."

"Okay," Stephanie said.

"While you're waiting for his computer, find out what's going on at the nuclear facility," Quinn said to Rashid. "Jayla, I'm glad you're still here. Put a national query out to all federal agencies to see if anyone else has a similar situation."

Jayla nodded, tucked her braids behind one ear and immediately began typing into her portable tablet.

"Once we've ruled out that this situation requires our involvement, all of us will get some sleep," Quinn said, glancing at his watch, his voice much softer and not all that convincing.

He left the conference room, took out his personal phone, and read a recent message from Holly asking him if he needed new shoes for the trip. Without hesitation, he typed: I don't need more shoes. I might be late tonight. Or I might not be home again. I'll let you know when I know. Sorry.

They had just averted one crisis, he hoped they weren't stepping into another. He debated calling the FBI Director for a briefing and decided to wait. The evidence wasn't sufficient enough to warrant the call. If luck was on their side, Raj Pivani's death might be a case for the CDC alone. His team would decide as soon as possible. In the meantime, visiting the CDC to see what Maddie's tests uncovered might be the best use of his time.

Chapter Thirty

San Fernando Valley
November 4th

Rick could barely see around the pile of PPE suits and evidence kits he carried. He stepped into the hallway and almost walked straight into Ken.

"Watch it," said Ken.

"Oh, sorry. You're back. Good timing."

Ken tossed the remainder of a protein shake into a nearby garbage. He wrapped his arms around Rick's pile and relieved him of half of the equipment.

"We're not just wearing face shields, we're going with full-blown pressurized suits and respirators." Rick sounded excited. "And the CDC set up a decon tent at the scene."

"Better safe than sorry. Got everything we need?" Ken asked.

"Yes."

"How do you know?"

"Because Quinn looked it over to make sure. I'll drive. I've got keys."

"Fine with me."

They walked in silence to the parking lot until Rick said, "You look refreshed." He lowered himself into the same car he had just driven from the airport.

"Looks can be deceiving." He shut the passenger door. "I hadn't lifted in a few days, so I did some quick sets. I showered. I was about to hit the sack when Quinn called."

"Go ahead and sleep. I've got the address. It's fifteen miles away and I'm told it will take at least forty minutes, which is unreal by the way. It's going to take me a long time to get used to LA traffic." Rick started the car.

"I'm not gonna sleep. I'll feel worse if I do." Ken leaned forward and adjusted the air conditioning.

"So, what do you think we'll find out there?" Rick turned to look over his shoulder and back out.

"We're hoping *not* to find anything to indicate this death is related to terrorism."

"But what do you think we might find to confirm it?"

"I don't know. It's rare to find an Islamic flag and an intricate map of the sewer system on the wall, if that's what you're thinking."

"That's not what I was thinking. Jeez." He glanced at the navigation screen. "Quinn said you were U.S. Army Infantry same as him before the FBI. How long were you active duty?"

"Don't take this the wrong way, but don't talk to me right now, okay? I have a headache." Ken turned on the radio and closed his eyes.

Rick ran his hand through his hair and kept his eyes on the road.

The next thing Ken heard was Rick saying, "Wake up," and turning off the ignition.

"That was quick." Ken rubbed his cheeks.

Rick stifled a yawn. "No, it wasn't. There was a wreck on the 110 overpass." He got out of the car and stretched his arms to the sky, taking in the police and barriers blocking the end of the modest, otherwise unremarkable street. Police tape cordoned off a small house from the road. The word QUARANTINE wound around the perimeter on yellow tape, from the edge of the back yard to the front, crossing the sidewalk and meeting the roadblock signs in the street. Signs posted all around the property sent a clear message. No Entry or Removal. Unauthorized Keep Off. Danger - Infection Hazard.

The agents exited their car carrying their PPE and evidence collection boxes. They approached one of the police guards and presented their identification.

"FBI, huh? Guys from the CDC just left with the body," the guard said. "Do you know what this is about?"

Rick said, "We're going to—"

Ken interrupted. "We're here to find out. We'll change and have a look."

Neighbors stood gawking from a safe distance as Rick and Ken slipped on alien-looking protective suits.

They awkwardly ducked under the yellow tape and headed across the front yard. "I'm already sweating in this thing," said Rick. "And you look like a giant beast. Like *The Thing* from the Fantastic Four. Hey, why was Quinn so freaked out about my PPE? He talked to me about it again before we left."

"Something happened when he was in the military, in Iraq. Whatever it was got him into bioterrorism. That's all I know. It's classified. But, your father will probably tell you if you ask him."

Rick frowned.

216

Walking up Pivani's front path, evidence of the man's violent sickness surrounded them. They maneuvered cautiously around dark streaks and splotches as if they were participating in a macabre obstacle course. They stepped across the blood-stained entryway and stopped on a patch of unsoiled carpet to survey the front room.

"This guy wasn't about to win any decorating awards. And he definitely wasn't a hoarder," Rick said.

"You don't need to provide a running commentary," Ken said.

The living room of the small ranch home contained a few pieces of simple furniture in good condition, aside from blood spatter. A framed college diploma hung on an otherwise bare wall. Rick lifted a framed photograph from its spot on an end table to take a closer look. Inside the frame, Raj Pivani stood between a bearded older man and a woman wearing a hijab.

"Raj and his parents, I presume." Rick set the frame down exactly where he found it.

"The majority of Muslims aren't terrorists, but every terrorist seems to be a Muslim," Ken said.

"That's random. Won't a comment like that get your ass in trouble?" Rick said.

"You're in the real world now, Rick. Life isn't a PC college campus. Islamic State supporters don't represent the majority of Muslims, but being a minority doesn't make them any less of a major threat."

"Timothy McVeigh, the Unabomber-Ted Kaczynski, Eric Rudolph, Dylan Roof. Not Muslims."

"Yeah, okay, but the ones from outside this country. And that's a short list you came up with, by the way. If people knew what we knew, if they sat in on the debrief meetings, they would be hiding in their basements, afraid to leave their homes, begging the President not to let anyone else in the country."

Rick frowned. "Immigration and refugee bans have a low statistical probability of preventing terrorist attacks. They might possibly prevent a few suicide bombers from sneaking in, but plenty of them are already here. And we can't read minds."

"Was that your college thesis or something?" Ken sneered.

Rick ignored him. "And we don't know if this guy, Pivani, is a Muslim anyway."

"Of course he is. Did you see what his mother was wearing in the picture?"

Rick dropped to his knees to peer under the couch. "Still, doesn't mean he is."

"What I said is the truth. Rashid would tell you the same," Ken muttered. "You sure don't sound much like your father. He made it pretty clear he wants to keep the Muslims out."

From the other side of the room, Rick raised his voice in anger. "That's not true."

"Someone turns grouchy when he's tired," Ken said.

"Are you talking about me or yourself?"

Ken snorted in response. He *was* in a bad mood. Tired. He'd missed two workouts and his body craved the endorphins those sessions generated. He was sweating like crazy under his PPE. And the text Quinn had sent didn't help any. Quinn had told him to look out for Rick. "Teach him all you can at Pivanis." Christ. He was essentially on babysitting duty. Clenching his jaw, he lifted the couch cushions one by one. He reached his gloved hands into the corners and along the edges. Finding nothing aside from lint, he stood next to an armchair in front of a small flat-screen television and looked around. No music, no videos, no DVDs.

Thick engineering text books, history books, and two Tom Clancy novels stood neat and straight on a small bookcase, lined up in order of height. Rick opened each book, holding the spines facing the ceiling. He carefully rifled the pages and allowed them to flick apart one by one.

"Good," Ken said, watching him.

The agents created grid patterns with their eyes, roving over every surface, floor to ceiling, making sure they hadn't missed anything in the sparsely-furnished room.

"Let's hit the kitchen. I see his computer." Ken picked up a laptop from the kitchen table, unplugged the cord, and slid both into an evidence bag from which it would be disinfected before being given to Rashid.

"I've got his cell," Rick said. He slid it off the counter, placed it in another bag, and added it to the evidence box.

"Stay here and check out the kitchen," Ken said. "I'll go look through the bedroom. Holler if you have any questions. Don't mess anything up."

Rick rolled his eyes. "It's not like I haven't had training."

"But that's all you've had."

An eerie breakfast tableau sat untouched in the kitchen. Two eggs congealed inside a pan on the cooktop. Dark drops trailed across the laminate counter and dotted a plate with toast.

Rick opened the kitchen cabinets to reveal well-stocked shelves with neatly arranged containers of peanut butter, cans of tuna fish, and boxes of pasta. The refrigerator held dozens of water bottles, and some basic groceries: eggs, milk, orange juice, butter, and a few labeled Tupperware containers.

"An organized planner," Rick said to himself. He closed the refrigerator door and noted the *almost* bare, white surface void of memos, mementos, and take-out menus. In the center of the freezer section, a single silver magnet held a Chargers football ticket.

Rick was looking under the sink when he heard Ken yell, "Oh! Shit!"

"Everything okay?" Rick said.

"Yeah. Apparently, the CDC thought the disaster in the toilet seemed worth saving. Don't ask me why Raj didn't flush it himself. He managed to get out of here okay and die on his porch."

"I've never died before. I couldn't tell you what he was thinking," Rick said.

"Someone has to flush the damn thing eventually." Ken pressed the lever and waited for the toilet to evacuate its messy contents. "Took three flushes to get it down."

"The other bathroom is clean, like no one has ever used it," Rick said.

"If he was a loner like everyone who knows him seems to think, probably no one has."

Inside the bedroom, Ken opened doors and drawers revealing undershirts, T-shirts, boxers, and shorts, all neatly folded, even the underwear. Several pairs of dark and khaki pants, white and blue dress shirts, two dark suits and a dozen ties hung from a bar in the closet. On the top shelf of the closet, Ken found a large shoebox. He lowered it down and opened its contents on the bed. The box contained photos of a younger Raj, surrounded by other young adults, in a college campus setting. "Looks like he had friends at some point," Ken said out loud. He emptied the photos into the collection bag in case they needed to contact the people in them. He opened another door. "Found a prayer mat in this front closet," he hollered to Rick.

"So what?" Rick yelled back. "That doesn't make him a terrorist."

"Makes him a Muslim though—probably. There's not much else. Gather his trash. We'll go through it back at the office."

Rick walked back to the kitchen, removed the bag of trash, and placed it carefully in one of his own biohazard bags. With the bag still grasped in his hand, he stared up toward the ceiling. "Humpf!" He snatched the ticket off the refrigerator and put it in an evidence bag. "You know . . . um, have you found anything to indicate he's a sports fan?"

Ken shook his head. "He doesn't seem to have any hobbies. No weights or exercise machines. Like no life outside work."

"Yeah, I got that feeling too. But he has a Chargers football ticket on his fridge."

"A souvenir?"

"No, it's for this Sunday's game. A really good seat too. Shame it's going to go to waste."

"You can't use it," Ken said.

"Yeah. I know that." Rick's tone made it clear he found Ken's comment offensive.

"It might be proof he wasn't planning on dying," Ken said.

"Maybe. Um, I'm going to look around one more time."

"Make sure we've got all the trash."

Rick walked slowly through the house opening doors and peeking in closets, searching for something to disprove his notion that the ticket was out of place. "No team jerseys or caps. No sports equipment of any kind in the house. The ticket is...odd."

"Maybe his employer gives away tickets as perks. I wouldn't know anything about that personally," Ken said. "But some companies do it."

"Eh. He worked at a nuclear facility. Do they entertain clients? I don't think so."

"I think we're done here." Ken looked around a final time to ensure nothing was missed.

After they were sprayed down in the decontamination tent and extricated from their PPE, Ken called Rashid and put him on speaker phone. "We're on our way back with Pivani's computer and cell. We'll drop them off and then hit the showers because we're drenched with sweat."

"What else did you find?" Rashid said.

"Nothing. If there's anything to find, it will be on his computer," Ken said.

"Okay. I'm waiting on it."

"Wait," Rick said. "Can you check something for me?"

"What are you going to ask him?" said Ken, at the same time Rashid said, "Sure."

"Can you see if there's any record of this guy attending football games or any other sporting events?" Rick said. "See if he purchased a Chargers ticket on his credit card, and if not, can you find out if his employers might have given away Chargers tickets?"

"Will do," Rashid said. "That all?"

"Yes. Thanks," said Rick.

Ken disconnected the call.

"He can do just about anything, huh? And I can't believe he didn't ask why," Rick said.

"Yep. He's amazing at his job because he has the necessary experience. Unlike you, he doesn't ask too many questions. In fact, if I didn't know better, I'd think you were a double agent, someone chosen to spy on us because we'd never suspect you."

Rick rolled his eyes. "Whatever, man."

Chapter Thirty-One

Paris

November 4th

Kareem bit his nails to the quick on the train to Paris. He prayed for strength almost continuously, yet almost missed his sunset prayers. He needed to pull it together, channel his energy into serving without doubts, fear, or guilt. None of this was about him. It didn't matter if he felt brave or terrified. Following through was the only act that counted now. His parents were dead. He had no wife or children. *This,* right here and right now, was the path Allah uniquely created by blessing him with everything necessary to make it happen—his American birth, his biomedical engineering expertise, his multilingual skills. *This* was all about Allah and honoring His plan. The events had been destined long before Al-Bahil found him. *Say all of that enough times and it will be believed.*

During his travels from Syria, he wondered about the bombs scheduled to detonate in Chicago, Philadelphia, and Boston. He had visited Boston when he was younger. He remembered Faneuil Hall, an enormous hollowed-out house crowded with food vendors and tables. He also remembered a mall with a giant escalator stretching from outside to indoors. Soon, people might be scrambling around Boston's busy streets looking over their shoulders, too afraid to gather along the Charles River or enter once crowded museums. They may never feel carefree riding the subways again. But that fear would be temporary. It was nothing relative to the fear his virus would cause.

Chaos and fear. Fear created a temporary feeling, one that needed to be reinstated repeatedly for the weak Americans. Unlike a subway attack, the fear caused by the spread of the virus would stay with them much longer. Maybe forever. Like their mantra for 9/11—*Never Forget.*

He wondered about the last big attack on America. He honestly didn't know what it was. So many organizations hated America. Any one of them might have recently succeeded in demonstrating just how much. He scanned his internet feed and found nothing about recent terrorism. He wanted to search for the information, but doing so would be incredibly stupid. The CIA or FBI or MI6 were always listening and watching. He wouldn't do anything to jeopardize the mission now. He didn't want to be nabbed when he stepped out of the airplane because of his internet activity. He wouldn't accomplish much from inside a jail cell. He turned back to his phone and internet browser. There was plenty of news about football, one of America's biggest obsessions. He'd been interested once. He vaguely remembered middle school arguments in which he'd participated over who was the better team, the Lions or Packers. Always the Packers. Those days seemed a long time ago.

In front of him, a young woman wearing earbuds waited to get through security. One hip jutted to the left in her tight jeans. Her short top revealed a few inches of her abdomen and a silver ring piercing her navel. The sight of her bare skin caused him to shudder: he was reminded of Al-Bahil's gift. He pictured the young girl's pretty face and how she looked on his bed. She'd had no choice. And now he felt sorry for her. Kareem wasn't symptomatic, so no one around him at the airport was at risk, but he'd had intimate sexual contact with the girl and exchanged body fluids. She was going to get sick. Something turned in the pit of his stomach. He felt filthy inside. He scratched at his neck. He wanted out of his body, out of his skin.

I hope Al-Bahil sleeps with her next.

His tortured conscious hoped Allah wasn't listening.

He scowled at the young women around him. They were scantily dressed, with no attempt at modesty. Westerners. He hated them. All of them. It was their fault he was in this situation. If they weren't such pigs, he would still be at the University of Damascus working in a lab full of hopeful young scientists.

Kareem lifted his gaze and pushed his shoulders back. What would he say to Amin when he arrived in Charlotte? He remembered the Islamic term *Taqiyya,* which condoned lying when necessary to advance the cause of Islam. The concept left him feeling instantly vindicated. Surely *Taqiyya,* justified by the Quran and other Islamic texts, was created for situations exactly like his own. The Prophet said, 'War is deceit." The Prophet was correct. He had deceived his cousin and he would continue to do so, until…well, he'd cross that bridge when the time came.

Once he passed through security, he put his shoes back on and entered the nearest men's room to wash his hands. He had the cure inside his bag. At this point, it was the only thing standing between him and certain death and there was nothing stopping him from taking it right now. The recruits could spread the virus and he could simply disappear, find a lab where he could work or a small University where he could teach. He had done his part. Surely Allah didn't need him to die too. How on earth had he let Al-Bahil convince him his own death was part of Allah's plan?

Shame flooded his senses, overwhelming him with a rush of heat and humiliation. There was a huge penalty in the afterlife for running away from a battle. Al-Bahil's ISIS videos had driven that point sharply home over the past year. And yes, he wanted the guarantee of a lifetime in paradise with virgins who were actually willing, not terrified and sobbing like Al-Bahil's farewell gift.

He curled his hand into a fist and smashed it into the wall. Pain shot from his knuckles up his arm and into his neck. A middle-aged man stopped cleaning his glasses, looked at him and quickly turned away. A worried looking teenager rushed past, gazing straight ahead.

Go ahead, stare at me. If you only knew...

He held his bleeding knuckles under running water before wrapping them in paper towels. Reaching into his bag, he could feel the plastic travel bottles containing the antidote. He clutched one and held on to it, staring at his unwavering reflection, barely recognizing the man staring back at him. After a minute, he lifted his chin toward the ceiling and closed his eyes. He released his grip on the antidote and reached around in his bag again, moving aside the virus keychain from Amin, his phone, and a pack of gum, until he found his bottle of morphine. He removed the cap and swallowed a tablet.

Give me the strength to continue.

Chapter Thirty-Two

Los Angeles
November 4th

While Rick and Ken were gathering evidence at Pivani's house, Quinn drove to see Madeline. The CDC didn't have offices in LA, so she had temporarily set herself up at the National Bioforensic Analysis Center, the closest maximum containment lab in the area. If Madeline had discovered anything to rule out his team's immediate involvement, he wanted to know as soon as possible so they could all move on and get some sleep. That's what he told himself as he merged into four lanes of slow moving traffic and headed to the lab.

At the front desk, he presented his FBI identification, cleared security, and walked to the office Madeline had been assigned. Her door was slightly ajar, and he could see her staring intently at her laptop screen, fingers poised on either side of her mouse. Tiny wrinkles of concentration crossed her brow. She lifted her hand and rested her index finger against the center of her lower lip. Quinn knew that gesture well. His gaze lingered before he made his presence known by clearing his throat and knocking.

Madeline looked up and her surprise was evident. "Quinn. Hi," she said, her voice edged with anticipation. She tucked her hair behind her ear on one side and smiled.

"Hey, Maddie. So, you'll be working in LA for a while?"

Madeline set her elbow on her desk, tilted her head to the side, and rested it in her hand. "Until we figure out what's going on, yes."

"Where are you staying?"

"The CDC has a few leased apartments nearby."

"Good. Well, I've got two guys at Pivani's house right now gathering intel. Have you discovered anything new about the virus?"

"Nothing conclusive yet. But soon. I sent samples back to my office in Atlanta. They'll do the same RNA tests I requested here. We'll see who identifies the virus first. I've got a team of epidemiologists flying in to help track its origin and prevent its spread. And on your end?"

"We'll know more once we go through his cell and computer. Rashid has them now. You've met him, right?" Madeline nodded and Quinn continued. "We know Pivani left the country four weeks ago, and there is no record of his activity once he landed. Almost three weeks of unexplained absence abroad."

"Oh." Madeline shook her head, her expression grave. "I knew he left the country, but no record of his travel on credit or debit cards?"

"Nothing. He was on sick leave from his job. It's possible he was receiving medical treatment somewhere. We don't know anything for sure, yet."

"I'm glad you're on this. When will you know where he's been? We can't assemble an epidemiological case and identify recent contacts unless we discover where he's been for the past four weeks."

Quinn nodded. "I know. So, you think the disease is something new?"

"Yes, I know it is. We've never seen this before or it would have registered in the DxH." Madeline took a deep breath and clasped her hands together. Quinn noted there was no ring on her left hand. "While we're waiting for the lab results, I'm going to examine the body. You can come with me if you're interested. It beats waiting."

Quinn tilted his head toward the door and said, "I'm in."

"Good. Let's get suited up."

In the changing room, Quinn had a heightened awareness of Madeline removing her clothes behind the partition. Their relationship was professional now. Most of their recent interactions had been over the phone and in crowded meetings. They hadn't been alone together in years, but he still easily remembered how she looked naked—amazing, and the feel of her skin when she was in his arms. The remembrance awakened his senses like an electrical current, followed by a wave of guilt.

When Madeline emerged, hidden underneath her biohazard suit, they helped each other hook up their air supplies and adjust straps.

"Let me check the seal," Madeline said, adjusting his respirator. She stood close enough to bring back distracting memories, like the wine tasting trip that ended with stripping and jumping into a hidden lake. Watching Madeline, graceful, indisputably brilliant, and capable, he couldn't help wonder if he had made a mistake.

Years ago, Madeline made her feelings for Quinn clear before she left to work on a CDC case in Africa. While she was gone, Quinn got serious with Holly. And soon after, he married her. He'd made his vows. For better or for worse. So, he should focus his energy on changing worse to better at home. But first, he had work to do. They needed to figure out the deal with

Pivani. If Madeline had found a case of bioterrorism, he wouldn't have time to worry about his marriage for a while.

"So, how are you?" said Madeline, her hands on either side of his face mask.

"I'm good, just, you know . . ." Quinn's answer said nothing, but Madeline nodded as if she understood.

"You look tired. Are you feeling okay?"

"I am. My team had a few crazy busy days. Everything ended well, that's what matters."

"Good. All right. Suits secured. This way." She led him through two sets of sealed glass doors. The first required a scan of her retina to open; the second brought them to an isolation room with negative pressure to prevent pathogens from escaping. Another man in a biohazard suit passed them carrying test tube samples. Madeline exchanged a few words with him before he left.

"An infectious disease expert," she said to Quinn. "He'll be back to join us in a few."

Bright light flooded the mostly white space. Atop a metal table lay Pivani's bruised body, looking like the only thing that didn't belong in the stark, sterile room. Quinn stood silently a few feet away from the table. A cooling mechanism inside his suit kept him comfortable as Madeline opened the body and conducted her examination. Quinn tried not to focus on the intermittent drip, drip, drip of bodily fluids dripping through a hole in the table and into collection containers below.

Madeline dictated into a recorder while she worked. Quinn didn't understand all the medical jargon, but he understood more than enough to be alarmed. In addition to the obvious jaundice, all indicators for blood clotting were inhibited. The pulmonary sack was filled with blood, the spleen was engorged, and the kidneys experienced complete necrosis. Quinn found it impossible to imagine that this man appeared healthy two days ago.

The infectious disease expert returned and Madeline summarized some of her findings. "The lab rushed some preliminary results while working on isolating the viral proteins. His white blood cell and platelet counts were extremely low. His liver enzymes extremely elevated."

"I'm not surprised," said the other physician. "Based on the internal examination, his body succumbed to an unusually accelerated breakdown. It's fascinating."

Madeline turned to Quinn. "Typically, with a hemorrhagic fever, death occurs six to sixteen days after symptoms appear. Raj's neighbors reported seeing him looking and acting normal two days ago. Assuming their testimonies are accurate, the progression is faster than any known viral agent. It's extremely aggressive and lethal."

"Just great," said Quinn, clenching his teeth.

After the exam, Quinn and Madeline waited to be disinfected and safely extricated from their suits, giving them more time to analyze the case.

"He's been back in the states for a week. Could he have caught the disease here?" Quinn asked.

She shrugged. "That is the million dollar question. The disease shared some markers with Ebola. The Ebola incubation period, from infection to manifestation of symptoms, is two to twenty-one days. The infection can't be spread until symptoms develop."

Madeline's phone rang again. She looked at her screen and held up one finger for Quinn. "It's the national lab," she whispered.

"Dr. Madeline Hamilton," she said into the phone, "I've been waiting for your call." She listened silently for several seconds before sounding incredulous, even angry. Her skin turned ashen and she pressed her hand against her cheek. She asked questions in rapid fire sequence, thanked the lab, and hung up. She stared at Quinn, her eyes wide.

"What did they say? You're scaring me with that look, Maddie." He waited, but she did not respond. Something about her eyes, the worried look directed back at him, made him repeat his question. "Tell me, for Christ's sake, what did they say?"

Madeline exhaled slowly. "It's bad, Quinn. They isolated the virus. Structurally it's filovirus in origin, but there's a reason it wasn't recognized by the DxH device." She lowered her voice. "Its molecular structure has been altered from a single-strand, negative-sense RNA. The viral RNA was crossed with a particularly aggressive common cold virus."

"Crossed, as in?"

"Synthesized. Man-made."

Quinn's jaw tensed and his legs felt weak. "The common cold? Does that mean—"

"Yes." Madeline clasped her hands together, her expression grim. "Not only is it highly contagious, but it's airborne—"

"A man-made airborne infectious agent," Quinn said softly, lifting his gaze to the ceiling. *Holy Shit.* "Could this virus have accidentally escaped from a lab in Los Angeles? Was anyone working on something similar here?"

"I don't know, Quinn. That's not information accessible to me. It would certainly be illegal, and it seems doubtful. Maybe, if Raj Pivani was a genetic engineer working in a biomedical lab somewhere…but he wasn't. I think if he contracted the disease here it would have to have come from some underground military lab. Wouldn't it?"

Quinn and Madeline stood, eyes locked, without speaking. A list of protocol flew through Quinn's mind. He shook his head to bring himself back to the present.

"We'll figure this out," Madeline said in a reassuring tone. "One step at a time, right?"

"We have to start the chain of communications on this. Can you type up something about what you said, those results, and send it to me? I'll share them with the National Biological Threat Characterization Center, so they can get started on countermeasures. We'll need detectors, drugs, vaccines, and decontamination technology." Quinn walked backward, suddenly in a hurry to get back to his office.

"Okay, or, you can just tell them to contact me." Madeline lifted her phone and asked to speak with the head of the CDC as Quinn hurried away from her office, already on his phone as well.

Quinn jogged to his car and called Jayla. "I'm headed back to the office. Please get the team together."

"What's going on?" she asked.

"We're dealing with a deadly weaponized virus. The stakes have been raised. Big time."

Chapter Thirty-Three

Boston

November 4th

CDC Medical Officer Amanda Cooney looked up at the treetops to admire the last traces of fall's grandeur. The trees still possessed some vibrant red, orange, and yellow foliage. Amazing how anything could collectively project such beauty before dying. Rarely did it happen with people. Not the ones she studied. With that thought, she stepped out of the glorious sunshine and into an apartment complex corridor. As a forensic physician and epidemiological expert on infectious disease, she and her assistant had flown from Atlanta to Boston at a moment's notice to examine the late Mike Spitz. The circumstances of his death had been deemed "out of the ordinary" by the medical team who found him.

She stopped herself from going directly to the victim's apartment, deciding to follow proper protocol precisely, something she did *most* of the time. She would wait on her assistant, who had to make a quick bathroom stop. In the meantime, she would speak with the woman who discovered Spitz, a young mother who lived across the corridor. Gathering her unruly brown hair into a bunch before securing her mask, Amanda knocked on the door of apartment 33A.

"Yes?" came a worried voice from behind the door.

"Hello. Jennifer Perkins?"

"Yes?"

"I'm Dr. Amanda Cooney with the Center for Disease Control. You may have been told not to let anyone in, but you can open the door for me."

Jennifer Perkins opened her door and stepped back, holding a Kleenex between trembling hands. Her eyes were red rimmed, her face splotchy. Her voice shook when she said, "You're wearing a mask."

"Just an extra precaution," Amanda reassured her. She chose the simple face mask so she wouldn't terrify Jennifer. Based on what she was told about Spitz's body, she would wear a suit with a respirator when she checked on him. It may be overkill, but if she underestimated the situation and was wrong, it could prove her last opportunity to be right or wrong ever again.

"I understand you found Mike Spitz?"

"Yes. Am I going to catch what he has? I have two daughters." Fresh tears sprang from Jennifer's terrified eyes and she pulled at strands of her brass-colored hair.

"I hope not, but that's why we've asked you to stay inside your apartment, until we find out for sure. The medics who were dispatched have also been isolated while we run more tests. Do you have someone else who can take care of your daughters?"

"My mother is picking them up from school. They don't even have any of their things," she sobbed.

"And their father?"

"He's not in the picture."

"It's going to be okay, if your priority remains keeping your children safe and monitoring your own health."

235

Jennifer sniffled and moved her head up and down in acknowledgement.

"I know you've already told the police, but please tell me everything you can remember about your neighbor this week, leading up to finding him."

"Okay." She took a deep breath that seemed to calm her. "I didn't see much of Mike lately. We don't talk or anything, but, you know, I see him going in and out during the week. I thought he moved out without telling me. Then I saw him again. Taking out his trash."

"What day would that have been?"

"It was just…Wednesday. It was Wednesday because I went for a walk with my girls."

"Did Mike look sick to you on Wednesday? In any way?"

"No. I don't think he looked sick at all. He looked fine then. I think. He's a big tough guy. I wasn't really looking at him though." She moaned and pressed her hand against her mouth.

"So how did you learn he was sick? How did you know to check on him?" Amanda asked.

"I didn't. I didn't know he was sick until I found him in his apartment. Dead." She strangled the sob rising in her throat and seemed to hold her breath. Amanda waited patiently for her to continue.

"I'm the building manager, I have to knock on doors and remind everyone to pay their rent if it doesn't come on time. Well, I'm supposed to deliver letters but it's easier to knock on their doors and anyway, my printer ran out of ink. Mike's rent was overdue. He's paid on time, mostly, for three years, so I thought something was up. I thought maybe he had gone out of town, or moved without giving notice, you know, because like I said, I had hardly seen him around lately." She twisted her hair around her finger then dropped her arm, pressing her palms tight against her sides.

"Do you know where he was?"

"No."

"Okay. So, you went to his door?" Amanda prompted.

"When he didn't answer his door, I started keeping an eye out for him. Then today, when I knocked, I noticed a wicked bad smell. I knew something wasn't right inside there. I have a key to all the apartments, so I let myself in to check on him."

Her eyes darted back and forth as if reliving her disturbing discovery. Amanda remained patient. She was anxious to examine Mike Spitz, but he wasn't going anywhere.

"I could tell something was wrong right away, before I even saw him. We had a dead possum under our house when I was a kid. His apartment smelled worse than the dead possum. I was going to walk through his living room and open a window to let in fresh air. Then I saw him on the couch. I didn't touch him, but I moved close enough to see he wasn't breathing. He was dead, and from something terrible. Wicked terrible. I can't get it out of my head—the way he looked. Like something out of a nightmare." She brought her hands to her mouth and shook her head. "I wish I had never gone in."

"Did you touch anything at all, besides the door knob when you were in there?"

"No. I don't think so." Hysteria rose in her voice. "I came back to my apartment and I scrubbed my hands with hot water and lots of soap. Then I called 911." A look of pure terror settled into her features. "You said the paramedics who came here have to be isolated too?"

"Yes, as a safety precaution. Hopefully none of you have anything to worry about, but of course, we want to be sure so you and your families stay safe. Please do not leave your apartment until you hear from us. This card has my assistant's number. Please call her if you think of anything else you want to tell me about Spitz." Amanda removed a card from her coat pocket with her gloved hands and handed it over.

"What if I start to feel sick?"

"Call the number on that card right away."

Amanda said goodbye to Jennifer, wishing she could say something to ease the woman's fears. Until she knew what they were dealing with, no comforting words could be found. Her assistant, Karen, walked up behind her, putting an end to her thoughts.

"Hi, I'm here." Karen stopped at the edge of the corridor. "Should I wear a suit?"

"Just wear gloves and a face shield for now. You won't need to touch the body."

Karen helped Amanda get dressed into her PPE. They entered Spitz's apartment together.

"Whoa," Karen said. "Be glad you can't smell anything. It's bad."

"Jennifer Perkins almost opened the windows. Thank God, she didn't. Until we find out what type of sickness we're dealing with, we can't risk exposing anyone else."

"What?" said Karen. "It's hard to hear you when you're wearing the headgear."

"Never mind." Together they walked into Spitz's apartment and found his body on his worn, tweed couch wearing only boxer shorts.

"Good God," Karen said, looking around.

Dark splashes and spatters coated the floors of the living room, bedroom, and even the lower walls of the bathroom, evidence of violent sickness. A toppled glass lay atop a side table surrounded by a puddle of water. Below, a dark stain marred the carpet. A blood-tainted shirt and plaid flannel pants were balled up on the floor near the couch as if they had been ripped off and thrown to the ground.

Amanda moved closer to the couch. "Well-established rigor mortis, which puts his death over 24 hours ago. That's my estimate. Whatever he has, it's ravaged his body."

"Wow." Karen stood a few yards away, unable to take her eyes off the body, "This is bad."

Severe conjunctivitis marked his eyes and bloody mucosal membranes allowed a trickle of blood to escape his nose and harden into crust. A hemorrhagic rash fanned the fair skin of his torso like a bright red spider web. A chill ran down Amanda's spine. She had hoped the medics were mistaken. Although she'd been warned, she wasn't expecting this.

"Have Mass General—"

"Can't hear you," said Karen.

Amanda spoke louder. "Have Mass General set up a monitored quarantine unit for Ms. Perkins and the medics who were here earlier. Asking them to stay inside isn't enough. Not until we figure this out."

"Okay," Karen said.

Amanda scraped a drop of blood from Spitz's cheek and applied it to her DxH device. She stared intently at the device until it beeped. She read the results and pursed her lips. "Inconclusive match for any known viruses, but enough markers to indicate a hemorrhagic fever of some sort."

"I still can't hear you well. Did you say *of some sort?*"

"Yeah. I don't know what this is."

Karen stepped carefully around the human detritus. There was something particularly disturbing and mysterious about Mike Spitz's death, which is why they had been called out to his apartment in the first place. She took short, shallow breaths. Regardless of precautions, infection was still possible. She located a wallet on the floor, wet from the spilled water, and opened it to glimpse inside. Her gloves made the simple task more difficult, but using a small metal file to separate the contents, she identified cash, a football game ticket, receipts, a license, and two credit cards. On the floor next to the bed lay a cell phone. She placed it in an evidence bag just as Amanda's own phone rang.

"It's Ron Greene," Amanda said with a hint of reverence and surprise. She could see the lit screen, but couldn't answer it without risking contamination.

"If the CDC director is calling you, it must be important."

"Yeah, but I can't answer it now."

The ringing stopped and started again after a few seconds. "Karen, decontaminate your hands, step outside, remove your gloves, use the sanitizer and then call him back."

Karen nodded.

"Be careful. Take your time."

A few minutes later Karen called from the doorway. "Amanda?"

"Yes?" Amanda answered with a sharp voice, irritated about her thoughts being interrupted. She was so focused on Mike Spitz, she forgot about the director's call.

"Ron has some questions for you. I told him you were suited up. He said it can't wait."

"What is it?" Amanda raised her voice so Karen could hear her through her mask.

"He wants to know if your findings support Spitz having hemorrhagic fever."

"Like I said, it sure looks that way. I'll know more after we get the samples back to the lab. Why is he asking?"

Karen repeated Amanda's comments to the director. "He wants me to put him on speaker phone." She pushed the speaker button and held the phone out closer to Amanda, at arms-length, without stepping forward. Amanda walked toward her.

"Victim's name is Mike Spitz, correct?" Ron asked.

"Correct."

"He's Caucasian? Early twenties?"

"Yes."

"Hold on. I'm searching his background."

Amanda waited, wondering what was going on, until Ron spoke again. She could hear the change in his voice. "Mike Spitz left the country four weeks ago, and returned on October 28th."

"West Africa?" Amanda asked, assuming he picked up the virus there.

"No. Paris."

Paris? No one contracted hemorrhagic fever visiting Paris. "Ron, may I ask why you're checking in with me?"

"The FBI issued a national alert asking about similar cases. A man was discovered this morning in Los Angeles. Also with a form of hemorrhagic fever. Also left the country for Paris four weeks ago. He—hold on." He paused. "I'm going to call you back."

Amanda continued her examination, dictating her observations to Karen, who stood, masked, with her back to the apartment door. The director called back fifteen minutes later. Karen put him on speaker phone again.

"Link the preliminary results from your DxH to the CDC contact in LA. I'll send her number to Karen. Send them immediately."

"Yes. Will do."

Amanda and Karen exchanged a look. Karen said, "What's going on?"

Amanda shook her head. "I don't know, but it can't be good."

Chapter Thirty-Four

Los Angeles
November 4th

Madeline Hamilton shook her head in frustration. Their investigation of the newly named virus, E.Coryza 1, or E.C.1 for short, was getting nowhere. A team of experienced epidemiologists sat around a large table, anxious to get to work on understanding the situation and preventing a national epidemic. Unfortunately, with their current data, or lack of it, to be more precise, it was impossible to establish a case. They should have been interviewing everyone who had been exposed to Pivani over the past few weeks, as well as anyone who had direct contact with those exposed to him, and so on, isolating anyone found to have E.C.1.

"We have no information on where Pivani has been for the past four weeks?" said a woman with gray hair and glasses. "Obviously, we need data to figure out *when, where,* and *how* he contracted the disease. Without that information, we'll never know who he encountered after he became symptomatic. We'll never figure out the origin of E.Coryza 1. The disease could be spreading like wildfire this very minute with infected people leaving and entering countries."

243

"So, right now, the only data we have represents time from symptoms to death, based on the testimony of his neighbors? One day, maybe two, from symptomatic to death. Which is…unbelievable," said a tall scientist.

"It appears he went to great trouble to stay out of sight and avoid any sort of paper trail. I mean, who goes to Paris without using credit cards? We need more invasive search methods to track down his activities abroad. Are other agencies helping? I mean, do they realize this is monumental? Unprecedented?" said the grey-haired woman.

"Absolutely,' Madeline said. "The FBI is working on it. Working around the clock. And I know they'll contact us as soon as they learn anything new. Let's focus on the little information we do have."

"No one else from his place of employment is sick, but they have all been asked to self-monitor and call us immediately if symptoms develop," said the tall scientist.

"Our French counterparts are on alert, but so far, they haven't identified anyone with a similar disease. For right now, we'll need to focus on the disease itself," said Madeline.

Of course, if Pivani's illness represented some form of bioterrorism, an intentional infection, which was looking likely, Pivani could possibly be *the* index patient. His recent unexplained whereabouts certainly cast suspicions. Madeline had correctly assumed something wasn't right when she arrived at Pivani's house and called Quinn immediately. And that *was* the reason she called him, she told herself. It had nothing to do with wanting to see him. Nothing to do with the way she felt when they were working together. Yes, she was pleased he'd come to her office earlier in the day. He could have just called her back, but he drove across the city to speak with her in person, even though he was clearly exhausted. She sighed. Why was she doing this to herself? She knew he was married. He made his choice. And despite the rumors she'd heard about Holly's behavior, he appeared to be sticking with her. Unfortunately, his loyalty made Madeline respect him even more.

"The good news is we haven't found anyone who was exposed to Pivani since his symptoms appeared," said the youngest member of the team.

"It's not good news if we aren't sure," said the tall man.

A phone call from the director of the CDC made Madeline pause. "Excuse me. I better take this."

She answered her phone and heard, "Dr. Hamilton, this is Ron Green. I just got off the phone with a CDC physician in Boston. She's in an apartment complex right now examining a body similarly affected to the one you found in Los Angeles. I need you to quickly determine if it is the same cause of death. From what we've learned so far, I'll be surprised if it's not. This man also left the country for Paris and returned in the same timeframe. We'll need to find the connection as soon as possible. We could have something big here. I've sent you the physician's information, her name is Amanda Cooney."

"I know Dr. Cooney. We've worked together before," Madeline said.

"Good. The Boston office will share everything you need. Let me know if there's a correlation as soon as you have the results. I'm about to notify authorities in Paris of this second case. Like it or not, their city appears to be involved."

After the call ended, Madeline updated the epidemiologists.

"A similarly diseased body across the country in Boston?" said the youngest. "Wow."

"And both deceased men traveled to and from Paris around the same time?" said the grey-haired woman. "Hopefully we'll finally learn what they were doing in Paris."

Madeline wondered if Quinn knew about the Boston discovery yet. She'd check with him in few minutes, but she couldn't waste another second before calling Amanda Cooney. It might be too late to focus on how the disease was contracted. They might need to concentrate all their efforts on stopping its spread.

Chapter Thirty-Five

Charlotte, NC
November 4th

Amin walked away from the Charlotte Islamic Center disappointed. The service underwhelmed him. He understood every word, but the message lacked the urgency and the buzz of energy he had grown accustomed to in Syria. The beauty and holiness of the services abroad had reached him at a deeper level. The contagious intensity was missing at home.

During the service, he didn't notice Isa's father kneeling only a few yards away, but Isa's father had seen him. He speed-walked until he caught up with Amin on the sidewalk outside. "Hello," he said, out of breath. "I've been hoping to see you for weeks now."

"Hello. How is Isa? When is her big day?" Amin tried not to project any ill will.

"Ah, well. Slightly embarrassing, that." He looked at the ground before meeting Amin's eyes again. "It seems I got slightly ahead of myself where Isa is concerned. Isa isn't engaged. The man I introduced is only a good friend of hers. She seemed particularly upset that I misled you." Isa's father studied Amin's face as if searching into his soul. "I shouldn't have

247

gotten involved. I jumped the gun, as they say. It's quite different here. A father just wants his daughter to be happily married."

"Really? Oh." A wave of relief spread through Amin's body. Isa wasn't engaged! A sharp pang brought him back to reality. This wasn't the right time to involve Isa in his life. He was currently unemployed, and he might have something to take care of first—this thing with Kareem. But still, his heart soared with the good news. Isa was still single. If only he hadn't avoided her, he would have known this weeks ago.

"I know that at your age it can be a constant challenge to balance a devout Muslim life with American values. It's hard, but it can be done. I'm in a study group that meets here once a week on Thursday nights. We also do community outreach. Would you like to join us?"

"Yes, I would. Thank you for the invitation," Amin said sincerely. Isa's father's comments rang true and the study group sounded like just the thing Amin needed to stay on track spiritually. His life appeared to have turned the corner on possibilities.

Isa's father walked away and Amin turned his phone back on. Three voice mails had accumulated. Doug, Melissa, and Kareem had all called during the past hour. He walked to a nearby park and sat on a bench facing a pond. His finger hovered over the delete button for all the messages, until his curiosity got the best of him. He pressed play.

"Hi. Amin. It's Doug. Uh, if you're still looking for a job, a new opportunity opened at the bank. I've recommended you. Melissa wrote a peer recognition review and suggested you, so it's her you should thank."

The last of the rush hour traffic zipped by, but Amin hardly noticed. He tried to figure out his thoughts on returning to tedious spreadsheets and long hours. He closed his eyes. After a moment of reflection, he still had mixed feelings about the offer.

He played another of his messages.

"Hi Amin, it's Melissa. I hope you're doing well. I don't know if Doug has called you yet, but there's a new finance position open in the credit card division and you're a perfect fit for the job. I think it's a bump in level too, which is always nice. I hope you'll come in and interview. Let me know. Maybe you've already found something. That would be great too. Either way, keep in touch."

Hmmm. It was nice of Melissa to think of him. He hadn't missed sitting in his cube every day, but he needed a job. Melissa said this one was a good fit. He trusted her judgment more than Doug's. He called Melissa, and was surprised when she answered and spoke to him as if they were good friends. Maybe they were and he had missed it. After all, he wasn't the best at reading people's emotions, at least he had figured out that much over the past few weeks. In less than five minutes, he had been transferred to HR and had an interview scheduled for the following Monday. He sat on the bench for ten more minutes, watching people walking dogs, jogging, and feeding geese. He speculated about returning to the bank. All of it was a means of procrastinating before he listened to the message from Kareem. A quote by Nelson Mandela popped into his mind because Melissa had it pinned to her cube wall. *"The brave man is not he who does not feel afraid, but he who conquers that fear."* He never thought it was the most appropriate quote for the finance department, but it did fit with his current situation. Finally, he pressed play on the third message.

"Call me, cousin. We need to talk."

His body automatically responded to Kareem's voice with alarm, the same sensation he would expect if he heard there was a fire in his apartment building. He didn't call. He wasn't sure if he could handle Kareem. It would depend on what Kareem had in store for him. He didn't know if he was more afraid of not being able to stop Kareem from whatever he planned to do, or of stopping him and permanently severing all ties with his cousin. Which fear represented bravery and which was cowardly? How could he conquer either if he wasn't sure?

An image of Isa played around the edges of his thoughts, and helped him answer his own question. He could and would do whatever was needed to prevent her from harm. Kareem was family, but some things were more important than family. If only he knew what, exactly, Kareem planned to do.

Recently, Amin read in the newspapers about an angry and confused young man in Miami who had gone on a rampage in a grocery store with an assault rifle. He murdered five innocent people and wounded others before someone shot and killed him. An investigation revealed the perpetrator's bedroom was stockpiled with guns and ammunition. The public aimed their outrage at his family, three other adults who lived in the same house. Didn't they notice his private arsenal? Why didn't they alert authorities? There were plenty of clues something wasn't right. Their proactive cooperation could have saved lives. Amin did not want a repeat situation. But, after three weeks of living with Kareem, he hadn't seen a single weapon. And he didn't think there was any way for someone to enter the country with a weapon or weapon making supplies anyway. Amin's worries only stemmed from his cousin's growing hatred for America. And America was one of the few places on earth where people could hate aloud without fear of persecution, so he really had nothing to report.

But just in case, when he got back to his apartment, Amin booted up his old Dell and typed in *how to report suspected terrorism.*

A knock startled Amin from sleep. Instantly alert, he felt around in the dark for his phone. Eleven pm. No one knocked on his door this late. In fact, no one knocked on his door ever, except for the time Julia showed up in her pajamas at night. She'd gotten locked out of her apartment and needed to use his phone. He flicked on the light and grabbed his glasses, shorts, and a T-shirt. After hurriedly dressing, he tiptoed halfway to his door, stopped, and walked normally the rest of the way. He peered through the peep hole and saw Kareem.

He had expected this moment could happen. He had thought about what he would do when and if it happened, so it could hardly be considered a total surprise. He'd mulled over scenarios in his head, asking himself if he should act like their last conversation never occurred or if he should confront Kareem and demand answers, like he wished he had done before he left Syria. Despite all his previous ponderings, it was hard to believe the moment had now arrived. Kareem stood outside his door, looking much changed—younger and more hip— in jeans and a black hooded college sweatshirt. He looked so...*normal.*

Amin opened the door wide and stood aside. "Hey."

Kareem's eyes roamed over what he could see of the apartment.

"Well, come in," Amin said. "You've come all this way. Come in. We need to talk." Up until now, he hadn't decided how he would behave toward his guest. It was happening in real time.

"I wasn't sure if you would welcome me. And I did leave you a message earlier today. Maybe you didn't get it." Kareem finally stepped forward. "Big place."

Amin felt awkward greeting his cousin without an embrace, but he couldn't. Not until they resolved things. "Sorry there was no one to meet you at the airport with a car and stack of cash, but you didn't tell me when you would be here. And I guess you managed to find your own way." He hoped his tone relayed his sarcasm. "Where are your bags?"

"You're looking at them." Kareem let his backpack fall to the floor. His gaze settled on Amin's couch. Amin gestured toward it with a tight smile, sensing his cousin's fatigue.

Kareem crossed the room and dropped into a slouched, seated position. A thin sheen of sweat covered his forehead and cheeks. He folded his arms across his stomach. "Before you say anything. Let's just forget about what happened before you left. Our conversation."

"It's not something to forget about. We need to talk about it."

"When you came over, I thought things would be different. I thought you might be more interested in committing to our faith. It was my mistake and I'm over it."

"I *was* committed. I am, I mean—committed to deepening my faith and finding some purpose. I believe Allah wants everyone to live peacefully. And I could never stand back and allow anyone to jeopardize innocent lives. Not that you actually ever said you were going to harm anyone, but it seemed like you were hinting at it."

Kareem crossed his arms and leaned forward, rocking slightly forward and back. "Okay. Okay. So, let's just forget about it."

"Huh? Seriously? I can't pretend it's not a huge thing. Can I even trust you, or should I be calling the police?"

Kareem didn't answer. Instead, he kneaded his fingers against his temples.

Amin spoke again. "Look, normally, I would be happy about having you here. But right now—I'm leery."

"Me too. I'm not exactly feeling welcome. Look, you're my only family and I don't want bad blood between us."

"Neither do I. But this isn't an argument over who broke the window or something."

Kareem looked up and laughed and it sounded genuine. "I remember the argument. Fourth grade." He laughed again. "*I* broke the window."

"I know you did, because I knew *I* didn't." Amin allowed himself to smile briefly. "I don't know what it is you were talking about doing. But I'm prepared to stop you if there is something. I already know who to call."

Kareem looked sorrowful when he spoke. "There's nothing to stop. I'm not going to blow up anything. You have my promise." Then he smiled. "I want to make the most of my time here. Explore the city. Eat some greasy food. Have a good time. Like we used to."

Amin held Kareem's gaze and believed he was sincere. "Okay, then. Good." He sighed, relieved to hear Kareem say he wouldn't be blowing up anything, which was a very strange thing to be relieved about. Had the situation become *that* out of hand, or had he overreacted, imagined something that wasn't even true?

Kareem yawned. He shook his head like he was trying to stay awake, but the shake turned into a visible shiver and traveled down his body. His shoulders drooped forward. He removed a handkerchief from his pocket and blew his nose.

"You're exhausted," Amin said. "We can talk in the morning. I have an extra bedroom, but I use it as an office. It doesn't have a bed. Do you mind the couch?"

"The couch is fine." Kareem patted the cushion beside him.

"I'll get some blankets and a pillow. The bathroom is over there. Help yourself to whatever you need. There's not much food. I never have much food. It's a problem I need to work on. We can shop tomorrow. By the way, you look good without the beard."

Kareem nodded. He stood up but lost his balance. Amin extended his hand and helped him up. "Whoa, careful there. The bathroom is that way." He pointed. "I'll see you in the morning. Okay?"

"Okay. I'll get cleaned up and pray. I'm beat."

"Oh, I almost forgot. An envelope came for you. The one you sent. It's on the table there."

Kareem glanced over at the envelope. "Perfect. That's my thank you gift for you." He left the envelope on the table and walked to the bathroom.

Amin retrieved his extra bed linens and proceeded to make up the couch as best he could—stretching a fitted sheet around the cushions and smoothing down a flat sheet. Things were a little weird, but he believed they could also be smoothed out in the morning. His circumstances were improving. The prospect of a new job, Isa still available, and a reconciliation with his cousin. His future looked promising after all. *Life is good.*

Chapter Thirty-Six

Los Angeles

November 4th

By the time Rick and Ken returned to the field office from Pivani's house, their team was aware a man-made virus had killed Pivani. Their investigation ascended to a new level of urgency. The pace of their work quickened and they ignored their minds' and bodies' need for sleep. Rick and Ken delivered Pivani's cell phone and computer to Rashid and Stephanie, who would comb through all the files, activity, and communications, looking for an explanation of how he ended up dying from a weaponized virus. Rick carried everything else in the collection boxes to an evidence room.

"I guess our showers have to wait," said Rick.

"Yeah," said Ken. "But before we start sorting through the trash, do you have any aspirin?"

"Not on me. I could use some myself. I'll grab some. I'll be quick. Be right back." Rick left the room and walked briskly toward the kitchen where the team kept an adequate supply of basic over-the-counter pharmaceuticals. He waved his hand at Quinn when he walked by his office.

"Rick, wait. Come in here for a minute," said Quinn.

Rick walked backward a few steps and leaned against the doorjamb.

Rick reminded Quinn of a puppy. His hair looked damp and mussed as if he'd just finished a hard work out. His tired eyes still beamed with eagerness. He might as well have been wagging a tail.

"How did it go at Pivani's?"

"Great. We were careful if that's what you mean. And now we're going through his stuff."

"How much do you know about hemorrhagic fever?" said Quinn.

"Some, and I just googled it earlier." Rick grinned. "Something specific you want to tell me?"

"I was about your age when I had my first real life encounter with bioterrorism. The situation didn't end well. But it's why I'm here. It's one of the reasons I do this job." Quinn's tiredness allowed his memories to come flooding back.

Quinn had volunteered for a tour in Iraq and spent weeks patrolling a Turkish border. He had witnessed the rampant black market sales of food, oil, and even, he suspected, people. Walking through a Kurdish refugee camp, he understood the origin of the words "huddled masses." The refugees slept crowded together on bundles of filthy clothing, exhausted by their current conditions. Some of the men stayed awake through the nights, sitting shoulder to shoulder on the hard ground. They spoke Farsi and Hudu in hushed voices. The foul and unforgettable stench of the camp overwhelmed his senses. Yet he marveled at the strength reflected in hundreds of ravaged faces.

One night, as Quinn and his close friend, Owen, readied for their night shift just outside the main gates of the refugee camp, their commander ordered them to his headquarters.

"Listen up," said the commander. "New intel says a pro-Saddam militant has plans to infiltrate the refugee camp. We had eyes on him this morning, leaving Kachivan. He should be here by tonight, if he makes it this far. Word is, he's not in good shape. Keep watch for him."

"How will we know it's him?" Owen asked.

"He has a bad limp. A useless left leg he drags along."

"Sir, too many of the refugees fit that description with their missing limbs and injuries," Owen said.

"He's not even five feet tall," the commander added.

"Should we apprehend him when he arrives, sir?" said Quinn.

"No. Don't stop him. Your orders are to follow him into the camp, if that's where he goes, and see who he communicates with. Let him walk in like we know nothing about him. They think he has a message to deliver. Find out who he's coming to see."

Hours later, Quinn's night vision goggles cast an olive-colored shade over the rickety gate topped with barbed wire and the long rows of canvas tents that served as temporary homes for the refugees. The wind stirred up the dry ground and sand blew into his ears, nose, and mouth, making the goggles a necessity even without the night vision they provided.

"Shit, it's cold," Owen said, shivering.

"It's colder at home," said Quinn. "You said you grew up in Michigan."

"Yeah, but at home I don't stand around outside freezing my balls off," Owen said. "So, what do you think is the deal with this guy we're watching for?"

"I don't know. Maybe he's a courier delivering a message to someone important. Maybe one of Saddam's henchmen is hiding inside the refugee camp."

"Yeah. That could be. Like a spy who is supposed to get intel from the military. We'll probably never know. Anyway, the commander doesn't like us," Owen said. "He knows we volunteered for this tour, and he doesn't understand why anyone would do that. And he's not the brightest bulb out there."

"You're right. Let's just help make sure he doesn't drop the ball on anything."

"Like that game against Navy when you fumbled at the twenty?" Owen jabbed Quinn in the arm as he laughed.

"Where did that shit come from, buddy? Out of nowhere you thought reminding me of a major fumble would be a good way to pass the time? I'm so glad you watched all my games." Quinn shook his head, but kept scanning his surroundings.

Owen laughed again. "I only saw you when you played Navy, since my brother was there. Most of it was good."

"Oh, ya think?"

Owen lowered his voice. "Hey. Over there." He tilted his head toward the right while stepping farther back into the shadows.

Step-drag, step-drag, step-drag. In their eerily colored view, someone in barefeet moved slowly over the border like a Zombie in a horror movie. Narrow shoulders slumped forward under a tattered coat several sizes too large. The word *pitiful* entered Quinn's mind. He or she, it was impossible to tell, stopped momentarily to lean against a post before staggering through the camp gates.

"Fits the description, but I don't know. It looks like a child in bad shape." Quinn frowned. "How on earth did he make it this far?"

Owen shook his head. "He's about to collapse."

The person eventually reached the gatekeeper and fell against the makeshift table. His head hung to one side as if he lacked the strength to keep it upright. The gatekeeper pointed deeper inside the camp. He stood up to help the new entrant turn and move in that direction. A group of refugees noticed the newcomer's condition. They quickly surrounded him, offering a shoulder to lean on and an arm to steady himself. They waited patiently while he stopped, overcome by a fit of coughing, only moving on when he could breathe again.

"Probably taking him for medical attention," Owen said. "I'll follow and see if he's our guy. Sure not what I was expecting."

Owen stopped at the gatekeeper's table. "A boy. Alone. Very sick," the Kurdish gatekeeper told Owen in his broken English.

"Be right back," Owen shouted to Quinn. He walked further inside, his gun pointed down so he wouldn't frighten any of the refugees.

Was it Quinn's imagination, or was the chatter inside the camp increasing? Yes. Something was happening. The ever-present buzz of an unfamiliar language morphed into a broiling crescendo of noise. He thought he detected fear. He heard shouts. Accusatory voices.

What was going on?

Looking over his shoulder as he left his post, Quinn entered the camp, striding in the direction he had last seen Owen.

Up ahead, the boy lay on the ground. Two women knelt next to him. A man pulled at one of the women's garments. They looked like they were arguing. Both women stood up and stepped away, clutching at their own clothes and looking worried. Quinn tried to make sense of the scene.

Owen stepped into the space the women vacated and picked the boy up, cradling him in his arms.

Another woman grabbed Owen's arm. Small and frail, she spoke urgently into his face, her features scrunched with the need to make him understand. Owen's body tensed, even as he held the boy in his strong arms.

Something's wrong here, thought Quinn. *Why is that woman touching Owen? What's she saying?* The woman moved aside and was replaced by a man, his face smudged with dirt. He spoke to Owen with that same imploring look.

Quinn stepped closer. "What's going on?"

The man's eyes begged Owen and Quinn to understand him. He spoke barely passable English. "The boy. He tell sorry, send here sick. Make sick. Kill us."

The boy was dead. Quinn could see that now. His glassy eyes were open and unblinking like a doll's. Broken red vessels surrounded his irises.

"Oh, shit," said Quinn, taking a step back. He and Owen locked eyes until Owen looked down at the child in his arms.

"What was wrong with him?" Quinn said.

"I don't know. He's bleeding from every opening. Shit. I didn't see it at first."

"That's not good," said Quinn out loud. "If he was sent here to kill us, he must be contagious."

"Shit," said Owen.

"We have to separate everyone who touched him." Quinn looked around. "That's what we should do."

Owen nodded, still holding the child.

Quinn blocked a strong urge to flee the camp and concentrated on what he thought needed to happen. "Who touched the boy?" he said. "Move over here to this side if you touched him. Or if he touched you."

Owen, moved to the side with the child. "Can you get me a sheet or a blanket to put over him?" Owen asked the man who spoke some English. The man nodded and turned away.

"Everyone who touched the boy needs to move over here," Quinn said, pointing to where Owen continued to stand, alone, his head dropped forward.

Quinn was bigger than all of them, menacing-looking with heavy boots and a large rifle. The refugees looked anxious to do whatever he was telling them to do. They looked to each other for clues, but only ended up staring back at Quinn with confused expressions. He pointed to the boy and began acting out his words as if he was playing a game of life and death charades. No one moved. Quinn looked around frantically for the man who spoke some English, wishing Owen hadn't sent him away to find a sheet.

"There you are," Quinn said when the man returned carrying a blanket. "Tell everyone who touched the boy to move over there." He pointed to Owen. "They need to be separated."

The man who spoke some English turned to the growing crowd, waving his arms and shouting instructions.

"I'll be right back," Quinn shouted to Owen.

Quinn was breathing hard when he reached the gatekeeper. "The boy died. He said something to convince the refugees he was infected on purpose and sent here to spread disease. We can't let it spread. Close the gates. Don't let anyone else in or out? Clear?"

The gatekeeper nodded, his eyes wide, and began pulling the rickety gates closed from inside until they screeched and clanged shut.

"Put the locks on," said Quinn. "While we figure out what to do."

The gatekeeper secured the locks. He looked at Quinn and opened his mouth as if to speak, but closed it and turned away.

"What is it?" Quinn narrowed his eyes.

"I touched him too."

"Oh. Um, okay. Then come with me."

He hurried back to the center of the camp with the gatekeeper. Owen stood next to the small group of refugees who had come in contact with the boy. Most of them were women. The boy lay on the ground again, a small blanket-covered mound surrounded by unoccupied space like a moat. The refugees wrung their hands and stared at the tiny bundle as if the boy might rise from the dead. Owen kept his hands down and away from his sides, attempting to distance the rest of his body from contamination.

There were hundreds of refugees inside the camp. Quinn wondered what they would do when they learned he had locked them inside. He radioed his commander and told him what had happened.

"Are you inside or outside the camp?"

"Inside, sir. Owen and I are both inside. I closed and locked the gates, but if people get scared and try to get out, the gates won't be able to stop them."

"Okay. Try to keep things calm. Use force if you must. Wait to hear from me."

His commander responded minutes later.

"I have an infectious disease physician conferenced in. He wants you to describe the boy's symptoms."

Quinn described the boy's yellow eyes, the blood leaking from his body cavities, and the rash covering his neck, a rash that appeared to extend down under his clothing. He wondered what the descriptions might mean to a doctor.

"What is he saying? What does he have?" shouted Owen from several yards away.

"He hasn't said yet," said Quinn, moving his mouth away from his radio.

"You did the right thing, separating those who touched him," said the physician. "Keep everyone like that. Keep everyone away from his body. Did you touch him?"

"No, but Owen did."

Quinn heard the commander say, "Shit" in the background and then, "Good job, there, Quinn. Tell Owen he's done a good job too. Hold tight. I'll get back to you as soon as I can."

Their connection ended.

Quinn waited, pacing in the dim light, wondering what would happen next, aware of the separation between him and Owen. His skin felt itchy and tingly as images of the dead boy flashed into his mind without warning. Maybe they should have taken the body out of the camp. He hadn't thought that far ahead when he had decided to try and contain the disease. After thirty anxiety-filled minutes, the sound of large engines broke the silence outside the camp. Glaring cab lights illuminated the darkness through the holes in the fence, as they zoomed to a stop outside the refugee camp.

"What the hell?" said Owen, shielding his eyes from the bright light.

"I'll go see," said Quinn. He jogged to the gate so he could see through the holes. Military and commercial trucks had arrived. One with a giant biohazard symbol on the side. Doors opened and men jumped to the ground.

His radio squawked again. "We're throwing masks and protective suits inside for you and Owen. Walk to the front gate."

"Okay, I'm here," he said, wondering what they had learned. "But what about everyone else?"

He didn't receive an answer, but he caught the masks and packages intended for him.

"Do you know what's going on?" he asked an officer on the other side of the fence.

263

"Only that it's some sort of fuckin' emergency and no one is allowed in or out of the camp for now. Especially not out. We have directives to shoot to kill if they do. Sorry."

Bile rose up his throat. Quinn thought he might be sick. Forcing his panic away, he opened the tightly-folded contents of the package and discovered an extra-large protective suit. He delivered one to Owen, tossing it to him from the other side of a makeshift divide, then moved back to the gate so he could see what was going on. Awkwardly, he pulled and stretched the suit on over his heavy gear and attached the mask. He secured his gun belt to the outside of the suit. Through the holes in the gate he could see men wearing similar masks on the other side of the fence. His eyes darting around desperately, he watched them surround the camp and assemble a second layer of fencing. When they were finished, other men followed quickly behind, securing a large yellow banner around the perimeter of the new gate. An unfamiliar Arabic word stretched across the banner, repeating itself in large black letters.

"What does that word mean?" Quinn yelled to one of the soldiers hanging the banner.

The soldier answered, "Quarantine."

Inside the camp, the refugees spoke in hushed tones and Quinn tried to imagine what they were saying. They weren't freaking out like he'd expected, as if they had accepted their lives were beyond their control. Quinn passed on the meal he was entitled to eat. He felt alone, alienated, not just because of the language barrier and because he was military, but also because of the constricting protective suit and mask and because Owen had to be feeling even more alone than he. One small bit of comfort, the suit helped keep him warm.

Before the sun rose, he and Owen alone were released, decontaminated with a series of chemical washes, and sent to different rooms enshrouded in plastic. A medic took samples of his blood. He sat in a quarantine tent for three weeks, more than enough time to analyze his entire life, pray hard, and monitor every small twinge or ache with a heightened, panicky awareness. Had he done something brave by locking everyone inside, or had he done something cruel and stupid? With the dawn of each day, Quinn continued to feel fine while Owen grew sicker.

After three long weeks of waiting, Quinn was free and Owen was dead.

The government said it took courage to close the gate with himself inside, to protect the rest of his unit. The disease was highly virulent. Instead of being contained, it could have spread across the country. He received a Bronze Star. Owen received his posthumously.

Iraqi Sunnis under Sadaam claimed responsibility for sending the infected child in hopes of sickening the Kurdish refugees and especially, the U.S. military. Quinn never learned how the boy became infected, if he just happened to be fatally ill, or if he was made that way. The image of Owen cradling the child in his arms was seared into his memory. He intended to make good use of the life he had been spared. Protect others. Make Owen proud.

Now, fifteen years later, something about Pivani's situation made Quinn's experience feel acutely relevant. He had never shared his story with anyone, and he wasn't about to share it with Rick. Instead, he said, "Just remember that we can't do our jobs if we become victims. And if anything happens to you, especially to you, our whole department, no, the whole entire agency will be in deep shit on account of your father. The media will go crazy with the story."

Rick laughed. "I hear you. No worries. Ken and I are about to go through Pivani's trash right now. I was just grabbing some aspirin first."

"Good. Drop off a handful for me when you come back this way."

In the evidence room, Rick and Ken put on masks and double gloves and got to work.

"This is some of the cleanest garbage I've ever seen," said Ken. "Last year, I searched an insane amount of garbage from an ISIS group who had been hiding inside a house for months. Somehow food was coming in, but nothing was going out. Disgusting."

Ken picked out a plastic microwave container and put it aside. He did the same with an empty carton of orange juice. After removing a few other empty food containers, the bag was almost empty.

"All that's left is this envelope." Rick held it under the fluorescent light. "The stamp and postmark are from Paris. The return address is the Paris Yoga Institute. Was it possible the *prayer mat* you saw was a yoga mat?" Rick asked.

"I guess." Ken shrugged. "But this envelope is our first clue about what he might have done when he landed overseas."

"Here's a thought," said Rick. "If he had lupus like he claimed, maybe he went to this institute for some sort of holistic healing thing."

"You're all about innocent until proven guilty, in a big way," Ken said.

"Maybe." Rick lifted the envelope off the table with tweezers and deposited it in a bag. "I'll take this to be tested for fingerprints."

"There's shredded paper on the bottom. Some with ink. A letter maybe," Ken said. He tilted the plastic bag so the pieces fell together. Rick moved closer to look.

"Let's bring it to the lab too. They can piece it together, right?"

"Sometimes. It depends."

"People with lupus feel so tired they can barely get anything done. Everything becomes a monumental effort. Did you know that?" said Rick.

"Yeah. And?"

"That's what I'm starting to feel like."

"Same," said Ken.

"Finally, we agree on something."

"I think we can also agree that neither of us smells too fresh right now."

Ken snorted a laugh. "Let's get some caffeine and then go sit down close to Stephanie and Rashid. That ought to wake them up."

Chapter Thirty-Seven

Los Angeles
November 4th

Quinn had just stepped out of his office and into the hallway after speaking with Rick when his cell rang. His mind preoccupied, he answered without looking to see who it was.

"Good afternoon. This is Laura Purvis from the Los Angeles Times. Cynthia Fryberg is representing the Muslim Rights Organization. She said you were in charge of apprehending Dylan Redman. Can you please comment on—"

"I'm sorry. I don't have any comments for you."

"Wait. Mr. Traynor, can you just tell me—"

"I'm sorry, Ms. Purvis, I can't tell you anything."

He hung up just as another call came through. He saw it was Madeline and pressed accept.

"Quinn, it's me."

"Hi, Maddie. Did something new turn up from the exam?"

"Not yet. We have a second victim."

"Already? Same neighborhood? Or from the nuclear facility?"

"Not even close. He's in Boston."

"As in, Massachusetts? How do you know they're connected?"

"Because of you. Well, I mean, we wouldn't have known so quickly if you hadn't sent an alert to all agencies asking about similar cases. I sent something through the CDC, but your message got attention."

"My alert wouldn't have gone out if you hadn't thought to call me so quickly."

"Thanks. Anyway, the victim's name is Mike Spitz. A neighbor discovered him today. Paramedics called the CDC and an investigating physician found him in a similar condition to Pivani. We've already established the connection. The DxH device readings and our preliminary results indicate the viral strain is identical. It's the same engineered virus."

Quinn logged into his computer. Sure enough, a response to his earlier alert had been posted from the CDC in Boston. He wrote down the name Mike Spitz and said, "I'm having a hard time believing a second body was found clear across the country. How many more bodies are we going to find? We might already have an epidemic on our hands." His heart beat faster as adrenaline coursed through his body.

"Tomorrow, we *might* have an epidemic. Right now, we only have two dead bodies. Unfortunately, the second victim was also dead when he was found, so we still don't have information on where he contracted the E.C.1 virus. I wish we had a crystal ball."

"What type of exposure are we looking at from these two?" Quinn asked.

"We don't know, Quinn. On the positive side, Pivani's illness came on quickly. We haven't identified anyone who got

269

close to him once he had symptoms. As far as Pivani is concerned, it's possible we have this under control."

"And the second victim?"

"Six people we know of came in close proximity to Mike Spitz after he died. For all of them, contamination is possible, but not probable. They're currently isolated. Detectives interviewed everyone in the apartment complex. So far, they haven't turned up anyone who saw him when he was symptomatic."

"Sounds too easy," Quinn said.

"I agree. There's too much we don't know. If there's been exposure, a significant loss of life could occur. It all depends on the infectivity and lethality of the agent and the length of time it takes to detect and treat those who are exposed or have become ill. All factors we're working on."

"You said treat? There's no cure for a hemorrhagic fever. Unless something's changed?"

"I guess by treat, I meant isolate. ZMapp is still under development. We used it in 2014, but we're not even sure if it's effective, or safe. Ebola still kills about half of those infected. We have supportive therapies, like hydration and oxygen, but that's all. We've already begun working on something specific to this unique virus, but it will take months, at least. And if we were successful we just might end up with something to lessen the severity and decrease mortality."

"We don't have the luxury of months." Quinn paused. "We've got two bodies, three thousand miles apart."

The ensuing silence allowed them to appreciate the terrifying nature of the situation.

"Find out what Pivani and Spitz were doing in Paris, Quinn. Find the connection between these guys so we can stop this disease from spreading."

"I will."

"Call me as soon as you know anything else. I'll do the same."

Quinn's phone rang again immediately. He typed an urgent message to his team while he listened to the FBI director confirm what Madeline had already told him. He instructed Rashid to stick with Pivani's computer, and told the rest of the team to research Mike Spitz. They would meet in the conference room at 1700 hours. He stared at his monitor, concentrating momentarily on all the questions needing answers. Who was responsible? Could an engineered virus have accidentally escaped from a lab or a pharmaceutical company? Were the two deceased men innocent victims, terrorists, or victims of terrorists? Thoughts raced through his head in a continuous loop like a fever dream: *Information. Containment. Communication. Manage the media. Epidemic. Pandemic.* His fingers gripped his mouse as if it might sprout wings and fly out of his grasp. *One step at a time. Who else needs to know about the situation right now? Will we be able to handle it? Is it already too late?*

Rashid, an expert at multi-tasking, followed the links in Pivani's browsing history at the same time he called the CDC in Boston. "I'd like to speak with Dr. Amanda Cooney, please," he said.

"Dr. Cooney is not available. Can I take a message?"

"I'm calling from the Los Angeles FBI field office on a matter pertaining to the body Dr. Cooney discovered today. Our office sent the national alert on the first victim. It's important I speak with her. Do you know if she was at the home of the deceased?"

"She was there with her assistant, Karen Smith."

"Would they be the ones who gathered evidence from the scene, or did someone else do that?"

"I can't answer your question. Would you like to leave a message for Dr. Cooney's assistant to call you back?"

"Yes, I would, please." The thought of leaving a message and waiting for a call back was unacceptable, but perhaps he would only have to wait a few minutes. And he still had plenty of information to go through on Pivani's computer.

"Hold on, I'll connect you."

He didn't need to leave a message or wait for a call back because Karen answered after two rings.

"Karen, this is Agent Usman with the FBI's Counterterrorism division. I'm working on a related investigation."

"Yes. The CDC director informed us that another body with the same virus was identified in Los Angeles."

"That's correct. He was found this morning. I understand you examined Mike Spitz."

"Well, *I* didn't examine him. Dr. Cooney examined him. I saw him, but my job was to collect the evidence we might need from his home."

"Perfect. I know this sounds strange, but could you look through what you collected and see if by chance you found a ticket to an NFL game. And if you didn't, can you let me know who I can—"

"I don't have to look. I know he had a football ticket in his wallet."

"Can you tell me which team it was for, and what day?"

"Umm, sure. It will just take a few minutes for me to get down to our evidence room. Can I call you back at this number?"

"Please do," Rashid said. "I need you to scan both sides and send them to me. And run it for fingerprints. Please. It's urgent."

"May I ask why you want to know about the ticket?"

"I'm trying to establish a connection."

"Okay. I believe you when you say it's urgent. I saw Spitz. The sight of him . . . It's not something I'll soon forget. I'll go look right now."

At seventeen hundred hours, Quinn called his team together in the conference room. One person was missing. "We'll wait another minute for Rashid," he said.

"Would you like me to get him?" Jayla asked, pushing her chair away from the table.

"No. Thank you, Jayla. In fact, let's get started."

Ken spoke first. "We had just finished sorting through Pivani's trash when you called about Spitz. The only—"

Quinn didn't let him finish. "Hold up on that. First, quickly share everything we know about this second victim."

Rick spoke up. "The deceased, Mike Spitz, was a twenty-three-year old, Caucasian male. Single, no children. Born and raised in Cherry Hill, NJ. Two parents, both deceased, and one much older sibling. Graduated high school and attended a year of community college. Lived alone in his apartment for the past three years while working at Logan airport. He was responsible for checking airplane fuel, pressure levels, and refueling planes."

"And he had access to the Secured Area of the airport?" Quinn asked

"Yes. He cleared the Security Threat Assessment and the Criminal History Record check," Rick said.

"Just because someone hasn't done anything criminal yet doesn't mean they aren't going to," Ken said. "Remember the terrorists who plotted to blow up the underground fuel lines for JFK airport? They worked there for years, I don't remember how many, but more than three anyway, plotting away. Spitz could

273

have secured the job at the airport waiting for an opportunity to strike from the airport. Maybe a different opportunity came along."

"Is there any evidence of what Ken suggests. Has Spitz been biding his time for the past three years, waiting to play his part in some attack?" Quinn asked.

"Nothing I've found," Rick answered. "But I didn't get to his employment records yet. Spitz recently applied for a passport and traveled to Paris. He left a few days after Pivani and returned on the same day. That was his first trip out of the country. He's three generations of American. No religious background of any sort. He was in trouble once for a minor assault, but never convicted of anything. I think it could be a coincidence that he contracted the same disease through exposure."

"I did a quick check of his bank records and found the same situation as Pivani," said Ken. "No record of purchases during the time he was abroad. He dropped off the grid. That's all the proof I need to think he's a terrorist. He's an ideal candidate for some group to recruit. No close friends, no family, no significant other. Maybe he was picked on in junior high school."

"But we don't know how or where he contracted the disease," Stephanie said.

"The CDC is working on that," Quinn said. "We need to find out what both of those men were doing abroad."

The door flew open and Rashid hurried into the conference room, wrinkled shirt untucked and skin flushed, looking like he would bust if he didn't soon share what he had learned. "I'm late. Sorry. BIG news. And it's not good. You know how Rick thought there was something up with the football ticket?"

Rick leaned forward and gave Ken an I-told-you-so look.

"Spitz had a ticket too. For the Patriots. I got the info from the Boston CDC examiner's assistant, the one who searched his house."

"Fifty thousand or more men in Boston have that same ticket in their house. You would know if you followed sports, Rashid," Ken said.

"Maybe, but…I used the identification numbers on the tickets to track their purchase. Get this, both were bought online from the same ticket broker. At the same time."

"Excellent work. An indisputable connection," said Quinn.

"So, they were going to go to the NFL games and spread the virus through the crowds," said Rick.

"That's certainly what it looks like," said Rashid.

"But were they terrorists? Did they even know they were infected? If someone gave me the most expensive seat to an NFL game, I'd use it no matter who was playing. Wouldn't you?" Stephanie said.

"You have a point," said Rashid. "With both men dead, we may never know if they were aware they were infected."

"Average attendance for the Chargers is 67,000 per game toward the end of the season. Can you imagine the number of people who might have become sick if they walked around coughing, running their hands along all the banisters?" Rick said.

Ken and Stephanie responded at the same time. Rashid finally managed to interrupt them. "Wait. There's more. The credit card was only used for a single transaction, the tickets, and tracing the card was a dead end. But, there weren't just two tickets purchased. There were four."

"Four?"

"The Patriots in Boston, the Chargers in LA—"

"We know where they play," Ken said, popping his knuckles.

"And two for the Panthers, in Charlotte, North Carolina."

The silence that followed added gravity to the situation.

"All four tickets are for games held on the same day— Sunday, November 6. They're the most expensive seats available for purchase," Rashid said.

"That's great," Rick said. "If we have their ticket numbers, we can find them at their seats."

"Rick, what the hell is wrong with you?" said Ken. "If they make it to their seats, it's too late to prevent this thing from spreading."

"I just meant—"

Quinn interrupted. "Did someone pick up the tickets? Were they mailed?"

"All four were mailed to a company called the Yoga Institute of Paris, which has a Paris address," Rashid said.

"Yes!" Rick said. "That's the same—"

"We found an envelope with the same return address in Pivani's trash," Ken spoke over Rick. "I sent the envelope to be tested for fingerprints."

"So, someone at the Yoga Institute of Paris mailed tickets to Los Angeles and Boston. It's most likely a dummy company," Stephanie said.

"Send the address to our agents in Paris," Quinn said to Rashid.

"I already have."

Quinn turned to Jayla. "Get Charlotte's Special Agent in Charge on the phone. Tell him it's urgent. We need to find whoever has those two Panther's tickets."

Chapter Thirty-Eight

Charlotte, NC
November 5th

Amin woke up feeling disoriented. The sound of running water came from the bathroom. Who else was there? It took a few seconds for his head to clear, for the pieces of his world to settle into place. He got up and headed to the kitchen, peering into the bathroom as he walked down the hallway. With the door ajar, he saw Kareem standing in front of the sink with a towel wrapped around his waist. Kareem took something small out of his hand, placed it on his tongue, and swallowed. Looking into the mirror, Kareem caught Amin spying on him. Kareem looked startled, but recovered quickly. "Hey, good morning. I'm taking advantage of your luxury accommodations."

"Pffff. Hardly luxury," said Amin. "Your parent's house was much nicer when you lived in Detroit." He immediately regretted mentioning his aunt and uncle and stirring up sad thoughts, but Kareem's grin never faltered.

"How are you feeling?" Kareem asked.

"Me? Fine. Over my jet lag. But you looked pretty worn out last night."

Kareem took a deep breath and puffed out his chest. "I might be coming down with a cold. Hey, I'd like to see Charlotte. Can you show me around?"

"It might be like the blind leading the blind. Let's eat breakfast. It will give me time to figure out where to take you."

"Sounds good. Morning prayers first."

The cousins kneeled in the direction Amin indicated and fell silent. Acutely aware of Kareem breathing beside him, inhaling slowly through his nose and exhaling through his mouth, Amin called forth his personal list of important issues. He prayed he and Isa would soon be a couple, that his spiritual enlightenment wouldn't take a nosedive now that he was back in Charlotte, and for his new job to have an office instead of a cube. Pausing, he took a quick sideways glance at Kareem and noticed deep lines of concentration across his forehead, his eyes focused into slits, and his hands pressed so tightly into a steeple that his fingertips were white. Amin added an extra intention. *Please Allah, let Kareem's thoughts be peaceful. Please guide him down the right path.*

When finished, Amin said, "I'm going to scramble some eggs and make some toast. I've got eggs and bread. A small miracle."

"Sounds good. How far are we from downtown? Can we walk from here?"

"Downtown is called uptown here. Long walk, but less than a fifteen-minute drive. There's a Panther's football game tomorrow. Traffic will be bad around game time."

"I'd like to see the stadium."

"How come?"

"I hear it's impressive. And I guess I miss all the American sports hype."

"I don't know if we can get inside." Amin cracked the first of four eggs into a pan. "We can walk around it."

Kareem nodded. "That's fine. Do you go to many games?"

"I've been to a few football games and one or two Hornet's basketball games, all work-related, you know, with colleagues."

"You're not much of a sports fan, huh?"

"Never have been."

Kareem looked suddenly downcast. "I guess I should have known that about you."

Amin shrugged. He stared into the frying pan and resisted the urge to apologize.

"Just don't plan anything for tomorrow. That's when we're doing my surprise."

Amin rubbed the back of his neck. "What kind of surprise?"

Kareem laughed. "You'll find out in the morning. I guess it won't be as good a surprise as I thought. But we're still going."

Amin tried to smile.

"Let me tell you what I did the night before I left." Kareem's mischievous grin appeared in full force.

"What?" Amin suddenly felt nervous and took a drink of water.

"I had sex with a very, very pretty girl."

Amin almost choked on his water. He set his glass down, wondering if he'd heard correctly. "You did what?"

Kareem was still grinning. "You heard me."

"I'm just...surprised. I thought you said an unmarried woman can be stoned to death for having premarital sex."

"Only if someone finds out."

"Then I hope for her sake that no one ever finds out."

279

Kareem's smile disappeared. "Don't worry. If they find out the way I think they might, there won't be much anyone in the compound can do about it."

Chapter Thirty-nine

Los Angeles
November 5th

Quinn sent a classified message with *Threat of Immediate National Concern* in the subject line. Since 9/11, communication between federal agencies had greatly improved and extensive communication protocols existed for national emergencies. This new threat warranted all command and communication centers be notified. Department heads would demand additional information to pass on to cabinet members. The names, faces, and titles of the many people who needed to be informed flew through Quinn's mind and were mentally sorted into categories: *yes—now*, *yes—not yet*, and *no*. The Governor of North Carolina. DHS. The U.S. Embassy in Paris. The CIA. The military. French Intelligence Services. Maybe the NFL commissioner. He hoped he didn't miss any key agency. Before he racked his brain any further, he dialed Madeline's encrypted secure line.

"Maddie, Hi. Have a minute?"

"Hi, Quinn. Yes."

"Everything okay?"

"We've raised our response level to green so we have assistance from the agency's Emergency Operations Centers."

281

"Good. You still have classified clearance, right?"

"Yes.

"Okay. Here's what we've got. Both Spitz and Pivani were in possession of NFL tickets for November 6th games. The tickets were purchased with the same credit card, used exclusively for the one purchase, and mailed to a company in Paris. We believe Pivani and Spitz were infected with the intent of spreading the disease in the stadiums." After an extra beat of silence, he said, "Maddie, did you hear me?"

"Yes, I'm just trying to—this is worse than I thought. Can you imagine how many thousands fill a stadium? My God!" A soft whistling noise escaped her lips.

"We believe there are two more carriers. Two additional tickets were purchased with the tickets we already found. The other two are for a game in Charlotte, North Carolina."

"Wow. At least you know to look for them. Make sure anyone who might get close is protected. I'm praying you find both long dead."

"You'll be the first one called when we find them. I mean, you know, to identify the viral samples."

"There's something I'm curious about. Both the carriers isolated themselves after their return from Paris. Thank God. But, why would they do that? Why didn't they do the opposite and walk around spreading the disease, if infecting people was their objective?"

"Two scenarios I can think of. The first—they weren't intentional carriers. They might not have known they were infected. Doesn't mean they're completely innocent, although maybe they are innocent victims, but perhaps they didn't understand what they got themselves into."

"Evidence against the theory is neither called a doctor or an ambulance when they became ill. Not even when they were violently ill. Makes me believe they were expecting it to happen," Madeline said.

"Good point."

"Although, if the onset was as quick as it appeared, it's possible they were delirious and not able to think clearly to call for help. Not likely, but possible."

"Maybe," said Quinn. "The second scenario—they knew they were infected. Volunteered for it. They were told to wait for the November 6th games for maximum effect, to spread the disease so the greatest number of people would be stricken at once. But the symptoms came on too early and were so incapacitating, they didn't get the chance. They died before they could cause an outbreak."

"That's terrifying. Of course, with both dead, we're just making logical guesses. And with an engineered virus, there's no way of knowing how it's going to affect people—onset, intensity, and duration—unless they've already tried it out."

"Wouldn't you have heard about an outbreak of this nature, regardless of where it happened in the world?" said Quinn.

"Yes, of course, animal outbreak or human, unless it happened in a military-like setting and could be kept quiet and contained."

Quinn shuddered as images of the Nazi concentration camps crossed his mind. "Like a controlled experiment."

"That's what I'm thinking. Did you find anything on the computers of Pivani and Spitz to help us track down their recent whereabouts?"

"Nothing," Quinn said. "Not yet."

"Nothing relevant in their emails? How were they communicating? How did they make plans to go to Paris, or wherever they went after that?" Madeline's voice rose. "Do you know where they stayed when they were there? Who they stayed with? Shouldn't you have leads and connections by now?"

Quinn dropped his head, rubbed his temples. "Whoa, Maddie." His stress level forced out a nervous laugh. "You just asked me five or six questions. Look, our only lead is the address where the tickets were sent. We should have intelligence coming in from Paris agents any time now."

"I'm sorry, I'm just frustrated, and concerned, as I'm sure you are too. Every minute matters here."

"I know," Quinn said. "The other two carriers isolated themselves in their apartments. They got sick and died sooner than expected. Like you said, best case scenario, we find the next two have met the same fate and they too stayed isolated."

"Agree."

"I didn't mention this to you before, but the entire defense system just busted their asses around the clock for weeks to prevent several ISIS-planned attacks. We were successful, but now I think those attacks were decoys, meant to wear us out before the main event."

"Really?"

"Unfortunately, yes. ISIS literally spends every minute of their waking day and all of their energy planning ways to screw with us."

"Thank you, Quinn, for all you're doing behind the scenes."

"I have a great team."

"Can you send me the Paris address? I'll alert my counterparts there."

"I'll send it now."

"This *is* all classified info? I mean, you're not alerting the public to any of this yet, correct?" said Madeline.

"God, no. The only way this ends well is if the public doesn't have to find out about any of it."

"That's what I thought. The CDC is operating under the same opinion."

"Okay. I've got to go."

"Good luck, Quinn."

Chapter Forty

November 5th

Charlotte, NC

The day was dark, damp, and chilly in uptown Charlotte. The sky threatened to dump torrents of rain at any moment. Amin led his cousin through the most interesting uptown streets, past giant sculptures and into connecting glass-tunnel walkways. Kareem acted like a manic-depressive fitting a year of bipolar behavior into one day. He prayed fervently, his behavior alternating between intense and morose, yet he also made Amin laugh by bringing the expression "taking it all in" to a new level. He explored the uptown buildings and hotels as if he'd had one too many drinks and didn't have a care in the world. He turned heads by tottering across a fountain and climbing onto a sculpture, in general, acting younger than his years.

"That's the Continental Bank building where I used to work." Amin pointed upward when they were near the skyscraper.

Kareem tilted his head back to stare up at the tallest building in Charlotte. "Let's go inside and meet your former boss."

Amin snorted. "Doug. Why?"

286

"I want to meet the man who fired you so I can thank him. Otherwise you would never have come to Syria."

"I'm probably going back to work there."

Kareem stared.

"What?" said Amin.

"I just want to meet him. Shake his hand."

"We can't access the elevators without passing through the retina scanner. There are turnstiles to keep people out."

"We can vault over them. Let's do it."

"There are also security guards. Besides, it's Saturday. Doug won't even be there."

The sky darkened and a heavy rain began to fall. Amin moved under an awning to stay dry, but Kareem stayed in the rain, tilting his head up to the sky.

"There's a theater over there. Let's see what's playing," said Amin.

Kareem chewed on the inside of his cheek before agreeing. They bought tickets to see a movie that had started five minutes earlier.

"This movie sucks," said Kareem, after twenty minutes inside the theater.

"Eh, it's not the best."

"Come on. Let's get out of here."

"It might get better. It's only just started."

"I don't want to waste any more time on it." Kareem stood up and Amin followed him out of the theater and onto the sidewalk. The rain had stopped.

"I want to go in here," Kareem said, gazing into the Mexican restaurant next to the theater.

Amin laughed and shook his head at his cousin's eagerness. "It's not even five and we've already stopped twice for food, and you hardly ate any of what you ordered. Save a restaurant or two for the next few days."

Kareem went in anyway. "Seat us by the window, please," he said to the hostess.

At Amin's suggestion, Kareem ordered a sweet tea. He gulped it down, chasing two pills.

"What are the pills for?" Amin asked.

"My back," said Kareem, staring out the window at the wide variety of people passing by.

"You never mentioned you had back issues before."

Kareem shrugged. "There's a lot we don't know about each other."

Long before dinner, Amin was glad Kareem had come to Charlotte. They were having fun. It hadn't been that way in Syria, with Kareem spending so many hours in his lab and Amin feeling like a suspicious outsider. Amin set his mind to finding more things they could do together over the next few days, or weeks, however long Kareem planned to stay. If things continued like they had today, the longer the better.

After a full day of touring Charlotte, the Sarif cousins returned to Amin's apartment.

"I'm beat. I need to sit down." Kareem laid back against the couch and closed his eyes.

"Long trip and the time difference," Amin said. "We can watch some TV. I'll be right back."

Amin was only in his bedroom for a few minutes, but when he returned to the living room, he found Kareem already snoring.

Amin couldn't help but laugh, and also feel a bit disappointed. But tomorrow was another day. He didn't have to plan anything, since Kareem had reserved the day for his "surprise." Amin filled a glass with water and returned to his room to watch television. The local news played the weather report followed by a piece hyping the next day's Panthers versus Falcons game. He changed the channel to an old episode of Seinfeld, but failed to register what was happening on the show. Unresolved issues had his mind spinning: returning to work at the bank, a second chance with Isa and, most surprising, his cousin's presence— dreaded for so many days but turning out to be fun.

Yet, with Elaine yelling at George on the television in the background, and Kareem snoring on the couch, doubts lingered. Had Kareem changed his mind about whatever it was he meant to do? Changing convictions was no easy task, had it really happened as if it was nothing? And what about Amin's own spiritual convictions? What could he do to keep from slipping back into a spiritual oblivion? What would happen to his spiritual gains if he returned to spending each day inside the bank working on spreadsheets, the only change being a different cube? He didn't know because he couldn't know. When in doubt, pray. That's what a good Muslim would do, and that's who he wanted to be.

And verily, whosoever shows patience and forgives that would truly be from the things recommended by Allah.

Amin tried to focus on this passage from the Quran, one of his favorites. He had forgiven Kareem, Doug, Shelly from HR, Isa's father for saying she was engaged when she wasn't, whoever was responsible for siphoning his gas, those who killed his aunt and uncle, and the Muslims in Syria who prayed for most of the world's population to suffer. Who else should he forgive? He wondered if anyone needed to forgive him. Five minutes after he began, he stopped praying because it felt forced and insincere. He got up and grabbed the business card Isa had given him with her work email address. He returned to bed with his laptop. Once it booted up, he composed a note to Isa. Business writing was something he did often and it came easily,

289

but pouring his emotions into a heartfelt note, without sounding strange, presented a challenge. He did his best to channel a lighthearted vibe, calm and composed, yet interested and genuine.

Dear Isa,

So much has happened since I met you at the mosque with your father and decided you were the woman of my dreams. At first, none of it was good. At the mosque social, I was about to ask your father about dating you, when he told me you were engaged. A few days later, I lost my job. Not for poor performance, but just because. So, I visited Syria to help save my scientist cousin from becoming a jihadist, and to console him over the sudden death of his parents, my aunt and uncle. Sounds crazy, I know. Maybe it was.

Things unexpectedly took a turn for the better in Syria. I spent weeks repairing a mosque and attending service every day. I strengthened my faith by focusing on creating something beautiful and reflecting in silence, not by spending most of my day working on spreadsheets. When I returned, I discovered, again from your father, you weren't engaged. Right away, I wanted to contact you, but with no job and some worries about my cousin, I hesitated.

My cousin is here in Charlotte now, and my concerns seem to have been unwarranted. Maybe you can meet him soon. We explored the city today and walked through your building. That's when I decided I would be a fool to wait until my life was perfect to ask you out. Besides, I think I have a new job starting soon in a different department at Continental Bank. I interview on Monday, but I was told it's only a formality.

Amin read over what he'd written and frowned. He would never send it to Isa. She didn't need to know the embarrassing stuff, like his concerns about Kareem or how he was fired. Not before she got to know him. He could revise the letter the next day, or forget about it and see her in person, like he originally planned. As terrible as his note was, it served as an outlet for his emotions, and he suddenly felt drained. His eyes had grown heavy while he was writing. The first of three sneezes from the other room startled him. Amin's hand slipped on his mouse when he went to click the save icon. He shut down his laptop and lay down to sleep, believing he had saved a draft. Except that's not what happened. The message was on its way to Isa's inbox.

Chapter Forty-One

Los Angeles
November 5th

Quinn paced behind the conference table, unable to sit. He glanced at his watch. Fourteen hundred hours. Seventeen hundred hours on the East Coast. Too much to do and not enough time.

"Who do we still need to communicate with?" Jayla asked.

"I need another call with the National Security Advisor. And the Governor of North Carolina. Right after we get the search for the two ticket holders underway."

Quinn's tired team sat slumped in their chairs. They were still capable, but noticeably worn, less sharp, like the errant hairs frizzing out of Stephanie's usually smooth ponytail. He had to make a quick decision over their involvement going forward. If he gave them the choice, he knew what they would choose. The same way he would if he was in their shoes. The same way he had already decided for himself. He wasn't sure if he should let them, but he knew what they were about to do, again, preventing a major terrorist attack, was the very reason each of his team members had coveted this job.

He put the decision square in their corner. Addressing the team, he said, "Every Federal Agency has a stake in this case, but the emergency timeframe doesn't leave time for politics to play out, so it's ours. However, I can request it be turned over to another office right now. You can go home and rest, take the showers some of you desperately need, and jump back in tomorrow and help. But if we keep this, sleep is out of the question for a while. So, are all of you up to this?"

"I'm not going home," Stephanie said.

"Me either," said Rashid.

The other three, Rick, Ken, and Jayla, shared similar sentiments.

Quinn lowered his head and smiled without opening his mouth. "I thought so. Just monitor yourselves. We can't make a mistake. No matter how we're feeling, we need to be able to give one hundred percent."

"Of course," Stephanie said.

"How we handle this could be the difference between preventing a worldwide epidemic...or not. Until the remaining ticket holders are identified, everyone in the United States is at risk."

"If the public finds out, it's going to be an unprecedented shit-storm," said Ken.

"North Carolina will need to activate large scale precautionary measures in case we don't find these other two before morning," said Stephanie.

"What did the DHS representative say about—"

"Have you called the CDC to see —"

Everyone spoke at once, their questions and comments aimed at Quinn. His thoughts were sharply interrupted by a haunting flashback: children from the Kurdish refugee camp during his final tour in Iraq, then students at a local high school he and Rashid visited in the summer, followed by the random thought—*Remember to text Holly that I'm not coming home.* He needed to block out everything not related to the case and focus. They had to get started. He thumped the table with his open hand.

"I just spoke with Charlotte's SAC. The Counterterrorism Hostage Rescue Teams are loading into helicopters now. They'll be on the ground there within the hour. It's our job to have a list of suspects ready for them by the time they land."

Heads nodded around the table.

"Based on the incubation timeframe for hemorrhagic fever, we'll work with the assumption that these carriers, like the other two, were infected outside the country and entered the United States recently. Two hundred and eighty thousand people arrive at our international airports each day. Our primary objective is to narrow those arrivals down to our two terrorist weapons."

"Who may or may not know that's what they are," Stephanie quickly added.

"I want three lists of suspects. Priority A, B, and C. Stephanie, I want you and Jayla to develop the A list. Here are the criteria."

Jayla typed as Quinn spoke.

Priority A Criteria

- departure = Paris
- final destination = Charlotte
- entering U.S. = 10/24-11/3
- primary nationality = American
- secondary nationality = Middle Eastern= Syria, Saudi Arabia, Iran, Iraq, Jordan, Egypt, Sudan, Somalia, Libya, Turkey
- age = 17-30
- marital status = single

- traveling alone
- gender = male

"With that criteria, we would have missed Spitz," Stephanie said.

Quinn nodded. "I know. But we have to prioritize. We need to have names ready for the field agents and the HRT when they hit the ground. Jayla, I need you to track down the addresses as Stephanie comes up with the names. Ken, you'll work on the B list. Ready for that criteria?"

Priority List B

- departure = Paris
- final destination = Charlotte
- entering U.S. from 10/24-11/3
- age = 17-40
- marital status = all
- nationality = all
- gender = all

"What if they don't live in North Carolina?" Rick said. "For example, South Carolina doesn't have its own football team. What if he or she lives somewhere in South Carolina and plans to drive up to Charlotte for the Panthers game?"

"We'll accommodate for that scenario with the C list that the rest of us will work on researching," said Quinn.

Priority List C

- departure = all international airports
- final destination = all SC or NC airports
- date range = 10/24-11/3
- age = 17-40
- marital status = all
- nationality = all
- gender = all

"This will be a long list, but it's our safety net. After we deliver the A and B list names to the field agents, we'll continue researching everyone else—census records, voting records, medical records—anything that moves them to the top of the candidates. The entire Intelligence and Analysis department is available to help with the research. We need to know these people inside and out so the right ones are singing out to us."

"I'm on it," said Rashid.

Rick raised his hand. He quickly pulled it down and asked his question when Ken sneered at him from across the table. "What if we put out an alert asking anyone who has certain symptoms to come forward so we can treat them? Or, we could ask for the people with those tickets to come forward? We could offer them an even better incentive. Like a big-screen TV? I know that would only work if the carriers aren't real terrorists, but is it worth a try?"

"No." Ken leaned back in his seat and stared at Rick as if he'd never heard anything so stupid. "No, for so many reasons. If they are real terrorists, we've just tipped them off that we're looking for them, and they might change their target. And even if they aren't, you think we can put something on social media asking anyone in Charlotte who has signs of hemorrhagic fever to call us? Yeah, that would go over real well. We might as well do the terrorists' jobs for them and scare the hell out of everyone."

"Okay. Just brainstorming ideas."

"Don't," said Ken.

"Hey, guys, be nice. We're supposed to share ideas and challenge each other," said Stephanie. "That's why we're a team."

"Stephanie is right," said Quinn. "We don't have time for this. You're showing how tired you are. Just get to the lists."

In less than an hour, Stephanie and Jayla created an A list with forty names and more than forty addresses including home, work, and second and third homes.

"Send it to the HRT teams and DHS in Charlotte," Quinn said. He finished scanning the list and looked at his watch. Current time: 2100 hours on the East Coast.

"I finished the B list," Ken said, getting up from his chair. "Jayla, I just sent it to you. Can you get their addresses? Damn, I need more coffee. And some food."

"I'm doing something first," Jayla said. "Use the Intelligence analysts from another office. They're all available."

"We all need food and coffee," Quinn said. "Order something for everyone, Ken. After you get the addresses."

"Eating slipped my mind," said Stephanie. "But this isn't an episode of 24 where no one ever needs to use the restroom."

For the first time since he started working on the suspect list, Rashid turned away from his monitors to watch Stephanie hurry from the room.

"Oh, shoot. What time is it?" Rick looked at his phone. "Oh no. Be back in a few minutes."

"What, did you have a date?" Ken asked, a sneer apparent in his tone.

"Something like that. Had a date set up yesterday, but I cancelled and rescheduled for tonight. I'm about to find out just how understanding she is when I cancel again. Wish me luck." Rick was half way across the room when he stopped and turned back to Rashid. "Rashid, why don't you ask her out?"

"Are you talking to me? What? Who?" Rashid said.

"You know who. It's sort of obvious."

"I don't know what you're talking about, man." Rashid waved Rick off. "But *this* isn't the time."

"I'm just saying, the only opportunities we regret are the ones we don't take."

"That's not true," Ken mumbled. "If you were older you'd know. There are plenty of actions we eventually regret."

Rick shrugged. "Surprise yourself," he said to Rashid before sprinting away.

Chapter Forty-Two
Los Angeles
November 5th

With less than 24 hours before the Panther's kickoff, Quinn's team propelled forward on fumes of exhaustion, working against the clock to abort the attack in time. Jayla rushed from her desk to Quinn's office to deliver a message.

"There's a National Security Council Meeting in five minutes. It was called to discuss the deployment of additional forces to the Middle East. I got you, Dr. Hamilton, and the Governor of North Carolina added to the call," said Jayla.

"Perfect," said Quinn. "If we don't succeed in tracking down the two carriers before sunrise, the list of people who need to know is going to explode."

Jayla nodded. "I'll route the call into the briefing room."

"I better get over there." Quinn stood up, grabbed his sports coat from the back of his chair and a tie from one of his desk drawers.

"Here's a list of names and titles, the people on the council." Jayla handed him a printed list as he strode past her.

She frowned as her eyes quickly assessed him. "Wait. One second, I have some Visine in my bag. Let me give it to you."

"No time." Quinn hurried to the intelligence briefing room and stood at the head of the table, alone, tightening his tie. He had less than a minute to glance at the list of attendees. Included were the President, the National Security Advisor, the Director of Central Intelligence, the Secretary of Defense, the Chairman of the Joint Chiefs of Staff, the Secretary of Health & Human Services, the Secretary of State, the DHS Cabinet member, the Attorney General, the Federal Emergency Management Agency Director, the Federal Bureau of Investigation Director, the Governor of North Carolina, and Madeline.

The Secretary of Health and Human Services kicked off the video conference. She was ex-military. Even seated, her posture was straight and strong. A Band-Aid covered part of her chin and Quinn remembered hearing she'd been in a minor car accident earlier in the day.

"With us for the beginning of this call are Assistant Special Agent in Charge Quinn Traynor with the FBI's Counterterrorism unit, Dr. Madeline Hamilton from the CDC's Outbreak Response Team, and Trent Silvers, the Governor of North Carolina," said the Secretary. "Mr. Traynor is going to update us on an escalating threat of national concern. Go ahead, Mr. Traynor."

Quinn wasn't sure how much everyone on the call already knew about the situation. He swallowed, aware of his heartbeat, unusually fast and strong, and a slight tremor from too much caffeine. "I'm ASAC Agent Quinn Traynor." He realized immediately that his words were unnecessary because the Secretary had already introduced him. He needed to focus.

"And this makes two times in one week that I'm hearing from you, Mr. Traynor," the Secretary said, adjusting her glasses. "You prevented the mass transit attacks, so let's hope for the same success."

300

Quinn nodded. "Thank you, everyone, for allowing us to join your call. We believe our country is targeted for a bioterrorist attack and we have less than 24 hours to respond before it is carried out. To give you some background—as you know, yesterday, our country's defense successfully prevented an ISIS cell from detonating explosions in three of our city's subway systems. We now believe those were decoy attacks meant to distract us and spread our resources thin before a larger and more widespread attack with a viral weapon." He reorganized his rushing thoughts as someone asked a question.

"What do you mean by a viral weapon? What type of virus?" The Chairman of the Joint Chiefs of Staff made a fist and brought it to his lips.

"E.Coryza 1 or the E.C.1 virus. It's a genetically altered strain of Ebola. Ebola viruses, those that affect humans, are spread through contact with bodily fluids. By crossing Ebola with the common cold, this new strain can now spread through the air via coughing and sneezing, even breath, without physical contact," said Quinn.

Around the conference table expressions grew more solemn.

Quinn continued, keeping his voice calm and in check, even though the urge to *hurry, hurry, hurry* threatened to choke him. "Four human carriers have been deliberately infected to disperse this weaponized hemorrhagic fever."

"Excuse me, Agent Trayor, how do you know there are four carriers? Where are they?" the Secretary of State asked.

"To the best of our knowledge, there are four. Two of them, both U.S. citizens, have been positively linked. They were each discovered today. Deceased. One in Boston, one in LA. The CDC is working to control an outbreak, but the risk of spread from those two, at this point, is low."

"And why is it low?" The National Security Advisor looked puzzled.

"E.C.1 is highly contagious, but not until symptoms develop. The onset of symptoms, in the case of the two deceased men, was so sudden and violent, they weren't able to spread the virus before they died."

"And the other two?"

Quinn wasn't sure who posed the question. "The FBI is working to identify and locate them now. Ideally, we will find them incapacitated but still alive so they can be questioned. We believe the exposure target is the Panthers football game in Charlotte at thirteen-hundred hours tomorrow and that the infected individuals are somewhere in the stadium's vicinity. Facing the possibility of a nation-wide epidemic with unprecedented public health and economic impact, we can't overemphasize the importance of locating these individuals."

"How are we doing that?" the Secretary of State asked. "We certainly don't have much time."

"Less than an hour ago, my team developed a profile and identified a list of matching candidates. Field agents and the HRT have been deployed to personally screen each of them in Charlotte."

"And if we don't find them?" the National Security Advisor said.

The FEMA Director answered. "Defense agencies are currently working together to establish our contingency plan."

"When will we notify local law enforcement and the public?" asked the Chairman of the Joint Chiefs of Staff.

"It's imperative this information remains classified for now. If the carriers are alive, they are isolated. If word gets out about our search, and about the other two dead patients, we've provided motivation for them to start spreading the disease immediately," Quinn said.

"What about your field agents? If they're outfitted, won't they be noticed and cause a panic?" the Joint Chief of Staff asked, looking at the FBI director and the Attorney General.

The FBI Director spoke. "The field agents are *not* wearing protective suits, precisely to avoid a panic situation. They have the gear with them and will use their judgment about when and if to put it on. The HRT team will take additional precautions if they believe the suspect they were sent to apprehend is infected."

"There are plenty of groups who would do this, but who *could* do it?" said the President, looking around his conference room table.

Madeline spoke up. "Mr. President, Ebola is stored in numerous biological labs across the world – from pharmaceutical companies to universities. Even the simplest biotech facility has the ability to harvest and alter the virus, if they have a skilled virologist."

"So, we don't know who is responsible?" The President puckered his lips and stared at Quinn through squinted eyes.

"The defense agencies are all working together to determine responsibility. We suspect ISIS. We suspect the attack is retribution for the death of Anwar Al-Bahil who was killed by the U.S. military on November 6th last year. But no one has claimed responsibility yet. And that's good. If the information stays classified, whoever is responsible doesn't know two of the infected men are dead and we've discovered their bodies. As long as they don't know, we have more time to find the terr…I mean, carriers."

"What about shutting down the Panthers game?" the Secretary of Health and Human Services asked.

"Quinn and I worked this out earlier today," said the Governor. "If we haven't located the infected men by ten am tomorrow, I'll shut the game down and declare a state of

303

emergency. It would be a last-minute call and would coincide with alerting the media."

"Prior to that time, we will *not* be notifying anyone at the venue, including the NFL board and local law enforcement. Inciting a panic situation could be more detrimental, at least in the short term, than the threat of contagion. The infected carrier would likely find another location: a mall, an airport, anywhere with crowds of people," added Quinn.

Several people had differing opinions as to how long they should wait before alerting the public. The DHS Cabinet member prevailed. He said, "If the carrier isn't located by eleven am, we'll alter the scope of the mission to alerting and protecting the public. The Governor will mobilize a state response and prepare the hospitals."

Images of what might happen flashed through Quinn's mind—uncontrollable panic, irrational behavior, stampedes. His stomach tightened.

"What about shutting down all of Sunday's NFL games as a precaution? And how do you know there aren't more carriers?" said the Secretary again.

Quinn answered. "We're pursuing every lead to find out. At this time, we have no evidence of additional carriers. We are certain tomorrow's Panther game in Charlotte is a target. I'll provide an update as soon as we hear something from the agents in Charlotte."

The President closed his eyes for a brief second. "How fast can we formulate a public health response?"

"We're implementing an emergency front-line training protocol to make sure first responders have the necessary training and equipment," said the FEMA director. "All reserve hospital workers and EMTs may be needed."

The governor spoke. "I've already activated the hospital disaster plan for North Carolina. I've called it an emergency training drill. If necessary, tomorrow morning we'll have isolation tents set up in Charlotte, on the location of a former NBA arena. We've already started, again, under the auspices of an emergency drill. The tents look like a giant outdoor market and shouldn't cause alarm."

Madeline's composed image filled the screen on Quinn's wall. "The CDC has a highly experienced hemorrhagic fever response team on their way to Charlotte."

"What about vaccinations?" the President asked. "Don't we have Ebola vaccinations now?"

Madeline answered. "The vaccinations are still in testing stages, but E.C.1 is new, altered. Our current vaccinations *might* reduce the severity of the disease, but would not prevent contraction. We're working on altering the vaccine, but it still needs to be tested and manufactured on a large scale. So, for the short-term, vaccination is not an option."

"How is our stockpile of PPE?" The Attorney General looked to Madeline and then the FEMA Director.

Madeline answered. "I conferred with the other government agencies on this. It's not at the level required if the attack is carried out. For all medical personnel, we'll need level four gear, head to toe covering, face shields, and respirators. No skin can be exposed because decontamination will require chlorine spray. We have enough for primary care givers and it can be delivered in less than 24 hours. It takes twenty full-time staff to care for one patient with advanced hemorrhagic fever. If the disease spreads, we're going to have a severe shortage of PPE and caregivers. And the emotional toll an outbreak will take on primary caregivers should not be underestimated. It's difficult to be mentally and psychologically prepared for the amount of suffering they could witness."

"What about body bags? Storage for corpses?" said the Attorney General.

"We can discuss that after the call," said the FEMA director, without looking up.

The CIA Director glanced at a notebook in front of him. "What is the incubation period for the disease?"

"With a known hemorrhagic virus, it could be between two and twenty-one days, depending on the individual. Again, this virus has been altered," Madeline said.

"That's not an answer." The CIA Director shook his head.

"We don't have the data to provide an exact number. We only have two victims to study, both were dead when we discovered them, and we don't know when they were infected," Madeline said.

"Why don't you have the information yet?" The Secretary of Health and Human Services frowned.

"Bottom line. We don't know," Quinn said, jumping in.

The President cleared his throat. "If and when the Governor declares a state of emergency, I'll address the nation at the same time. I'll initiate the Pandemic Plan and authorize travel restrictions, along with military deployment and media control. We'll have to deploy the National Guard, won't we?"

Nods all around the table.

"This is unprecedented territory." The Secretary of State clasped his hands. "We're used to restrictions to keep people out, not keep them in."

"The only way we avoid a national disaster is to find the remaining ticket holders before the morning," the FBI director said, stating the obvious.

"I hope we find them alive," said the Attorney General.

"And believe me, when we find them, they're going to wish they were dead." The President slammed his fist on the table.

Holly paced around the empty house, her anger intensifying.

Where the hell is he?

She glared at the numbers on the wall clock. They were supposed to board a red eye to Spain in a few hours. Her bags were packed, but Quinn still wasn't home and he hadn't done a thing to prepare for the trip. Holly clenched her fists. A tingling feeling built inside her nose until she sneezed with so much force it rattled her brain.

She had already left Quinn several messages and texts, each one angrier than the last. Running out of patience, she called his assistant

"Quinn Traynor's office," Jayla answered, sounding rushed.

"This is Holly Traynor. I need to speak with my husband. Do you know where he is?"

"He's busy right now, but I will make certain he gets your message."

"We're supposed to be on a flight to Spain tonight and I need to know if he's going to come home in time. He never came home yesterday. I'm starting to wonder if he's even alive."

"Oh, no. I'm so sorry. None of us made it home yesterday. But Quinn is fine, Mrs. Traynor. He's not able to talk right now. He's in the secure briefing room. I'll make sure he gets your message."

A slight growl escaped Holly's throat. She pressed the "end call" button as hard as she could, wishing for a more satisfying way to disconnect and convey her frustration. "Damn it!" She stormed into the kitchen. Leaning heavily on the counter, she opened one of her canisters, selected a pill, and stared at it in her open palm. So much power contained in something so tiny.

She easily remembered why she started taking them. They made her loneliness ache less. They made Quinn's perpetual absence more bearable. But right now, she wanted to hang on to her anger, its magnitude felt critical, essential to surviving the next few hours. She made a fist around the pill. Maybe she wouldn't take one after all. But…she also felt like crap. She opened her palm, tossed the pill into her open mouth, and swallowed.

Why had she allowed herself to believe she could count on him this time? If she hadn't raised her expectations, she wouldn't be in this position, feeling hurt, foolish, and betrayed. "He's not going to ruin this for me. I don't need him. I'm going to Spain no matter what," she said aloud.

Her eyes itched. She stomped to the bathroom, and fished around in the cabinet for the antihistamines. After finding the bottle and swallowing yet another pill, she returned to the bedroom and sat down to think about her next move.

Stephanie was on the verge of bursting into the briefing room when Jayla stopped her, just in time.

"Quinn is briefing the National Security Council. Including the President."

"Ooh." Stephanie raised her eyebrows. "Okay."

"It shouldn't take long."

"I'll wait." Stephanie repeatedly ran her hand over the top of her head and down her ponytail, fidgeting until the door opened. She began speaking immediately. "We did more research on the A list candidates. One person rose to the top. He's a banker and lives in Charlotte. I already sent his name to Rashid, who accessed his computer—" Stephanie's eyes darted away for an instant. "Obviously, we didn't have time for approvals."

308

"I don't care." Quinn shook his head. "It's fine."

"He found recent searches about the Islamic State in the man's browsing history."

"Damn. Let me see what you have."

She handed Quinn a piece of paper. "We didn't write up anything formal."

"Because we don't have time for formalities."

"There's his name and address." Stephanie pointed.

Quinn picked up his phone. "I'll tell the Hostage Rescue Team."

"Please let this one be alive, so we can find out if there are others." Stephanie lifted her gaze toward the ceiling.

Quinn nodded to her as the HRT answered his direct call.

Stephanie returned to the work room.

"We're down to the last few names," Rick said.

"We should all take a break while they confirm the banker is our guy," Ken intertwined his fingers and pressed his hands forward, away from his chest.

"We need to keep going through the list. Just in case," Stephanie said, raising her voice. Her nerves were frayed. Rick appeared to be holding up the best, which Stephanie attributed to his youth.

"In case we're all wrong about the number one suspect? The guy who fits all the criteria? Whose search history reeks with ISIS?" Ken said.

"Yes. Besides, he's only one guy and we need two," Stephanie said, her voice harsher than she intended. "Oh, God, I'm beginning to sound like an angry, exhausted mother. Sorry, Ken." She closed her eyes and gently rubbed them.

Ken let his head drop backward as far as it would go. "No prob. Take a break."

"We're all tired, Ken. We're all really, really, tired. Wired. Can you just move on to the next name, please?" She glanced over at Rashid, who was still working at a feverish pace. She wanted him to see her eye roll, but he was too busy concentrating.

The sun in Los Angeles dipped into the horizon. At the same time, just a few miles from uptown Charlotte, moonlit darkness provided some cover for the mission. The unsuspecting Charlotte neighborhood was still and quiet until a breeze stirred crispy brown leaves into the air and four men wearing biohazard suits approached a row of high-end condominiums.

From their headquarters, Quinn, Stephanie, Ken, Jayla, and Rick watched the HRT in action. They had a larger-than-life birds' eye view on the wall monitor, streaming from an unarmed predator drone. Hundreds of other defense agency employees were watching the same feed around the country. Quinn took a deep breath and wrapped his hand around his chin.

"They're wearing full protective suits," said Ken. "I thought they weren't going to. Anyone could step outside to walk a dog or something. What are they thinking? We're screwed if the media catches wind of this before they get him. All-out panic. And the terrorists will head to plan B."

"We know," said Stephanie. "But if this is the guy, they need to be protected."

"This better be him," said Ken. "How can it not be?" He sat down and bounced his knee before standing up again.

With the speed and choreography of a well-rehearsed performance, the HRT surrounded one condo and stopped, poised to burst through the doors. With their bodies fully covered, they looked like a band of Martians. One of them backed up against the neighbor's door and kicked two pumpkins out of the way.

Quinn thought—*pumpkins—something about the pumpkins rolling down the stone steps.*

Then—*Oh, no! Holly.*

Our vacation.

Oh Shit.

He grabbed his personal phone from his pocket and typed a text message.

Chapter Forty-Three

Los Angeles
November 5th

Holly's head throbbed like her temples were being pushed out from the inside. She moaned and fell back to sleep. Finally, the urge to pee forced her awake. She rubbed her eyes and pressed her fingers against the sides of her head.

"Quinn?"

Silence.

Where is he? Where is my husband? She looked at the clock. "Shit! Shit! Shit!" She hadn't meant to fall asleep. Her flight to Spain would be boarding before she reached the airport. She grabbed her phone, a shaky tremor running through her entire body. Intense anger could do that for sure, but she also needed to eat and probably, on top of everything else that was going wrong, she was coming down with a cold.

Quinn had left two text messages.

I'm so sorry. I'll explain later. I'll change our flights and we'll go a few days later.

Please forgive me. I'm so sorry.

She yelled at her phone, "Fuck you, Quinn!" and threw it down.

Rage coursed through her. Her suitcase, packed for their trip, remained at the door where she had placed it. She grabbed the suitcase and tossed it on its side. Snatching the zipper and yanking it down, she pulled out the contents, item by item, flinging them behind her. Her new hat—wouldn't wear it in LA. Her sexy new lingerie—what a joke it turned out to be, carefully choosing those. Her new walking shoes. Two bottles of pills. The rattling sound they made hitting the wall only fueled her fury.

How could Quinn do this to her? How could he? And how could she have allowed him to disappoint her once again? She stood up with her hands on her hips, legs spread wide, only slightly distracted by an episode of dizziness. To hell with him! She was done with Quinn. So done!

Her head ached and her legs were a little weak, which threatened to derail her psychological victory. She used the bathroom and then returned to the kitchen canisters to make the headache stop. She gulped a full glass of water, her thirst as powerful as if she'd been parched in the desert for a day. Bending over to snatch up her phone made her throbbing head worse. She couldn't think about that now. She had to call Reese.

"Hi, honey," Reese said.

Holly burst into tears.

"Oh, my God. Holly, what's wrong, sweetie? Why are you crying?"

Her cries turned to sobs.

"Holly, answer me, please. You're scaring me."

Holly sniffed, snorted, blew her nose, and finally pulled herself together enough to speak. "I'm okay. No. I'm not, I have a cold, damn it, which would have ruined my vacation if Quinn hadn't ruined it already. I'm done with him."

"What did he do to you, hon?"

"We're supposed to be on our way to Spain right now, and he never came home last night. And he's not home now. I have no idea where he is."

"Oh, my God! I forgot. Your vacation. What a bastard. I can't believe he did this to you. Do you think he left you?"

"No. I think he's at fucking work where he always is." Holly sobbed, coughed, and reached for another tissue.

"You sound terrible. Hold on. Stay there. I'm coming. I'll be there as soon as I can. Don't go anywhere, Holl. Promise me."

"I won't," Holly said. "I feel like shit."

"Take some medicine and get in bed. Get some rest. I'll be there soon. It's going to be okay."

Holly sat down on the couch, put her feet up, and fell asleep.

When Reese arrived, Holly struggled to get up and walk through the house to let her in. Every step was a monumental and dizzying effort. She opened the door halfway. Reese grinned and held up a champagne bottle. The top of another bottle peeked out from the large bag on her shoulder. Behind her stood four or five other people Holly barely knew.

"Reese, I told you I wasn't feeling well," Holly whispered. The effort of speaking burned her throat.

"And, voila! We're here to make you feel better." Reese pushed the door open the rest of the way, gave Holly a tight hug, and marched inside with her friends. "And there's one more person coming too. Just the one you need to make you feel appreciated."

Chapter Forty-Four

Charlotte, NC
November 5th

Scott Hussan's North Carolina issued driver's license still held his given name, Sadam Hussan. For obvious reasons, everyone had called him Scott since his high school days in Atlanta, where he lived until college. Although he hadn't made the time to officially change his given first name, as far as he was concerned, it didn't exist. He'd built a reputation around his work ethic, his intellect, and for being a nice and fair man. He wanted to avoid any association with one of the most hated men in recent history.

Even though it was a Saturday, Scott had spent most of the day inside his Charlotte office, not unusual for a young investment banker and part of the reason he had way more money than time. Lately, he hadn't been feeling his usual invincible self. He had recently returned from visiting his girlfriend, Genna, in Paris, where she was completing a semester of graduate work. The amazing week flew by. He didn't want to leave her. An unwelcome melancholy hovered over him, beginning the moment they parted with a prolonged kiss at the airport. October 28th at two-twenty in the afternoon to be exact. He'd done his best to keep the something-is-missing feeling at

315

bay by immersing himself in work. As long as he stayed busy and at the office, he didn't have time to miss her. But at home, in his townhome with the city skyline view, her absence invaded his every pore. His longing became almost a tangible feeling he could grab out of the air and squeeze. He closed his eyes and imagined Genna's soft skin, the way her kiss sent a shiver through his body. This is what it felt like to love someone. What should he do about it?

He poured himself a glass of Moscato. He preferred beer, but sweet, white wine was Genna's drink of choice, and he had a compelling urge to surround himself with anything reminding him of her. Sitting down on his leather couch, he grabbed the remote and aimed it at his DVR. Sixteen recorded episodes of the Big Bang Theory awaited him. He would watch one even though he'd seen it before because it was her favorite show.

In the scene he was watching, Sheldon wrote quantum physics equations on a white board and Leonard questioned his calculations. Scott sighed and took a sip of wine.

CRACK!!!

"FBI!"

His front door splintered down the middle. What the…? A large man wearing a space suit appeared in the doorway, legs apart, reminding Scott of an astronaut. Another appeared behind him. Scott's mind, sharper than average, reached an unprecedented level of confusion. The bizarre notion of an alien invasion presented itself as the far-fetched but only explanation to represent the scene unfolding before him. How else could he explain it? But did they say FBI? They didn't look like FBI.

His back door shattered with a piercing crack. He jerked his head around to discover more men in space suits lined up outside. He jumped up and dropped his wine glass to the floor. Fear of the unexpected and unexplained flooded his system, jarred his nerves, and prevented him from screaming. He froze, mouth agape, in front of his Chesterfield couch surrounded by shards of glass, a snapped wine stem, and a small pool of Moscato.

"FBI! Don't move!"

Chapter Forty-Five

Charlotte

November 6th

Amin woke in the middle of the night to terrible retching sounds, which brought back memories from his childhood. On his eleventh birthday, his family ate at a local family restaurant. The food didn't agree with his parents. That night, after cake and presents, he lay in bed, staring at the solar system on his ceiling, listening to his mother and father throwing up. His parents suspected food poisoning. They had all ordered the same meal, but Amin was fine, yet one more example of his body's amazing immunity. He was also reminded of his college roommate puking his guts out, as they used to say, on two different late-night occasions. As far as Amin could remember, those were his only experiences with vomiting. He had never thrown up before. He never got sick.

The toilet flushed. Kareem's feet padded across the living room floor. A choking noise interrupted his steady footsteps and he hurriedly returned to the bathroom. Primitive, heaving sounds accompanied another round of vomiting.

The long trip must have worn his cousin down. Amin considered checking on him to ask if he needed anything, but decided to respect Kareem's privacy. No one wanted an audience when they were puking. He didn't know from personal experience, but he'd heard, and could certainly imagine truth in the statement. He turned on his side, pulled his comforter right up to the edge of his chin, and put a pillow over the side of his head to drown out the sound. Pretending he hadn't heard Kareem being sick seemed like the most considerate thing to do. Eventually he returned to sleep.

Amin woke up later than usual. At first, he stayed comfortable under his covers with only a vague recollection of his sleep being interrupted numerous times during the night. He rubbed his eyes, eventually recalling the events of the past two days. His cousin had traveled from Syria and was there now, sleeping on the couch. They'd had a great time uptown. Kareem got sick during the early morning hours. Amin hoped whatever had inflicted Kareem sounded worse than it was. He was half-dressed when he heard a low moan from outside his door. He yanked his pants up and buttoned them before peering into the hallway. Outside his bedroom door, the apartment reeked of fresh vomit. Amin pinched his nostrils closed and hoped he had some Lysol spray under the sink.

Kareem moaned again and Amin hurried down the hall, feeling terrible now about not checking in on his cousin during the night. "Kareem, are you okay?"

"Yes. Fine." Kareem's words ended with a coughing spasm.

"You don't sound…" Amin stopped midsentence and stared at Kareem on the couch. "Holy shit," he blurted in a whispered breath.

"I'm fine!" Kareem didn't exactly yell, he hissed, which made the situation more surreal.

The urge to back away thwarted Amin's compulsion to help. Kareem lay naked on top of the blankets. Amin was horrified by the sight of him. The whites of Kareem's eyes were red. Strange bruises splotched his dark skin. Amin didn't know what to make of it. And where were his clothes? That's what popped into his head—as if it mattered—what did Kareem do with his clothes?

"What time is it?" Kareem asked.

"What time is it?" Amin echoed. An absurd question. He didn't know the answer and it hardly seemed to matter considering his cousin's condition. It took a few seconds to pull himself together and calmly say, "We need to get you to an urgent care doctor. There's one nearby. Just—just hold on—I'll get you some clothes and take you."

"I'm—." He gagged. "I'm fine. I've got pills—." He turned to face the couch cushions and coughed, sharp and painful sounding. "It's the trip . . . or I have the flu."

"No, I think it's more than that." Amin stared at a large rash on his cousin's back. He needed to temper his reaction. He didn't want to scare Kareem, but there was something going on way beyond a run-of-the mill flu. Kareem wasn't freaking out, thank goodness, but perhaps he had no idea what he looked like.

"We have to go to the football game," Kareem said, his words slurred.

"Football?" Amin said. "What?" Thinking his cousin must be delirious, he backed away. He went into his bedroom, his mind a jumbled mess of frantic thoughts, opened his dresser drawer and stared at his neat pile of boxer shorts. He had to think, figure out what to do. What sort of sickness did Kareem have? It didn't seem normal. This wasn't at all how he imagined the morning. He returned with some of his own clothes for his cousin to wear.

"I need water," Kareem said, his voice a strange croak with a gurgle. "Get my pills." He hacked like something had dislodged from his throat. "Help me up."

"I'll get the water. Can you put these on?" Amin held out a shirt and shorts. He looked down, feeling unsure of everything he did and said.

Kareem remained limp on the couch. Suddenly he shot up to a seated position and sneezed. The force sprung his body forward like a jack-in-the-box. A spray of blood splattered the wall.

"Holy shit," Amin said again before he could stop himself. His hand flew to cover his open mouth. The wall resembled a murder scene. The urgent care clinic now seemed woefully inadequate for whatever was going on with Kareem. They needed an ambulance to come and get him. And quickly.

"We're going to the Panthers..." Kareem said, before moaning again. He struggled to sit up but didn't seem to have the strength.

"Panthers?" Kareem's nonsensical babbling only intensified Amin's fright. Amin knew he should help, do something, but he couldn't bear to touch Kareem's mottled body.

Kareem managed to push himself upright, onto his elbows. He stared at Amin, who shuddered at the drop of blood trailing from his cousin's eye.

Amin stepped closer to his cousin to offer reassurance, but didn't dare touch him.

Kareem laughed, a weak and pathetic sound that turned into a choked gurgle deep in his chest. He looked insane. He tried to sit up all the way. "My gift to you. Panthers tickets. We're going." He fell back against the couch as if he had used up his last bit of energy.

"They'll know how to help you at the hospital," Amin whispered. With trembling hands, he picked up his phone and dialed 911. He couldn't tear his gaze away from his cousin, as if watching him intently might prevent the sickness from escalating.

"911. What's your emergency?"

"My cousin is bleeding from his eyes and nose. And he was throwing up last night. I don't know what's wrong with him. He's not making sense. I need an ambulance. Hurry. Please."

"What is the address of your present location?"

"9413 Sharon Court, Apartment 5."

"Does he have any medical conditions?"

"Not that I know of."

"Is he conscious?"

"Yes."

"Do you know what's causing his sickness?"

"No. I don't know. I really don't know. But it's bad," Amin's kept his voice low so Kareem wouldn't hear him, but Kareem didn't seem to be processing his surroundings anyway.

"Has your cousin recently been out of the country?"

"Yes. He has. He's from Syria. He arrived in the country yesterday. I was there too."

"Hold on. An ambulance is on the way."

"Gonna rest one minute. Then go," Kareen mumbled in Arabic from the couch. "Allah, give me strength. Unless you have a different plan for me after all."

Chapter Forty-Six

Los Angeles

November 6th

Quinn drained another can of Coke. His voice rang in his ears, like an echo, when he spoke. Random thoughts, some of them maddeningly irrelevant—the number of hours since he last slept, the Band-Aid on the Secretary of State's chin, does diet soda really make people fat—crossed his brain like sequences from a dream, mixing together with the current unfolding events. He struggled to focus on the pertinent thoughts, not the spam generated by his sleep-deprived brain. Time was running out.

He had to summarize the bad news to his team. "Scott Hussan isn't the guy. The HRT knew from the moment they entered and found him scared senseless. They still bundled him into a containment suit, as we saw, and took him back to an isolation room in the FBI building. They interrogated him and tested his blood. He isn't sick. He has no trace of infection. He was visiting his girlfriend in Paris. She's doing graduate work on the Islamic State. Everything he explained was true and verifiable. He isn't a carrier."

"And they've checked on everyone else, all the names from the other lists?" Rick strummed his fingers on the table.

"Everyone on the A and B lists has been tracked down and ruled out. They're almost through the C list." Quinn's body felt heavy, his chest tight.

Across Charlotte, the few remaining people from the Priority C list were being drawn from their beds and breakfast tables to be questioned by field agents. Meanwhile, Panthers players and thousands of their fans awakened to a beautiful fall morning and started their pre-game routines and rituals. Families packed their trunks with ham biscuits, shrimp cocktail, and gallons of sweet tea to get an early start on tailgating. In less than two hours, Quinn would need to admit defeat by calling the Governor of North Carolina and updating the Security Council. The public would be informed of the situation, to some extent, and the country would be thrown into an unimaginable panic. Quinn and his team had failed.

"We're going to have to let a fully-rested team take over from here. They'll probably focus on executing the contingency plans," Quinn said, rubbing the back of his neck.

Ken nodded, without lifting his head. Dark circles rimmed his eyes.

"Okay," said Stephanie, sounding dejected.

"Just finish documenting what you've done so I can transition our work," Quinn said before leaving the work room.

"This can't be true," Rick said. "The world is about to learn there's a deadly disease on the loose in Charlotte? What will they be told?"

"FEMA will have prepared written statements," said Stephanie. "There are entire divisions to coordinate the dissemination of information." She stared at the wall. "I can't believe this is about to happen."

Rashid remained focused, his fingers moving across his keyboards, slightly slower than usual but nonetheless precise—selecting, linking and cross-checking keywords, statistical probabilities, and red flags from hundreds of databases. His knuckles grew white and his key strokes suddenly stopped. With a significant correlation to all his newly-modified risk factors, one name leapt from his monitor. "I've got something!"

Stephanie, Rick, and Ken turned their weary eyes to Rashid.

"Amin Sarif. He's twenty-seven, born in America, parents are immigrants from Iraq. He recently traveled in and out of Amsterdam, but when I pulled up his credit cards, he purchased nothing for three weeks."

"How do you spell the last name? S A R I F?" Stephanie said.

"Yes. His aunt and uncle were killed in a recent attack in Mosul by a U.S. security firm. There's potential motive. He has a cousin. His name is Kareem. Kareem Sarif."

Ken and Rick locked eyes.

"*Redman's Kareem?*" Stephanie quickly returned to tapping her computer keys. "This has to be our guy,"

Ken worked his keyboard, his eyes darting across multiple screens. "It could have been a work trip, all expensed on a corporate card. I'll look that up. We can't waste any more time on the wrong person."

"No. He's recently unemployed. I've got his income records." Rashid raised his arms and interlaced his fingers, resting the back of his head in the cradle they formed. He scanned through the information on his monitor.

Staring at her computer screen, Stephanie's voice rose with excitement. "The cousin, Kareem Sarif, is in his twenties. He left the United Sates for Mosul eleven years ago. He holds a Ph.D. in Molecular Biology from Damascus University. He might be *the* scientist behind this. He entered the country two days ago. He was out of our entrance date range by a day!"

"Guys!" Rick yelled, nearly breathless. "I cross-referenced Amin Sarif's address. An ambulance was *just* dispatched there. A man is bleeding from his nose and eyes."

"Yes! Quinn! Quinn! Wait!" Stephanie jumped out of her seat and ran from the room. "Quinn!"

"I'll locate the dispatcher so they can alert the ambulance," said Rashid. "Good job, Rick."

Rick stood up, his eyes beaming. He placed his hand on Ken's shoulders and forced out a loud exhale. "We just found the carriers. We found both of them."

Ken smiled and made the sign of the cross. "Holy Mother of God. I think we really did."

Chapter Forty-Seven

Charlotte
November 6th

Julia answered an unexpected knock at her apartment door wearing a T-shirt and pajama pants. She shuffled back a few steps when she saw a uniformed man with a shaved head and bulging muscles standing in her doorway.

"FBI, ma'am. We have to clear the area. You need to come with me. Right now."

"What is this about?" Julia said, without moving.

He reached for her arm. She attempted to pull it back but he held firm.

"We need you to leave your apartment. Now. For your own safety."

"Wait, I…" Her eyes moved to the figures in white suits and helmets preparing to barge into Amin's apartment. "What's going on?"

"An emergency. Come with me."

"Amin? I think you have the wrong person." She tried to plant her feet. "He's an accountant at one of those big banks."

"Ma'am, you're holding up a federal operation." He continued to pull Julia away.

Just outside Amin's apartment, a man yelled, "FBI! Stay back! Don't move!"

Amin's door splintered into large pieces. "Don't hurt him!" Julia screamed from across the parking lot.

As the door smashed apart, Kareem turned his head to the side and moaned, "Nooo."

Amin gasped. He stood next to his cousin holding a shirt, boxers, and shorts in his trembling hands. He couldn't believe what was happening. His cousin was dying before his eyes and two people covered in plastic suits with face shields had burst into his apartment. Not medics. An icy coldness gripped his core.

The intruders looked at the blood-spattered wall and then focused on Kareem.

"He's sick." Amin's voice shook. Was their forced entry a result of his call to 911? Where were the medics and the ambulance? What was going on?

A third person entered the room in one of the same suits.

"Don't move!" One of the strange men grabbed Amin's arms, twisting them behind his back. The clothes fell from his hands. The man snapped on handcuffs, dropped a shielded helmet over Amin's head, and pushed him into a seated position on the floor.

One of the other men inserted an IV line in Kareem's arm and shouted, "Keep him alive!"

Amin sat rigid, his heart racing and his arms tightly constricted over his lower back. Two sets of eyes stared at him from behind their hard, plastic masks. They were large men and their voices meant business.

"What is your name?"

"Amin Sarif."

"This is your home?"

"Yes."

The other man pointed to Kareem. "Who is he?" Kareem was surrounded by the men in their bulky suits. Amin could barely see him. He glimpsed a tube trailing from one arm.

"He's my cousin."

"His name?"

"Kareem Sarif."

"Does he live with you?"

"No. He arrived from Syria two nights ago. He got sick last night. He's really sick." They obviously knew, anyone could tell, but Amin could hardly think straight. His world had become a real-life horror movie. "What's going on? Why am I in handcuffs?"

"Is this his?" one of the men pointed to Kareem's bag on the counter.

"Yes," Amin answered.

The man ran some sort of wand over the duffel and unzipped it. Amin held his breath, suddenly expecting to see a giant assault rifle or something else incriminating, but only clothes tumbled out onto the floor. A black baseball cap, a black and turquoise Panther's football jersey, boxers, a pair of socks.

Large gloved hands lifted Kareem's letter from the counter and carefully peeled it open. "I found the tickets," the man yelled into a mouth piece. "These are the guys. Both of them. One is sick. I don't know about the other."

"I'm not sick," Amin said. "But my cousin needs help." He almost said, *Please, he hasn't done anything wrong,* but stopped himself because he didn't know if the statement was true. Yesterday he thought so. Today, anything was a possibility. "Are you going to take him to a hospital?"

No one answered.

Fear tightened his throat. "Why are you here? Why did you come to my apartment?" His voice sounded shrill. The men looked his way, but again, no one answered. They were busy communicating with others through ear pieces and microphones hidden inside their space suits. He'd never felt so helpless and afraid. And alone. He felt very alone.

Kareem moaned from the couch.

Amin became aware of a barrage of noises outside. Banging on doors. Shouts of "FBI!" Assertive voices commanding his neighbors. "Grab what you need and leave immediately."

He heard, "For how long?" "What's going on?" and "Why do we have to leave?"

What was happening? What had Kareem done?

"How were you infected?" a man shouted at Kareem.

"Infected?" Amin shifted his gaze to his cousin. Suddenly, puzzle pieces clicked together in his mind, although the picture was far from complete. He turned his head toward the wall and squeezed his eyes shut, wanting to run and hide from his memories as well as the scene currently unfolding in his apartment. Had Kareem deliberately infected him with a deadly virus in Syria, that night after Amin refused the so-called *vaccination*? Amin shivered. Was he sick too?

"Do you know who infected Kareem?" one of the men said.

"I don't know." Amin dropped his head. "Someone in Syria. Maybe someone he works for."

"Where does he work?"

"He's a microbiologist in a lab in Syria. He does research to find cures for diseases. I think."

"What is the lab called?"

"I don't know."

"Who does he work for?"

"Someone named Al-Bahil." Finally, he had one relevant answer.

"Muhammad Al-Bahil?"

"Yes, I think so."

"Kareem Sarif works for Muhammad Al-Bahil," the man said to whoever was listening on the other end of his earpiece. "When did your cousin arrive in the States?"

"Friday night."

"Where did he go from the airport?"

"I think he came straight here. I don't know."

"How did he get here from the airport?"

Amin shook his head. "Cab?"

"Was he sick when he got here?"

"He was tired. I don't think he was sick until late last night. This happened very quickly."

"Who else has he been in contact with since he arrived?"

"No one really, I mean he hasn't been too close to anyone besides me. Except…Oh! This is before he arrived, but I just remembered, he had sex with a girl the night before he left Syria."

"What's her name?"

"He didn't tell me. She's in Syria. That must be how he got sick."

"Hmfff. Yeah—that must be how." The FBI agent shook his head as if he was disgusted. "Stand up! Don't touch anyone!"

The agent lifted the helmet off Amin's head and pulled protective material over his body, including his cuffed hands, like a giant garbage bag. Only his head and feet stuck out. The helmet was replaced. "Let's go," he said, pushing Amin forward.

Kareem moaned incessantly as two more suited men entered the apartment. They carried a stretcher inside a sealed tent. They lifted Kareem onto the stretcher and zipped the covering, sealing him inside.

"Ant-ta-da!" Kareem suddenly yelled out what sounded like garbled nonsense. Amin thought it might be Arabic. "It's in my bag—" he said, before coughing spasms racked his body.

"What?" one of the men said. "We can't understand you."

"Amin. Two shampoo bottles!" At least that's what Amin thought he heard Kareem scream from under the heavy plastic as the men carried him out of the apartment.

"Delirious," said one of the two men carrying the stretcher.

"Sure is," said the other.

Chapter Forty-Eight

Los Angeles
November 6th

Holly's gaze moved painfully across her living room taking in the mess: L'Amore Production DVDs on the floor in front of the television, beer bottles, the onyx Sophie vase overturned, an open, almost empty suitcase, clothes scattered around. Everything about the moment, including her pounding head and nausea, reminded her of college, waking up inside a fraternity house at UCLA. She closed her eyes. What had happened?

Quinn. Damn, Quinn.

He was the reason for all of this. He blew off their vacation. He hadn't been home in days. Where the hell was he?

Her head began to clear. Recent memories returned. At least, some of them. Like throwing everything out of her suitcase. Calling Reese. Reese coming over to cheer her up with a group of friends in tow.

Then what happened? Holly remembered champagne. Coughing and sneezing. Not being able to keep her eyes open. Having trouble standing. Her last memory from the evening was of Christian helping her lie down and telling everyone to leave.

Christian? In her home? Yes, she distinctly recalled him shooing Reese and her friends away. Reese said he was being rude, but Holly was grateful. They needed to go.

Morning sunlight streamed in through the windows and burned her eyes. She wasn't feeling any better. In fact, she felt much worse. The pain pills would help minimize her discomfort. She needed another. And now.

Unable to think clearly, she stumbled from the living room couch toward her bedroom. Her body felt strangely detached from her brain like they weren't working together. Yet, her nerves were sharp, frayed threads of pain. She couldn't remember ever feeling this way—this terrible—in her whole life.

I might have gone too far this time. This is my warning. It's time to stop using, before the drugs affect my looks and health.

A powerful gurgle inside her lower intestines propelled her toward the bathroom. She stopped half way there to lean on her dresser and the feeling dissipated.

When did I eat last? I must be dehydrated. There are electrolyte waters in the refrigerator.

But the refrigerator seemed miles away. Reaching the kitchen seemed the equivalent of trekking the final peak of Mt. Everest.

Find my phone and call the cleaning lady—tell her to come right away—but first—go back to sleep.

She was desperately tired, every bone in her body ached with exhaustion, but she was also shaking, which didn't seem right.

Tainted pills. One can only be lucky for so long. Need to call Reese and warn her.

She edged across the room, made it to her bed, and collapsed across it, unable to move. After a few hours of restless sleep, she woke, drenched with sweat. The sheets and

334

pillowcases were soaked. She got out of bed, every slow move painful. A fleeting glimpse of her reflection in the mirror shocked her. She quickly looked away. Her eyes were red. Her face had a strange rash, visible even under her smudged make-up. Never in her life had she ever looked so wild and ugly. She limped forward, keeping herself upright by holding onto the wall. Every few steps she paused to catch her breath like an old woman plagued by arthritis.

Suddenly, Quinn appeared. He stood in the bedroom doorway. He wore only his boxers, the navy ones with the shamrocks. His broad chest was smooth, lean, and strong. He smiled, which seemed strange. *Why is he smiling at me? Can't he see I'm not okay?* He opened his palm. It held a small pile of pink pills. He offered them to her.

She shook her head. "I don't need any," she tried to say. Her throat burned.

Quinn's smile grew tight. "A young woman died when you and Reese ran her off the road. Did you know?"

"What?"

"A young woman died on her way home. She died because of you. Because you and Reese didn't stop to see if anyone needed help."

"No. No one died, it was just a fender bender. There wasn't even a mention in the news." Holly wasn't sure if she was speaking out loud or if her words were stuck inside her head.

Quinn shook his head.

"I didn't know...I didn't think anyone was hurt, I..." Holly struggled to justify her past actions. She couldn't think. She could hardly breathe. Why was he bringing this up now?

Like vapor, Quinn vanished as suddenly as he had arrived.

What the—? Oh my God. I'm hallucinating. She choked back her tears. Leaning heavily against the wall, sweat dripping

335

down her back, she reached for the tissue box on the table. Her fingers shook so violently she couldn't control them, but finally she succeeded in grabbing a handful of tissues. She blew into them, alarmed by the sensation of liquid flowing from her nostrils. She forced herself to look. The tissues were stained a dark red.

Holly gasped with fear. *Too much coke. But wait...no....I haven't...*

Mustering the courage, she staggered back to the mirror and lifted her chin. Her eyes weren't merely bloodshot like she'd had a rough night, they were jaundiced and bloody, like the creepy addict she saw when she visited Christian in the valley. *We must have gotten the same batch of tainted pills. Christian did this to me!* She hyperventilated, unable to avert her gaze. Red capillaries had burst along her tongue. Her frantic heartbeat hammered her temples.

"What is happening to me?"

Her brain struggled to overcome her fear and confusion. She needed to see a doctor, but she couldn't call 911 because she didn't want anyone to know about her terrible drug reaction. She didn't want to be arrested. But she also didn't want to be alone. She spotted her phone and reached to grab it with her quivering hand, but instead sent it tumbling to the floor behind the night stand. She dropped to her knees, moaning like an inhuman creature, and crawled across the carpet, searching. The carpet fibers felt like knife blades under her fingers. She patted the space under the bed and under the nightstand, desperate to find her phone.

Her vision blurred.

Quinn. I need you. Help. Please help.

The room spun. Dark grey clouds flooded her sight. Something roiled inside her stomach. Her pain escalated, transporting her into a state of shock.

Just before she passed out, she thought, *I forgive you. Just come home. We'll go to Spain once I get better.* And then, *I don't want to die alone.*

Her eyes flew open, and then closed a final time.

Chapter Forty-Nine

Los Angeles

November 6th

In the Los Angeles field office, the counterterrorism team finally slept for a few hours, collapsing immediately once they lay down. Except Quinn.

The Governor of North Carolina called on a secure line from outside the Panther's stadium.

"I just want to thank you, Quinn. It's a picture-perfect day. Thousands of people are trailing through the security lines into the stadium right now, excited for the big game. If they noticed security being tighter than usual, no one has mentioned it. I just can't believe…To say I'm relieved is the understatement of the century."

"That makes two of us," said Quinn.

He hung up with the Governor and called Holly, his fourth call in less than an hour, but still no response. He knew he had screwed up as far as she was concerned. But making amends would have to wait a bit longer. He had to provide updates on the case, starting with the National Security Council. A few moments later, he was on a video-conference call with most of its members.

"We found the two carriers," said Quinn. "American born cousins, Amin and Kareem Sarif. They were located before they had the opportunity to spread the disease. Kareem Sarif passed out on the way to the hospital and was DOA. Amin is still alive and under interrogation. We've also confirmed E.C.1 originated from an ISIS group, specifically Muhammad Al-Bahil, presumed to be the current leader of ISIS, the brother of former leader Anwar Al-Bahil. The CDC is currently conducting an emergency risk assessment."

"Good work," the Secretary of Health and Human Services said. "Did ISIS officially take credit? Or did the surviving terrorist claim responsibility on behalf of ISIS?"

"No to both questions. We have yet to hear from ISIS, but Amin Sarif confirmed his cousin worked for Muhammad Al-Bahil. He also saw the first two infected men, Pivani and Spitz, in Syria on the day he left. However, Amin Sarif is vehemently professing his innocence and ignorance of the threat."

The secretary laughed. "Innocent? Hardly. But that's original. He's the first Islamic-extremist terrorist I've ever heard of who didn't want credit as a martyr."

"He's not symptomatic yet, but he tested positive for E.C.1. He may have more to say when he becomes ill."

Ken was waiting outside the briefing room when Quinn finished the call and stepped out.

"We found more evidence linking all of the carriers together," said Ken. "Kareem's fingerprints were on the envelope we found in Pivani's trash. That envelope was from the Yoga Institute of Paris."

Quinn nodded.

"Rashid got remote access to Spitz's computer. He compared the browser histories for Spitz, Pivani, and Redman. The one site they had in common was The Yoga Institute of Paris. The French police had already raided the building. They found nothing unusual. It looks like ISIS was using it as a dummy company, to route mail through from the United States on to ISIS networks."

"Hard to believe they were communicating through the U.S. Post office," Quinn said.

"The company's website has class names and class times, most of it in English. Made to look like they're a real yoga studio offering classes, which they are. But it's also where they put all their recruiting info. Their inspirational quote of the day and their practice of the day are all coded instructions. The website asks for a login password and a code, which must be sent through the mail. We think it's all done to make the recruit feel part of something very selective."

"Great work," Quinn said. He stepped forward and almost lost his balance. He steadied himself against the doorframe. He'd been too focused to realize how tired he was, but suddenly, he couldn't ignore his exhaustion. "I'm going to go home," he announced. With all the excitement, everyone had forgotten about the vacation he missed. Good thing. The way he was feeling, he couldn't deal with anyone giving him a hard time, or worse, feeling sorry for him.

Chapter Fifty

Los Angeles
November 6th

Quinn called Holly again on his way home. No answer.

"Damn," he said to himself.

He had already checked to see if she had flown to Spain without him. Holly's ticket had not been used. He understood why Holly was furious, but was it fair? It's not like he went out drinking with friends and lost track of time. His mind was groggy and his eyes were irritated. He blasted cold air through the car to stay alert, and braced himself for the fury waiting. There was no way to prepare for it. He would have to ride it out until it eventually dissipated. The sooner he faced her anger, the sooner they could move past this episode. He hoped. After they spoke, he would call the airlines and try to switch the tickets. If not, he would buy new ones. Just as soon as the FBI and CDC established beyond a doubt that E.C.1 was no longer a threat to the public.

He parked his car next to Holly's and closed the garage door. He expected her to burst into the garage, eyes blazing with anger. He took sidelong glances at the door, dreading what was to come. The door stayed shut. Craving sleep, he crossed his arms over the steering wheel and leaned his head against them. A few precious moments of peace. Without meaning to, he closed his eyes and fell asleep.

An hour later, he woke with lower back pain and a cramped neck. The events of the past few days flooded back to him. He looked at his watch. His first instinct was to check on the case—to get an update on viral containment from Maddie and see what had been learned from further interrogation of Amin Sarif. But he knew what he still had to do at home.

He lifted his stiff body out of the car and entered the house without further hesitation. He'd get it over with like peeling off a bandage. He thought of the Secretary of Defense and her conspicuous Band-Aid again. The Security Council would be needing another update soon. He opened the door and almost tripped over an empty suitcase. Clothing was scattered all around it. Blankets trailed from the couch onto the carpet. An uncorked champagne bottle, make that two of them, and glasses were spread across the counter.

He crossed the living room, alert to sudden movements, and walked toward the bedroom, where he expected to find his wife. He hadn't announced he was home, but she must have heard him come in. So far, she had done nothing to acknowledge his presence. Strange. What did she have planned to demonstrate the depth of her anger? Fear of the unknown had his nerves on edge. Ridiculous, he told himself, after the real danger he had witnessed at work. Yet reprimanding himself did nothing to alleviate his apprehension. He stepped cautiously down the hallway and into the master bedroom like the lead character in a horror movie.

And then, with no warning, *he was.*

Holly lay sprawled out across the floor, next to the bed. Her eyes were closed. She was almost unrecognizable. Not the Holly he knew with meticulous hair and makeup. This Holly looked deathly ill, ravaged by disease. Her appearance made him gasp. He called out, "Holly!"

I'm dreaming. I'm still asleep in the garage and this is a bad dream. My work life mixing with my home life. Wake up!

He squeezed his eyes shut and opened them only to confirm the scene was real.

"Holly." He said her name quietly at first. Then he screamed it. "Holly! Wake up! I'm here! Wake up!" When she didn't move, he pressed two fingers against her carotid artery and her cool bruised skin, still begging her to wake up. He moved his hand under her breast on top of her heart, searching again for a pulse. He felt for breath. There were no signs of life. Tendons bulged in his neck and forehead as he pressed down hard on her ribs for the first chest compression. Blood streamed out from her nose and mouth as if her body had become a giant sack of liquid. He jumped back in time to avoid contact, his own heart leaping like mad in his chest.

His training kicked in with his attempts to revive her. She was his wife. Of course, he'd do everything in his power. But he had ignored the part of his training telling him to take precautions and avoid exposure to an unknown illness, the possibility of a deadly virus or bacteria.

Quinn paced the room with his arms crossed and hands stuffed under armpits. He stole glances at Holly. From behind, it looked like she was resting on the floor. It felt wrong to leave her there. Wrong not to rush back over to help her up. He choked back a wave of painful emotion, sat down on the edge of his bed, and dropped his head into his hands. Holly was dead. Beyond help. No point in calling an ambulance. With a trembling hand, he called Madeline.

He swallowed hard to keep his emotions in check. "I need your help. I need you to come to my house."

"Quinn. Hi. I just got into the office and we're so busy, as you can imagine, trying to make sure E.C.1 is contained. I'm about to step onto a conference call. Is there someone else you can call? I mean, what is it you need?"

343

"My wife is dead. I think she was infected with E.Coryza 1. She's on the floor. She's dead."

"What? What do you mean?"

"I came home and I found my wife dead. Her body looks a hell of a lot like Pivani's. Like she hemorrhaged to death. There wasn't anything wrong with her when I saw her last." He could hardly believe what he was saying.

"Oh, my God. Are you okay? I'm so sorry."

"I need to know if she's dead from the virus."

"Okay. I'll get there as soon as I can. Let me think. When did you see her last?"

"I don't know. It's been a few days because… You know, this fucking ISIS virus! But she would have told me if she wasn't feeling well. She hates being sick. She can't handle it. She would have let me know. She'd have said something about it in her messages at least. We were supposed to be in Spain right now." He paused, realizing he was grieving to Madeline about his personal loss. "I'm sorry. I called because I'm not sure…. I can't . . . She's dead. And unless I've lost my mind, she has E.C.1."

"I'm coming. Stay there. Don't touch anything." Madeline paused. "Did you touch her? Were you wearing PPE?"

"I checked to see if she was still alive. And no, I wasn't expecting to find her dead so I wasn't wearing protective gear. I don't think I came in contact with any of her fluids." He lowered the phone and studied each of his hands and arms. No blood. "And she wasn't breathing. But I don't know. I wasn't thinking about…that."

"It's okay. Text me your address. I'll be there as soon as I can."

Quinn spoke quickly, his words rushed together. "Thank you, Maddie. Thank you."

"If you can, try and find out where she's been for the past two days, who she's been with. Maybe we'll finally find out how the carriers were infected. I mean, if that's what's happened. It seems...never mind. I'm coming. And I'm so sorry."

Quinn let out a huge breath after speaking with Madeline. Someone else would be in charge now, and he could let his grief take over. But Holly hadn't fallen down the stairs or slipped in the shower. It appeared she had died of the same virus he thought they had under control. How was that even possible? There wasn't time for personal grief or guilt. He needed to function before the situation escalated. It was imperative to determine who Holly had seen while she was sick. Everyone she came in contact with should be isolated immediately. He spotted her phone on the floor, partway under the nightstand. He ran to the laundry room to grab a pair of rubber cleaning gloves and used them to pick the phone up and look through her most recent calls. Her last contact was Reese. He pressed the call button.

Quinn gritted his teeth through five rings before Reese answered.

"Hi, babe. Are you feeling better? Did that asshole ever come home?"

"Reese. This is Quinn."

"Quinn? Why are you calling me? I'm not sure if I want to talk to you."

He couldn't tell her everything. He needed to choose his words with caution, or he would incite the panic he had just helped the country avert.

"Reese. Listen carefully. This is serious. Holly is sick. What she has is highly contagious. I need to know who she's been with the past few days. I need to know if you're sick too."

"Do you think I'm stupid, Quinn? Who she's with is none of your business. If she wanted you to know she would tell you herself. And if you were around like you should be, you wouldn't have to ask. You're supposed to be in Spain right now. Do you even know that, Quinn? Do you? God, you're an asshole. I'm not telling you anything about Holly. She'll tell you, if you're lucky enough to ever speak with her again."

Quinn choked back his rage. Was this really happening? Holly dead, permanently and irrevocably dead, and Reese insulting him? The good news, at least, was that Reese sounded full of energy and venom. She didn't seem to be sick, at least not yet. He tried to control his emotions. "Just tell me if you saw Holly in the past two days."

"Yes, Quinn, I did. I saw her when she called me, devastated about you blowing off the trip she planned. Who does that, Quinn? Who does that? You are an asshole!"

Quinn ignored most of her words. She *had* been with Holly recently. "Listen, Reese. I'm going to send someone to your house to speak with you. I need you to stay there. Don't leave your house. You need to be checked and we need to make sure you don't get anyone else sick."

"Fuck you! Don't you dare send anyone to my house. What the hell is wrong with you? You had so many chances. Just walk away. She's so much better off without you. She doesn't need you."

Reese hung up the phone. Quinn's nostrils flared and his nails dug into his clenched fists. That had not gone well. He couldn't handle this. It was too personal. Madeline's team would have to deal with Reese. He prayed to God that Reese, and anyone else who had recently been in contact with Holly, stayed inside.

Chapter Fifty-One

Los Angeles
November 6th

Madeline parked her rental car in front of Quinn's home. Nothing about this was real. Here she was putting on an impermeable gown, double gloves, and a face shield to see him. She walked to his front door, unsure of what to expect. She was surprised he lived in such a large and opulent home, and so close to the ocean. Quinn opened the door and stepped aside for her to enter. Madeline felt a lump form in her throat. He barely resembled the man she knew. He wore a rumpled dress shirt, needed to shave, and his red-rimmed eyes looked tired and wild at the same time. It hurt Madeline to see him so emotionally pained. She pushed back against the flood of sympathy threatening to derail her professionalism.

"I'm so sorry, Quinn."

The muscles of his face contracted, but he didn't look at Madeline. And he hadn't really looked at her when he opened the door. Madeline got the sense he couldn't bear to see her, even though he had called and asked her to come. "This way," he said gruffly, walking with his shoulders slumped forward.

Madeline followed quietly, passing impressive originals on the grey walls, a reminder of Holly's connections in the art world. She noticed the disarray, which made her think there had recently been a party, but she didn't know for sure. Perhaps it was the usual state of the home.

Quinn stopped outside a large master bedroom with an unmade king-size bed in the center. "There she is," he said, in a voice Madeline didn't recognize.

Holly lay on the floor next to the bed. Madeline knew Holly only from pictures she'd seen long ago, and she'd done her best to erase those images from memory. Lush red hair fanned out around Holly's head and across the carpet. Even with bruised, jaundiced skin, her beauty was still evident. Madeline crossed the room and crouched down beside the body. The moment seemed surreal. Putting emotions aside, she did her job, using a swab to place a drop of Holly's blood onto the DxH device. She waited silently while Quinn paced around the room wringing his hands. When the DxH device beeped, she lifted it close to read the results and swallowed hard before speaking. "Of course, we won't know for sure without the lab tests, but it appears you're right. I'm sorry. I just…This is horrific."

Quinn stopped pacing. He stared at a spot on the wall, his eyes blazing with anger. "How the hell did this happen? Was I personally targeted somehow?"

"I had the same thought. It's too coincidental. Unless…?"

"Unless what?"

"Unless people are stricken with the disease all over the country. Were we wrong in thinking the carriers didn't infect anyone before they died?" Something bitter moved from her stomach and into her throat. She forced herself to stay calm. "We need to find out if any new incidences have been reported. Without being too specific. We can't put the healthcare community on alert without causing panic. Or, maybe, I don't know…maybe it's too late to worry about that."

"I'll find out right now," said Quinn, removing his phone from his pocket. "And I sent you the address of her friend, Reese. She was here with Holly last night." Quinn focused on his phone and didn't look at Madeline. She couldn't imagine what he was feeling, and she kept that in mind. Still, he made her feel like she had personally done something to make him angry. As if she might somehow be responsible for his wife's death. Although diseases were her livelihood, she had no part in Holly's death. But if Quinn's grieving process demanded she be the target of his anger, so be it. She resisted the urge to put her hand on his arm and offer him a gesture of comfort. She only wished she could help him through his pain.

Three other CDC epidemiologists met Madeline on the street in front of Reese's apartment building. Together, they put on masks and walked to her front door.

"We're not going to tell her Holly died," whispered Madeline. "We need her to be thinking clearly. Time is of the essence. Chances are good she's infected. And this virus progresses lightning fast."

Reese answered her door barefooted, wearing yoga pants and a hoodie. She looked over each of the people standing on her doorstep wearing surgical masks. "What's this about?" She gaped at their masks and then frowned. "Is this Quinn's idea of a joke? He said he was sending someone over, but this? Guys, it's too early for Halloween."

"I'm Dr. Hamilton from the CDC. We're here because Holly Traynor is sick."

"This is for real?"

"This is for real," said one of the epidemiologists, keeping his voice professional. "We need to ask you some questions and examine you. What Holly has is highly contagious, so we also need to find out about anyone else who was at her house yesterday."

"This is fucking unbelievable. Is it because of Quinn's job? Did he make her sick?"

"We don't know how Holly became infected. That's what we need to find out, and quickly. Please, let's start with you giving us names. We'll follow up with each of them."

"What does she have? And what's going to happen to me?"

"We'll tell you everything you need to know and we're here to help you. But first, I need you to give me the names. *Now.* We need to prevent others from becoming sick."

"Well, if she's sick, then I'm sick too. I was trying to console her and she was coughing and sneezing all over me. Damn it. I have a trip I can't miss next week. For work. You need to tell me what sort of *sick* we're talking about. Like pneumonia?"

Madeline did her best to hold her temper. Did Reese actually believe the CDC made house calls wearing masks when someone contracted pneumonia? Even though it was hardly relevant, she couldn't help thinking, *this was Holly's best friend?* On the outside, Reese was incredibly beautiful, but on the inside, there was clearly room for an attitude adjustment. It made her wonder if Holly had been as shallow.

"Who else was there, at the Traynors' house?" Madeline asked.

"Oh, for shit's sake, you're not going to answer my questions, are you? Fine. Well, first off, you should know about Christian. I called him to come over and help cheer her up. If anyone got sick, it would be him. They were having an affair."

"Oh?" said Madeline, her surprise evident. She hadn't meant to say anything out loud.

"That's right. A purely sexual relationship. Some of my other friends were there too. I thought a little surprise party might lift her spirits."

"I need first and last names. Phone numbers and addresses if you have them."

Reese rattled off five other names. "I brought champagne. I poured a few glasses and we passed them around. So, whatever she has, we probably all have it. Fucking unbelievable. You need to tell me what it is." Reese scrunched up her nose, turned her head to the side, and sneezed. The epidemiologists exchanged subtle but wary glances.

"You're going to have to come with us," Madeline said.

"What right do you have to—"

"Can you handle this from here?" Madeline asked her colleagues, ignoring Reese.

Both nodded.

"Thank you, in advance, for your cooperation. You'll be in good hands," Madeline said to Reese, before turning and walking away with one of her associates. The other two epidemiologists would stay behind to let Reese pack a bag and get her to the hospital where isolation units were already being set up.

Once she'd returned to the car, Madeline checked in with the CDC and with Quinn. No other new incidences of E.C.1 had been reported. She fanned herself with her notebook. She had expected a busy day, but not like this. It appeared Quinn had been intentionally targeted. Somehow, his wife had been infected. But Madeline didn't have time to dwell on that aspect. Her next step was to track down the other partygoers, call them, and tell them to keep away from others until they could be officially quarantined.

Madeline glanced out the window as she drove to the San Fernando Valley to see Christian Towson. In the seat next to her, a CDC field agent spoke to him on the phone. Madeline felt compelled to call Quinn back and console him, but she didn't think she could do it, not with him acting like she was to blame. Maybe it was best to give him space.

The passing landmarks were vaguely familiar. She was either experiencing déjà vu or she had driven down these neighborhood streets before.

"Well, we got lucky," the agent said, hanging up his phone. "Christian Towson is home. I told him Holly Traynor was sick and we were on our way there. He sounded confused, understandably, but cooperative. He doesn't have any symptoms. At least, that's what he said."

"He may be asymptomatic at the moment, but he's the most likely to be infected, based on his sexual contact with Holly. Assuming Reese told the truth." Madeline had to admit she was curious to see who was having sex with Quinn's wife.

At the next stop sign, she pointed to a blue house with a giant sunbeam sculpture hanging below the roofline. "I remember that house. The last time I was out this way, I was at Pivani's."

"Hmmm," said the agent.

Eventually they passed Pivani's house, still surrounded by quarantine tape.

"There it is." Madeline pointed.

"We're only a mile from Christian's address," said the agent. "Coincidence?"

"I'm thinking not."

Three minutes later, they parked outside Christian's house.

"Quiet street," said the agent. Madeline agreed.

They knocked. Christian opened his door to face the two strangers wearing masks. He looked worried. His wide-eyed gaze moved between them. They showed him their identification.

"This is, you know, strange. What's wrong with Holly? Can I see her?"

"Unfortunately, no. She has a contagious virus. I'm sorry. We're here to determine how she became infected, and who else might be at risk," Madeline said.

"Whoa. Is she going to be okay?" Christian eyes continued to dart back and forth between the CDC agents. He fidgeted with the top button of his shirt.

"Anything you can tell us might help," said Madeline.

"Okay." He bit his lower lip. "I mean, where do you want me to start?"

"When did you see her last and did you notice she was sick?"

"Just yesterday. She wasn't feeling well. She thought she might have the flu. But she was also very upset. See, she's married." Christian coughed and looked away toward the horizon. The CDC agent took a quick step backward. "She was supposed to go to Spain with her husband on vacation, but he blew her off. Didn't even call, hadn't come home in a few days."

Madeline's hands tightened into fists. She struggled to keep quiet while listening to Christian talk about Quinn as if he was an irresponsible, careless man.

"She was really down," said Christian. "I wasn't sure if she was sick or super upset. Her friend, Reese, called me and some other people over to help cheer her up, but I could tell Holly wasn't in the mood. As soon as I got there, I told them to leave. She fell asleep on the couch before I left. I tucked her in, but I didn't want to disturb her sleep. She needed it. I should have stayed with her, I wanted to, since she was sick, but...I guess I didn't know when her husband would finally show up."

"Where have you been since you left her house?"

"Nowhere. I mean, I came straight home and I haven't left the house yet."

"Good. Can you remember the last time Holly came to see you here? The exact date?" Madeline said.

"She's only been here once. It was last Thursday. Why?"

Madeline and the epidemiologist exchanged looks. Last Thursday. The day before they found Pivani.

"Do you know a man named Raj Pivani who lives a few blocks from here?" said Madeline.

Christian shook his head. "No. Why are you asking about him?"

"We're fairly certain he has the same virus Holly has."

"Is his house the one with the yellow tape around it? Wait, is he Indian?"

"Yes. He wa—yes, he is," Madeline said. "So, you do know him?"

"No, but when Holly was on her way here, she saw him. She thought he was an addict. She only told me because she thought he was gross."

Yes, gross would have been an adequate description if he was symptomatic, thought Madeline. "She didn't call to get him help, or alert anyone to his condition?"

"Um, no. I don't think so. Why aren't you asking Holly these questions? Is she quarantined too? I called her after you called me, but she hasn't answered."

Madeline responded in a gentle voice. "Holly Traynor and Raj Pivani are both dead."

Christian's mouth fell open. He stumbled backward until his back hit the entryway wall. His hand clutched at his chest. "Dead? Holly is dead?"

Madeline nodded. She allowed Christian time to process the news before she spoke again. He couldn't help them if he couldn't think straight.

354

After a minute, Madeline said, "It's an aggressive virus. We need your help to prevent others from becoming sick. Is there anything else you remember about the day she came out here? Did she actually speak with Pivani, or just see him?"

Christian wiped a tear from the corner of his eye. His face had turned pale. "Holly thinks I don't listen—oh God! She *thought* I didn't listen, but I always did. She didn't just see him. Her phone battery died. She stopped and asked Pivani for directions. She said he coughed on her face when she was in her car."

Relief hit Madeline like a wave of fresh air. Finally, they had a rock-hard connection, a solid explanation for transmission between victims. Holly Traynor had not been targeted because of her husband's role in the FBI. She had inadvertently encountered Pivani and experienced an air-borne transmission. Madeline wanted to let Quinn know immediately.

"I'm surprised you didn't call a doctor for Mrs. Traynor, or take her to urgent care," said the CDC agent.

Although it was probably a damn good thing he had not taken her out of her house, thought Madeline.

Christian looked stricken. He shook his head. "Like I said, I knew she was sick, but she was really upset. And..."

"And what?"

"It was hard to tell what was going on with her because she was using. More than usual, because she was down. I guess you'll discover that anyway, if you do an autopsy."

"Was she sharing needles?"

"No, never. Nothing like that. Just pills. I think."

"We aren't concerned with drug use in this investigation, unless it's related to the spread of the virus. We have a much bigger problem on our hands," said the agent.

"So, if Holly was infected on Thursday and died, when, this morning? This disease can kill someone that fast?" Christian lowered his forehead into his open hand and closed his eyes. Suddenly he looked up. "Shouldn't I go to a hospital and start the treatment now?"

Behind her mask, Madeline's face softened. She didn't want to respond and make Christian even more afraid. There was no good way to tell someone there wasn't a cure.

Chapter Fifty-Two

Los Angeles
November 10th

Quinn had plenty of time alone to analyze recent events, personal and professional. Best case scenario, he faced twenty-one days of isolation and quarantine inside his now thoroughly decontaminated house. If he became infected, he wouldn't have that much time. History was repeating itself. But unlike Iraq fifteen years ago, this time there would be no Bronze Star waiting if he made it through alive. Not for screwing up and allowing his wife to die.

Specifics of the case circled round and round inside his head while he worked out in the garage, microwaved and ate the meals dropped off for him, and communicated with his team. The recent events leading up to Holly's death boiled down to one heart-wrenching mistake. One. Just one decision. You only had to be wrong once to change the course of many lives.

Holly contracted E.C.1 on the day she asked him to have lunch with her, the day he refused. He knew that now. If he had left the office and met her, she wouldn't have driven to the valley to meet another man. She would still be alive and, most likely, no one else in the Los Angeles area would have died from the virus. The irony lashed relentlessly at his conscience.

357

He had been trained to detect suspicious behavior, yet he hadn't known his own wife was cheating on him. He'd thought something was up recently, but he didn't know what, and he hadn't taken the time to find out. The night Holly came home soaking wet and acting weird, he knew there was something going on. She said she'd been with Reese, meeting her new boss. He shouldn't have ignored his instincts. But he hadn't gotten around to thinking about it again, because he was so involved with work.

If Holly were still alive, maybe he would be angry about her affair. But she was dead. Dead because he wouldn't leave work and have lunch with her. No, he wasn't angry at Holly. Not at all. He'd reserved all his anger for himself.

He finished a grueling set of pull-ups and wiped the sweat from his brow. His phone rang.

Holly's father. He gave Quinn an update on Holly's funeral arrangements, a funeral from which Quinn would be noticeably absent due to his quarantine status.

Quinn's head was still in his hands a few minutes later when his phone lit up again.

"Mr. Traynor?"

"Yes?"

"I'm calling from the CDC. Just a courtesy call. Someone is on their way to your house to test your blood for E.C.1 markers. They should be arriving shortly."

"Okay. Thanks for letting me know."

The caller wasn't Madeline. And it wouldn't be Madeline coming. Good. He didn't want to see her. Couldn't even look at her when he saw her last. She hadn't done anything wrong. In fact, just the opposite. She'd done everything right. Her timely call after examining Pivani was the main reason the FBI was able to stop an ISIS cell from starting a pandemic. Quinn and his mistake were the only reasons people in the LA area were now infected. Madeline served as one more glowing example of Quinn's miscalculated decisions. He should have chosen her years ago. He didn't. He chose Holly. And now, considering Holly had just died, his inability to keep that realization at bay disgusted him, flooded him with fresh guilt. No, he couldn't look at Madeline and be reminded of all his mistakes. His guilt already weighed him down like a ton of rocks. He hoped she was already back in Atlanta.

He chugged from his water bottle, doing his best to keep hydrated, prepping his body for the severe illness that could hit at any minute. It would start with a sniffle or two, a cough or a sneeze, and then his body would begin to break down, cell by cell. At least the process would be rapid. Although he deserved to suffer.

His phone rang again. Rashid. Quinn eagerly answered. Focusing on the case helped dispel his other problems.

"Ready for this?" Rashid said.

"What have you got?"

"It's about Amin Sarif. He's at the CDC in Atlanta."

"Right."

"Since the HRT found him, he's claimed to be innocent. Claimed he had no part in his cousin's plans to destroy America, even though he appears to be the textbook candidate for terrorist recruitment—lonely, unemployed, looking to fit in somewhere, his browser history loaded with extreme Muslim sites."

"Uh, huh."

"Well, he's telling the truth. He really didn't know what his cousin was doing."

"How could you ever come to *that* conclusion? What did you find?"

"I watched every interrogation tape, and I have to admit, he'd already convinced me after the first few minutes. But then I found a letter to, get this, *the woman of his dreams* on his laptop. He wrote it the night of November 5th, the night before we found him and his cousin. The letter proves everything he's said. It's a powerful testament to his innocence along with his mind-blowing ignorance. We've already questioned the girl. She knows nothing."

"You're sure about his innocence?"

"Yes, unless he's so clever he wrote it as a potential defense. But, why would he? If you're going on a suicide mission, would you have a plan B to pretend it was a big misunderstanding in case you got stopped?"

"No. Jihadists still want credit from above even if their attempt fails."

"Exactly," said Rashid. "And he's been extremely cooperative. He's told us every detail he can remember about his time in Syria and Al-Bahil's compound."

"Is he sick yet?"

"No. Not yet. Still waiting for it to hit."

Quinn briefly closed his eyes. For a few minutes, while talking to Rashid about the case, he'd forgotten he was *also* waiting to see if he became sick.

"Oh. Quinn. Damn, I'm sorry. That was…insensitive."

"It's okay. You know, at first, I didn't care if I got sick. Two days ago, I thought a random cough was the beginning of my death sentence and I was like, bring it on. I thought I deserved it. But now, I guess my attitude is changing."

"Good."

"I want to see Muhammad Al-Bahil captured."

"It's the President's number one priority. He promised the world Al-Bahil will soon be located and destroyed."

"The country needs someone to blame for E.C.1. A *live* person. So, you really believe Amin Sarif is innocent?"

"Yes. He may be a fool, but not a terrorist. Still hard to swallow, but it's the truth. He's having a tough time accepting that his cousin was willing to murder him. He wants to believe Kareem was forced into coming here."

"If Kareem was infected against his will and wasn't a willing participant, then why didn't he ask for political asylum when he got here? Why didn't he isolate himself? Kareem is guilty. He's the one who engineered the damn virus!"

"Amin says he must have been forced."

Quinn laughed. "Don't forget, when we arrested Dylan Redman, he told us Kareem tried to sell him on some big sinister plan. Amin may be a fool, but I'm not. I, um…" Quinn almost choked at the end of his sentence as his words sunk in. Because of Holly's indiscretions, he might be the biggest fool of all for not knowing his wife was having an affair. Everyone knew now that Holly and Christian formed the center of the CDC's epidemiological case and were mentioned in every news segment about E.C.1.

Quinn bit down on his lip and forced himself to focus back on work. "So, as you know, I've assigned Stephanie and Ken to the task group charged with finding Al-Bahil."

"Yep. Oh. Hey, I need to jump on this call about the shrapnel bombing in St. Petersburg. They asked for my help on something."

"Oh. Sure. Wait! One more thing. When you're in the office, try and keep Rick busy with something until I get back, but nothing critical. And keep an eye on him."

"Will do. And Quinn?"

"Yeah?"

"We're all looking forward to your return. Lots of prayers going out your way."

Chapter Fifty-Three

Atlanta

November 11th

Amin opened his eyes when he heard the clink of keys and someone moving around outside his make-shift cell in one of the CDC's quarantine centers. What now? The endless interrogations were over, and for that he was deeply grateful. They had left him physically and emotionally exhausted. He'd passed all his lie detector tests, according to his attorney. His attorney also assured him that any charges he faced in America were likely to be dropped, eventually. But his case was complicated. Amin's biggest mistake was accepting the false passport, which the authorities might not have even known about if he hadn't told them. He hoped his cooperation would work in his favor.

He sat up and peered through the heavy, thick sheets of plastic. Another medical professional had arrived, her face partly concealed under a face shield and a protective suit. But Amin recognized her eyes—Dr. Cooney. This woman had been particularly kind to him. She seemed to be one of the few who believed him when he professed his innocence.

Amin couldn't hear Dr. Cooney, but he saw her speaking to the burly marshal and the FBI agent who guarded his cell. And just two short months ago, he'd thought it was overkill when Continental sent a guard to watch him clean out his desk.

The marshal unlocked the door outside the isolation cell, maintaining the maximum distance possible between himself and Amin, even though the marshal wore a mask and gloves and Amin still had no symptoms. Amin couldn't blame him though, not with the images of Kareem's illness seared into his memory.

While the heavy plastic was unsealed, Amin rolled up his shirt sleeve before his hands were cuffed together.

"I'm not taking blood today. I'm only here to talk," said Dr. Cooney, who couldn't enter the cell until the guard had restrained Amin.

"Okay," said Amin, surprised. He put his hands together behind his back and was roughly handcuffed. The guard stepped back and Dr. Cooney entered.

"I have good news and bad news. Which do you want first?" she said.

"Whichever you prefer."

"All of our testing indicates you're an asymptomatic carrier."

"What does that mean?"

"It means you've contracted the E.C.1 virus, it's living inside you, but the good news for you is that it probably won't ever make you sick or you would have become sick by now."

Amin nodded. "I never get sick. I've got super-immunity. So, what's the bad news?"

"Even though you probably won't ever contract the disease, you can transmit it to others."

"I can? How?"

"Any exchange of bodily fluids."

"Oh," said Amin. Immediately an image of Isa popped into his mind, along with the intimacy they could never share. Then he laughed, a harsh but sad sound. What was he thinking? He was in quarantine. His cousin had quickly become the most hated man in the news and he wasn't sure what was being reported about his own involvement. The spread of the virus was under control, but many people had died after a small party at the home of an FBI agent. Even if Amin didn't have the virus, it was unlikely Isa would ever want to come near him again. With what had become of his life, an opportunity to ever accidentally infect Isa, or any other woman for that matter, was highly unrealistic.

"You'll always be a risk to society," said Dr. Cooney. "One misplaced cough, or if you ever cut yourself and shed a drop of blood, any exchange of bodily fluids, and someone could die."

"So, I'm stuck in a quarantine cell like this until the World Health Organization or the CDC come up with a cure?"

Dr. Cooney lowered her eyes before meeting Amin's imploring look. "A cure could take years. Big pharma isn't going to get involved in this. There's not enough money in it, not with E.C.1 basically under control."

"So, even once I prove I'm innocent, I'm still stuck here?"

"Well, not here exactly, but someplace like here. We're going to need to study you."

Amin dropped his head and closed his eyes.

"I know that's hard to hear, and I'm sorry. Just let me know if you have any questions." She paused. "Oh, and you have another visitor. She can speak to you from outside the plastic."

Amin lifted his head in surprise, eyebrows raised. He'd already spoken with his attorney, and his parents said they wouldn't be back until the day after tomorrow. They were meeting with a few other legal representatives, just in case. "Who is it?"

Dr. Cooney shook her head. "I didn't ask her name. A good friend, apparently."

Amin thought he detected a smile in Dr. Cooney's eyes, but that might have been wishful thinking.

"I'll see you soon," she said, exiting through the heavy plastic sheets.

"You have to keep the cuffs on," said the FBI agent. "Even though *your friend* is staying on the other side of the plastic with me."

Amin nodded and sat down on his bed. *Was a friend really waiting to see him, or were they screwing with him?*

Amin looked up when he heard footsteps. The marshal had returned and he wasn't alone. Amin's mouth fell open. He could not have been more surprised if Kareem had returned from the dead.

She wore a long-sleeved black T-shirt and jeans. "Hi, Amin," said Isa.

"Isa?" Amin blinked. "I can't believe you're here."

"I got your email."

"My email? I know I wrote you one, before all this, but I didn't think I sent it."

"You did."

Amin wasn't sure what to say. There really were no appropriate words. Under normal circumstances he would have been embarrassed about the email, but relative to his current situation, it was nothing. Their eyes met and held without speaking.

"You've really got yourself in a mess, haven't you?" Compassion filled her eyes.

Amin smiled slightly, for the first time in days. He couldn't help himself. He had nothing to lose. "And I thought my chances with you were all over when I realized I was carrying a roll of toilet paper around when we spoke. This . . . well . . . it's worse. I guess you really do sort of like me."

Isa nodded, her smile was sad, but still, it was there. "This is definitely worse than the toilet paper." She shook her head and smiled again, in spite of herself. "The FBI has already had a—how should I say it—a few words with me. I know you're innocent. What can I do to help?"

Chapter Fifty-Four
Los Angeles
November 11th

Traffic moved smoothly through the palm tree lined Los Angeles streets. The notorious LA traffic had all but disappeared. Fewer people walked the sidewalks. Those who did wore surgical masks or scarves over their mouths and noses. Wearing a loud Hawaiian shirt, a young man walked briskly to a car carrying a grocery bag, perfectly normal looking aside from his gas mask. Men like him had capitalized on the prevailing fear, charging hundred percent mark-ups to deliver bags of food from the grocery stores still open for business. The Governor had declared a state of emergency for Southern California and implemented a sundown to sunrise curfew to prevent looting. Military personnel patrolled the business areas wearing helmets with face shields. Grim expressions conveyed their worry.

Rick stopped at a red light and waited, alone, at the intersection. Trash spilled over the sides of a dumpster surrounded by a two-foot pile of garbage. Sanitation crews weren't willing to risk their lives for their jobs. Everyone was afraid of becoming infected. With a silent killer on the loose, there was one natural response—fear. No way to know who might already be sick and who might be next.

Rick's cell rang.

"Dad," said Rick, with a grin, excited to speak with his father. For once, he actually possessed important information the Senator did not have.

"Are you okay?" said his father.

"Yeah."

"I wish you had let me get you out of there."

"No one allowed in or out of Southern Cali, which includes me. Most everyone is holed up inside their homes anyway."

"What is it like?"

"Apocalyptical. Deserted. Eerie." He shook his head and looked around while he drove. "You know, I expected an FBI career to be interesting, but the past few weeks have been unreal. Insane." He didn't say frightening, no need to increase his father's worry. "We thought E.C.1 was contained until my boss finally went home and all hell broke loose."

"His wife's death is a tragedy. It's also a PR disaster for the agency."

"Maybe, but her friend is to blame for this current nightmare." Rick gritted his teeth thinking about Reese. "She's not responsible for the outbreak, obviously, but she's responsible for the chaos. The CDC allowed her to make calls to her family while she was in isolation. She texted pictures. A few images of her looking like hell with bruised and bleeding gums next to a pretty hot *before* picture went viral."

"Big mistake, and heads rolled over the incident," said the Senator.

"Well, she's dead now. And so is the man who was sleeping with my boss's wife. It's really awkward for everyone who knows Quinn. All the E.C.1 deaths are spread out like a web from his wife and her friends. The media and news shows are salivating."

"It's a shame they're sensationalizing this thing. E.C.1 is under control. The media is acting irresponsibly. The bans and curfews should be lifted by the end of the week, if not before."

"Doesn't matter, Dad. Even though everyone who had exposure to the virus was isolated, the terror is escalating here. Nothing short of a miracle cure or vaccination is going to stamp out the fear. The CDC and the World Health Organization are scrambling. Hey, Dad, gotta go. I'm at work now. Took me less than half the time it usually takes to drive here."

Rick was still thinking about the incredible events of the past week when he entered the FBI office. "Morning, Jayla," he said, passing her desk. Her braids were gone and her hair was surprisingly short, making her look like a different person altogether.

"Hold up," said Jayla. "I've got something for you to do. From Rashid."

Rick turned around quickly and walked back to Jayla's desk. He knew he'd been pushed aside for a bit. Quinn had probably told everyone to keep him occupied with unimportant busy work. Until Quinn returned, he didn't expect to have much to do. And Quinn's return hinged solely on being lucky enough to have avoided infection.

"Kareem Sarif's belongings have been shipped here. They're going to remain in our evidence storage room, but first everything needs to be labeled and cataloged," said Jayla.

Rick nodded. "Okay." Not exactly high priority work, or they wouldn't have let him do it alone, but something.

"We have to dot all the I's and cross all the T's on the case. Our records will be analyzed by a special commission. They'll determine what could have or should have been done differently. And I don't think it's going to be kind to us. Poor

Quinn." Jayla shook her head. "Anyhow, the box is waiting in the evidence room."

"I'm on it." Rick walked straight to the evidence room and located the box. The neon stickers stuck to the outside indicated the box and its items had been decontaminated. He put on gloves and began to empty the contents. A pile of clothes. A keychain with a virus symbol. A toiletry bag. A bottle of pills— they already suspected the pills were morphine based on Kareem Sarif's blood tests. A bar of soap wrapped in a cloth. A container shaped like a stick of deodorant, its label in Arabic. Two travel-sized shampoo bottles filled with a cloudy liquid, presumably Syrian shampoo.

Ken popped his head in the door, startling Rick.

"How is it going?" he said. Ken had been strangely nice to him in Quinn's absence.

"Fine," said Rick. "I'm labeling Kareem Sarif's stuff."

Ken surveyed the items on the table. "This crap might sell on the black market some day for millions. Like Hitler's things. Know what I mean? Kareem Sarif's deodorant available to the highest sicko bidder."

"Right."

"I don't want him to ever have that attention. I'd like to throw all his shit into the incinerator," said Ken.

"I'm not throwing anything away."

Ken raised an eyebrow and frowned. "I wasn't serious. I said I wanted to. There's a big difference. Don't throw anything away."

"I know."

"Just label everything, enter it into the computer, and then put it in storage. Don't make any mistakes. Let me know when you're finished. You can help me with some data."

Rick nodded and Ken left.

Rick stared at Kareem Sarif's belongings without moving. He felt unmotivated. Uncertain. Exactly how the terrorists wanted him to feel, as if his everyday tasks didn't matter anymore, as if everything he did or planned to do was futile and inconsequential. Well—enough! He wasn't going to give them what they wanted. Even though his tasks seemed insignificant, he would do his job as if it mattered. Pressing his shoulders back, he carefully labeled everything and entered the information into the computer. He put the pills, the deodorant, the soap, and the shampoo bottles in a separate bag. He didn't take them to the storage room with the other items. He walked them to the lab for testing. Just to be thorough. Just to cover all the bases.

Chapter Fifty-Five
Syria
November 12th

From a distance, the compound looked like a modest American subdivision aiming for privacy with a tall stucco wall. Located in the middle of nowhere, it was essentially hidden, and far nicer than the average Syrian community. After traveling miles without detection, the Special Operation Forces soldiers moved cautiously toward the wall, disguised in burkas that covered their machine guns but not their heavy boots. They scaled the back wall with ease and in silence. Once inside, they saw the building with the arched stone entrance, the structure Amin had described as Al-Bahil's main office. The black Mercedes he mentioned was parked in front. Nearby was a large school surrounded by new playground equipment. So far, everything matched Amin's report of the IS compound. They had found it.

"Don't forget, Kareem Sarif slept with someone from the compound on the night before he left. The infection may have spread. Don't let *anyone* get close to you," the commander whispered.

One of the men finished taking the pictures needed in case they had to return. They assumed their practiced formation.

"Let's do it. We're going to capture Al-Bahil alive." The commander led his team toward the building but stopped after a short distance. Crouched down and hidden, he signaled to his men, touching his finger to his ear. Something wasn't right.

There was no noise.

He pointed to the carrion birds circling the skies overhead.

They crept forward again, their backs against the side of the building. Their guns protruded out in strange shapes under the burka fabric. One of the men gestured toward an unmoving body on the ground, then a second body and a third. Each showed signs of death from E.C.1.

"They can't infect us if they're dead, as long as we don't touch them," said the commander, needing to reassure himself as much as his men.

Alert for any movement, they entered the building without making a sound, muscles tense, hearts pounding. Large drops of sweat slid down the commander's face. They cleared room after room, all empty except for the body of a teen-aged girl inside a large bedroom. Her blood had stained the white sheets around her head. The king-size bed resembled a giant modern art canvas with deep red paint.

"This way to the stairs," whispered a soldier.

The scent of death grew stronger as they descended to the underground bunker. At the bottom of the stairs, a heavy, locked door blocked further entry.

The commander listened for over a minute for any sign of life behind the door before signaling for his men to back up against the walls. He fired his gun, shattering the lock, and slammed the door open. His men had their weapons ready.

The heavy door opened into a waiting area. Two large men dressed in black clothing sat slumped against a wall, one on each side of an open door. The one with the bullet wound in his

373

head still held a gun. Splattered brain matter covered the wall behind him. The lifeless, jaundiced eyes of the second man stared straight up at the ceiling.

On the other side of the door, a vomit-covered body lay sprawled across a velvet chaise. A black flag wound around his hands. A deep scar ran down one side of the man's bruised face, from his temple to the edge of his thick black moustache.

"That's him." The commander sighed, clenching his teeth in disappointment. "I sure don't think Al-Bahil intended to infect his compound. But once the symptoms start, it's too late to do anything about it."

"At least he got what he deserved," said one of the soldiers.

Everyone was dead.

Epilogue
One year later

Amin sat uncomfortably straight on the plush couch, trying to remember how to look relaxed. Chin up. Shoulders down. Unclench his jaw. Stop his knee from bobbing up and down. A bright, hot light shone above him. He glanced down at his hand, wrapped around Isa's. He looked up and smiled at her, then turned to face the interviewer, ABC News Correspondent Virginia Foster. *Please just talk about the foundation*, he said to himself.

"Action," said a voice behind him.

Virginia's face suddenly lit up with a professional smile. "Welcome everyone. We're here with Amin Sarif, founder of the Islamic Peace Foundation and the cousin of deceased ISIS terrorist, Kareem Sarif."

Amin felt muscles twitch reflexively around his eyes but he didn't let his expression change.

"First, let me congratulate you on your recent engagement," said Virginia.

"Thank you." Amin and Isa smiled at each other. Isa lifted her hand and a square cut diamond sparkled under the set lights.

"Amin, before the bioterror attack, you were not a public figure. Am I correct?" said Virginia.

"No, I wasn't. Far from it. I was a financial analyst at a bank."

"Considering the objective of your recently-established foundation," she glanced down to read from a card, "to spread the truth and peace of the Muslim religion, did you feel personally betrayed by last year's bioterror attack on our country?"

"Yes. I felt betrayed, as you suggested, and horrified. But a few bad apples do not spoil the entire bucket. I believe Allah gave me certain experiences to provide a platform to share my message with the world. Islam is a beautiful, holy, peaceful religion."

"You say a few bad apples, but to put it in perspective, millions of ISIS militants claim to be Muslims."

"Yes. Unfortunately, you're correct. And my foundation is trying to reach them."

"Just how will your foundation reach them?" Virginia tilted her head and narrowed her eyes.

"The same way ISIS and other extreme factions reach them. The internet via social media. With movies, videos, and ads aimed at those searching for a higher purpose. Each time the terrorist groups produce something new, we target the same audience, counteracting with Allah's true message of peace."

"Hmm. And you think that will be effective?"

"Yes. I hope it will be effective. The alternative is to do nothing. My unwitting involvement in a terrorist attack has inspired me to do what I can. I mentioned the media, but of course, if we find more effective methods to counteract their movement, we'll use those methods."

"I understand your foundation has lots of international support, both financial and with the media. Congratulations on your successful campaign."

"Thank you. Let me say that Isa's father has a lot to do with it."

"So, let's talk about the events that led you to start your foundation. Your cousin, Kareem Sarif, was an esteemed microbiologist before he became radicalized, before he engineered the E.Coryza 1 virus that killed hundreds of people in southern California. Is it true that you were in Syria with him just before he came to America to spread the fatal virus?"

"Yes." His jaw tightened. "My cousin was a brilliant scientist. His life's work was developing vaccinations and cures for virulent diseases. What happened to him shows how powerful ISIS is. They're able to manipulate and brainwash intelligent people."

Virginia's smile faltered before she found it again. "In spite of the foundation you've established, and your cooperation with law enforcement, some people are having a hard time believing you didn't know what was happening, that you didn't understand this attack was coming. What do you want to say to those people?"

Amin shifted his weight in his chair. Isa squeezed his hand. He had answered that question countless times. He could channel a sense of calm and purpose and hold on to it, at least until he was away from the public. "I can't make anyone believe me, but it's the truth. I didn't know what Kareem did to me, or what he planned to do to my country."

The interviewer shook her head slightly, her smile remained plastered on her face. An uncomfortable and intentional silence followed.

"Amin, do you have anything you'd like to say about Rick Webster? For those of you who don't know, Rick Webster is the son of Senator John Webster. He's the FBI agent who discovered the cure Kareem Sarif carried into the country."

Amin's smile was genuine. "Because of Rick Webster, and so many others at the FBI, DHS, and the CDC, I got my life back. I'm immensely grateful. I spent months in quarantine being tested and often wondering if I would ever be able to leave, wondering if I would spend the rest of my life there. I believe the CDC and other scientists would have eventually developed the same cure my cousin did, but it might have taken years. The very first experimental dose of my cousin's vaccine eliminated all traces of E.C.1 from my system." He paused. "If you don't mind allowing a shift in subject, Isa and I would like to talk about the foundation."

"Did you see Amin Sarif interviewed on the news yesterday?" Stephanie said.

"No, but I don't need to. I watched hours of his interrogations and interviews last year when you were working on locating Al-Bahil," Rashid said.

"The interviewer mentioned Rick. He's gotten a lot of credit for sending a few bottles down to the lab." Stephanie laughed.

"I'm sure his father's PR team has something to do with it. It will help with his next election."

Rashid lifted a section of Stephanie's long blonde hair and placed it gently behind her shoulder. "You may have already forgotten, but I didn't—we agreed not to talk about anything work related tonight." He took hold of her hand and smiled. "Two seats just opened up at the bar. Let's go, before someone else gets them."

On Saturday night, Quinn was in the kitchen of his new condominium. It was cozy and small compared to the beachview mansion he'd recently sold. Two bedrooms, and a yard just big enough for his new dog, a mixed breed who barked to alert him to someone approaching the door.

Quinn reached down to stroke her neck as she walked next to him toward the front entrance. He looked up, through the glass, and stopped short when he saw who was on the other side.

Madeline.

Her hair was longer than the last time he'd seen her. She wore a form-fitting T-shirt and jeans. She looked beautiful.

"Hi. Are you going to let me in?" she said.

"I'm sorry. I just…"

"You weren't expecting me, I know. I took a chance that you might be home."

He opened the door and stood aside. "Come in. Please. It's been a long time."

The dog's tail slapped against the wall in her excitement to greet Madeline. "Hey there, fella. What's your name?" Madeline crouched down to rub between her ears.

"Um…her name is Maddie," Quinn said sheepishly.

Madeline looked up and narrowed her eyes. Quinn felt heat rising to his face. She lifted the dog's heart-shaped tag and sure enough, the word MADDIE was etched into the silver metal. Madeline laughed. "Hmmm. I'm not sure what to think about that."

"Well, um, she's new. I just picked her up at a shelter a few weeks ago. We're still getting to know each other. So far, so good."

"I love that you rescued her from a shelter." Madeline was still smiling.

Quinn shifted his weight and crossed his arms. "So, what are you doing here? In LA, I mean."

Madeline stopped petting the dog and stood up. "I'm working on a case." She took a few steps inside and set her laptop down on the kitchen counter. "I thought you could help."

"Yeah?"

"Mm hmm, but also—I wanted to see you. Things were really difficult when we last—"

"I know."

"I guess that's why I showed up without calling first. Hey, is that—?" She pointed to a bottle of Merlot sitting on the counter. "We visited that winery, remember?"

"I do." Quinn looked wistful. "Believe it or not, that's one of the bottles we bought."

"Seriously?" She picked it up and read the label. "Wow! How about that. Although, we did buy a few cases, didn't we? Nicely aged."

"We could open it. Finally. While you tell me about your new case."

"Sounds like a plan." Madeline sat on one of the bar stools and leaned her elbows on the counter.

Quinn removed two wine glasses from his cabinet. "I'll open the bottle and then we'll get to work."

Madeline nodded.

"So, what have you been working on?" said Quinn. "Here, let's sit on the couch."

Madeline moved over to the couch and began telling him about her most recent project. Quinn handed her a glass of wine and sat down next to her. He asked questions fueled by genuine interest, and shared what he could about his team's recent work. Wine glasses were refilled. The conversation moved from work to exercise routines, caring for a dog, and movies. Two hours passed quickly with Quinn and Madeline growing more comfortable with each other.

"Can you excuse me for a second?" Madeline stood up. "Bathroom?"

"That way." Quinn gestured in the direction of the powder room.

Quinn finished the wine in his glass, surprised at how much he was enjoying Madeline's company. It had been a long time since he'd had a social visit of any sort.

Madeline returned and Quinn said, "So, tell me, what is it you thought I could help with?"

Madeline smoothed her shirt sleeves before sitting back down. "I lied, Quinn. I made up an excuse to come see you. I *am* consulting on something in LA, but it has nothing to do with bioterrorism. There is no project I need your help with. The truth is... I haven't stopped thinking about you for the last year and I wanted to see if you were okay. Your new place and your cute dog make me think you've moved on with your life. That's good. It's really good."

Quinn reached for her hand and held it. Madeline's lips slowly formed a smile as she looked down at her hand in his.

"I *have* moved on," said Quinn. "I've had a lot of time to reflect on things. Tonight, being with you—well, I'm pretty sure of what I want."

"And what's that?"

"I want another chance with you, Maddie."

"Oh." Madeline laughed.

"Why is that funny?"

"It's not. It's just...well...you don't know how happy I am to hear you say that. I was thinking—"

Quinn cut Madeline off by pressing his lips against hers, catching her off guard and leaving her breathless. He leaned back slowly, their eyes locked together, savoring the perfection of the moment, the memories it stirred and the future it promised.

"Thoughts?" said Quinn. He touched her face, letting his finger trail gently down her cheek.

Madeline smiled, her eyes bright, and finished the last sip of her wine. "I'm wondering if I can get another kiss."

From the Author

Two ideas sparked the concept for *Only Wrong Once*. The first inspiration hails from years ago, when I was a graduate student in Epidemiology and Public Health at Yale Medical School. One of the top floors of the building held a secure and restricted room for advanced research. The lab inside was rumored to hold the most dangerous of diseases, including Bubonic Plague, Polio, and hemorrhagic fevers. Studying those samples required the utmost precautions and I remember people actually whispering out of reverence when talking about it. My work never took me inside that room, but just knowing those samples existed, so close to our day to day classrooms, always struck me as wildly disturbing and fascinating.

The second flicker of a concept evolved because of my brother, a DHS agent. Like Quinn, he has a year's supply of food and water at his house. Though he doesn't share the details of his career, I do know he's privy to some frightening intelligence regarding terrorist activities. Just the thought of it makes me nervous, but it also makes me appreciate the agencies committed to stopping terrorists before they cause harm.

Note to Readers

Thank you for reading *Only Wrong Once*. I hope you enjoyed the story. If you did, I would deeply appreciate a review on Amazon or Goodreads. I learn a great deal from them, and I'm always grateful for any encouragement. Every review matters, even if it's only a few words.

Other Books by Jenifer Ruff

The Brooke Walton Series

Everett

Rothaker

The Intern

Thrillers

Only Wrong Once

Young Adult Suspense

Full-Out

Printed in Great Britain
by Amazon

48034043R00221